Nefertari's Narrative

Text copyright 2017 Fiona Deal

All Rights Reserved

This is a work of fiction.
Names, characters, places and incidents
either are the product of the author's imagination
or are used fictitiously.

Chapter 1

Early summer 2016

It's a funny thing, when you've been invited – somewhat forcibly – to leave a country to be begged virtually on bended knee to return.

I was sitting in an office in the behind-the-scenes part of the British Museum surrounded by Egyptian men. My fixed-term contract at the museum had been extended when the employee whose absence I was covering decided she wanted to take an extra year off after her maternity leave. But now it was drawing to a close. I was due to leave next month.

Even so, the offer on the table right now needed careful consideration. My immediate instinct was to leap at it. But I've been working hard to curb my natural impetuosity. I realised it may not be in my interests to appear too eager. Besides, the reasons that had kept me in London for the last three years were good ones, and very little outside of my immediate employment prospects had changed.

The men in question were Rashid Soliman, senior Egyptologist at the British Museum, Director Feisal Ismail from the Ministry of State for Antiquities in Cairo, and a third Egyptian gentleman I'd never met before. Mr Zahed Mansour was from the Egyptian Tourism Authority, here on the orders of the newly appointed Tourism Minister Yehia Rashed. So I was in exalted company. And then there was Adam. While he's British of course, there was no way I was meeting three such powerful Egyptian men without back-up and moral support from my husband, also an Egyptologist at the museum.

'The tourism industry in Egypt is in free-fall,' Zahed Mansour said in thickly accented English, shaking his head mournfully. He was brown-faced, bald-headed and round-cheeked, with wide-set eyes and fleshy lips. What caught my attention most, looking at him, was his forehead. One could hardly call it lined. Yet it had three permanent-looking creases, set in the shape of a smiley face. With his bald head, it rather gave him the impression of a man with two faces: the worried-looking one that was real and, above it, the smiley face that made him look a bit cartoon-like.

'Who could have foreseen that the jubilation of the Arab Spring would prove so short-lived?' Rashid Soliman intoned. Rashid was a large and lugubrious Egyptian who spoke faultless English with all the formality of a High Court judge handing down a sentence. Jowly and flabby, his notable feature was his thickset, bushy eyebrows, which met in the middle above heavy-framed glasses. In contrast to the rather comedic look of the junior Tourism Minister, it gave him the appearance of a permanent scowl, not helped by the down-turned corners of his mouth. I'd been quite in awe of Rashid Soliman when I first arrived at the museum, and still wasn't sure I felt completely at ease around him. A man with a short fuse, he could flare up in an instant then simmer down again equally quickly.

Getting no response from what I presumed was a rhetorical question, Rashid added, 'Or that the political turmoil of Mohamed Morsi's appointment to the presidency and subsequent removal from office would turn out to be the least of Egypt's worries.'

'It has been a turbulent few years,' Director Ismail agreed. A tall, urbane man with closely cropped black hair, greying at the temples, he exuded an air of quiet authority.

'Turbulent is putting it mildly!' Zahed Mansour exclaimed. 'Some people are saying our tourist industry is only one disaster away from total wipeout! The question is, can Egypt's tourism recover from this latest blow?!' I'm not sure he realised he'd punctuated every sentence with an exclamation mark. Not knowing him, I could only take it as an indication of how emotionally exercised he was about the situation.

Adam frowned. 'It's still not clear whether the EgyptAir jet that dropped out of the sky over the Mediterranean a couple of weeks ago was the target of terrorism or a terrible accident.' He referred to the latest tragedy.

'Either way, the Egyptian economy will suffer,' Zahed Mansour prophesied glumly. 'If it's terrorism, it will reinforce the view of holidaymakers worldwide that Egypt is not a safe place for a vacation. If it's a technical fault, people and the media will blame Egyptian incompetence. So, if it turns out to be an accident it will hardly be any better for tourism in Egypt. People will still say it's not safe to travel. It's a huge problem for the Egyptian tourism business, particularly with the events that have taken place in the recent past.' The deep pessimism of this outlook was in stark contrast to his smiley-faced forehead. I tried to concentrate on what he was saying and not let the duality of his appearance distract me.

'After the ousting of Mohamed Morsi in July 2013, tourist travel to Egypt fell away sharply,' he went on. 'In our boom years of 2009 and 2010, fifteen million holidaymakers visited Egypt. Tourism employed more than one in ten of the country's workforce and generated the equivalent of £8.5bn British pounds in revenue. By 2013 tourists had dropped by a third to less than ten million. It has slumped further since then. Last year's revenue from tourism was just under half the 2010 figure at £4.2bn. And we've seen a further drop of 44 percent of visitors from last year to now. This latest disaster promises to be the final nail in the coffin.'

I couldn't help but wonder if it was this unrelentingly optimistic outlook that had won him his job as a junior minister in the Egyptian Tourism Authority! But, to be fair, he was speaking no more or less than the truth. These were troubled times for Egypt.

Zahed Mansour, perhaps feeling my gaze on him, lifted his eyes to meet mine and attempted to tug on my heartstrings. 'It's terrible news for all ordinary Egyptians who rely on foreign visitors for their livelihood: hotel workers, tourist guides, taxi drivers and stallholders in the local souks and bazaars.'

When I didn't react, Director Ismail leaned forward. 'It is indeed true that the only ones whose interests are served are the armed Islamist groups determined to inflict economic damage and destabilise the government under Abdel Fattah el-Sisi.'

'It's understandable that foreign holidaymakers are reluctant to set foot in Egypt,' Adam said levelly. 'In light of the recent attacks on Western tourists, and with large swathes of neighbouring Libya controlled by so-called Islamic State, it's hard to blame visitors for staying away.'

I knew what it cost Adam to say this. We considered Egypt our home-from-home. We'd been devastated, forced to abandon our fledgling business venture offering tailored Nile cruises aboard our newly restored Victorian dahabeeyah when the tourist industry imploded. We were no longer living the dream we'd envisaged. Adam might have a romantic soul, but he's also willing to face facts. I knew he was referring to the pro-Islamist tourist stabbings that had taken place in

Hurghada back in January. So while our hearts may feel wholehearted sympathy for ordinary Egyptians caught up in the recent turmoil, our heads recognised and understood the very good reasons for the tourist decline. The trouble was plane disasters and the ongoing threat of Islamic terrorism had brought Egypt's beleaguered tourism industry to its knees.

Zahed Mansour twisted his hands together in a gesture reminiscent of our friend Walid Massri, also given to hand wringing when distressed. 'Things were looking promising back in 2014,' he said. 'We opened the replica tomb of Tutankhamun with high hopes that it would help attract visitors. Even though the world's media ran the story, it was overshadowed by the rise of ISIS. And then of course we had the suicide attack at Karnak in June last year.'

I was horribly well acquainted with this since our police pal Ahmed had been injured in the explosion. Three men had approached a barrier at the entrance to the temple complex. When confronted by Ahmed and his colleagues, one of the attackers detonated an explosive belt he was wearing. Ahmed's colleague shot a second man dead, and Ahmed himself, while suffering burns, was able to bring down the third. Two civilians plus Ahmed and one of his colleagues were injured but no tourists hurt. It was an incident that could have been far worse if not for the quick action of Ahmed and his unit. But it was cold water poured on the hopeful sparks of a resurging tourist trade.

And a salutary lesson that terrorism could strike way too close to home for comfort. Until that moment, I'm not sure I'd ever seen Ahmed's job as especially dangerous. While he'd sometimes courted a certain amount of personal risk, it had usually been alongside Adam and me, and of his own choosing. Terrorism was different – indiscriminate and chilling. Thank God, Ahmed assured us he'd made a full recovery, with just some scarring to his hands and forearms. But just how close a call it had been was lost on no one.

Zahed Mansour wasn't done. Still wringing his hands, he seemed almost to take some bizarre masochistic pleasure in enumerating Egypt's woes. 'The attack at Karnak was nothing compared to what happened in November when ISIS downed the Russian Metrojet plane, blowing it up over the Sinai desert as it flew from the resort of Sharm-el-Sheikh, killing all 224 people on board.'

There was really nothing any of us could say in response to this. It was a terrible, mindless atrocity, as incomprehensible as it was shocking.

'And of course, since then, Russian tourists are staying away and your British government has suspended all flights to and from Sharm-el-Sheikh indefinitely,' Zahed Mansour finished. 'It is possible they may re-start in the autumn, but at this point nothing is certain. And so, Egypt suffers.'

When again nobody responded – it was difficult to know what to say – Zahed Mansour turned his brown-eyed gaze on me. 'Mrs Tennyson-Pink, you haven't said a word,' he chided.

'Meredith,' I said. 'Please, call me Meredith.' I'd decided in a work environment, my full name was more professional than the abbreviation employed by friends and family. And I still wasn't used to having a double-barrelled surname. But, when it had come down to it, I'd found myself curiously reluctant to relinquish the crazy last name my poor father saddled me with.

'Meredith,' he repeated with a small incline of his bald head. 'You have been very quiet throughout our discussion.'

I met his gaze as squarely as I could. 'You've just set out, with frightening clarity, all the reasons why any sane person would give Egypt a wide berth at the moment,' I pointed out as politely as I could. 'And yet you seem hell bent on persuading me to drop everything here in London to go back with you and accept a job with the Egyptian Tourism Authority. I'm struggling to see the enticement, I don't mind admitting.'

He sighed. 'I regret I am unskilled in the gentle art of marketing. What I *can* tell you is Egypt is investing heavily in security. We have enlisted the help of a British firm recruited to deliver a new aviation security programme for Egypt's airports and train 7,000 new security staff over the next six months.'

I thought of the deadly suicide bombings that took place in Brussels airport in Belgium earlier this year. I wasn't sure any amount of airport security was necessarily protection against crazed and radicalised Islamists pathologically intent on destruction.

Director Ismail crossed his long legs, flicking at an imaginary speck of dust on the knife-crease in his suit trousers and leaned forward to re-join the conversation. 'There was some hope British Egyptologist Nicholas Reeves might help kick-start our declining tourist trade with all that excitement last autumn over the possibility of hidden chambers behind Tutankhamun's tomb,' he said. 'As you may recall, Meredith my dear, the world's media went into a frenzy over the speculation that secret chambers may turn out to be the hitherto undiscovered tomb of Queen Nefertiti.'

I met his gaze and we spent a few moments locked in a silent communication. He knew as well as I did that, even if there should turn out to be hidden chambers behind Tutankhamun's tomb, the chances of them containing the earthly remains of Nefertiti buried among a stash of Amarnan treasure were nil.

Adam and I had debated this endlessly when the story broke in September last year. Nicholas Reeves, renowned authority on Tutankhamun, had long believed – and published academic papers to support his claim – that many of Tutankhamun's grave goods had in actual fact been made for a female pharaoh whom Reeves posited came to the throne on the death of Akhenaten, contending this was none other than the pharaoh's Great Royal Wife, Nefertiti. He reported that in studying images of the boy king's tomb, he'd spotted faint lines behind the painted plasterwork, which may reveal hidden doorways.

In late September 2015 Nicholas Reeves arrived in the Valley of the Kings – in the company of the previous Tourism Minister, a delegation from National Geographic and a press contingent – to search for Nefertiti inside Tut's tomb.

The world's media went into overdrive. Adam and I knew they wouldn't find her. He and I held the dubious distinction of being the ones to discover Nefertiti's tomb. It was hidden behind Hatshepsut's mortuary temple in Deir el Bahri in the Theban hills. She was resting there even now, alongside her husband, the enigmatic pharaoh Akhenaten, who'd thrown Egypt into a tumult almost as chaotic as the one it was facing now.

'But we can't be one hundred percent sure it's her,' Adam had said at the time. 'We never actually lifted the lid on her sarcophagus.'

I'd stared at him in open disbelief. 'Adam, her royal titles are carved all around its rim. Just about every artefact in the tomb is a treasure from the Amarnan court of Akhenaten and Nefertiti. If she's not the one inside the smaller sarcophagus inside the burial chamber, I'd sure as hell like to know who is.'

'One of Akhenaten's lesser wives...?' he'd hazarded. 'There was a wife called Kiya whose burial site is unknown. One of their daughters...? History never recorded what happened to a couple of the younger ones. It's possible one of them might be buried alongside their father.'

I'd accepted that however much I didn't want to believe it, this could well be a possibility. The "precious jewels" we'd found had never actually been named in the papyrus we'd translated that led to our discovery of the tomb. The sarcophagus made for Nefertiti may simply have been recycled for the secret burial in the cliffs behind Deir el Bahri. So we'd waited with bated breath while ground-penetrating radar scans were taken of the walls of Tutankhamun's tomb. It was hoped these would identify and map any voids on the other side.

The two-day survey took place in late November 2015 in the presence of Egyptian government officials, Nicholas Reeves, and over twenty other people including two TV crews. At the subsequent press conference the then Tourism Minister said that as a result of the survey he was "90 percent positive" there was a hidden chamber beyond the north wall of Tutankhamun's burial chamber. He also said the scans suggested a further hidden door in the west wall of the tomb. He speculated that the open spaces beyond could contain artefacts and grave goods to surpass Tutankhamun's, and possibly the mummy of Nefertiti.

The media went nuts with headlines around the world. It was catnip to the international news media, and also the Egyptian authorities desperate to reboot the ailing tourist industry.

But just last month reports started to emerge that a second survey had failed to replicate the results of the first. National Geographic brought in an electrical and a mechanical engineer to test the findings. They worked overnight in Tutankhamun's tomb after the Valley of the Kings was closed to visitors, and out of sight of the world's media. Far from providing more fuel for the fire of speculation about fresh treasures, the new data provided the coldest of cold showers. The engineers challenged the findings of the radar scans, claiming ground-penetrating radar was not capable of distinguishing "organic" material, as cited in the previous press releases. Their own surveys revealed no empty spaces behind the walls, and no suggestion of treasures, human or otherwise.

The world media reported with rather less fanfare that Tutankhamun's tomb contained NO hidden chambers.

I continued to meet Director Ismail's eyes. 'But, despite the media storm, Nefertiti is still missing,' I tested, noticing his gaze didn't waver from my face. *Ok,* I thought. *So, that's how it is. We're hanging onto our secret.* I levelled my tone and

14

went on, 'The fabled queen is almost certainly not to be found in any secret chambers behind Tutankhamun's tomb, mostly because it now appears these simply aren't there.' *And because we know exactly where to find her*, I added silently with my eyes.

'The only way to find out for sure if there are indeed cavities behind the walls of the most famous tomb in the world would be to drill a hole in the wall.' Zahed Mansour offered with eagerness in his voice.

Rashid Soliman sat forward. 'Quite naturally, the whole world is up in arms at the very *thought* of *that*,' he said sternly.

'More infra-red scans are planned,' Director Ismail said smoothly. 'I think it's fair to say the Egyptological community has not given up hope.'

I shrugged. 'But the conclusion right now is that the Nicholas Reeves and the world's press, not to mention the Egyptian Tourism Authority,' – glancing quickly at Zahed Mansour – 'have had their hypotheses thoroughly dashed.' I turned my head to smile at Adam, gratified that I'd been right to hang onto my belief that Nefertiti remained nestled inside her stone sarcophagus behind Hatshepsut's temple.

He returned my smile, silently acknowledging my small triumph. Then he turned serious and levelled his gaze on Director Feisal Ismail's impassive face. 'So, in the absence of a spectacular royal tomb to catapult Egypt into the international headlines and lure tourists back, you're rooting around for another marketing angle, something to put the land of the pharaohs firmly back on peoples' bucket lists.'

I realised Adam was testing the Antiquities Director every bit as much as I had; perhaps reluctant to accept an impression that hadn't been confirmed to him directly. His words presented Director Ismail with a gift of an opportunity to tell us that, no, the reason he was actually here was because he'd had a change of heart and wanted to go public about our tomb – let's face it, three of us in the room were perfectly well aware there was indeed a spectacular "undiscovered" tomb ripe for the picking! Instead the antiquities director simply stared back, silently communing with Adam as he'd done with me. I could only conclude he was far less concerned with rescuing Egypt's crippled tourism industry than he was with protecting its greatest ever discovery. In this, he was as one with our dear friend Walid Massri, so I could only silently approve his decision.

After a long, weighty pause, Director Ismail let out a heavy sigh; perhaps realising he had to say something for the benefit of Rashid Soliman and Zahed Mansour, both regarding him expectantly, and without the benefit of our secret knowledge. 'Indeed,' he said. 'I think we have just been treated to a most embarrassing – or most enjoyable, depending on one's point of view – masterclass in the perils of archaeology by Media. Now the Egyptological community has egg on its face to add to its many other tribulations. The situation has become politically toxic. Senior heads have rolled.' He was undoubtedly referring to the replacement of the out-going Tourism Minister with Zahed Mansour's new boss. 'We have left the realms of archaeology and history and entered the arena of statecraft and political jockeying. It is as I always feared if a major discovery were to be made in Egypt to rival Howard Carter's. I'm just not sure we have the governmental stability to cope.'

With these words, I knew, he was telling Adam and me why he'd elected to continue to keep our secret. That Islamic State was operating on his nation's doorstep may also feature in his reasoning, I felt sure. As Walid had said so often after wrestling long and hard with his conscience, these current unstable times did not lend themselves to the announcement of great discoveries.

Director Ismail added, 'So all in all I don't mind admitting I find myself somewhat relieved that Tutankhamun's tomb has so far revealed no hidden secrets.' He must have caught sight of the horrified look Zahed Mansour shot him, for he quickly corrected himself. 'Which is not to say, of course, that the Egyptian Tourism Authority does not need all the help it can get to entice tourists back to our wonderful country.'

I leaned forward, 'It seems to me,' I said, 'that rather than search in vain for new tombs or hidden chambers, you could do a whole lot worse than re-open some of the ones you've already got.'

I saw Zahed Mansour and Feisal Ismail exchange a confused glance.

'Take Seti I and Nefertari,' I pressed on. 'Theirs are the most spectacular in the Valley of the Kings and Queens respectively. And yet they've both been closed to the public for decades. It strikes me there might be people out there who'd consider a chance to see their tombs a very good reason indeed to visit, or perhaps re-visit, Egypt.'

Zahed Mansour was looking at Director Ismail as if this was an idea that had never occurred to him, but now it had taken hold it wouldn't let go.

'You should target people who've been to Luxor before in your marketing,' I advised. 'Give them a reason to go back. Opening the replica of Tutankhamun's tomb a couple of years ago was all very well. But it was no incentive for those who'd already seen the real thing to return.'

Director Ismail sat back. 'You have given us something to think about,' he murmured. 'But I wonder if this alone will be enough.'

Adam shifted on his seat. 'I think it's about time you cut to the chase and told us exactly why you're here and how you want to enlist Merry's help,' he said flatly.

Rashid Soliman, who had been unusually quiet, now sat up straighter and lifted his chin. 'Our esteemed colleagues have observed the phenomenal success of the Belzoni exhibition,' he said proudly, reminding me once again of Ahmed, who has a similarly puffed-up way of speaking.

'It's true,' Director Ismail admitted with a small smile that revealed a golden molar. I'd forgotten about his gold tooth. But now it was hard to tell which gleamed more brightly: his tooth or his eyes as they regarded me steadily. 'The Ministry of State for Antiquities keeps a watching brief on the Egypt-related exhibitions of all the major museums of the world. Yours, here at the British Museum last year, profiling the remarkable achievements of Giovanni Belzoni proved to be one of the most popular ever staged.'

'It's Adam and Dr Soliman who deserve the credit,' I said quickly when his gaze didn't shift from my face. 'Adam's the one who came up with the idea of taking a leaf from Belzoni's book by creating an exact replica of the finest chambers from Seti I's tomb as part of the display. And Dr Soliman arranged for the long-term loan of the alabaster sarcophagus from the John Soane Museum.' I didn't need to add that the exhibition had been a triumph. Adam had even persuaded Rashid to employ actors to stage little dramatic vignettes at interludes throughout the day. These re-enacted the moment of the tomb's discovery by the one-time circus strongman, a giant of a man dressed in a turban and flowing Turkish robes. It had imbued the exhibition with the breathless thrill of early Egyptian exploration. Visitors clamoured for tickets, many returning for repeat visits, and bringing friends and family with them. Indeed, it had been such a sell-out the museum had extended its run, only bringing the curtain down last month to allow enough time for Rashid and Adam to finalise preparations for the next exhibition about Egypt's lost underwater cities due to open in August.

'Ah, yes,' Director Ismail acknowledged, smiling briefly at Adam and Rashid before returning his attention to me. 'But it was your accompanying articles, Meredith, and the visitor's guide you wrote that really brought the Belzonis' story to life. I saw the reviews. Many said it was like reading a novel and seeing the characters step off the page.'

Zahed Mansour leaned forward. For the first time the expression on his face and forehead matched as he smiled at me. 'The astonishing success of your Belzoni exhibition just goes to prove that Egypt has lost none of its appeal. I've seen for myself the Egyptian galleries here thronged with people at all hours. It's the same in all the major museums of the world.'

'*Ancient* Egypt has lost none of its appeal,' Adam corrected him gently. 'And of course in the museums of the world, visitors can get up close and personal with your nation's ancient treasures without fearing for their lives.' He glanced sideways at me. Adam has always contested that it's better to see the relics of the first and finest civilisation in the world in the display cases of a museum than not see them at all. In view of the events of recent years, I'd found myself leaning increasingly towards his point of view.

The smile dropped from Zahed Mansour's face. 'All I ask is for the opportunity to employ Meredith's talents in the service of the Egyptian Tourism Authority's marketing campaign,' he said sourly.

'In Egypt,' Adam pressed. 'You want Merry to come and work for your Tourist Board in Egypt.'

'Well, yes,' Zahed Mansour nodded. 'I fail to see how she can follow in the Belzonis footsteps if she remains here in the UK.'

Chapter 2

'So, what's the big idea?' Dan asked that evening. We were having dinner with Dan and Jessica in the tiny house in Greenwich they'd bought shortly before the birth of baby Polly last year. It was clear Dan's bachelor pad wasn't suitable for a growing family. But luckily he'd had it long enough to sell at a profit in the burgeoning London property market sufficient to enable them to afford this small but perfectly formed Victorian home near the Cutty Sark.

We'd fallen into the habit of joining them for supper on an almost weekly basis as Jessica made the most of her maternity leave to indulge her newfound love of cooking. It was a constant source of amazement to me that such an elfin, golden-haired and pixie-featured creature could turn out culinary feasts seemingly at the drop of a hat, often with a baby strapped to her, and yet stay as tiny and waiflike as she'd been when we first met.

'I got out of the cooking groove during my time as a club singer in Cairo,' she admitted.

I daresay her disastrous first marriage, to a silver-tongued but criminally inclined villain hadn't helped. The never-to-be-forgotten day of our meeting occurred four years ago when we'd rescued her from a sleazy apartment block in

Cairo, locked in among antiquities stolen from the Egyptian Museum by her now-dead husband and his also-now-dead brothers.

The fact that all three of this unholy triad of thieves had crossed over to the afterlife was something in which I took no small measure of personal satisfaction. I'd been on the scene for all three deaths, although not actually responsible for any one of them I hasten to add. That Jessica was now happily married to my ex-boyfriend of ten years was equally something I could quietly rejoice in. It had released me to fall in love with and marry Adam after all.

Jessica was Ted's daughter. Ted was a professor of Egyptology and Adam's former tutor at Oxford. Since his retirement he'd become something of a father-figure, or, at the very least, a favourite uncle. The professor had joined us on a number of our adventures in Egypt. As he joined us now, taking a delight in his new granddaughter that was a joy to see.

At just over a year old, Polly was teething and attempting to take her first tentative steps on her fat little legs. We all adored her.

But right now she was in bed. Jessica had just re-joined us at the table, bringing the baby monitor with her. Dan was brewing coffee.

It was Adam who answered Dan's question. 'The Egyptian Tourism Authority wants to ride on the coat tails of the Belzoni exhibition. The idea is for Merry to re-trace the Belzonis' steps through Egypt, writing a blog-cum-travelogue that can be published online and in all the major travel magazines, not to mention National Geographic and those focused on Egyptology and archaeology.'

I accepted the mug of coffee Dan poured for me, and elucidated further. 'As you know, the British Museum opened the Belzoni exhibition last year as 2015 was the two-hundred-year anniversary of the Belzonis' arrival in Egypt. But Giovanni Belzoni's major discoveries in the Nile Valley took place in 1816 and 1817. I think the plan is that I follow in the great man's footsteps two hundred years after him and bring his story back to life, while giving potential tourists an insight into all the major heritage sites along the Nile to encourage tourists to see Egypt as a holiday destination once again.'

Dan sat down heavily at the table. A big, gangly chap with long limbs and a stomach that gave away his fondness for beer, his expression as he gazed at me was a familiar one. I wasn't surprised to observe the scowl. In the latter stages of our long relationship it was an expression his features had settled into with increasing frequency. The upside of this was the proof Dan cared about me enough to be annoyed by what he saw as my recklessness. The downside was that we were clearly incompatible. Put it this way, Adam entered my life and Jessica Dan's just at the right time.

His scowl now proved Dan still cared about me. We were among the lucky few whose affection endured though our relationship didn't. 'And just how did the Egyptian Tourism Authority come to learn about you?' he asked with a deep note of suspicion in his voice.

Adam smiled. He never reacted to Dan's tone the way I did. It's possible he didn't hear the subtext, for he answered the question at face value. 'It seems the junior Tourism Minister Zahed Mansour was bemoaning Egypt's beleaguered tourist trade to Director Ismail at some ministerial shindig in Cairo. His hopes that secret chambers in Tutankhamun's tomb might help kick start things had turned to dust, and he was casting about for another marketing angle to entice tourists back. Director Ismail knows Rashid Soliman, and was keeping tabs on the success of the Belzoni exhibition. He'd read all the articles Merry published on the British Museum website. And, of course, he already knew who Merry was, thanks to the tomb.'

He had no need to explain this last remark. Dan and Ted had been there when Director Feisal Ismail relieved us of responsibility for the tomb (which is another way of saying he'd banned us from it, and from his country, and slapped a gagging order on us). Jessica, of course, knew all about it. She'd been part of the original rescue party that saved Adam and me from permanent entombment after we found ourselves

25

trapped inside on the night we discovered it. So we could speak freely among ourselves.

'So you're saying Feisal Ismail contacted Rashid Soliman, who invited the two bigwigs from Egypt to come and offer Merry a job,' Ted said, nodding as events leading up to today's interview became clear. 'And the British Museum is willing to sponsor this travelogue project?'

'Yes,' Adam confirmed. 'It's a way of garnering more interest in the museum's Belzoni exhibits and likely to attract even more visitors through the doors.'

'You'd be mad to go,' Dan said abruptly, looking at me. 'And Adam, I'm surprised if you're encouraging her.'

Jessica smiled gently at me and laid a small hand over her husband's on the tabletop. 'He's going to start telling you Egypt is a political no-go zone given to street riots and civil strife,' she smiled.

I was quite pleased to see the scowl Dan directed at her was every bit as fierce as those he sent my way. Perhaps Jessica wasn't immune after all. But then his eyes softened. 'No, that was last time she insisted on going native,' he said in growling tones that actually held traces of humour. 'This time it's the godforsaken terrorists I'm concerned about.'

Adam and I had already had this discussion. I was able to meet Dan's gaze squarely as I took a sip of my coffee and put the mug back down in front of me. 'While Egypt has suffered perhaps more than its fair share of attacks, it seems to me I could be a victim of terrorism just about anywhere on the planet right now. Let's face it, in recent years all the major cities of the world have come under fire. In the last year alone Brussels and Paris have been hit, and beyond that, New York, London, Mumbai, Tokyo, Sousse in Tunisia ... would you like me to go on...?'

Dan met my gaze. 'I accept any one of us could be in the wrong place at the wrong time and be caught up in one of these atrocities. But, Pinkie, why go courting trouble...? Just think for a moment. It's one thing to know there are dangerous animals in the world, quite another to get into their enclosure with them.'

I chose to ignore this last remark. I was sure it was intended to rile me. Dan had once left me sitting in an open-topped jeep in the middle of a pride of lions on a safari game reserve as one of his despicable practical jokes. He'd bribed the ranger to pretend we'd run out of petrol. He knew full well I'd freaked out at the time. I was a far jumpier character back then. Or perhaps he brought out the worst in me. 'There's no Foreign Office ban on travel to Cairo, Luxor or the Nile Valley,' I pointed out coolly, challenging his gaze with mine. 'It's only Sharm-el-Sheikh that's off limits at the moment. I reached for Adam's hand under the table and held it, voicing the opinion we'd come to after long discussion this afternoon. 'It strikes me that if we stop travelling to places like Egypt then fundamentalist groups like Islamic State are getting exactly what they want. We're playing into their hands.'

Adam returned the pressure on my hand with a reassuring squeeze and smiled at Dan across the table. 'I want to support Egypt to get on her feet again. And, let's be honest, if you don't like crowds, now's a great time to go. Ahmed says the sites are all but deserted. There's nobody there.'

Dan arched one eyebrow. 'The reason nobody's there is they're all in rubber dinghies paddling to get *here*,' he said ironically, referring to the current refugee crisis from the Middle East.

'That's more Syria and Libya than Egypt,' I pointed out. 'Besides, it's not something to joke about.' I frowned at him, and went on. 'I agree with Adam, the best time to visit Egypt is now. The sites are amazing without crowds of tourists everywhere. It's possible to imagine the tombs and temples as they were when Belzoni and his contemporaries dug them out from the sand.'

Dan started to interrupt me, but I held up my hand to forestall him. 'As for terrorism,' I said. 'You're more likely to win the lottery twice in a row than be involved in a terrorist attack.'

Dan's eyebrows swept downwards as he met my gaze. 'Err, the fewer players the more chance there is of your number coming up!' He spoke as if this flaw in my logic was blindingly obvious. Dan has never hesitated to pick holes in my arguments given half a chance.

Despite the habitual awareness of my hackles rising in response to his hectoring tone, I faltered hearing that if I'm honest. It brought crashing back to the forefront of my mind the one consideration I'd been wrestling with since agreeing to go away and think about the proposition put before me today.

I took a hasty gulp of coffee and decided I may as well own up to the main issue concerning me. 'It's just the ethics of the whole thing making me hesitate,' I confessed. 'I can think of nothing I'd like more than to retrace the Belzonis' footsteps and be paid for the privilege, whilst also writing up my experiences as I go. Given that, I can accept the personal risk of going to a politically unstable country with a very real threat of terrorism. But I'm not sure how I feel about putting my name to a campaign whose fundamental aim is to encourage tourists back to Egypt. What if I'm successful and, because of something I write, people venture to Egypt who may otherwise have stayed away, and then get caught up in one of these awful terrorist incidents? How would I live with myself?'

It was a very real fear, and I felt myself shrinking away from the prospect.

Dan stared at me as if finally I was seeing the light. Adam held my hand tightly, wordlessly in tune with my anxiety, not seeking to persuade me either way. It was Ted who leaned forward, pulling my attention to his face with the movement.

'My dear girl, you can't possibly take responsibility for other people's decisions.' He held his glasses on the bridge of his nose with his forefinger and peered at me intently through them. A small, neatly attired man with silver hair and pale blue eyes, he spoke with a soft seriousness that lent gravitas to his tone. It's possible he'd learned that note of solemnity as an Oxford university lecturer back in his pre-retirement days. If so, he employed it now to great effect to add weight to his words. Or it might simply have been his advancing years lending him added authority. Ted was in his late seventies. Adam and I loved him as a mentor, a dear friend, and the closest thing to family it was possible to be considering we weren't actually related. So when Ted talked, I listened. Fixing me with an intent gaze, he went on, 'If somebody reads your travelogue and decides to visit Egypt, it will be because they have made that choice for themselves. You won't have contacted their travel agent or purchased their flight tickets. They will have done these things of their own free will. You have to assume they are as cognisant of the risks as you are. It's not your job to point out those risks. If we start trying to play parent and nursemaid to people who are perfectly capable of reading the newspapers and making their own choices and decisions, then we are indeed playing into the terrorists' hands. It means we are colluding in allowing a culture of cowardice and fear to thrive. That's what Islamic State wants, and that's what we'll be giving them.'

'Well said professor,' Adam concurred.

'You're right Dad,' Jessica said quietly.

Dan said nothing, but his features settled into that oh-so-familiar frown. I'm not sure he and the professor had ever wholly hit it off. Dan's warped sense of humour had been an early test to their relationship. Sadly there wasn't anything humorous in the subject under discussion now.

Ted wasn't quite done. He took a sip of coffee and glanced at each of us in turn, his eyes finally coming to rest on his son-in-law's scowl. 'You young people may not remember it, but I'm sufficiently long in the tooth to recall the Lockerbie disaster.' And he went on to elucidate. 'Just before Christmas 1988 a Pan Am flight was blown out of the sky when a bomb exploded onboard over the Scottish town of Lockerbie. Those killed were not just the people onboard. Many were folk simply sitting in their living rooms watching TV when chunks of flaming fuselage smashed through their homes.'

We all stared back at him with grave faces. In actual fact, I did have a vague recollection of the Lockerbie bombing. I'd have been about eleven at the time. I could see the others dredging it up from their memory banks too.

'Colonel Gadafi took responsibility in the end, if I remember rightly,' Adam said.

'He did.' Ted nodded.

'So, you're saying we should stand against Islamic State in the same way we stood against Gadafi's Libya,' Adam added.

'Partly, my boy,' Ted agreed. 'Partly. But more than that, I'm saying there's nowhere wholly safe in the world. Those poor souls in Lockerbie were killed with their suppers on their laps, no doubt watching Coronation Street or something equally banal on television. To me, that stands as a lesson that one should never stop living one's life or rejecting opportunities for fear of the risk of terrorism. Lockerbie proves it can strike in the apparent safety of one's own home. I'm no great fatalist, but it does rather make me wonder whether if one's number is up then it's up, simple as that. So why give up on a dream just because of the danger of something that *might* happen. That smacks to me of handing over one's life to the enemy with or without being caught up in one of these dreadful atrocities. It gives these despicable fanatics victory on a plate.'

Dan knew he'd lost the argument and had the grace to look abashed.

He reserved his final word on the subject for the hug he gave me as Adam and I were departing a little while later. 'Well, at least there's one thing I can be thankful for,' he said as he released me.

'What's that?'

He looked down into my eyes with a self-satisfied smirk. 'I'm no longer the one who has to face Puff the Magic Dragon!'

He was referring to my mother of course. I knew my family would need some persuasion to support my return to the land of the pharaohs. But I could also hear an echo of my Mum's voice in my head saying with an air of fatalistic resignation that she'd realised a long time ago she couldn't live her children's lives for them. I also knew she was realistic enough to recognise I was every bit as much at risk travelling to work every day on the Tube as I was likely to be in Egypt. In that acknowledgement she and Ted were very much in tune.

It's fair to say my mind was made up.

The next day I met with Zahed Mansour, Feisal Ismail and Rashid Soliman and named my terms.

* * *

It was agreed I'd return to Egypt in early September, about six weeks after the end of my contract at the British Museum. I'll admit to a bit of a wobble about my decision when in mid-July scores of people were killed and injured in Nice. A crazed pro-Islamist drove a 19 tonne cargo truck into crowds along the promenade. The victims were out celebrating Bastille Day at a seafront firework display. Islamic State claimed responsibility for the attack, describing the killer as a "Soldier of Islam".

Watching the News footage and reading the newspaper reports, my anxiety was swiftly replaced by a blood-boiling anger. If anything, this latest horror simply served to reinforce Ted's view that nowhere was safe from these extremist murderers. I decided I might as well take my chances in Egypt than kid myself I was safer staying away. It felt like a small but important act of defiance, two fingers up to the warped ideology waging war on our Western way of life. I could feel the Bulldog spirit kicking in my gut. It made me super-determined not to be cowed. Egypt was my destiny. At least, it had certainly felt like it for a number of years. I refused to allow fear to control my actions and my life. It was time to go back.

In the meantime, there was the small matter of my leaving do to attend. Carrie Kinsella made all the arrangements. Carrie, my colleague in the public relations and marketing team at the museum was a firm friend, although the truth is we got off to a rather shaky start. Her unwitting assault on Adam in the early days of our employment no doubt had something to do with it. You may well ask how it's possible for an assault to be unwitting. This would be a perfectly reasonable question. I'll excuse her by saying she didn't realise it was Adam she was attacking from behind with her brolly. She was in a state of panic at the time. The mother of all thunderstorms was unleashing its fury overhead. She was also in the thrall of a devious antiquities trafficker masquerading as a museum Egyptologist.

With so much mitigation, I'd found it in my heart to forgive her. Adam, naturally, had been of the opinion from the start that there was nothing to forgive. But then Adam has always been a sucker for a damsel in distress. It makes his passion for me all the more mystifying. Not that I'm complaining. Adam and I are soulmates. I don't need him to rescue me. In fact I sometimes wonder if it's possible *I* might have been the one who rescued *him*. Adam was at a point in his life when I walked into it where nothing was certain except his love of Egypt. That this was a shared passion, then as now, remains a constant source of joy. It's led us on adventures too numerous to mention.

But I digress. So, to my leaving do.

Carrie arranged it in the Great Court Restaurant at the museum. This was where Adam and I held our wedding breakfast a little over eighteen months ago, when we were 'officially' married. Of course, we'd considered ourselves husband and wife ever since our impromptu exchange of vows while trapped inside our secret tomb three years ago. But the ceremony in the replica of Seti I's tomb created for the Belzoni exhibition (plus the legal version at a local Registry office the following day) made the whole thing bona fide and lawful.

Adam and I had actually married each other three times. Three times lucky, I like to say. So my leaving do in the Great Court Restaurant in the museum was laced with a heavy dose of nostalgia and not a little sense of the bittersweet.

I was eager and excited (whilst a trifle nervous) to return to Egypt. But I'd loved my couple of years at the British Museum. Frankly, I still couldn't believe my luck that I'd landed a job – no matter how temporary – at the nation's pre-eminent cultural attraction, and one with an unrivalled Egyptian collection. I was sorry to be leaving. But I'd signed up knowing my position was time-limited. So there was no point bemoaning the end of my contact now it was upon me. I'd been fortunate to squeeze a further year out of it.

Even so, I couldn't help but feel a tug of regret knowing my identity badge and security card would no longer grant me employee admission. The museum had been a great place to work.

Everyone was there to see me off and wish me well. As it was after hours, the dining tables had been rearranged, so the vibe was more one of an exclusive bar than a posh museum restaurant. Jazz played from a sound system set up in the background, and waiters and waitresses (who'd signed up for overtime) came among us with platters of canapés.

Pippa, my sister-in-law, one of the invited guests said, 'Wow, Merry! This is a lot of trouble and expense to go to for someone on a fixed term contract!'

My boss Ruth Farriday happened to overhear her. 'We're sorry to see Meredith go,' she said. Ruth was a business-like woman in her middle years. Stout with a short professional haircut, and dressed in a no-nonsense suit, her single nod to femininity was the colourful silk scarf she'd arranged artfully around her collar. 'She played an enormous part in the success of our Belzoni exhibition. Giovanni Belzoni and his wife Sarah sprang back to life under the creative flair that flowed from her fingertips and onto our website. Our visitors were mesmerised. I've never known them so rapt about one of our showcases.'

'You weren't able to offer her something permanent here on the back of a track record like that?' Pippa challenged gently. I knew she wasn't especially thrilled at the prospect of my imminent return to Egypt.

'Sadly not,' Ruth admitted with a note of genuine regret, which touched me more than I liked to show. Ruth had proved herself a tough taskmaster. I respected and admired her, and knew I'd been fortunate to have a boss who challenged me to give of my absolute best every day. 'Our employment rules preclude it. That's why we wanted to give Meredith the best possible send off.'

With a lump in my throat, I accepted my beautifully wrapped leaving gift – a rather nice silver bangle patterned with engraved hieroglyphics. These spelt out the words "Good Luck Meredith", a lovely personal touch. There was also a card, signed I think by just about everyone on the staff team. As farewell parties go, I have to say I was extraordinarily affected by the generosity and warm-heartedness of mine.

'We'll miss you, Merry.' Carrie said simply. 'You've made your mark on the place. It won't be the same without you.'

I was pleased to see she was here with her new boyfriend. Graham was deputy head of the security team at the museum. He'd been appointed to the role a year or so ago after the museum conducted a root and branch review of its security systems in the wake of events that led to the imprisonment of Carrie's former flame. It amused me to see her switch her affections from poacher to gamekeeper. Graham was a gregarious chap with a ready smile and laughing eyes. He was far more deserving of her quick wits, sunshiny nature and pretty face than the dastardly Simon Kingsbury had ever been. That her ex was serving a long custodial sentence for his crimes was a source of some personal pride since Adam and I had played a part in putting him behind bars.

'We've had some fun, haven't we?' I acknowledged, hugging her. 'And we'll stay in touch.'

And then it was over. I was a British Museum employee no more.

There was one big advantage to being unemployed for a few weeks before my departure for Egypt. August turned out to be beautiful weather-wise: hot and sunny throughout. This is such a rarity in the UK. Usually as the schools break up for summer holidays the rainclouds descend. Not so this year. This meant I was free to enjoy that oh-so-rare thing: a perfect English summer.

I made the most of it, sunbathing in London's parks, where the grass was turning yellow through lack of rain, and spending a few days in rural Kent at my parents' country cottage. As predicted, my mum and dad accepted my decision to return to Egypt with concern but not challenge. Reassured by the terms I'd negotiated for my new job, they made no attempt to talk me out of it, for which I was grateful. They just told me to be careful, and that was fair enough.

I made sure I was back in the capital in time to watch the Olympics with Adam, Dan and Jessica. Four years ago London hosted the games. The four of us had yelled ourselves hoarse cheering our athletes to their storming victories, watching the action on a gigantic screen set up in Hyde Park. This year it was the turn of Rio, and we watched events unfold on Dan and Jessica's television. It was thrilling to watch as Team GB's gold medal tally rocketed even beyond its 2012 total, making Rio our most successful games ever. We became the first country to out-perform its own record at the games subsequent to being host nation.

Pride gripped Great Britain, and the Olympics became the talk of bars, restaurants and coffee shops. It made a nice change from the political theatrics that had dominated the earlier part of the summer as Britain voted to leave the European Union and hurriedly replaced David Cameron with our second female Prime Minister Theresa May.

All in all, it had been quite a summer. The UK was a happening place to be. Nevertheless as the weeks passed my thoughts turned more and more to the prospect of what lay ahead of me in Egypt.

After all, for me personally there was more to going back than simply taking up my new role on behalf of Egypt's Tourism Authority and following in Giovanni Belzoni's footsteps. Secretly, I was far more interested in the opportunity it presented me to retrace the journey of Belzoni's wife Sarah.

Chapter 3

As wedding presents go, mine from Adam was really rather special. He'd used what remained of his hard-earned savings to purchase a set of papers bequeathed by Sarah Belzoni to her one-time servant and lifelong friend James Curtin. That the purchase was made via Adam's ex-wife Tabitha was a small detail I was happy to overlook.

Adam and Tabitha were in the final stages of their divorce when I met him. So there was nothing to get het up about there. That Tabitha had chosen to leave Adam for a wealthy wine merchant who just happened to be a direct descendent of James Curtin was one of those strange quirks of fate to which I'm becoming increasingly accustomed. It's happened a few times now that destiny seems to have grabbed me by the gut and given me a damn good squeeze. I've stopped asking myself about the science of coincidence or happenstance, call it what you will, and learned simply to accept it as part of life's rich pattern.

Anyway, on James Curtin's death Sarah's papers passed generation to generation through the male line of descent until they reached Richard Curtin, Tabitha's new fiancé. A man with no historical curiosity, genealogical bent or apparent familial sentimentality, Richard Curtin had little interest in the bequeathed papers. In fact they languished forgotten in his attic for years after his father's death. He and Tabitha rediscovered them when they cleared out Richard's attic in preparation for buying their new home as a soon-to-be married couple.

As the bequest contained some small ancient Egyptian artefacts and fragments of papyri, Richard spotted a potential money-spinner. Tabitha, with a "thwarted" (in actual fact newly-qualified) Egyptologist as an ex-husband, enlisted Adam to help value the small collection for sale via an auction house. Adam, wonderful man that he is, recognised the opportunity to make an offer for the papers and other bits and pieces and kill two birds with one stone: give Richard and Tabitha a fair price for Sarah Belzoni's bequest, whilst also securing for us this unique insight into how Egypt's lost civilisation was rediscovered. Despite Adam's generous offer, Richard and Tabitha still proceeded to auction. To my way of looking at it that said a lot about the glint of greed in their eyes. That Adam, forced to bid for the Sarah Belzoni papers, managed to secure them for a fraction less than his original offer was vindication enough. That he then chose to give them to me as a wedding present simply served to reinforce (as if I needed it) how lucky I am to have met and married my soulmate.

He knew the Sarah Belzoni papers would be the perfect wedding gift. I can think of none finer or imbued with such meaning. Having said which, I'm quite sure Adam was not entirely innocent of wanting to flesh out the little mystery we'd stumbled across and felt the papers might be our best chance. Considering this was my deepest desire, it served simply to underline just how in tune Adam and I truly are.

Sarah Belzoni already held the accolade of being the first European woman to travel through the Nile Valley. She accompanied her husband, the flamboyant and publicity-savvy Giovanni Belzoni on his travels through Egypt and Nubia spanning the years 1815 to 1819. She was there when he first visited the temples of Abu Simbel covered in drifting sand, and when he discovered the most beautiful royal tomb in the Valley of the Kings: that of the New Kingdom 19th Dynasty pharaoh Seti I.

What the world was yet to learn was that Sarah Belzoni, intrepid to the last, made a bid to mount an expedition of her own to Egypt after her husband's untimely death. Giovanni Belzoni met his premature end in 1822 on a reckless and ill-fated mission to West Africa in search of the lost city of Timbuktu. He contracted dysentery. It was a sorry end for the larger-than-life character, particularly one who'd done so much to bring Egypt's ancient history back from oblivion.

Reluctantly forced to admit that, this time, her husband would not be returning from his explorations, and staring penury in the face, Sarah Belzoni made a bold plea to the Trustees of the British Museum to sponsor her return to Egypt.

Her bid was to recover unique artefacts for the museum's collection. The Frenchman Jean-François Champollion had just cracked decipherment of the hieroglyphics and published his *Précis*. Using Champollion's publication to undertake a crash course of self-study, Sarah was convinced that on her travels through that antique land with her husband she'd spotted textual evidence to shed light on a story of ancient Egypt now emerging from the sands of time.

The trustees dismissively stonewalled her. Undeterred Sarah took her case elsewhere and ultimately secured funds from William John Bankes. A gentleman traveller of independent means, Bankes had been in Egypt at the same time as the Belzonis. He'd commissioned Giovanni Belzoni to transport a magnificent obelisk from the temple of Philae, near modern Aswan, to his family seat in Kingston Lacy, Dorset. It stands there proudly to this day.

I have no idea whether, when Bankes recommended a certain 'Samuel Bane' to the antiquarian Robert Hay, whose expedition to Abu Simbel took place in 1825, he realised the young man in question was in actual fact Sarah Belzoni in disguise. That he gave Sarah money was not in doubt. Our friend, National Trust Volunteer Margaret Rylance happened across the critical record in the Kingston Lacy archives of Bankes' posthumous payment to Giovanni Belzoni's widow of a sum more than adequate to compensate the recently bereaved woman for her late husband's trouble. Bane was

Sarah's maiden name. And of course it took no great mental leap from Sarah to Samuel. As I'd once said to Adam, it was simply a case of clocking the initials.

Sarah already had a track record of personal adventure and disguise. She'd dressed herself as a male Mamluk in order to take herself off on an independent tour of the Holy Land during her husband's explorations in Egypt, with just James Curtin, her young servant, for company.

Adam and I had indulged already in a suspicion that Sarah Belzoni might have returned to Egypt to join Robert Hay's expedition in 1825. Tabitha turning up with the promise of personal papers of Sarah's dated to around the same time was too good an opportunity to pass up. So Adam shelled out for Sarah Belzoni's bequest when the public auction failed to meet the list price, and then gifted it to me as a wedding present.

But that wasn't all. We also had access to the diary Sarah had written on her original trip to Egypt and Nubia alongside her more famous husband. This journal had seen adventure enough of its own having been stolen from Sarah in London during the months of her fruitless appeal to the British Museum trustees.

The culprit, we learned subsequently, was Henry Salt, British Consul General in Cairo, and Giovanni Belzoni's bitter enemy. Their enmity was thanks to a falling out over ownership and sale of the antiquities Belzoni found and transported from Egypt to England. Salt claimed them for himself, demoting Belzoni to the ranks of hired help. This meant Salt received all the proceeds from the sale of the antiquities to the British Museum while Belzoni got nothing. Belzoni was furious, and the two men had an acrimonious and very public quarrel from which their relationship never recovered.

It seemed that in London after Belzoni's death, Salt got wind that Sarah may have recorded a significant find from the smaller temple at Abu Simbel into her journal during her sojourn there with her husband in 1816. This was the temple dedicated by Ramses the Great to his queen Nefertari. Only later, when she'd learned to translate the hieroglyphs did Sarah recognise she may have come across something of value; hence her appeal to the British Museum Trustees.

I can only assume Henry Salt's hatred of Belzoni, even after the latter's death, was stronger than his moral principles. He stole Sarah's journal and thus deprived her of her personal record of the treasured times she and her husband spent exploring and excavating in Egypt. I daresay he imagined he could take this despicable theft a step further and steal a march on the widow who'd made such a brazen bid to mount an independent expedition back to Nubia. It seems clear he wanted to claim for himself whatever it was she'd stumbled across in Nefertari's Temple and recorded in her diary.

Much good it did him! Henry Salt returned to Egypt but was plagued with ill health and never made it further south than Thebes; modern Luxor. He died in Alexandria at the age of only forty-seven. But not before Sarah's diary had been stolen back from him. *Hah*! I thought with satisfaction.

The guilty party was an Egyptian ghaffir named Abdullah, hired by Henry Salt as his *reis* – a sort of foreman-com-guard-com-guide – during his excavations in Thebes. Abdullah had worked for Giovanni Belzoni during his travels in Egypt. He'd borne witness to the remarkable period when Belzoni discovered no less than six royal tombs in the Valley of the Kings. He'd also befriended Sarah. A talented artist, he'd illustrated her journal with sketches of the monuments they visited on their travels.

Perhaps Henry Salt hoped some of Belzoni's almost supernatural luck would rub off on him when he hired Abdullah. If so, his plan backfired. Abdullah had good reason to know of the hostility between the Belzonis and Salt, having spent so many years with Giovanni and Sarah. He was also clear where his loyalty lay. When he spotted Sarah's treasured journal in Henry Salt's possession he rightly suspected foul play. Suffering no qualms he promptly stole the diary back. Whether this was to scupper Salt in his nefarious intent, or to keep for himself a memento of his own cherished times with the Belzonis is impossible to say. All we know for sure is that Sarah's diary, illustrated with Abdullah's sketches, was lovingly passed down through the future generations of his family, until it came into the possession of his descendent Rashid Soliman, who happened to be Adam's boss.

You'll have gathered by now why I've stopped questioning the whims of providence. It may seem far-fetched beyond all imagining that Adam and I should have access through Rashid (reluctantly, I'll admit) to Sarah Belzoni's original journal, and also now own (with rather more alacrity on the part of Tabitha and Richard Curtin) the diary of Sarah's second journey to Nubia. On this latter occasion, disguised as a young male epigrapher, she joined the Robert Hay expedition to Abu Simbel in 1825. Far-fetched it may be. It's also the truth.

To say Adam and I devoured the contents of both journals in the weeks after our wedding would be to wildly understate it.

The key section in the original journal, dated to 1816, recorded Sarah's discovery in the smaller temple at Abu Simbel of a set of stone stele. From Abdullah's drawings and Sarah's faithfully transcribed hieroglyphics these appeared to tell the story of Queen Nefertari's family background. Sadly Sarah only copied fragments into her journal, not the whole text. It was enough to whet the appetite but not to answer the questions that had puzzled Egyptologists for decades about Nefertari's elusive origins.

The second journal, written during the Robert Hay expedition in 1825, was a hard one to decipher. I can only imagine the intrepid widow was exercising extreme caution in what she committed to paper so as not to blow her cover. And of course the romance was missing since this time she was travelling solo, bereft of her beloved husband. Gone was the flowing, descriptive prose of her earlier diary. In its place was a terse, abbreviated record of daily copying and 'squeezing' of the wall reliefs. Perhaps worrying that if her journal should happen to be read by any other member of the party she'd be thrown out as an imposter, she decided to remain circumspect in everything she wrote down.

For Adam and me this proved extremely frustrating. It was a fascinating record nonetheless of a pre-Victorian exploration, valuable for its own sake if not for any secrets it might reveal. There was just one entry that seemed to give the clue to Sarah's own frustration and disappointment.

"If ever there were stone tablets to be found here recording this temple's provenance or shedding light on its owners' history, they are here no longer. All that remain are a few scrolls of papyri, perhaps considered trifling and undeserving of notice by previous visitors. My colleague and compatriot Joseph Bonomi has permission to take these for his own collection in part-payment for his services."

The Joseph Bonomi collection had been bequeathed to the Ashmolean Museum in Oxford as recently as a couple of years ago. Ted had been coaxed from retirement, given the opportunity to catalogue it for the museum's archives. As yet, nothing from this collection had been put on display beyond a few assorted artefacts: carved scarab beetles, a few small bronze statues, some clay ostraca, and suchlike. It seemed museum visitors were less attracted by the chance to pore over papyri. Presumably this was owing to the fact that to the majority of people these were faded scrolls of quirkily attractive but nevertheless meaningless gobbledygook.

Not so to Adam and Ted. It's quite handy having an Egyptologist for a husband, not to mention a professor of philology as a friend-cum-favourite-adopted-uncle. The three of us had spent many happy hours perusing the papyri.

The scrolls teased and tantalised us, but didn't really answer our questions. Nefertari was described variously as *'granddaughter of the royal house'* and *'hereditary princess'*, but nowhere as *'King's daughter'*, which was the usual way of describing a direct descendent of the pharaoh and his great royal wife.

This was more of a clue to Nefertari's opaque origins than historians had been able to piece together before. Even so it was insufficient to enable us to make any bold claims about her heredity. It had always been assumed that Nefertari was a high-ranking member of the nobility, not necessarily of royal blood. The Bonomi papyrus suggested otherwise. But there was a world of difference between a suggestion and a statement. The royal titles were the strongest evidence yet of a royal lineage, but not the same thing at all as actually knowing the line of descent.

I felt sure the set of stone stele Sarah Belzoni had first seen in the smaller temple at Abu Simbel in 1816 must have told the story. But they were no longer there when she went back to look for them in 1825. To say Adam and I shared her disappointment and frustration was putting it mildly. It was a terrible anti-climax.

'So what happened to them?' we'd asked each other.

'The trouble is, any number of early explorers visited Abu Simbel in those first years after Belzoni cleared the sand from its façade,' Adam said. 'Any one of them could have found the stele and removed them.'

'Then why haven't they turned up in one of the important international Egyptological collections?' I frowned. 'You'd think if the stele spelled out Nefertari's family tree they'd be on display among the most prized of all antiquities – just as Sarah Belzoni believed they might be if only she'd managed to secure them for the British Museum.'

Adam shrugged. 'It's possible of course they were simply destroyed, possibly by local tribesmen, and probably by accident.'

This was such an undesirable outcome I was unwilling to entertain it. 'Is it possible,' I ventured, 'that those stele might have found their way into one of the major Egyptian

51

collections of the world without anyone registering their significance?'

'Highly unlikely,' Adam said dampeningly.

Even so, he and I had used up our annual leave entitlement over the last year or so making long-weekend visits to as many as possible of the cities of the world that housed notable ancient Egyptian collections. We visited Berlin, Munich and Saxony in Germany; Turin, Florence and Bologna in Italy; Paris obviously; and spent our 10-day summer holiday last year in America touring all the main collections housed in New York, Boston, Berkeley and Chicago. We scoured all these national museums, searching for any sign of the stele, or anything that might indicate they'd ever existed. Adam's credentials as an Egyptologist employed by the British Museum granted us access to the storage vaults, always accompanied of course. We'd resolved to be completely candid about the purpose of our visit, openly saying we were seeking to corroborate suggestive evidence posed by the Joseph Bonomi papyrus about the origins of Queen Nefertari.

But despite the interest and willingness to help this sparked in all those we approached, our tours of inspection failed to turn up anything of note. Well-travelled though we might now claim to be it was only insofar as we'd made whistle-stop tours of the major European and North American archaeological and antiquities collections. It's fair to say our heads had been firmly in Egypt the whole time. Sadly this left little time to really enjoy the countries we visited.

It also left us no further forward than when we started, and with sadly depleted bank balances.

'There's one obvious place we haven't checked out,' I'd said to Adam on our return from the States.

'Oh?' he'd turned his lovely blue eyes on me.

'What about the Egyptian Museum in Cairo? We've seen the behind-the-scenes part of the museum. The place is positively packed with artefacts that have never seen the light of day, or even been properly catalogued. You've said yourself, there's almost as much in storage as there is on display!'

His eyes gleamed, deepening from blue to violet as he regarded me. I knew this meant he'd caught my drift and would need no further convincing. Adam's eyes always seem to change colour when his bloodstream starts to fizz with the excitement of a new possibility. 'We should get Walid and Shukura on the case,' he'd said, mentioning our Egyptian friends who worked at the Cairo Museum. Walid is the senior curator in charge of the ancient Egyptian collection. Shukura is a PhD doctor of numismatics, the study of ancient coins. So in fairness making a search for Ramesside stele couldn't really be described as her specialism. Even so, I knew for a fact she'd be thoroughly put out not to be included.

Still regarding me with the light of possibility in his eyes, Adam went on, 'The Grand Egyptian Museum will be opening in Giza in the next couple of years, all being well. Surely they must be making a start on sorting through the storage vaults in preparation for the move. It's the perfect opportunity to search for the stele.'

We'd put Walid and Shukura on the case of the missing stele months ago, with disappointing results. If the tablets Sarah Belzoni had seen and noted into her journal in 1816 were languishing forgotten in one of the storage vaults of the Cairo Museum, they were very well hidden. Walid's slow and systematic searches had so far failed to turn them up. Still, I had not yet given up hope.

I clung to a faint belief that the reason the stele hadn't come to light was because nobody had yet thought to look for them in the right place. I refused absolutely to countenance the possibility they had been broken or smashed no matter how accidentally in the early days of Egyptian exploration. The first Egyptologists were little more than treasure seekers, Belzoni included. It was unconscionable to me that any of these adventurers could have failed to recognise the historical value of textual tablets found inside a temple that had been covered in drifting sand for millennia. And if the natives had claimed them then they too, I felt sure, would have done so as a means of making a swift profit, selling them onto the burgeoning antiquities market as the era of Victorian exploration proper got underway.

My instincts told me that if the stele did indeed still exist, then there was a possibility they were still in Egypt. Of course there was absolutely no way of knowing where to start looking. If Sarah Belzoni aka Samuel Bane had failed to locate them, there was no reason why I should be any more successful.

I just had this crazy feeling of destiny taking me by the hand and tugging at me. It felt as if I'd been handed all the other pieces: Sarah Belzoni's two journals and the Bonomi papyrus. The stele must surely be the last piece of the jigsaw. And now I'd been gifted the opportunity to return to Egypt and follow in Sarah Belzoni's footsteps.

Others may scoff at what I call my female intuition or Egyptological sixth sense. But I've learned to trust it, and to pay attention when I hear echoes of ancient Egypt resounding down the centuries.

So I felt quite sure this totally unexpected and wholly unlooked-for career opportunity with the Egyptian Tourism Authority was more than just chance. Egypt had come knocking. There were secrets she still wanted to share with me and I was eager to find out what they were. It felt like an old romance flaring to life again. I couldn't be happier. I was going home. And Adam, perfectly naturally, was coming with me.

Chapter 4

I'd been quite specific in naming the terms of my return to Egypt. The first: I wasn't going alone. Adam, unlike me, was on a permanent contract with the British Museum. He'd been confirmed in the role when his despicable erstwhile colleague, the antiquities-trafficking Simon Kingsbury, was put safely behind bars.

But if I was going to Egypt then Adam was coming too. It was as simple as that. Happily Adam was as adamant as I on this being my opening gambit for negotiating the acceptance of my job offer. I'd been afraid he might baulk at the prospect of walking away from his first – and, let's be honest, prestigious – paid employment as a qualified Egyptologist. Thankfully he made it clear from the off that there was no way on earth he would sanction me going back without him.

'For a start, neither Dan nor your mother would ever forgive me; and I'm not sure which I'm more frightened of,' he'd joked. 'But seriously, Merry; if it's as potentially dangerous as everyone seems to think thanks to the terrorist threat, then some husband it would make me to even contemplate letting you go on your own.'

So it was settled. I made it clear to Director Ismail and Zahed Mansour that the first non-negotiable proviso for my acceptance of their offer was that Adam would be joining me. Adam similarly braved an audience with Rashid Soliman to tender his resignation.

Rashid's response surprised us very much. He invited Adam to take a twelve-month sabbatical from the British Museum, '...so you may accompany your wife on her journey retracing Belzoni's travels.' (Even though I wasn't there to hear him say this, I had no trouble imagining the sonorous tone in which he delivered this small speech). 'After all, Meredith will need an Egyptologist intimately acquainted with Giovanni Belzoni's history to ensure her travelogue is accurate in every particular. Who better than the man responsible – jointly with myself of course – for staging the British Museum's most successful exhibition?'

Damn cheek! I remember thinking. I credit myself perfectly able to conduct the research necessary to provide a historically faultless reprisal of the Belzonis' life and times in Egypt. But then I recalled my mother drilling into me never to look a gift horse in the mouth. Rashid was bending over backwards to be accommodating, and here was I bristling defensively at what I imagined he might be implying. Silently I gave myself a damn good talking to, and gracefully held my tongue.

That Rashid was willing to hold open Adam's job for a year was an unexpected bonus. He even went so far as to offer to pay Adam's reasonable expenses, since the British Museum was sponsoring the trip, although Adam himself wouldn't be salaried. It was more than we could have hoped for and we were duly grateful. So, it was decided. We were all set to go.

* * *

I don't mind admitting I was a little less relaxed than usual on the flight from Heathrow to Cairo on board the EgyptAir jet. As we landed and taxied down the runway, I scanned the airport precincts for any sign of unusual activity. I was a bit cross with myself about these obvious signs of the jitters. But I guess I'm only human, and it was perhaps only natural to feel a sense of trepidation in view of recent events. But as the captain switched off the fasten-seatbelt sign I forgot my unease in the simple excitement of being back in Egypt.

The first thing to hit me when we stepped out of the aeroplane onto the wheel-up steps was the enveloping heat. I'd forgotten the almost physical quality to it. But here it was, pressing me into a suffocating embrace. Along with the blinding sunlight it was an aggressively forthright welcome.

The second thing to strike me was the deafening holler Ahmed let out from the tarmac where he stood waiting to greet us. He was standing there in full uniform, legs akimbo, big booted feet planted on the runway, barrel-chest puffed out and arms flung wide in the joyful exuberance of his welcome.

Ahmed was the second non-negotiable condition of my new employment contract. 'There's no way I'm signing up without a personal security guard,' I'd told Director Ismail and Zahed Mansour unequivocally. 'And I know exactly who I want you to appoint.'

They'd assured me earnestly that arrangements for my personal safety were already in hand. But I'd refused point blank to be shifted from my resolve. A few hasty telephone calls later I was duly informed that Mr Ahmed Abd el-Rassul was to be seconded for the duration of my assignment from his current role in the Tourist and Antiquities police in Luxor and would be sent to meet Adam and me when we arrived in Cairo. It was a small but important victory. 'We can be the three musketeers all over again,' I'd said to Adam joyfully.

Ahmed himself was so eager to pull us both into a welcoming embrace every bit as forceful as that of the stifling temperature he didn't even wait for us to reach the bottom of the aircraft steps. Instead he bounded halfway up them to greet us, forcing the other disembarking passengers to manoeuvre around us. He grabbed us each in turn to crush us against him in a bruising bear hug that made me wonder if I ought to reroute Adam and myself straight to the local hospital to check for broken ribs. 'Adam! Merry!' he yelled, making my ears ring. 'I have been counting my own heartbeats until you are returned here safely to your ghostly home!'

'I think you mean spiritual, mate,' Adam wheezed, recovering his balance after extricating himself from Ahmed's vicelike grip while I drew a careful breath testing to see if my lungs still worked.

Ahmed ignored him, or perhaps he didn't hear him so caught up was he in the rapture of our arrival. 'Welcome my friends! Welcome to Alaska!'

This was a favourite catchphrase of the locals. The caleche drivers and felucca sailors in Luxor employ it all the time; their ironical little joke with the tourists about the blazing Egyptian temperatures.

I reached out and grasped both of Ahmed's huge hands; pulling them towards me so I could examine the scarring on them and his forearms. He was wearing a short-sleeved crisp white shirt with gold and black epaulets on each shoulder, so I had no difficulty in observing the rippling indentations on his dark skin where the burns from the explosion had healed.

'It is nothing,' he assured me, squeezing my hands before releasing them and taking my carry-on luggage from me so he could take it down the steps. 'The damage it is small, and the pain, it did not last long.'

'It's hardly nothing,' Adam argued. 'You stopped a group of suicide bombers getting into Karnak!'

61

'You were incredibly brave,' I echoed.

Ahmed brushed off our praise, although I could tell he was secretly delighted by our concern. 'It was my duty to stop those men,' he said. 'You are here now and that is what is important. No longer do you stay away. And I will protect you with my life!'

'We know that, mate,' Adam smiled. 'You've done so before. Why do you think Merry was so determined to get you released from the day-job?'

Ahmed puffed out his chest. 'You do me great honour,' he said grandly. 'It will be just like ancient times!' He flashed his beaming megawatt smile and announced, 'Khaled, he comes on the Nile from Luxor! Tomorrow, he arrives in Cairo. Queen Ahmes, she sails with him.'

Our police pal's pronunciation is so much better than it once was. But when excited he still has a tendency to lapse into a kind of pigeon English, with an excessive use of exclamations. I call it Ahmed-speak and I don't mind it one little bit. Besides I knew exactly what he was trying to say. It proved just how badly Director Ismail and the junior tourist minister wanted me to take up their job offer.

Anyone listening in on this conversation – and they could've done so from at least thirty feet away if they were so minded thanks to the sheer volume of Ahmed's voice – might wonder what on earth an ancient Egyptian queen could possibly have to do with things. But Ahmed's mangled

English made perfect sense to me and I felt my excitement mount to match his at the prospect of seeing her again.

I'd placed two final caveats on my acceptance. Firstly, that for the whole of my time in Egypt I insisted on travelling and living aboard the dahabeeyah owned jointly by Adam and me. She was called the *Queen Ahmes*. Already named before we made an offer for her, we'd known immediately she was part of our destiny. It was thanks to Howard Carter's portraits of the real Queen Ahmes (an elusive figure from ancient history, married to Thutmosis I, and Hatshepsut's mother) that Adam and I got together in the first place. So we had good reason to feel sentimental about the dahabeeyah when we were introduced to her. It was love at first sight. She'd played a significant role in our adventures since then and it had been a bitter wrench to leave her when we departed for England three years ago.

We'd left her mothballed in dry dock near Luxor in the hope of our eventual return. I don't mind admitting there were times when I thought the happy day may never come. That it was tomorrow was a dream come true.

In negotiating terms with Director Ismail and Zahed Mansour I'd made it clear their agreement to our use of the *Queen Ahmes* would include payment of all reasonable living expenses. This seemed perfectly fair to me since there would be no need for them to put Adam and me up in a succession of hotels. Secondly, I specified that I required someone employed and paid a fair wage to sail her and keep her in tiptop shape while we journeyed the length of the Nile.

Khaled was the man who'd lovingly restored the *Queen Ahmes* to her former Victorian splendour in the first place. He'd also put her back to rights after the heart-wrenching (and deliberate) fire that broke out on her upper deck during one of our run-ins with a previous (and now thankfully dead) nemesis.

I couldn't imagine being back in Egypt on an open-ended ticket and not staying on board the *Queen Ahmes* with Khaled at the helm. Ok, so it wouldn't be as the owners of our own business offering luxury tailored Nile cruises to discerning travellers. But it was surely the next best thing, and without the constant worry of how to make ends meet or drum up trade. You can be sure I negotiated a perfectly acceptable salary for myself into the bargain.

I'd had to put up with a fair bit of teeth sucking from my prospective Egyptian employers as I stipulated these last two conditions of my return. I could see they weren't wholly thrilled at the independence I was striking out for. But then, as I'd reasoned patiently with them, it was a job offer I was negotiating, not terms for their control of my whole life. Besides, while the Belzonis travels in Egypt and Nubia pre-dated the Victorian era by a good few years, I pointed out that it was surely more authentic for me to retrace their passage through this antique land on board a historic sail boat on the mighty Nile as opposed to using the more modern and far less evocative transportation offered by trains and cars and planes.

Eventually I think I wore them down – either that or they really did have very high hopes for my potential impact on future tourist traffic. Either way, they granted my wishes. Khaled and the *Queen Ahmes* were duly dispatched from Luxor at about the same time as Adam and I were saying our last farewells to friends and family in readiness for our trip.

So I can happily report Director Ismail and Zahed Mansour accepted all of my prerequisites. Having said that, they also named one or two terms of their own.

It had been decided we'd start out in Cairo, primarily I think so I could take a full briefing from the newly appointed Tourism Minister, who was ultimately my big boss. This was ok. It was normal enough employment practice to clarify my job description and agree a few core objectives for the assignment. Besides, the Belzonis – after a brief period of quarantine in plague-ravaged Alexandria – also spent time in Cairo before accepting the commission from Henry Salt and journeying south. I was eager to start my travelogue in the same place it all began for Giovanni and Sarah.

But before all of that, there was the small matter of the welcome-home party Ahmed and our friends had organised.

* * *

'Welcome back, my dears. Welcome back. My goodness, how we have missed you both! Things have seemed positively dull without you. And of course our poor beleaguered country has suffered the slings and arrows of outrageous fortune since your departure. So much political upheaval! So many clashes on our streets! Soldiers killed at our military checkpoints! And now, of course, the ongoing terrorist threat from ISIS, which operates so alarmingly on our borders. Poor Mr el-Sisi, he presides over a sinking economy. As tourists stay away – and it is hard to blame them – there are not enough jobs for our young people. Once it was said that Egypt's would be one of the biggest growth economies of the twenty-first century. Not so any longer, I fear. With so little employment here in Egypt, our young men take extraordinary risks with their lives to cross the Mediterranean in search of opportunity for a better life in Europe. It is enough to make one shudder at the very thought of their boats capsizing. But enough of all this doom and gloom! I will make you question why on earth you were ever persuaded to return! You have been having exciting times at the British Museum in London, I hear! The most successful Egyptian exhibition ever! Adam, you are a genius! And, Merry, you have put the Belzoni story out there for the world to read! Clever girl! My dears, it gladdens my heart to have you both back. Maybe now we can cherish some small hope of a turnaround in

Egypt's fortunes. Or at the very least, a little bit of fun to enliven these desperate times!'

I'd swear Shukura delivered this entire monologue without once pausing for breath. Dr Shukura al-Busir, expert in numismatics at the Egyptian Antiquities Museum was a force of nature and a motor-mouth. To look at her, she was a fairly typical Middle-Eastern professional woman of a certain age. She squeezed her ample frame into a too-tight navy suit for work, favouring comfortable black pumps on her feet. She let her personality shine through in the brightly patterned headscarves she wound around her face and shoulders and, as now, the flamboyant kaftans she favoured when not at work. She also wore quantities of dark kohl around her eyes and numerous chunky gold rings squashed onto her pudgy fingers. If her general appearance was unremarkable – allowing for these small concessions to character – her voice most definitely was not. She always spoke volubly and at full throttle whether in Arabic or English. The surprise when she switched into our language was her faultless Home Counties accent. This was courtesy of her time studying for her PhD in Oxford. It had taken me aback when I'd first been introduced to her but I was used to it now, happy to be swept along on the gushing tide of her discourse.

I was left almost as breathless from the hug she swept me into at first sight as I'd been after Ahmed's bone-crushing welcome. It was something of a relief when she released me to launch into speech so I could test for bruises.

I smiled weakly at her. 'We're delighted to be back,' I said with as much breath as I was able to muster back into my compressed lungs. 'We've missed you too.'

Adam kissed her cheek, making her blush. I think she has a soft spot for Adam. He's always at his most charming around her. 'We're very much looking forward to Merry's new assignment,' he smiled. 'Although whether we'll be the panacea for Egypt's ailing tourism industry that everyone hopes remains to be seen.'

'But, dear Ted is not joining you on this occasion?' she frowned, remarkably managing to restrict herself to this single question.

Ted and Shukura had once, long ago, enjoyed a brief flirtation on an archaeological dig after Ted's wife died and before Shukura met and married Selim. They bore an enduring affection for one another that was touching to observe.

'He's absolutely besotted with Polly,' I grinned. 'I think it will take more than the lure of following in the Belzonis' footsteps to prise him away from his baby granddaughter!'

'Yes, he sent me a photograph,' Shukura nodded. 'Such an adorable little girl.'

'We've promised to look in on his apartment,' Adam said. 'Not that I hold out much hope for the survival of his pot plants after all this time.'

Walid Massri, an individual who resided at the opposite end of the forcefulness spectrum from his colleague, now stepped forward to greet us personally. 'I have looked forward to this day for a very long time,' he said earnestly, clasping first Adam and then me by the hands. 'It is most certainly true that things have not been as interesting around here without the two of you.'

Poor Walid! I don't doubt Adam and I were responsible for some of the deep creases on his brow and the sorry lack of hair on his head. He'd always had wispy hair, which he'd combed carefully from one side of his pate to the other in a largely unsuccessful attempt to disguise his sadly receding hairline. Now there was no camouflaging it. Walid was as bald as an onion, and a similar shade of brown.

I felt a tinge of guilt, looking at the fork lines across his brow and the absence of hair on his head. I was quite sure we'd taken years off his life with the stress of the occasions he'd 'borrowed' genuine Tutankhamun treasures – not once but twice – to rescue Adam and me from a long and agonising death entombed with the mummies of Akhenaten and Nefertiti.

'We've been counting the minutes,' I assured him, leaning forward to kiss his cheek in the way Adam had

Shukura's. He blinked at me and squeezed my hand even tighter.

'Your wedding seems five minutes and yet a lifetime ago,' he said, referring to the last time we'd all been together when they'd made the journey to London to see us married. 'It seemed then we might never have the pleasure of welcoming you back.'

'Home,' Adam corrected him. 'You're welcoming us home.'

'Please, come and sit down.' Selim, Shukura's husband, who'd been standing respectfully in the background while the hugs and kisses took place now stepped forward and ushered us into the lovely spacious apartment he shared with Shukura and their three children. 'As you might imagine, Shukura has prepared a feast to mark your homecoming. Our kids have been told to make themselves scarce tonight so we can have a proper catch-up and find out about all your plans. We have champagne to celebrate your arrival. Ahmed, my friend, you can do the honours popping the cork.'

As the only non-Muslims in the room, Adam and I would be the ones drinking the champagne. But I knew it was a gesture meant to emphasise just how truly thrilled they were to welcome us back. And, let's be honest, it's never a hardship to have half a bottle of premium champagne to oneself.

Selim, unlike his wife, spoke English with a pronounced Arabic accent for all that his command of our language was flawless. A handsome man with greying hair at the temples, he was courtesy personified. I knew he took great personal pride in hosting our homecoming party with his wife. I could well imagine that Shukura had been slaving over a hot stove all day.

Before long blissful reality took over from hopeful imagination. Ahmed did indeed perform the honours with the champagne, bellowing with shock as the cork hit the ceiling and ricocheted back into his face (thankfully missing the beautiful set of new teeth Selim had fitted not so long ago). Uncorking champagne was a skill our big friend sorely lacked. But Shukura's skill in the kitchen could not be doubted. Dish after dish of the finest Egyptian cuisine was brought to the table to tempt, tantalise and totally fulfil us.

'So, you are here to recreate the journey through Egypt and Nubia undertaken by Giovanni Belzoni and his wife two hundred years ago...' Walid said as a succession of sumptuous savoury dishes gave way to a selection of desserts. 'What exactly does that entail?'

Walid spoke careful English, also with an accent but with a precision that betrayed dutiful and plentiful study.

I smiled. 'My mandate is to bring his travels alive for a modern audience and reignite a fascination with Egypt in much the same way Belzoni's was to excavate statuary and antiquities to entice visitors to the British Museum, then in its infancy.'

'Actually,' Adam piped up alongside me, 'the British Museum is still keen to muster all the publicity it can from Merry's travelogue. Why else would it sponsor her trip and grant me the pleasure of coming too…?'

'But you'll be employed by the Egyptian Tourism Authority?' Selim questioned.

I nodded. 'Yes, just as Belzoni was employed by Henry Salt – not that he was ever willing to concede it.'

'Salt, as British Consul General, was authorised to collect antiquities on behalf of the British Museum,' Walid said. 'He'd determined he wanted to claim the fallen head-and-torso statue of Ramses II, then known as The Younger Memnon, from the Ramesseum in Luxor.'

'Yes,' Adam nodded. 'By all accounts Belzoni talked himself into the job after the failure of the water-wheel project that took up the best part of his first year in Egypt in 1815. The trouble was, Salt viewed Belzoni as a simple employee, whereas Belzoni saw himself as more of an independent consultant, engaged on behalf of the British Museum to make his own discoveries. It's a shame they didn't clarify the status of their relationship from the start since it led to so much misunderstanding and such a bitter falling out further down track over the ultimate sale of the collection.'

Shukura gleamed at me, 'So, Merry; which are you? Employee or consultant?'

'Very much the hired help I fear,' I admitted. 'I've been left in no doubt at all about the concessions I'm expected to make as part of my conditions of service.'

'Oh?' Shukura queried, miraculously limiting herself to a single word question.

I sent a lightning glance at Ahmed under my lashes. That he was enjoying his dessert of pears poached in Middle-Eastern spices and served in thick vanilla custard way too much to be paying much attention to the conversation was evident from the blissful expression on his face. I smiled and launched my missile. 'Director Ismail has insisted that someone from the Ministry of State for Antiquities should be assigned to accompany me every step of the way,' I said. I didn't add that the Director had taken me pointedly to one side, setting out in an undertone that he wasn't prepared to take any chances with my propensity to make ancient Egyptian discoveries. He wanted someone on hand 24/7 to claim any rogue finds for the Ministry, no questions asked. 'He's appointed Habiba Garai to the role.'

Ahmed choked so violently I thought he was truly in danger of spattering Shukura's lovingly poached spiced pear all over Adam, sitting opposite him. Thankfully, and with a supreme effort of self-control, he clamped his lips shut and managed to keep the contents of his mouth inside it.

'Habiba will join us onboard the *Queen Ahmes* tomorrow evening,' I finished.

Poor Ahmed! It was hard enough for him that I'd demanded his employment as my security guard, which meant sleeping aboard our dahabeeyah with the Nile as his bedfellow. Ahmed is a man who likes dry land beneath him and has no love of boats or aeroplanes. Now his equilibrium was further shot to pieces by the news that the love of his life was to join us on our journey. I couldn't say for sure what the nature of the relationship was between those two. I was quite certain Ahmed was besotted with the sultry Egyptian Ministry Inspector. But even though he'd followed her to England when she was sent to expose the antiquities trafficking ring a couple of years ago – a grand romantic gesture – and they'd attended our wedding together, I was still wholly unclear whether there was anything official about their relationship. I daresay long distance romances must come with their challenges. Ahmed worked in Luxor and Habiba in Cairo, so I suppose it couldn't be easy to put things on a regular footing.

But his reaction now told me there was much to look forward to in the weeks ahead.

'And that's not all,' Adam said. 'Zahed Mansour has assigned a photographer to the project. As this is a major tourism marketing campaign intended to be published throughout the world, he wants Merry's prose to be accompanied by a stunning set of pictures.'

'That shouldn't prove difficult,' Shukura remarked. 'Egypt is surely one of the most photogenic countries in the world. But, are you saying the expectation is for the photographer to travel with you on board the *Queen Ahmes*?'

I nodded a bit glumly. 'I think Zahed Mansour saw an opportunity to turn my demands to his advantage. Sailing the Nile on board the dahabeeyah presents some fantastic photo opportunities. Yes, the photographer will travel with us as our guest. So Director Ismail and Zahed Mansour have each made sure they've put a spy in our camp, although I'll trust Habiba not to play both ends to the middle.'

I noticed Ahmed stiffen, perhaps wondering what I might be implying. But he didn't glance up from his dessert bowl.

'I've told Merry to try to look at it positively,' Adam said. 'It's an opportunity for us to get used to having a stranger on board the *Queen Ahmes*. We'll need to be accustomed to that if things ever perk up enough to allow us another shot at our business venture.'

I'd acknowledged the sense in this, although I'll admit I was a little piqued to have been foisted with an uninvited guest. Habiba didn't count. I was perfectly happy to include her in our little party since I considered her one of us; and was sure I could trust her to tell us if for any reason she found her loyalties divided. But I was a bit miffed about the photographer. It meant that even during the hours I was off duty and ostensibly 'at home' I'd have a colleague for company, a set of eyes and ears for the Tourism Authority.

'True,' I conceded. 'But I'm pleased Zahed Mansour only demanded we take one permanent houseguest. I'm to report to some chap who's the Authority's Marketing Manager rather than to Zahed Mansour directly. Zahed omitted to give me his name, just said he'll be sent to meet us at each of the main Belzoni-related archaeological sites rather than travelling with us. I imagine he has a day job the Minister is unwilling to release him from. Apparently he'll rendezvous with us for the first time tomorrow at the Giza pyramids.'

'Habiba and the photographer will be there too,' Adam said. 'We're to meet them all just before sunset.' I saw him glance at Ahmed, finishing his spiced pears and vanilla custard with an air of studied concentration but perhaps less enjoyment. The pyramids at sunset sounded impossibly romantic to me. If Ahmed thought so too, he wasn't letting it show. His expression was unusually inscrutable.

'It's my first official travelogue destination. Belzoni went on an overnight camping trip to the pyramids when he first arrived in Cairo,' I volunteered, deciding the nature of things between Ahmed and Habiba would become apparent soon enough. Ahmed's fixed expression made me disinclined to start fishing for information here and now.

'You have an exciting day ahead of you, my dears,' Shukura nodded. 'And to be reunited with the *Queen Ahmes* too; what a lot to look forward to!'

Chapter 5

If it were possible for a dahabeeyah to speak, I wonder what tales the *Queen Ahmes* might tell about her first visits to Cairo in the heyday of the Victorian Nile cruises made popular by Mr Thomas Cook. As Adam and I walked hand-in-hand through the modern docklands, I tried to imagine the wharves as she may once have known them, busy with dahabeeyahs and barges and no doubt teeming with vagrants and beggars, and rats.

Thankfully today there were no rats to contend with, at least none that I could see. The dockside had been smartened up with a twenty-first century facelift. This was where the modern cruise boats now docked since it had become possible a few years ago to once again travel the whole length of the Nile from Cairo to Aswan. Sadly, the number of cruisers moored at the dockside served only to reinforce what desperate times these were. Cruise boats without passengers did not denote a thriving industry – quite the opposite. Maybe that explained the knots of scruffy young men standing around, some in galabeyas and turbans, some in shabby jeans and shirts. Perhaps they were once crew onboard these luxury vessels, hanging about here now because they had nowhere better to go thanks to the economic downturn. They watched us a bit suspiciously as we made our way towards the jetty. I glanced at them a trifle nervously, wondering if I could rely on the same friendliness I'd always taken for granted in the locals before. Thankfully I didn't sense hostility, just hungry eyes.

Adam tossed a coin towards the young man closest to us. I watched a sad sort of pity as he snatched it from the air and shouted his thanks in Arabic. But then I forgot all about my surroundings in the simple delight of being reunited with the *Queen Ahmes* after such a long separation.

Khaled was steering her towards the jetty with both her enormous sails unfurled. She was a joyous sight to behold. My eyes filled and my throat clogged as I watched her come closer.

Adam slipped an arm across my shoulders and pulled me against his side so we stood locked together waiting to greet her. 'She really is quite splendid, isn't she?' he said with an audible thickness in his voice.

When finally I trusted myself to speak, I squeezed his waist and whispered, 'Beautiful.'

Then it was all action as Khaled manoeuvred the vessel alongside the jetty, shouted a greeting and tossed across a length of rope for Adam to catch and secure her at the quayside. I pulled a second rope tight and hooked the loop over one of the mooring plugs, so she was safely tied to the landing platform. A couple of the scruffy onlookers cheered, and I felt a thrill of pride that she attracted such an admiring audience.

That Khaled had lavished a bucketful of care and attention to get the dahabeeyah ready to welcome us back was evident the moment we stepped off the gangplank he hastily lowered, and on board. My senses swam with the competing aromas of beeswax, brass polish and the pungent perfume of fresh flowers. The wood panelling gleamed; the brass railings shone and vases of flowers brightened every surface.

Khaled was overjoyed to see us. He pumped first Adam then me enthusiastically by the hand, thanking us profusely for the opportunity to work for us again. I gathered from this his paid employment had been scarce or possibly non-existent during the time we'd been away. Like Shukura, Khaled is another one whose accent comes as a surprise, as do his bright blue eyes in his walnut-brown face. His mother was Scottish, and he'd spent his childhood and early teens in those chilly northern climes, returning with his father to Egypt when his mother sadly died.

'I've spent the last week getting her ready for your arrival,' he said as I ran my hand lovingly over the small reception desk, reacquainting myself with the feel of the woodwork. 'The engines have been freshly oiled, I scrubbed the canvas awnings, beat the dust from the oriental rugs, touched up some of the paintwork; and my wife laundered all the linen and made up the beds in each of the cabins. You'll find everything just as you left it.'

'She's looking wonderful,' Adam approved. 'And probably a damned sight cleaner than she was when we said goodbye. We've missed her, and you. It's great to be back.' He expelled a great sigh of happiness.

Khaled led us along the small corridor behind the compact reception area. We glanced into each of the cabins as we passed, complimenting both Khaled and his wife on their care and attention to detail. (I should have guessed the flowers were unlikely to be Khaled's idea). Each luxuriously appointed bedroom was individually decorated with a nod to Victoriana in its furnishings and décor, whilst also being fitted with all the latest mod cons.

We paused to drop off our bags in the cabin we'd claimed as our own. My gaze skimmed over the familiar muslin drapes, the iron bedstead complete with Egyptian cotton bed linen, and the antique furniture I'd painstakingly selected, all in white to complement the teak flooring and wooden shutters. I let out a sigh of pure pleasure.

Adam poked his head into the tiny en-suite bathroom, then turned and grinned at me. 'It's when you see her through the fresh eyes of long absence you realise how truly magnificent she is, don't you think?' he enthused.

And nowhere was this truer than up on the sundeck under the wide canvas awning, with the majestic sails still unfurled on their long diagonal poles fore and aft. We'd come through our semi-circular lounge-bar-cum-dining room, its shape following the curve of the stern. The deeply cushioned sofas and chairs upholstered in rich patterned silk looked as inviting as ever. Our small library of Egyptian history and picture books lined one wall. Khaled had clearly taken them out of storage and positioned them back on the shelves. I made a mental note to do a little re-arranging later, but couldn't fault his preparedness. Then we'd stepped through the glass-panelled French doors, onto the small external landing that linked the guest space with a few steps leading down to the kitchen and crew quarters. But instead of going to inspect these areas right away, we climbed the spiral staircase and stepped up onto the upper deck.

It was resplendent with rattan furniture, antique steamer-style recliners furnished with deeply padded cushions, potted palms in deep brass containers, and Turkish rugs scattered hither and thither across the wooden floorboards. Every surface that wasn't varnished wood or polished brass gleamed with the soft calico-white of newly touched-up paintwork.

'Khaled, you are a miracle-worker!' Adam congratulated him. 'She looks even better than when we finished decorating and fitting her out the first time! And if I told someone we'd had a fire up here they'd never believe me!'

Khaled's broad smile split his face. 'If she is to feature in a travelogue to be published in Europe and America, she'll need to be looking her best,' he said in his broad Scot's brogue.

I stood at the handrail, my back to the Cairo docks and still-staring onlookers, drinking in the sight of her, and letting memories tumble across my inner eye. This sundeck had been the setting of many of my happiest times with some of the people I loved best in the world. I felt the warmth of welcome envelop me, as if the *Queen Ahmes* herself was drawing me into an affectionate embrace. A spreading sense of peace stole over me as I realised I was truly here, exactly where I was meant to be. The past and the present came to meet each other and I wondered how long it would take until I felt I'd never been away. Whilst I'd been in London my adventures in Egypt had taken on the hue of make believe. Now I was back I wondered if the last three years in England might soon also start to take on that same hazy dreamlike quality of a distant memory that somehow didn't seem quite real anymore.

Adam came and pulled me into his arms, planting a lingering kiss on my lips. 'We're home, Merry,' he breathed. 'At last.'

* * *

We spent a few hours happily settling in, re-acquainting ourselves with every nook and cranny, and re-familiarising ourselves with the little details we'd forgotten – like how to work the water purifier.

Ahmed came to join us in the early afternoon, bringing with him an overnight bag with the few essentials he reckoned on needing until we reached Luxor and he could pick up the rest of his stuff. His joy at being given the opportunity to reprise our roles as the three musketeers was definitely muted by the prospect of living on board our 'overgrown felucca', as he rudely referred to the *Queen Ahmes*. Despite all the hours Ahmed had spent on board the dahabeeyah in the past, he'd never once spent the night; always preferring to return to terra firma. Even so, I knew he was thrilled to be commissioned as our personal bodyguard, especially since he'd been allowed to keep his police-issue gun. It was big and black and I had no doubt absolutely deadly.

'I will be even better than Kevin Costner!' he boasted proudly. Ahmed is a man who loves the movies, and has a tendency to picture himself as a film star in the epic that's his own life. 'But it is such a shame that you do not travel over dry land,' he mourned.

'You may not like sleeping with 'de fishies of de Nile' under your pillow,' I said briskly – parodying one of his old complaints in an approximation of his former (pre-new-teeth) pronunciation – 'but I'm sure you'll get used to it.'

'You are teasing me,' he said with unusual perception.

'Perhaps just a little,' I admitted, relenting a bit as I could see he was trying not to look hurt. Ahmed does not lack a sense of humour, but he has a tendency to take himself a teensy bit seriously and doesn't enjoy being the butt of other people's jokes. 'I promise we'll always be moored up at night,' I assured him. 'You'll never be more than a few paces away from dry land.'

'I will buy myself a tent and sleep on the riverbank,' he grunted, eyeing me with mutiny in his expression.

I grinned at him, recognising that now he was the one pulling my leg. 'Touché!' I laughed, only to spend the next five minutes explaining to him what this meant.

We allocated him a cabin the mirror image of our own, although located on the opposite side of the corridor. The dahabeeyah is pretty well soundproofed, but I'd decided there were limits to the proximity one might wish to have one's closest friends co-habiting within. Habiba could have the cabin at the far end of the corridor next-but-one to ours. If Ahmed and Habiba chose to make alternative sleeping arrangements, whether it was sharing one or other of their double rooms – or indeed Ahmed's tent on the riverbank – that was down to them. I didn't think it my place to assume one way or the other. This way they could work it out for themselves. The photographer could take the cabin next to Ahmed's. That would leave one room for Khaled, and one free. I decided this, the cabin between ours and Habiba's, could be converted into a small office for the purposes of this trip; somewhere I could quietly write my travelogue-cum-blog, while watching the Nile and riverbank scenery drift silently by.

Setting out this plan over mid-afternoon coffee on the sundeck, Khaled surprised me by saying he much preferred to sleep in the staff quarters on the lower deck behind the kitchen if it was all the same to me. These tiny little cabins had barely enough room to swing a mouse let alone a cat. But Khaled was fiercely proud of them since he'd managed to fit each with a small hand basin, although there was also a shared bathroom below decks.

I was about to argue that I had no intention of treating him like the hired help, even though – strictly – that's what he was. But he forestalled me, asking if he could respectfully request a favour.

'I wondered if you might consider allowing my wife Rabiah to join us when we reach Luxor? She is willing to work as housekeeper and cook, and will expect no wages, since you have negotiated such a generous salary for me to accompany you.'

I'd known Khaled was married of course but had never actually met his wife. Previously when he'd taken the controls to sail us up and down the Nile he'd always come alone. But, to be fair, these had been short trips. This time the duration of my journey was open-ended. I supposed everyone was waiting to see how it went. I'd signed up for an initial six-month – renewable – contract. Six months – or more – was a long time to be away from one's spouse. It was also a long time to do one's own cooking and cleaning, especially with six people on board. Rabiah would be a seventh, and it suddenly occurred to me she would be very welcome indeed.

Khaled thanked me profusely, and said if I didn't mind, he would remove one of the stud walls between the cabins below decks, so he and his wife could have a slightly larger cabin, and their own privacy. He refused politely and point blank my offer of the luxurious double guest cabin on the main deck.

So with everything settled, all that remained now was to welcome Habiba and the photographer on board.

* * *

The Tourism Authority sent a car to collect and transport us to the pyramid plateau at Giza. I caught snatches of these vast and timeless monuments between buildings through the windscreen as we crawled through the gridlocked outskirts of the city.

I knew Tahrir Square had been sanitised and emptied of protesters, although our journey didn't take us anywhere near it. But elsewhere, Cairo was comfortingly hectic: roads crammed with every sort of vehicle, donkey-carts and camels chancing their luck among cars, motorbikes, vans and coaches. Apartment blocks bedecked with huge garish advertising hoardings overlooked choked freeways and flyovers. On all sides the pavements were crammed with bakers, grocers, spice and shisha sellers, and just about every other kind of shop you can think of.

Cairo is the most densely populated capital in Africa, possibly even the world. It's traffic-choked and noise-polluted. A permanent haze of exhaust fumes hangs over the city thanks to the sheer age of most of the vehicles crowding the metropolis. The thick air reverberates with the constant blaring of the car horns Cairene drivers use to compensate for the fact there are no discernible rules of the road. And every one of its fifteen-million-or-so inhabitants seems permanently on the move. The pyramids loom over it all, three points of eternity, stillness and silence bearing witness to the frenetic pace and ceaseless activity of twenty-first century living. They stand there mute and impassive as year by year the modern suburbs encroach further towards their base stones. Every time I see them I ask myself fancifully if they mind the intrusion. And I always tell myself the same thing. The pyramids have outlasted many of the ages of man. They'll no doubt outlast this one too, and have the last laugh into the bargain.

The pyramids were already well over a thousand years old during the New Kingdom of ancient Egypt when some of the most famous of the A-list pharaohs ruled their empire. Now at over four-and-a-half thousand years, I couldn't help but think they were truly a testament to the immortality craved by the early dynastic kings who built them.

As I climbed out of the car and rummaged in my bag for my sunglasses I succumbed to the usual shivery sensation across the nape of my neck as my brain tried to grapple with such an unimaginable passage of time. It never failed to impress on me a sense of my own relative insignificance. I was a mere pinprick along the timeline of these monuments' duration. But still I wanted to make my mark. And that, I told myself, was exactly what I was here to do.

I put on my sunglasses and was reaching back into the car for my straw hat when a young man stepped out from the shadow of the Great Pyramid looming across the plateau, and thrust out his right hand towards me to be shaken. 'Mrs Tennyson-Pink,' he said.

'Meredith,' I corrected, straightening and pulling on my hat before taking his proffered hand.

'Mrs Tennyson-Pink,' he said again, as if *he* were the one now correcting *me*. 'I am Saleh el-Sayed, Marketing Manager at the Egyptian Tourism Authority.'

Ah yes,' I nodded, smiling. 'Zahed Mansour said he would send you to meet me here. Hello. But, please, do call me Meredith. I'll be the first to admit my surname is a bit of a mouthful.'

He didn't smile back as I might have expected. 'Meredith,' he repeated carefully. Those for whom Arabic is their native language struggle with pronunciation of our English t-h's. Poor old Ahmed took years to master them. So I was aware my Christian name presented a bit of a challenge. That this man was keen to get it right first time was obvious from the way he took his own leisurely time over the syllables. He eyed me closely as he did so, a long appraising glance almost as if he was measuring me for size, working out my weight and wondering whether he might be strong enough to pick me up and throw me. I didn't feel wholly comfortable being scrutinized like some sort of museum exhibit, and withdrew my hand since he showed no sign of releasing it. 'Welcome back to Egypt,' he said abruptly. 'I trust your dahabeeyah has arrived safely from Luxor.'

'Yes, she has, thank you,' I murmured, surprised by his determined formality. This was unexpected, especially since he was younger than I'd imagined he might be. In his early thirties at a guess, Saleh el-Sayed was a nice-looking chap with slicked back black hair and the coffee coloured skin of Egyptians from the northern parts of the country. He was dressed in a smart slim-fitting linen suit with an open-necked blue shirt. He sported a rather nice pair of designer sunglasses and smelt strongly of an expensive aftershave I recognised as one Dan used to favour. I noticed he had an iPad in a leather case tucked under his left arm. I got the sense of a modern young businessman dressed to impress and perhaps also out to make a point.

Adam came round from the other side of the car and held out his hand. 'I'm Adam Tennyson, Meredith's husband. Good to meet you.'

I couldn't help but notice the handshake Saleh submitted to with Adam was a somewhat abbreviated version of the one he'd given me. 'Adam,' he repeated simply, not required this time to concentrate on getting the pronunciation right. 'Zahed Mansour has asked me to ensure you are both given free access to all of the archaeological sites you will visit as part of your commission with the Authority.' He delivered this in faultlessly precise English but in an entirely expressionless tone of voice, allowing for the slight accent.

'Thank you,' I said. 'We appreciate it. What is your role exactly?'

I saw him stiffen. I'd meant only to be politely enquiring, but it was clear my question caused him to bristle. I sensed a distinct undercurrent. At the same time I started to discern that the awkwardness of this first encounter wasn't just because he was concentrating on getting his English right and on making a professional impression. 'As Marketing Manager I am responsible for the Tourism Authority's website and overseas advertising campaigns,' he said tightly.

'A tough job in these straitened times,' Adam said jovially, picking up on Saleh's defensive stance in the same way I had.

'I am good at my job, Mr Tennyson,' Saleh said, pulling his shoulders back.

'I'm sure you are,' Adam said quickly. 'I don't believe anyone has implied otherwise. And, please, it's Adam. If we're going to be working together, we should surely drop the formality, don't you think?'

Unusually, Adam's easy charm failed to have the desired effect. There was no responding warmth in our new colleague's manner. 'I will ensure you have everything you need at each stop on your journey,' Saleh said stiffly. 'But I don't believe we are working *together*.'

His slight emphasis on the last word gave me the clue to his behaviour. 'Zahed Mansour made it clear I was to report to you,' I soothed, attempting to mollify him with a smile. I was quite happy to massage his ego and play the underling if that was what was required to get him to loosen up a bit.

Saleh el-Sayed's expression didn't change. He stepped back, a man standing on his dignity if ever I saw one. 'I have some introductions to perform,' he remarked, turning to beckon forward the young man hovering a few paces behind him, keeping company with a beautiful young woman in the lengthening shadow cast by the Great Pyramid as the sun dipped in the sky. 'Now, Miss Habiba Garai of the Ministry of State for Antiquities you already know, I believe…?'

I decided to ignore his studied civility and the ridiculous chip he appeared to have on his shoulder. 'Habiba!' I cried joyfully, closing the gap between us in a few swift paces and throwing open my arms.

'Merry!' she laughed, coming eagerly into my embrace. 'I have missed you! Adam!' She turned from my hug into his. 'It has been too long!'

I couldn't help but notice her glance over Adam's shoulder towards the car, where Ahmed was standing silently watching proceedings. He looked as solid and immovable as a granite statue. The expression on his face behind his sunglasses appeared equally hard. Something had happened between those two, I discerned, exchanging a quick glance of incomprehension with Adam.

Habiba looked stunning as usual. She was dressed all in cream, wearing silk trousers, nipped in at the ankle, with a long figure-hugging embroidered tunic, which reached down to her knees on top. A cream headscarf completed the ensemble, covering her hair and shoulders and framing her beautiful face. She was as coolly sophisticated as ever, and I rather regretted my cropped white cotton jeans and loose-fitting shirt.

Saleh el-Sayed cleared his throat to draw our attention back. 'And this is the photographer assigned to your trip,' he said, indicating the young man watching our reunion with Habiba with a smile on his face. 'Allow me to introduce Mehmet Abdelsalam.'

If I hadn't already known the young man was a photographer, the huge camera hanging from a strap around his neck, and the tripod he was carrying would have given it away in an instant. He immediately dropped the tripod onto the sand and came forward to greet us. His ready smile and open guileless expression was in stark contrast to the closed features of the Tourism Authority's Marketing Manager. 'It is my pleasure to meet you,' he said with a small bow once he'd shaken each of us by the hand. 'I must thank you for agreeing to let me travel with you on board your dahabeeyah. You are most kind. I am looking forward to this assignment very much.'

Guessing him to be a similar age to Saleh el-Sayed, his look and demeanour couldn't have been more different. He was nowhere near as good-looking as the Marketing Manager and didn't come anywhere close in the sartorial elegance stakes. A slight, plain-featured young Egyptian man with shaggy hair, uneven teeth and dark, slightly pockmarked skin, he was wearing cargo pants, a plain white T-shirt and dusty running shoes. But his bright, eager smile and open manner more than made up for his lack of physical charms.

I found myself heartily relieved it was he who'd be sharing our home, not the prickly Mr el-Sayed.

'I'm sure the pleasure will be all ours,' I said warmly. 'Now, Saleh,' I turned to the Marketing Manager, using his first name quite deliberately. 'I understand Zahed Mansour had a reason for suggesting this as the location of our first meeting...?'

He inclined his head towards me. If he'd happened to be twenty-or-so years older than me, I might have taken this as a benevolent gesture. Since he was a bit younger, I found his condescension extremely aggravating. 'Indeed, Mrs – er – Meredith.' He laboured his pronunciation of my name in the same slow insolent tone as the first time. It was almost as if he wanted to make an insult of it. 'You will be aware, I am sure, that Giovanni Belzoni made the usual pilgrimage here to the Giza plateau to visit the pyramids soon after his arrival in Cairo.'

'I imagine it all looked a little different back then,' I remarked, trying to ignore the fast food outlets and the modern-day detritus that littered the place: crisp bags, fizzy drink cans and empty plastic water bottles left to drift disrespectfully against the gigantic epoch-defying stones.

Adam shaded his eyes and tipped his head back to stare up at the awe-inspiring pyramid towering above the plateau. 'Belzoni camped here overnight then climbed the Great Pyramid before dawn to see the sun rise,' he said. 'He waxed lyrical about it in his *Narrative.*'

'Your Belzoni exhibition at the British Museum was its most successful ever, I understand,' Saleh said thinly. 'You are clearly very knowledgeable. But, I wonder, even given your success, is Giovanni Belzoni well enough known to entice tourists back to Egypt? It seems you are appealing to a niche – that is the right word, yes? – market of people who have some interest in Egyptian history. This appears to me to miss out the vast majority of people who come to our country for their holidays simply for the sunshine and hot weather.'

It takes a lot to rile Adam. Even so, I felt his hackles rise. 'You realise, of course, this assignment was the brain child of your boss Zahed Mansour?' he challenged. 'Surely Egypt's ancient history as the cradle of civilisation is its unique selling point. There are plenty of other places that can lay claim to sand dunes, beaches and wall-to-wall sunshine. Some might even say the ferocious heat here in Egypt is a distinct disadvantage during the British summer holidays. And, of course, those other places may also be considered a whole lot safer right now.'

I stepped quickly into the breach. I recognised Dan in Saleh el-Sayed's description of a typical tourist. My ex-boyfriend had never been enamoured of the archaeological or historical marvels of Egypt. He'd opted for the golf course, no matter how dry and barren, given half a chance. 'My assignment is simply an experiment,' I said, seeking to pour oil on troubled waters. 'None of us has any idea whether my retracing of Belzoni's adventures will encourage people back to Egypt. But it surely has to be worth a try. Now, Saleh,' I smiled determinedly at him. 'As you're the one with your finger on the pulse of tourism marketing, tell me, what's my best angle for promoting the pyramids to potential tourists?'

Saleh didn't answer immediately. It's fair to say I was starting actively to dislike this young man. 'Should we invite your security guard to join us?' he said instead.

Adam put his forefinger and thumb between his lips and let out a shrill whistle. 'Hey! Ahmed! Stop standing there like a flippin' obelisk and get yourself over here!'

'I will go and welcome him,' Saleh said unexpectedly, and started walking back across the dusty terrain towards the car.

Adam watched him go. 'Now there's a young man with his nose put thoroughly out of joint,' he murmured to me in an undertone so Habiba and Mehmet couldn't hear.

'I feel a bit sorry for him,' I said, trying to convince myself it was true. 'It's hardly his fault if despite his best marketing-campaign-efforts visitors are staying away. He's not responsible for the rise of so-called Islamic State or the absence of hidden chambers behind Tutankhamun's tomb. I can well imagine it must feel like a slap in the face to see the lengths his boss has gone to in order to entice me back to undertake a mission I daresay this Saleh chap feels he's more than capable of performing.'

'Even so,' Adam muttered. 'There's no need to take it out on you.'

'I'm a big girl,' I smiled. 'I can handle it. Besides, what's the worst he can do?'

As Saleh and Ahmed joined us, our police pal looking pointedly everywhere but at Habiba, Saleh said, 'I thought you might like to be one of the very few modern parties granted the privilege of climbing to the top of the Great Pyramid, as Giovanni Belzoni did. The Tourism Authority and Ministry of Antiquities have granted special dispensation to make this possible. The view is spectacular, especially at sunset. But I warn you, it's an arduous climb, and a long way to fall.'

Chapter 6

'Has anyone ever actually fallen off a pyramid?' I asked Adam breathlessly as we hauled ourselves up from one enormous stone block to the next.

'I doubt it,' he said. 'It's not exactly a sheer drop, is it?' That said, he immediately – and unnervingly – contradicted himself, 'Although I seem to remember reading a report of a man found dead at the foot of the Great Pyramid about thirty years ago having apparently fallen asleep and toppled from the summit. He was alone, and the authorities never came up with an adequate explanation for their assertion that he fell asleep before falling.'

I pondered this a moment, not feeling remotely reassured. 'When did the authorities slap the ban on scaling the pyramids?'

'Some time in the eighties, I think,' he said. 'They wanted to protect the monuments from further damage, and climbing them was also considered dangerous. But people have been flouting the ban ever since. We're among a very few lucky ones who get to do this legally, which makes a nice change for us, don't you think? It's an incredible honour to be granted official permission to climb to the top.'

'Hmm,' I panted, hoisting myself up onto another huge stone block, unsure as yet whether it was a privilege or a punishment. 'But do you think Saleh el-Sayed might be planning on pushing us off when we get there? He seems thoroughly put out by our being here. Legal is great, but add dead into the equation and I'll own up to preferring a life of crime.'

Adam grinned at me. 'I'm not sure he'd invite a security guard and a photographer along if that was truly what he had in mind,' he chuckled.

Joking aside, I could see why this climb was considered dangerous. At four-and-a-half thousand years old, the Great Pyramid was time-and-weather worn, with stones of uneven size, eroded and covered in windblown sand and loose scree. It made for a treacherous climb. After a while I concentrated only on looking upwards because each time I paused to look down my head swam and my knees buckled. The higher we went the sheerer the drop seemed below us.

'Actually, I think it would be very easy indeed to fall off,' I muttered as my foot slipped on loose chippings towards the top and I lost my balance. I grabbed at the closest stone block to steady myself, gasping with fright. It took a long moment for my heart to stop pounding. 'Put it this way, I don't think you'd bounce!'

Adam helped me up the last few stones. The blocks were cleaner cut up here, and smaller obviously. It had taken us a solid fifteen minutes of determined climbing to reach the top.

Mehmet Abdelsalam had scrambled up ahead of us, and was setting up his tripod on the summit when we clambered up to join him. Saleh el-Sayed and Ahmed were bringing up the rear. Habiba, possibly sensibly, had elected to stay behind.

The top of the Great Pyramid of the Old Kingdom pharaoh Khufu is actually a squarish platform with a relatively flat surface, though made up of uneven blocks of stone. I'd guess it at about thirty feet across. It's not possible to walk across the centre from one side to the other, however, as there's a triangular structure there that looks a bit like a TV mast secured to the apex. I'm not sure whether this serves any purpose or is simply intended to finish off the pyramidal shape.

'This was a favourite picnic spot for Victorian travellers,' Adam commented, standing straight and gazing around him. 'Wow! What a view!'

I joined him, taking a little longer to trust myself to stand upright and enjoy the panorama. For some reason my knees remained decidedly wobbly. I was supremely conscious of standing atop an estimated 2.3 million limestone blocks. I told myself that since they'd stood firm for the last four-and-a-half millennia there was no reason to think they might give way now. Even so, I took my time.

Adam smiled and slipped an arm around my shoulders as I finally plucked up the courage to straighten up. 'This pyramid held the record as the tallest manmade structure in the world for over 3,800 years,' he said. 'It was only when the spire on Lincoln Cathedral was completed in circa 1300 that it was shunted into second place. Not bad, huh, for what we might consider a pre-historic building project?'

With Adam's arm around me I felt secure enough to forget my vertigo and the lack of safety ropes and barriers and start to enjoy myself. I lifted my head for the first time and dared to look beyond the perimeter of the square stone platform. Looked, and caught my breath, and felt my knees go weak all over again. This time it wasn't my fear of heights making my head swim, but the sheer giddy intoxication caused by the sight my eyes were drinking in.

Some way off to the side of us another huge mountain of hand-cut rock thrust upwards from the plateau. This was the immense pyramid of Khafre, its granite casing stones still relatively intact at the top. It glowed golden in the slowly sinking sun, the sky shimmering pale blue behind it. It was a magical, spellbinding sight. I drew in a breath of pure wonder. 'My God, Adam; this is incredible.'

'Khafre was no fool,' Adam murmured. 'He built his pyramid on slightly higher ground than his father, and at a somewhat steeper angle. So, even though it's smaller than this one, at ground level and from a distance his appears taller. It's really only from up here you can get the proper perspective. It really is jaw-dropping, isn't it? Wow, Merry! What a treat! I never imagined we'd be invited to do *this*!'

The desert drifted off beyond Khafre's pyramid and the smaller one of Menkaure set slightly off-centre behind it, all but invisible from this angle. On our other side modern-day Cairo was a hazy smoke-coloured smudge, much more picturesque from up here in the cleaner air above the city smog.

'Thank you Saleh,' I said sincerely as the Marketing Manager joined us, still managing to look immaculate in his linen suit despite the energetic climb. 'This is very special.'

He pushed his sunglasses on top of his head and narrowed his eyes on my face. 'Well, I fail to see how you can write about Giovanni Belzoni's travels with any insight if you have not shared in his experiences.'

Chastened, I realised I'd forgotten about Giovanni Belzoni. The fear and thrill of my own adventure scaling the Great Pyramid wiped all thought of my purpose in being here from my mind. I looked about me, trying to visualise the giant onetime circus strongman enjoying this same spectacle.

'Looking in *that* direction, I imagine very little has changed,' Adam said, reading my thoughts, intuiting my discomfort and smoothly covering it. 'On his first visit here Belzoni was a simple tourist. Recording his visit he wrote about the distant view of the smaller pyramids to the south.

Look, Merry; across there near the horizon, you can just make out the other pyramid field; see?'

I squinted and followed the line of his pointing finger, and did indeed spot tiny pyramidal shapes far off in the distance. I knew this was Dahshur, site of the red pyramid and the famous bent pyramid.

I could see why Rashid Soliman had thought it would be to my advantage to bring Adam along on this trip. My husband was a walking encyclopaedia on the Great Belzoni. I smiled at him, wordlessly thanking him for stepping into the breach of Saleh's ill-concealed disapproval. I gazed at the encroaching metropolis. 'I'll bet Cairo is much closer and looks a whole lot different now than in Belzoni's time.'

'More a city of minarets and spires in his day, than of skyscrapers and tall apartment blocks,' Adam concurred.

Saleh didn't comment, just looked on with no discernible change of expression.

I decided to ignore him since there was a very real risk of him ruining this moment for me. And since this must surely count as one of the highlights of my life – and I've been lucky enough to have a few – I really wasn't in patience with his unspoken resentment. Instead I felt it might be time to showcase some of my own knowledge of the giant in whose footsteps I was walking.

'Belzoni might have been a tourist on his first visit,' I said. 'But he'd earned a reputation as an early archaeologist of some genius by the time he returned here to Giza in the spring of 1818. His major discoveries and achievements were behind him by then. He'd heaved the bust of Ramses II from the Ramesseum to the Nile for passage to Alexandria and ultimately the British Museum. He'd cleared sand from the façade of the Great Temple at Abu Simbel. And he'd discovered no fewer than six tombs in the Valley of the Kings, including the most impressive of them all, that of Seti I. But he still had a few tricks up his sleeve. Already conscious of cracks in his relationship with the Consul General Henry Salt,' – I cast a sidelong glance at Saleh el-Sayed (although I needn't have bothered because he was discourteous enough not even to be looking at me) – 'Belzoni took advantage of Salt's own excavations in Luxor to conduct what he called "a little private business". He headed here to Giza in search of pyramid treasure.'

I gazed at the majestic mountain of quarried and smoothed stone blocks rising in perfect symmetry from the plateau beneath us. Khafre's pyramid, viewed from the top of the Great Pyramid must surely rate as one of the sights of my life. I drew an awe-filled breath and continued, rather in the manner of a tour guide,

'Here, Belzoni's famous engineering skills were put to the test. As far as anyone knew, the Second Pyramid of Khafre over there had never been opened. Belzoni decided there and then he would be the first man inside.'

Sensing Saleh el-Sayed bored and unimpressed alongside me, I decided to cut to the chase. 'A month later after a great deal of digging and a couple of false starts Belzoni entered the burial chamber. The plain, polished granite sarcophagus was already open, its lid broken in two. The few bones he discovered inside turned out to be cattle bones – possibly the lunch of earlier tomb robbers. Frustrated and out-of-pocket, Belzoni scrawled his name and the date in the burial chamber and left.'

Saleh el-Sayed might be clouding the atmosphere with waves of barely concealed disinterest but Adam was the complete opposite. 'Sadly for him Belzoni had to settle for a modern re-entry into a tomb that had been thoroughly ransacked in antiquity.'

'That was the story of his life,' I remarked. 'He may have had the luck of the devil rediscovering tombs and temples buried for millennia in drifting sand. But unlike Howard Carter he never struck gold. Some ancient treasure-hunter had always pipped him to the post.'

For the first time, standing up here on this truly monumental mountain of hand-carved rock, I felt Giovanni Belzoni's ghost brush against me. All my senses quivered. It made me super-determined to bring him back to life for a modern audience.

If Saleh el-Sayed could be considered an example of my typical target market then I'd have to admit to stumbling at the first hurdle. He quite clearly had no atmospheric empathy or apparent interest in the magnificent history of his country. For a man whose job it was to promote said country to foreign visitors, I'd have said this was a distinct black mark. Surely there was more to Egypt than scuba diving, sand dunes, suntans and souks – although there was all of that too, of course.

'I am sure your readers will lap it up,' he said thinly. 'Although you realise, I suppose, that there are many who believe Giovanni Belzoni was in Egypt for no reason other than his own personal aggrandisement.' He allowed an uncomfortably long pause to draw out, ensuring I was left in no doubt he considered me guilty of the same thing. Perhaps his knowledge of history was better than I'd thought. It was clearly just me he objected to. Having made his point, he continued abruptly: 'Now, I suggest we allow Mehmet to take some more photographs while you make any notes or impressions you may wish to record. Then we can descend again. While the late afternoon light remains, you might like to take a camel ride out to the distant rock plateau. It affords the best view of the Giza pyramids, seen at their best at sunset.'

I wasn't quite sure how he managed to impart such an appealing suggestion with such an air of insolence. Coming from anyone else, I'd have taken this as a thoughtful and well-intentioned plan. Yet somehow Saleh el-Sayed managed to convey the idea with a subtle undertone of disrespect, almost as if daring us to take him up on the proposal, and put him to the extra work required.

'Thank you Saleh,' I said, perhaps rather over-doing the enthusiasm. 'That's a wonderful idea!' I wondered how hard I'd have to shove to send him toppling over the edge of the pyramid, caught myself in the thought, and was horrified at my instinctive inclination towards violence. It was only a little while ago I'd suspected him of luring us up here to perpetrate the very same thing on us, or me at least. I was mildly surprised nothing untoward had happened, and sorry to find myself disliking the Marketing Manager so much. It cast a pall on the eager anticipation with which I'd looked forward to this trip.

'I will go and make the necessary arrangements,' Saleh said formally, turning away and stepping back onto the gigantic staircase of rock. 'I will see you at the bottom. Please take care with your descent. The climb down is harder than coming up.'

'I can't make up my mind whether that sounded like a warning or a threat,' I muttered when he was out of earshot. 'Ahmed, I may need your help.'

Our police buddy who'd been standing off to one side staring fixedly at the horizon, now turned and cast me a panicked glance. 'When I promised to protect you with my life, I did not realise you had it in mind to scale the Great Pyramid,' he huffed his disapproval.

'I didn't,' I said. 'This was as much of a surprise to me as to anyone else. What's the matter? Don't you like it up here?'

'I do not enjoy the highness,' he said pompously. 'But where you go I must go too. This is what I sweared to that man from the Ministry. Even though I might fall and get a braked neck, I must do my duty.' He gave a hearty sigh that left us in no doubt how he felt about making such sacrifices with life and limb.

'Hah!' Adam said rudely. 'Ahmed, mate, you're as nimble as a mountain goat, despite your bulk. I'll bet you could scramble down there in five minutes flat if you had good reason to. Now, stop complaining and help Merry over the side. Aren't you looking forward to riding a camel?'

Ahmed's look of horror suggested he could think of nothing worse. 'Nasty, bad tempered creatures,' he muttered.

His poor opinion surprised me. I considered camels docile and submissive animals if I considered them at all. I remembered my fondness of Ramses the camel, resident at the Jolie Ville hotel in Luxor. He willingly took guests for rides around the hotel grounds, as placid as you like. 'These camels, they spit,' Ahmed added, apparently feeling the need to justify his denouncement.

I decided there and then to make it my mission to get Ahmed up on a camel before we left the Giza plateau this evening. Indeed my anticipation of this spectacle was enough to sustain me through the quite hair-raising clamber back down the pyramid. Saleh el-Sayed was absolutely correct that it was a trickier business going down. It took longer and it seemed there were far fewer hand and foot holds. I finally arrived at the bottom hot, dusty and dishevelled. Ahmed lifted me down from some of the larger blocks, while Adam helped Mehmet with his tripod and camera case.

While I will always count my climb to the top of the Great Pyramid as one of the most awe-inspiring experiences of my life, I was pretty glad to be back at ground level.

Habiba was standing a little way distant, in conversation with a woman scribbling into a notebook. The woman wasn't Arabic but Western in origin by the looks of her. Habiba waved as I looked towards her and beckoned me to join them. Glancing down at myself, I regretted the cropped white jeans, now caked in dust and streaked with grime, and was self-consciously aware of my shirt sticking damply in all the wrong places. Alongside Habiba I felt scruffy at the best of times. And right now, sweaty, unkempt and smarting from the disappointment of my first encounter with Saleh el-Sayed, I really wasn't sure I was in the mood for any further introductions. But I consider myself a well brought up girl and abhor rudeness. So, swiping at my filthy jeans, I crossed the rocky terrain towards them.

Habiba's companion glanced up from her notebook as I approached and looked eagerly, almost hungrily, at me.

'Wow! That must have been epic! Not many people get to climb the Great Pyramid these days. You lucky thing! I'd give my eyeteeth for a chance like that! What was it like?'

I was rather taken aback. British obviously, she delivered this like a rapid-fire machine gun. 'It was – er – epic,' I said.

She was a big girl, dressed in a shapeless denim dress that reached nearly to her ankles. It had the unfortunate effect of making her look somewhat tent-like; with flat, functional sandals peeping out from the long-line hem. I noticed she varnished her toenails, however, perhaps a nod to femininity or vanity, or individuality; it was too soon to say. Whatever, they were bright blue.

'What a privilege!' she enthused. 'The view from up there must be astonishing. Was it an arduous climb? Forgive me; yes, I can see you're a bit hot and bothered. But I'm sure it was well worth the effort. If you had to summarise the experience in just one word, tell me, what would you choose?' She peered expectantly at me with her pencil poised above her notebook.

I cast Habiba a quick frowning glance. She looked back apologetically with a small helpless shrug.

'It was – er – epic,' I said.

I watched the woman start to write the word then pause. She glanced up, narrowed her eyes on my face and started to laugh. 'Ah, I haven't introduced myself, have I? I've just launched straight in as I always do. Forgive me!' She stuck her pencil behind her ear and thrust out her right hand towards me. Her brown hair was clasped back with a grip. Sadly this had the effect of making her look more teepee-like than ever, a small head atop a pear-shaped body, draped in a long-line and loose-fitting tent of a dress. 'I'm Georgina Savage. Habiba here was just starting to tell me that you work for the Egyptian Tourism Authority, which explains your authorisation to climb the pyramid with a small party including a photographer in tow. But I'm afraid I didn't quite catch your name...?'

'That's because I didn't give it,' Habiba murmured at my side.

Undeterred Georgina Savage ploughed on, still with that look of bright inquisitiveness, and still pumping my hand. 'So, may I be so bold as to enquire...?'

Inexplicably, I found myself warming to her. Perhaps it was her energetic forthrightness I liked. It certainly contrasted starkly against the undercurrents of unspoken hostility emanating from a certain Saleh el-Sayed.

'Meredith Pink,' I said. 'Er – Meredith Tennyson-Pink,' I corrected quickly. One day I'd get used to it.

'Hello Meredith Pink-Tennyson-Pink,' she grinned at me, revealing neatly spaced but large teeth. 'That's quite a name you've got there!'

112

'Tell me about it,' I muttered. 'And you're a journalist obviously.'

'Freelance,' she clarified with a small nod. 'A fully *independent* journalist, just so you know. I think it's important to make the distinction these days. All the time mass media relies on advertising revenue, democracy itself is in peril, wouldn't you say?'

'Er – I'm not sure I've ever given it much thought.'

'You should,' she advised. 'Some of the major newspapers perpetrate fraud on their readers when they allow corporations to influence their content for fear of losing paid advertising. Concentration of ownership is another reason to question mass media's ability to represent a plurality of voices. Did you know, for example, that seventy percent of the UK News market is controlled by just three companies – News UK, Daily Mail and Trinity Mirror?'

'I had no idea,' I said weakly. The woman was a human bulldozer.

'I want to reserve the right to report on things as I see them,' she said. 'I object to being told what to put in or leave out because of the political affiliations of some Media Mogul or other. I was sacked from my newspaper job a year or so ago when I dared to put Israel's invasion of Gaza in the context of Palestine's off-shore gas reserves. It seemed essential to me to cover the geopolitics of environmental, energy and economic crises. But my bosses didn't like it.'

'Oh,' I said, not sure I'd followed a word of this. 'So, what brings you here to Egypt now?'

'I object to the way the Media reports it as a warzone,' she said bluntly. 'This may serve national foreign policy in the West, but it does nothing to enhance the lives of ordinary Egyptians struggling to make ends meet, don't you agree?'

'You care about the lives of ordinary Egyptians?' I asked with some surprise.

'I take an interest, yes,' she said. 'My family had links here generations ago, and it's always been my holiday destination of choice. Give me a tomb, a pyramid or a temple in preference to a beach, a sunlounger and a snorkel any day of the week.'

Now I knew I liked her, dodgy profession notwithstanding. 'So, you're seeking to bring a more balanced view of Egypt to cut through the bias of Western reporting, is that it?'

'Exactly!' she said. 'It's ridiculous that people are staying away for fear of terrorism, don't you think? That can strike you anywhere in the world. And the reports of the political upheaval and civil unrest here over recent years were, in my opinion, grossly exaggerated. People are too quick to take fright, I'm sure you agree? I want to show them what they're missing out on.'

'Then we share a common goal,' I said. 'I'm here with much the same purpose, if not for quite the same reason.'

'Oh?' She pulled her pencil from behind her ear and gazed at me with keen interest. 'Tell me more.'

Looking at the poised pencil I hesitated but actually was given no opportunity to elucidate. Saleh el-Sayed approached with a small crew of galabeya-clad men leading a train of gangly and despondent-looking camels. These poor creatures looked perfectly ridiculous decked out in pom-poms and tassels, and with little tinkling bells strapped to their bridles. If that was the decoration they had to submit to day in and day out I wasn't surprised Ahmed said they were bad-tempered and prone to spitting. I would be too forced to wear that get-up and listen to the incessant jangling.

'Your camels,' Saleh el-Sayed said shortly. 'They will take you and your party across the desert plateau to that distant outcrop of rock. You will find the view of the pyramids unsurpassed from there. Once you are ready and Mehmet has taken his fill of photographs, they will bring you back. There should still be time to go inside the Great Pyramid, should you wish – although I advise against it if you suffer with claustrophobia. The corridors are narrow and steep, and the air is hot and oppressive.'

'As a marketing man, you're not doing a great job of selling it to me,' I said lightly, hoping he might see the joke. Silly of me; the man was entirely devoid of humour.

'I am not attempting to sell it to you,' he said thinly. 'It will be entirely your choice, of course. I am merely pointing out the discomfort.'

If he was trying to put me off, perhaps in the hope of cutting short my visit, his words had the opposite effect. 'Thank you Saleh,' I said with forced politeness. 'I appreciate your concern. But I'm as keen as mustard to see inside.' I didn't care whether he knew this English expression or not. But the slight tightening of his features told me he did, and didn't appreciate my enthusiasm.

Satisfied I'd scored a hit, I turned back to Georgina Savage. 'Will you excuse me?'

'Of course, of course,' she said quickly, thrusting the pencil behind her ear again. 'I can see you have more exciting things to do than talk to me right now. But perhaps you won't mind if I hang about for a bit on the off chance of catching a few minutes with you later…?'

I was unable to reply since Saleh led the procession of camels in between us. I'm quite sure he did so deliberately. 'Which of you wishes to ride?' he asked solicitously.

'Not me,' Habiba said quickly, backing away.

'Ahmed!' I called over my shoulder, reminded of my mission. 'Adam! Mehmet! Over here!'

Adam was still carrying Mehmet's camera case and he and the photographer joined us quickly. Ahmed came slowly and with obvious reluctance.

One by one the camel keepers encouraged their charges to sit. They achieved this by pulling on the ropes attached to the beasts' bridles. Ungainly animals at the best of times the motion of sitting down does not appear a natural one for camels. I watched them lurch forward then back, and then fold their long legs underneath their bodies. It was impossible to say whether the jangling of their bells enhanced or detracted from this spectacle.

Ahmed watched too. I could tell he was thinking the animal he mounted would have to repeat this procedure in reverse with him on top to stand up again. And I could see exactly how he felt about the prospect. A big man, Ahmed was perhaps imagining the risk inherent in such a manoeuvre. 'If we must ride, why can it not be on a horse?' He indicated the line of scrawny-looking stallions, similarly bedecked and beribboned as the camels, standing a few metres away under meagre canvas awnings to protect them from the sun.

I risked a glance at Saleh el-Sayed, standing off to one side, wondering if it was worth me making a plea on Ahmed's behalf. His stiff stance and closed expression warned me against it.

'Come on, Ahmed; don't be a spoilsport,' I coaxed. 'You won't be the only one on a camel. We're all going together. It will be fun. Now, why don't you get on to this first one and show us how it's done? I'm sure you'll look magnificent! Quite the Omar Sharif!'

'Humph,' he grunted. I saw him dart a glance at Habiba standing a few feet away watching proceedings with a small smile playing on her face. I'm not sure what it was in this glance that changed his mind, but Ahmed stepped forward. Perhaps he realised the loss of face in standing arguing was equal to the potential loss of dignity in bestriding a camel while it lurched to its feet. Ahmed is not a man who lacks a backbone, and he likes to show off. Perhaps he saw an opportunity to impress.

The first camel handler stepped back as Ahmed came forward. Our friend stayed carefully out of spitting range, approaching the animal from the side. 'This camel is called Peter Pan,' the fellow shouted out for our benefit. I couldn't help but raise an eyebrow at this. The poor camel's name was every bit as absurd as its tassels. But I'd learned a long while ago that the Egyptians find it droll to foist crazy names on their animals, perhaps as entertainment for visitors. Still, I had no idea what might constitute a sensible name for a camel – Sahara, perhaps; or maybe Gobi – so I refrained from comment. Having performed the introductions, the camel handler helped Ahmed to mount the wide, blanketed saddle, telling him to cling to the pommel at the front as the camel made the pitching motion requisite in standing up.

This was achieved with no loss of dignity whatsoever. Ahmed clung as advised, his face set in grim determination as the camel tipped forward then lurched back, rising unsteadily to its feet.

'See? That wasn't so bad, was it?' I called out my encouragement. 'Ahmed, you look resplendent! Sit there, just like that so Mehmet can take a photograph of you. I'm going to frame it and send it to your mother as a souvenir! Another great memento for the Abd el-Rassul family archives!'

The words were scarcely out of my mouth when a gunshot rang out, practically in my ear. I jumped out of my skin and dropped instinctively to the ground. But my reflex reaction was nothing compared to the camel. It reared and bolted. Ahmed clung to the pommel for dear life as the panicked camel galloped off across the plateau.

Chapter 7

I darted a glance everywhere at once, trying to see who had fired, and why. Fear gripped my windpipe and cut off my breath. It was as if all my worst fears of a return to Egypt were being realised in my very first outing. I didn't want to believe I was unsafe, but it was hard not to succumb to an instinctive reaction to dive for cover.

I noticed a knot of ragamuffin boys a little way away, jumping around and yelling at each other. As a pair of security police ran towards them I realised they were playing with firecrackers. Not a terrorist incident after all. I slumped with relief, and then jerked my head up as I remembered Ahmed.

Still, I was too dazed with shock and fright to get to my feet. The same seemed true for the others. We were a frozen tableau for several seconds as the camel pelted away with Ahmed bouncing on top. Adam was the first to move. I have never seen a man run so fast. That it was in completely the opposite direction from Ahmed and the bolting camel confused me at first. Then I discerned his purpose. I watched open-mouthed as he sprinted past the little knot of men standing apparently rooted to the spot near their horses. He vaulted onto the closest stallion, thankfully saddled and untethered. And then he was off in pursuit, sand flying out from under the horse's hooves as he chased Ahmed and the charging camel across the desert plateau.

Whoever named the camel Peter Pan must have known it could fly. I had no idea camels could move so fast. I caught my breath, convinced Ahmed must surely lose his grip on the pommel at any moment and come tumbling off. It was a long way to fall from atop a camel. To be pitched from one travelling at high speed across a rocky desert plateau would, I felt sure, result in broken bones at the very least. A big man, Ahmed would fall heavily. I started to very much regret my cajoling. It seemed serious injury was unavoidable. It was my fault that he was up there on the dratted animal in the first place. I'd bullied him into it, and now there was a real possibility he may not make it back unharmed. It was enough to have me staring after him open-mouthed with horror.

The camel keeper – the one in charge of Peter Pan as well as all his mates – and Mehmet as well – started running in pursuit, shouting and waving their arms. I imagine they had some notion of attracting the bolting camel's attention and perhaps encouraging it to slow down.

I managed to get shakily to my feet and felt some small urge to follow them. But I realised there was absolutely nothing I could do except watch, and pray Ahmed could hold on tight. There were already enough people running wildly across the pyramid plateau, since a couple of guards had also joined in the pursuit. I'm sure their intentions were admirable, but it was quite senseless. I failed to see how running men could ever hope to catch up with a terrified camel. Indeed I started to wonder if all the yelling and arm waving might actually frighten the poor startled creature more. I could only hope Adam, furiously riding his scrawny steed, might have a better chance of averting disaster.

With my heart in my mouth I watched, convinced any second now Ahmed would lose his manful grip on the pommel, fall and be badly hurt. All my optimistic plans for the forthcoming trip down the Nile were out the window if Ahmed had a broken leg, or worse. I stopped myself thinking just how much worse if he should, say, come hurtling off and land headfirst on a rock. Fighting a sick sense of impending disaster, I almost stopped breathing altogether catching sight of the extra danger ahead of the galloping camel.

The pyramid plateau is not just rocky terrain covered in desert sand as the name might suggest. It's actually an excavation site littered with deep trenches and scattered tomb pits. I could see the running camel rapidly approaching a wide excavation trough. It was impossible to tell how deep it was, but it appeared to be a good six or more feet across. I had no idea whether camels were capable of jumping. However I was reasonably certain Ahmed would have no chance at all of staying in the saddle if it attempted the leap.

But of course Ahmed and the camel weren't the only ones hurtling towards the treacherous-looking ravine. I caught my breath and stared unblinking and aghast as Adam astride the horse he'd commandeered started closing rapidly on the panicked camel and its presumably even more panicked rider. I had no idea if he'd spotted the looming danger.

I wanted to scream out a warning but knew it was useless. He was too far away to hear me and had a thundering horse underneath him. Besides, with my breath stuck fast in my throat I doubt I was capable of screaming in any event.

As I stood watching, helpless to avert the imminent and surely inevitable catastrophe, Adam pressed his horse to a sudden burst of speed. He cut in front of the runaway camel and turned it on the very edge of the trench. For a few heart-stopping moments the two animals careered along side by side. Adam's horse appeared to be galloping on thin air, so close were its hooves to the crumbling edge of the excavation trough.

I watched in an agony of anxiety as Adam reached out for the camel's bridle. One false move and he risked sending them all – camel, horse and both men – toppling over the edge into the trench. I clutched at Habiba, who'd moved to stand alongside me. Or she clutched at me; I couldn't quite be sure which. Either way, we clung to each other while Adam performed his kamikaze rescue attempt, desperately working to bring the crazed camel under control.

At last, and not before I'd seen the very real possibility of having to abort this whole trip flash before my eyes, his heroic mission paid off. The camel turned away from the trench and slowed down. Then, with Adam still pulling on its bridle, it finally came to a stop. Ahmed promptly tumbled off sideways, or was thrown off by the camel, I couldn't tell which. Adam dropped to the ground too and crouched alongside our fallen friend. From this distance it was impossible to see if there was any damage done. Ahmed might not have fallen from the camel at speed but he'd still fallen.

By this time the runners were spread out all over the terrain, strung out as if in a long distance race. Mehmet was the first to join Adam and Ahmed at the scene, closely followed by Peter Pan's keeper, who took the loose bridle in his hands and, with barely a glance at Ahmed, started walking the creature back towards us. It was beyond my powers of comprehension to see how he could possibly see Ahmed as culpable in what had happened. But there you have it. People do seem to incline, however illogically, to those they consider their own.

The others all converged rapidly on the spot. One of the pyramid guards took charge of the horse, while the others clustered around Ahmed and Adam.

It was only as they started to move back that I saw Adam and Mehmet hoist Ahmed to his feet and move to support him, one under each shoulder, so he could limp back across the uneven terrain towards us.

Habiba and I both sprinted forward to meet them. 'Is he badly hurt?' I called out, still some distance away

'Twisted ankle,' Adam shouted back as we closed the gap. 'Sprained wrists. And wounded pride. I think he'll live!'

'Oh, thank God,' I breathed, heaving with relief and exertion as we raced up to join them. 'And you? Are you ok? Dammit, Adam, that was some crazy stunt you pulled off back there!' As on previous occasions when I'd seen him risk life and limb, my instinctive reaction to his survival was an overwhelming desire to berate him.

'I daresay I'll be a bit saddle sore tomorrow,' he grimaced. 'But no permanent harm done.'

'I didn't know you could ride.' I remarked rattily, reaching out to brush caked sand from his hot face. 'You didn't by any chance happen to grow up in the circus, did you?' I'd actually wanted to say how much I admired his foolhardy courage if not his crazy recklessness. But for some reason these words wouldn't come.

'All courtesy of a public school education,' he said with a small shrug.

Habiba held out a water bottle for Ahmed. But with no free hands for the moment since his arms were looped across Adam and Mehmet's shoulders, he shook his head in refusal.

'You are unharmed?' he asked me instead.

I looked at him in confusion. Now I could see there was no serious damage done and had harangued poor Adam for giving me the fright of my life (one of many, I might add), I was absolutely fine. Breathing heavily, but fine. 'Yes; shouldn't I be?'

'The gunshot,' he frowned. 'I was afraid the camel was kidnapping me just at the moment you might need my protection.'

The thought of anything remotely deliberate in the camel's actions gave me momentary pause. Ahmed's choice of words was often bizarre. But I could see his concern was genuine.

'It was just kids letting off firecrackers,' I explained. 'Silly young idiots. Look, the police are dealing with them now.' I glanced back at the spot, now some distance away, where we'd been standing at the foot of the Great Pyramid. Saleh el-Sayed was still there in exactly the same position as before, watching us, one hand raised to shade his eyes. It struck me as a bit strange that in all the pandemonium he was the only one who appeared not to have moved. Intercepting my glance, he started to walk forward as we crossed the plateau, finally stepping back into the immense shadow cast by the pyramid.

'You still wish to ride out to see the view?' he asked unceremoniously as we met halfway. He expressed no concern at all for Ahmed's misadventure or injuries, and made no comment about Adam's courageous rescue mission. 'There is time to visit the pyramid chambers if you still wish it?'

I found his lack of apparent concern astonishing, and suddenly couldn't wait to get away from him. 'I think we should call it a day,' I said firmly. 'Perhaps Mehmet can ride out and take some photographs, so we don't miss out altogether. But as for my look inside the pyramid, it can wait for another time.'

I thought I saw a ghost of a smile whisper across his lips. 'I will inform your driver to bring the car closer so your security man has less far to walk,' he said. Yet again, the solicitude of his words belied the grudging tone in which he uttered them. I had a sneaking suspicion he'd enjoyed how close to disaster we'd come.

'Thank you,' I said, determined not to let his oiliness rile me. 'Mehmet, will you be alright to make your own way to the docks and meet us there later?'

'Of course,' he said, with a gap-toothed smile. 'I need to collect my bag anyway. I'll take a few photographs and come after sunset. I have to say, miss, I wasn't expecting this assignment to be quite so exciting! Is it always like this?'

Ahmed, still draped over Mehmet and Adam's shoulders, let out a loud 'Hurrumph.'

Adam looked at me and grinned. 'My friend, you have no idea!'

***

I was surprised to see Georgina Savage waiting by the repositioned car when we got there. I'd forgotten all about her. 'Is your security man alright?' she asked, coming forward eagerly. 'My goodness! I saw the whole thing! That was some daredevil rescue you pulled off, sir!' she congratulated Adam. 'When I saw that dugout, I thought you were going to pitch headlong into it for sure! Thank God you were able to turn the camel! Now, I have some arnica and also bandages in my rucksack. Arnica is great for bruising, and we should really strap the poor man's ankle, don't you agree?'

I'd already noticed she had a tendency to finish every remark with either an exclamation or an invitation to corroborate what she'd just said. Perhaps it was a journalistic trick to somehow put words into other people's mouths. Even recognising this outrageous manipulation, I found myself agreeing to her suggestion as Adam and Mehmet eased Ahmed onto the back seat of the car, with the driver helpfully holding open the nearside rear passenger door. 'Yes, we should really bandage it before it starts to swell too badly.'

She hadn't actually waited for my response, already rummaging in her rucksack. 'Ah, here we are. Now then, if you could just help him remove his shoe and sock from the foot we need to strap… The left one is it, yes?'

Habiba stepped forward automatically to assist with this procedure, only to stop dead in her tracks. I was just in time to intercept the truly forbidding look Ahmed shot her. It silently commanded her not to come near, and certainly not to dare even think about touching him. I'm not sure I'd ever seen him look so thunderous.

Truly baffled now, I decided I really did need to find out what had happened between those two. Last time I'd seen them, in London for our wedding just before Christmas almost two years ago they'd both seemed smitten. I certainly hadn't had any sense of anything amiss whenever we'd spoken to Ahmed in the intervening months. But now I thought about it, he really hadn't mentioned Habiba much in any of our calls more recently.

Having rebuffed Habiba, Ahmed was struggling manfully to untie his own shoelace on the injured foot. I moved to help but Georgina Savage got there first. She bustled forward and crouched down purposefully with her first aid kit, drawing up the folds of her denim skirt into her lap. 'Now then, let me see how bad the swelling is on your poor twisted ankle. And strained wrists too, is it?' She lifted both his hands onto her knees, and let out a loud exclamation. 'Oh, my poor dear man! What on earth happened to you?'

Ahmed instinctively tried to pull his hands away but it was too late. She was holding him fast, staring at the very obvious evidence of burned skin.

Adam stepped forward. 'Did you hear about the thwarted suicide bomber attempt at Karnak last year?'

Georgina looked up at him, eyes wide. 'God, yes! The police on the scene averted what could have been an appalling terror attack!' She snapped her attention back to Ahmed. 'You were there?'

'He was one of the police officers who brought down the attackers,' I said proudly. 'Thankfully, he didn't take the full effect of the blast when the bomber detonated his suicide belt. And thank God nobody was killed – except the perpetrators of course. But, as you can see from the scarring, the collateral damage was bad enough.'

'And you had to be invalided out of the police?' Georgina jumped to the possibly inevitable conclusion.

Ahmed sat up straighter in the car doorway, pulling his shoulders back. 'I returned to my duties as soon as I was healed,' he said grandly. 'Now I am asked by the Tourism Authority to be bodyguard for this special assignation.'

'Assignment,' Adam murmured. 'And yet here you are injured on day one. I wouldn't blame you, mate, if you regretted the decision to join us.'

'I'm sorry Ahmed,' I said, crouching alongside him. 'It was my fault you were up on that damned camel in the first place.'

'Apology, it is not necessary,' he said solemnly. 'All, it is well. Never will I regret a decision to join you, no matter what I may suffer.'

I really was quite touched by this assertion. So much so, I couldn't speak for a moment.

'My good man, you really have been in the wars!' Georgina Savage exclaimed, starting to fuss over him with arnica and bandages. 'Now, I have some anti-inflammatories in here as well,' she indicated her first aid kit. 'You really should take a couple.'

Mehmet excused himself to take the promised photographs of the pyramids. There was clearly nothing more he could do here. Habiba stood back awkwardly as Georgina Savage ministered to our police pal, unscrewing the cap from a water bottle and passing him the tablets. Ahmed submitted with good grace but a stiff pose. I guessed he was in pain, or perhaps sitting on his manly dignity. Glancing between him and Habiba, it occurred to me that maybe the Karnak incident had somehow affected their relationship. Thinking about it, I wasn't sure I could recall him mentioning her at all since then. I determined there and then to give him a proper grilling later. I just hoped acceding to Director Ismail's demand that Habiba should travel with us on this trip wouldn't turn out to be a matter for regret. I loved Ahmed and, much as I liked Habiba, wouldn't see him discomfited for the world. Well, except for my insistence that he ride the camel, that is.

Georgina Savage talked incessantly as she wound bandages, first around each of Ahmed's wrists, and then around the heel and ankle of his left foot. 'We really need an ice pack, of course,' she said. 'You'll need to rest, keep everything bandaged for the compression, and ideally keep your foot elevated, and perhaps wear a sling to reduce pressure on the strains to your wrists. I know this will be awkward, since you've sprained them both, so maybe alternately?' she suggested.

She was quite the Florence Nightingale, I thought, watching her deft finger-work. For a big girl, she was surprisingly dextrous.

'You really must tell me more about this assignment of yours,' she said, glancing at me as she pinned the bandage around Ahmed's ankle to secure it in place. 'If you've been engaged by the Egyptian Tourism Authority on a project to market Egypt to potential holidaymakers, it strikes me we could scratch each other's backs, don't you think?'

'Oh?' I enquired, shooting a quick glance at Habiba. Either she'd given away more than I supposed, or Georgina Savage was remarkably quick on the uptake.

'With my media connections, I can bring your campaign to a far wider audience in the mainstream press than you might otherwise be able to reach.'

'And what's in it for you?'

'A story,' she said simply. 'I'm intrigued to know who you are, and how the Tourism Authority has managed to entice a British Egyptologist and a marketing expert from the British Museum to come and lead its campaign, complete with a dedicated security guard. It seems to me that could give me quite a good angle, wouldn't you say?'

'You seem to know quite a lot about who we are already,' I remarked ironically, casting another questioning glance at Habiba. She frowned back and shook her head, silently making it clear she had not been the one to divulge so much.

Georgina Savage chuckled; straightening up now Ahmed was thoroughly bandaged. 'I couldn't help but notice the attitude of your young Egyptian host over there,' she nodded in the direction of Saleh el Sayed, standing some distance away pointing Mehmet in the direction of the rocky plateau from which to take his photographs. 'Insolent civility is quite a tough behavioural combination to pull off, don't you think? To observe him so outwardly polite and yet so silently offensive told me immediately you'd put his back up somehow. It's not hard to get an Egyptian talking if he imagines a grievance.'

I realised she must have used the moments of Saleh el-Sayed's arrangements to relocate the car to thoroughly pump the Marketing Manager. And I could well imagine what he might have said. While I didn't doubt he'd restricted himself to the facts, I felt sure he'd imbued them with the full sense of his bitter indignation at being passed over in our favour.

'We're here to mark the two-hundred year anniversary of Giovanni Belzoni's travels through Egypt,' Adam volunteered, perhaps deciding that since she'd taken such good care of Ahmed and knew so much already, it couldn't hurt to talk to her. 'But I'm not sure we need more press coverage. The Tourism Authority has already lined up a series of articles with some of the premier magazines, National Geographic and the like. You might simply end up duplicating what we're already doing, and we'd hate to waste your time.'

'Why don't you let me be the judge of whether or not it's a waste of my time,' she smiled. 'Giovanni Belzoni, eh? Now there's a name to stir up debate and disagreement among those with more than a passing interest in Egyptian history. Was he a treasure hunter out for his own personal glory, or might we call him an early archaeologist, perhaps even the first Egyptologist?' She peered at me keenly as she asked this.

'I think he was a little bit of all of them all rolled into one,' I said. I hadn't really intended to be drawn into this, but Georgina Savage had a way of speaking that somehow demanded a response.

'He'd be exactly the sort of man who'd love the project to scan the pyramids that's going on here right now, wouldn't you say?' she went on. 'Searching for hidden chambers with muons is less intrusive than the battering rams Belzoni favoured, but the objective is the same. It will be fascinating to see if the Great Pyramid has any more secrets to divulge, don't you think?'

'Er, muons?' I said before I could check myself.

'It's a revolutionary technique developed in Japan,' Georgina explained. 'Japanese scientists use it to see through active volcanoes. It's exciting stuff, right at the cutting edge of technology.'

Adam nodded. 'As I understand it muons are like electrons on steroids. They were discovered by scientists researching cosmic radiation in a study of the fundamental laws of the universe.'

'Exactly right,' Georgina nodded. 'They're a bit like cosmic or gamma rays in their ability to pass through solid matter such as mountains or, as we have here, huge manmade pyramids.'

Habiba stepped forward, having overheard some of the conversation. 'The Scan Pyramid project is operating under the authority of the Ministry of Antiquities and coordinated by the Faculty of Engineering at Cairo University,' she said.

Adam grinned. 'I wouldn't mind betting the pyramids are still hanging onto a few secrets. How tantalising! You're right; it's exactly the sort of new discovery Belzoni would have loved. Perhaps an angle for your first article, Merry...?' he looked at me.

I didn't get a chance to respond. A sudden noise behind us alerted us to the fact that Ahmed was no longer sitting upright on the back seat of the car nursing his injuries.

'Dear Lord, the poor man has passed out!' Georgina exclaimed, seeing him slumped on the dusty ground alongside the car, having slipped forward from the back seat. 'Did he by any chance bang his head when he dropped from that camel?'

We all rushed forward. I was surprised to see Saleh el-Sayed a few paces from the vehicle. I can only imagine he'd sidled back over to us to join in our conversation before Ahmed tumbled unconscious from the car. I was even more surprised when the Marketing Manager now darted forward to help our fallen friend.

Ahmed groaned as, between them, Adam, Georgina and Saleh hoisted him back into the car. He muttered something in Arabic but didn't fully come round.

'We need to get him to a hospital!' I said urgently. 'Either that, or we take him back to the *Queen Ahmes* and call for a doctor.'

Somehow Georgina engineered it that the only way to get Ahmed fully inside the car was for herself to get in with him, pillowing his lolling head on her ample chest. Ahmed is a big chap, so once she had him there perhaps it truly was impossible for her to extricate herself out from underneath his bulk again.

I jumped in alongside him on the back seat since there was clearly not enough room for Adam with two such large people already there. Adam shrugged at me and climbed in the front instead.

'We really must go,' I said to Saleh el-Sayed from my position inside the car. 'Our security guard is clearly more badly hurt than we'd supposed.'

'I understand completely,' he responded, stepping away from the car with the closest approximation of a smile I'd seen on his face all afternoon.

I glanced apologetically at Habiba as I moved to pull the car door closed behind me.

'It's alright,' she said, interpreting my expression correctly. 'I'll come along with Mehmet a little later, after he's finished taking his photographs.' I saw her look worriedly at Ahmed's supine frame cradled in Georgina Savage's arms. And then she stepped back too as I closed the door and Adam gave the driver the nod to start up the engine. I didn't look back as the car pulled away from the Giza plateau.

Chapter 8

Once Georgina Savage was on board the *Queen Ahmes* it quickly became apparent it was going to prove extremely difficult to get her off again.

Ahmed regained consciousness on the drive back to the docks. Bleary though he still was, he was horrified to find himself pressed up against a strange buxom woman, no matter how soft and comfortable, nor how much she'd tended his injuries. He pulled himself straight with a muttered exclamation and sat stiffly upright with his eyes closed and his head against the backrest for the remainder of the return journey. He refused point blank to be taken to hospital, or to see a doctor.

'I am quite well,' he assured us. 'I wish only to rest. And to be left alone.' This last was said with a fierce look at Georgina and me. 'I do not need any fussing.'

With imperious reluctance he condescended to allow Adam to accompany him to his cabin and see him into bed. And it was Adam who unwound his bandages, treated his various strains and sprains with an ice pack, and bandaged him back up again.

'To be fair, he seems ok,' Adam said, joining Georgina and me in the lounge bar, where she was exclaiming over our small library of Egyptological books. 'I told him to rest with his feet up, and keep his arms elevated. We can take him in some dinner on a tray later.'

'Did he say why he passed out?' I questioned worriedly. 'I didn't think he'd bumped his head when he fell. I wonder whether we should call a doctor regardless of what he wants.'

'Perhaps it was just the shock of the fall,' Adam shrugged. 'I checked for bumps and bruises. Nothing. I suggest we let him have a good night's sleep and see how he is in the morning. He has no recollection at all of what happened. He said one minute he was sitting on the back seat nursing his injuries but otherwise feeling fine. The next thing he knew he was lying flat out – still on the back seat – but with his nose wedged firmly in the large lady's cleavage!' He caught himself; suddenly remembering said large lady was all agog listening in. He glanced apologetically at Georgina. 'Well, words to that effect,' he modified. 'I'm sure he meant no offence.'

'None taken,' she assured him breezily. 'Believe you me; it's been a long time since I had a handsome man's nose wedged in my cleavage, firmly or otherwise!'

Adam and I exchanged an embarrassed glance. 'It was very kind of you to accompany us back,' Adam said quickly to cover the awkwardness. 'But we really mustn't take up any more of your valuable time. Now, can I arrange a cab for you, seeing as the driver the Ministry sent barely hung around long enough to accept his tip?'

'Whether my time is valuable rather depends on where I spend it,' Georgina said brazenly, ignoring Adam's question. 'Right now, I'd say there's more value to be had here than in returning to an empty hotel room. I'm really quite concerned about your security man, and want to assure myself there's no lasting damage before I push off. Now, if you really want my time here to feel valuable, you could offer me a drink, what do you say?'

This direct assault on Adam's manners left him little choice. 'Er – yes, of course,' he stuttered. 'Tea? Coffee? Coca cola?'

'Would a gin and tonic be out of the question?' She glanced across at the bar. It wasn't as well stocked as it might be if we had our business up and running, but I'd noticed earlier all the essentials were there. Khaled, godsend that he was, had left no detail unattended during the time he'd spent getting the *Queen Ahmes* ready for our return.

Adam cleared his throat and darted a quick questioning glance at me. I shrugged imperceptibly. We're both way too well brought up to wish to appear rude. Yes, Georgina had foisted herself upon us but it was undeniably true she'd patched Ahmed up, and seemed genuinely concerned about him. A drink didn't seem unreasonable in the circumstances.

'Er – no; I mean; yes, of course,' he said hurriedly. 'I'll need to bring some ice up from the kitchen, if you could just give me a moment...? We've only just got the water purifier working again.'

'Of course; take your time,' she said graciously.

Adam bolted from the room leaving me once again alone with the ballsy and go-getting Georgina Savage. I was starting to discern that if she wanted something she went right after it, rather like a heat-seeking missile. I was a bit taken aback to glance across at her and catch her staring wistfully after him.

'That's a rather dashing husband you've bagged yourself there,' she remarked without preamble, intercepting my glance. 'Been married long?'

'It will be two years at Christmas,' I said with a smile.

'Quite a looker, isn't he?' she added, evidently having clocked Adam's combination of glossy dark hair and darkly lashed blue eyes. 'And brave with it; that was quite some feat he pulled off with the horse and camel; wouldn't you say? A man to hang onto, if you ask me.'

I hadn't; but she seemed perfectly willing to express her opinion with or without it being invited. 'That's why I married him,' I said levelly.

'Well, good luck with it,' she said, turning slightly and trailing her fingers along the spines of the books lined on the shelf alongside her. 'Never had much luck in that department, myself. Just signed my second set of divorce papers. It was my own fault, of course. Should have learned my lesson the first time around. Never was a good picker of men. Made the mistake – twice – of thinking it was a good thing to find a man devoted to his mother. Reckoned it showed a nice sensitive caring nature. Hah! Believe you me, if a man dotes on his mother it's because there's a horribly dysfunctional parental relationship in the background, and his mother's desperately looking to her son to fill the gaps. Devotion to a mother does not leave much room or energy left over for a wife. And a dysfunctional father is hardly the best role model for teaching a son how to be a good husband. I'm sure you agree?'

'Er – well – both Adam's parents died long before I met him; so I've never given it any thought.' I admitted. I was unprepared for her direct, uninhibited personal sharing, and uncertain how to respond.

'Then you are a lucky lady indeed,' she declared, leaving the bookshelf to plop herself heavily onto one of our – thankfully deeply padded – sofas.

'Lucky?' Adam said, re-joining us from the kitchen with an ice bucket held between his hands.

I decided not to comment on how apparently fortunate it was for me that he'd lost his parents. 'To be back here in Egypt and in paid employment on board our dahabeeyah,' I said smoothly. I was still grappling with Georgina's unlooked for revelations. I thought back to my long relationship with

Dan. As far as I could tell, he had a nice normal relationship with his parents. There were many reasons why Dan and I didn't commit to each other permanently, but to be fair none was because I felt I had to play second fiddle to his mother.

I didn't share in Georgina's experience, and couldn't help but wonder how much of it she brought on herself. I got the sense of a woman who would very much demand to be put first. Perhaps she was right and simply didn't know how to choose wisely. Even so, I sensed her forthright veneer covered a degree of vulnerability underneath. In our short acquaintance I'd learned she'd been sacked from her newspaper job; and it couldn't be easy to have two failed marriages behind her. My instincts told me she was a woman adrift in her own life right now and I decided there and then it wouldn't hurt me to be friendly.

Three gin-and-tonics later I heard myself ask if she'd like to stay for dinner. I'd dispatched Khaled with a shopping list while we'd made our trip to the Giza plateau. He could be relied upon to find a local supermarket and get everything we needed to see us through the first leg of our journey up the Nile. Judging by the truly appetizing aromas wafting up from below deck, he was also making himself indispensible in the kitchen before his wife joined us, stepping into her shoes domestically as both cook and housekeeper. Wonderful man.

My offer coincided with Habiba and Mehmet Abdelsalam arriving in a taxi at the quayside. Georgina accepted with alacrity. Adam raised an eloquent eyebrow at me but made no comment. So we made up quite a party for our first dinner back on board the *Queen Ahmes*.

Ahmed remained ensconced steadfastly in his cabin. Adam and I each checked on him at intervals, and quietly agreed he was suffering a major case of mortification rather than anything more serious. Having made a pair of spectacles (his words) of himself – not once but twice – he preferred to sit things out. Relieved it was nothing worse, I gave in and took him dinner on a tray.

Georgina proved herself a witty and entertaining guest, regaling us with stories from her journalistic days. Habiba seemed preoccupied, casting furtive glances at the door every so often. It's possible she imagined I didn't notice. Silly girl. I was watching her like a hawk. Mehmet Abdelsalam behaved as if he'd been awarded some special prize he wasn't quite sure he deserved. He thanked us lavishly and repeatedly for allowing him to travel on board our dahabeeyah, and promised us a photographic record of our trip to be proud of.

It wasn't until much later I was able to get Habiba on her own.

We'd moved up onto the open deck after dinner to enjoy a nightcap under the Egyptian stars. The ancients called these "the imperishables", and it wasn't hard to see why. Down here at the dockside we were a little way away from the bright lights of Cairo. The heavens above us were a twinkling mass. The ancients believed the imperishables to be the souls of their dear departed. Those that shone most brightly were the pharaohs who had crossed to the afterlife.

Looking up at the expanse of the night sky jewelled with these pinpricks of diamond light, I couldn't help thinking the ancients' belief quite wonderfully romantic. I preferred it at any rate to the scientific lecture Dan had once treated me to on one of our early trips to Egypt. He'd cut across me waxing lyrical about the eternity-laden magic of the Egyptian night sky to inform me bluntly that a star was nothing more than a luminous sphere of plasma held together by its own gravity. So much for romance!

After a couple of cups of coffee with liqueurs, Georgina declared herself 'pooped' and asked if we'd mind very much if she crashed out in the lounge bar as she simply didn't feel up to a cab ride back across town. Forced to admit we did, in fact, have a spare cabin, we gave in to the inevitable. In truth, I think I'd known from the moment she stepped on board we were stuck with her. It was too early to tell if I minded. Adam has on occasion accused *me* of being alarmingly forthright and single-minded. But I suspected Georgina Savage was in a league of her own.

Mehmet Abdelsalam said if we'd please excuse him, he'd like to check through his photographs of the pyramids before turning in.

Adam intercepted a meaningful look from me and offered to show both Georgina and Mehmet to their cabins. Khaled was already below decks clearing up after the rather delicious Kushari he'd served.

We'd all eaten well and managed to down perhaps more alcohol than was strictly necessary. At least, Georgina, Adam and I had. Habiba and Mehmet had stuck to the soft drinks demanded by their religion.

Perhaps it was the alcohol that made me especially direct when Habiba and I were finally left alone under the firmament. 'So, what's going on between you and Ahmed?' I demanded without prevarication, looking her straight in the eye. 'I never saw such a display of cat-and-mouse. Although, I wouldn't honestly like to say which of you was which.'

She sent me a hunted glance, possibly casting herself as the mouse, with me, this time, as the cat. Perhaps if I'd been sober I'd have reconsidered, apologised, told her it was none of my business, and let her off the hook. I'm British after all, and emotional gut-spilling does not come naturally. As it was, I ploughed on.

'The last time I saw you, in London for our wedding, I'd have put money on you two being the next ones up the aisle.' The look she gave me had me hurriedly amending my faux pas, 'Sorry Habiba, by which, of course, I mean to say the Muslim equivalent…'

She held my gaze for a long moment, looking impossibly beautiful in the starlight, her cream headscarf wrapped around her face emphasising the contour of her cheekbones, the soft curve of her chin and the dark pools of her eyes.

I thought for a moment she was going to stonewall me. Then sadness swept across her features and she dropped her gaze from mine.

'That's just the trouble,' she said. She left it hanging, forcing me to press her.

'Habiba?'

'He asked me to marry him,' she admitted, sounding choked.

I stared at her.

'After the terrorist attack at Karnak,' she amplified. 'He knew he was lucky to be alive. He said it was a wake up call and that he wanted to spend the rest of his life with me.'

I blurted out my next words before I could stop myself. 'But Habiba – that's *wonderful*!' I saw the expression on her face, and caught myself. 'Er... Isn't it?'

This time *she* stared at *me*.

'What?' I said. 'What am I missing? It's obvious you're made for each other!'

'*Are* we?" she questioned, looking pained.

'What can you possibly mean?'

'Ahmed is a traditional Egyptian man,' she said as if that explained everything.

I frowned. 'Yes?' I queried, not understanding.

'He'll want a stay-at-home wife who will give him babies,' she dropped her head forward miserably.

I started to perceive a glimmer of comprehension.

'That's not me,' she said before I could comment. 'So I refused him.'

I think it's fair to say I sobered up quite quickly at this point. Ahmed is one of my favourite people in the whole wide world. I love him, and I was pretty damn sure Habiba did too. This was quite clearly a conversation I needed to be wholly present-and-conscious in.

'Habiba?' I questioned again, deciding it was probably best not to jump to conclusions.

She leaned forward with her elbows on her knees, cupping her face in her hands, not looking any happier. 'I studied hard at university,' she said. 'And I've dedicated myself to my career at the Ministry.'

I knew this to be true. 'So...?' I pressed.

'I know I'm one of the lucky ones,' she admitted. 'Not many Egyptian women get the kind of break I've had. If I give it up for a husband and babies I'll feel I'm turning my back on all the Egyptian women who are looking to those like me to pave the way to proper emancipation and equal rights.'

Suddenly I understood. Egypt remained a male-dominated society. Habiba was one of the lucky ones. Her intellect, talent and natural ability to shine in a masculine world had brought her opportunity other Egyptian women could only dream of. Still, she was no Emily Pankhurst. At least, I hoped not.

'But, Habiba, you're still entitled to a personal life,' I said gently. 'This is the twenty-first century. You're allowed to be happy. 'You can have both.'

'That's easy for you to say,' she rebuked me lightly, looking up. 'You've grown up in the West. We're a few steps behind here in Egypt.'

I decided to cut to the chase. 'Do you love Ahmed?' I said.

She glared at me as if I'd challenged her faith.

'Yes,' I said quickly. 'I know you do. And he loves you too. That much is obvious. So why are you putting both of you through such misery? Surely you can be a career girl *and* a wife and mother. Isn't that an Egyptian role model worth aspiring to?'

'Easy for you to say,' she repeated mutinously.

'Possibly,' I conceded. 'You need to pave the way.'

She scowled at me this time. 'But where would we live?' she demanded, cutting to a more prosaic argument.

I frowned at her, genuinely not comprehending. 'Habiba, you have a job based in Cairo, from which your bosses have clearly released you for this trip. And Ahmed has a job based in Luxor from which his bosses have clearly released him for this trip. It strikes me you're both valued and could pretty much choose your assignments ... *if* you mean enough to each other.'

The look she gave me this time was truly poisonous, even for one so beautiful. 'Merry, you don't understand,' she said.

'What don't I understand?'

'I'm not at all sure I want children!'

'You and me both,' I said, laughing.

'No! You don't understand!' Her voice was rising in direct proportion to my apparent stupidity. 'In Egypt, when you marry, you're *expected* to have children. I'm sure it's what Ahmed wants.'

'And you truly don't...?'

Her eyes skidded sideways. 'I'm not sure. I'm not saying 'never'. But I don't want to give up my career. At least, not yet.'

'And did you tell Ahmed all this?' I said, deciding it was time to get to the heart of the matter.

'How could I? He has a right to expect a wife to put him at the centre of her world.'

'And his wife has the right to expect the same,' I said unequivocally.

'Spoken as a true Western woman,' she said bitterly.

'Habiba,' I entreated. 'You have the opportunity to have a trail-blazing career and a wonderful marriage if you will just see what's on offer and grab it! You're still young. The babies can surely wait a few years if that's what's needed. You just need to tell Ahmed how you feel, and what you're afraid of. I'm sure he'll respect where you're coming from.'

She looked at me with uncertainty writ large across her exquisite features. 'I wish I could believe you...' Then she smiled unexpectedly. 'You know, he holds you up as his ideal woman!'

I blushed, recalling a time when Ahmed had indeed admitted something of the sort – thankfully in front of Adam. 'If that's true,' I said slowly, 'then he'll respect your need for independence, even within your relationship. That's what Adam and I have, and Ahmed has seen that. You know what, Habiba? Ahmed might be a traditional Egyptian man, but he's subject to some pretty hefty Western influences. Far be it from me to tell you what to do, but it seems to me the very least he deserves is to be told why you've refused him. If you do that and he holds out for a stay-at-home wife and babies, you can enlist me to defend your corner. But at this stage it seems to me you haven't even given him the chance to respond to your concerns. You've simply rejected him outright. No wonder he's feeling bruised! And I don't just mean physically...'

Habiba looked up at the imperishable stars for a long moment. Then she levelled her eyes on my gaze. 'You've given me a lot to think about Merry,' she admitted.

Just in time, as Adam re-joined us to say Georgina and Mehmet were safely ensconced in their cabins and to ask if it was time for bed.

Habiba got up, sent me a rather watery-eyed smile, kissed Adam goodnight and headed for the spiral staircase. Adam plopped down into the rattan chair she'd vacated. 'Trouble in paradise?' he ventured.

'Ahmed asked her to marry him,' I said without preamble. 'After Karnak.'

I watched delight flood his features before he frowned. 'Why do I sense a "but"?'

'But she said no,' I confirmed. 'She's a thoroughly modern, well-educated Egyptian woman. She doesn't want to give up her career to become some barefoot bride bringing up babies.'

Adam's eyes widened. 'Ahmed told her she had to give up her job?'

'No, of course not! She's simply assumed that's what he wants, and it's spooked her. She expects the poor man to read her mind.'

'But Ahmed's not telepathic.'

'No,' I agreed. 'And neither is he the type to work it out for himself. Ahmed doesn't deal in all the stuff that goes on beneath the surface. He's too straightforward to read a load of subtext. She needs to talk to him.'

'Do you think I should have a word?' he asked worriedly.

'Absolutely not! This is something they have to work out for themselves. I don't think either one of them would thank us for interfering in their relationship. Besides, it's not as if they don't now have the perfect opportunity, thrown together here on board the *Queen Ahmes* for days on end while we sail up the Nile. I think all that's required of you and me is to take our ringside seats and watch with interest to see what unfolds.'

* * *

I'd promised Zahed Mansour to submit my first article, as well as get started on my regular blog before we left Cairo. The climb to the top of the Great Pyramid had fuelled me with inspiration. But it occurred to me I needed an angle, something more I could claim to share with Giovanni Belzoni. Considering my sunset trip had been cut short, I decided to revisit the Giza plateau next morning in search of an idea to get me started. I reckoned I could do worse than add my name to the people whose bucket list included a visit inside the Great Pyramid.

It galls me to admit Saleh el-Sayed was right. I didn't much like it. Claustrophobic is putting it mildly! If I didn't suffer curvature of the spine before I entered, I certainly knew what it felt like by the time I left. And, believe me, I sympathised.

Artificially lit, and equipped with handrails and wooden steps in the steepest parts of the ascending passage, the Great Pyramid nevertheless manages to convey the almost super-human skill of the ancient workmen who created it. What struck me most were the straight lines. Roman roads have nothing on the uncanny precision of those inner corridors, some only approximately three feet square. And to think I was in a perfect tunnel buried deep within more than two million huge limestone blocks was enough frankly to send chills down my spine.

I'm aware of the myriad theories put forward about the alternative purpose of the Great Pyramid by those who don't believe it was simply a tomb to protect the dead king's body while his soul travelled to the afterlife. I don't mind admitting that, inside, and panting with the exertion of the climb, I was perfectly willing to believe each and every one of them. I too felt I could discern some greater purpose; some grand plan we can only guess at today.

I visited the three known chambers within Khufu's pyramid, the Queen's Chamber, the King's Chamber, and the Grand Gallery, and couldn't help but wonder if the project to scan the pyramids might reveal more. That the Great Pyramid still held secrets seemed certain. And then I had my stroke of luck. Georgina had told me yesterday about the scientists using muon technology. But I hadn't expected actually to meet them.

Being myself, of course, it's because I tripped over their hi-tech equipment as I left the Great Pyramid with eyes adjusting to the harsh sunlight after the darkness and electric light inside. They'd arrived to set up for the day just as I was about to head back to the dahabeeyah.

'Hey! Careful!' some guy shouted. And so we got chatting.

Thanks to Georgina Savage, of course, I knew just enough to ask the right questions. Which perhaps helps to explain how I learned, almost a month before the general world press release, that the 'Scan-pyramid' project had identified two previously unknown cavities inside the Great Pyramid of Giza. Of course, it would take months more research to determine what these might prove to be. Nevertheless, how exciting!

And so, my first article ended up asking what Belzoni might have made of muons.

"*Belzoni employed the equipment of his day*", my article finished. "*To the modern critic, these took the form of palm leaves and, worse, battering rams. I can't help but think the engineer in Belzoni would have loved and embraced muon technology. But the showman in him demanded quick results. Belzoni didn't deal in months, but days. So perhaps the battering ram would have remained his equipment-of-choice even now..."*

I submitted it and kept my fingers crossed it hit the mark. Tomorrow we set sail for Luxor. My stint as a fully paid up member of the Egyptian Tourism Authority had begun. Little did I know then quite what it had in store for me.

Chapter 9

When Giovanni Belzoni left Cairo to sail up the Nile to Luxor in 1816, he was engaged on a mission directed by the Consul General Henry Salt to collect the bust of 'the younger Memnon' - that is the head-and-torso of Ramses II – from the Ramesseum, and secure it for the British Museum. Belzoni set sail accompanied by his wife Sarah, their loyal and limping servant James Curtin (injured in Belzoni's ill-fated water-wheel experiment), plus a Copt interpreter with an unfortunate fondness for drink, and a small crew of locals.

When I left Cairo to sail up the Nile to Luxor in 2016, I was engaged on a mission directed by Mr Zahed Mansour of the Egyptian Tourism Authority to write a travelogue – that is a blog and series of articles – to entice holidaymakers back to this ancient land. I set sail accompanied by my husband Adam; our loyal and limping friend Ahmed Abd el-Rassul (injured in an unlucky fall from a camel); plus a ballsy journalist with an unfortunate fondness for drink, and a small staff of friends and spies.

Naturally Habiba I counted in both categories. Khaled clearly was a friend. Mehmet Abdelsalam was friendly enough for sure. But it was too soon to say if we could trust him, or whether he'd been planted to watch our every move and report back.

Georgina Savage wasted no time in cashing in on our admission that we had a spare cabin. She was quick to claim it. 'I'll pay you the going rate for a five star hotel for my bed and board,' she bullied brashly. 'This trip is ripe with all sorts of back-scratching opportunities, wouldn't you say?'

I wasn't quite sure what she meant, but decided to let it go since she was prepared to pay good money, and up front too, for her board and lodging. If she drank us dry of gin and tonic it could at least be added to the bill. Let's face it; we needed the experience of paying guests if we ever wanted to get our aborted business up and running again. I decided we might as well cut our teeth on this unexpected and unlooked for custom.

In truth, I was just thankful my new nemesis Saleh el-Sayed had not been foisted on us as an extra houseguest. Now, with all cabins occupied or put to use, there was no chance of being required to play hostess to the young man or the gigantic chip he carried on his shoulder. It was bad enough knowing I'd have to grit my teeth at each of the main stops on our journey where he would be sent to greet us. Still, I told myself it was a small enough price to pay for this opportunity. And at least there would be a few days of sailing respite between each major site where I wouldn't have to put up with his excessively polite insincerity.

It was quite a party that gathered to wave us off from the quayside shortly after dawn next morning. Walid, Shukura and Selim came to wish us bon voyage. Zahed Mansour and Director Feisal Ismail were there of course. Saleh el-Sayed, dutifully in attendance, stood silently in the background on the dock while Khaled and Adam got to work unfurling the huge sails on their diagonal poles both fore and aft on the dahabeeyah. His impassive expression gave nothing away. But he did at least manage to raise his hand in a gesture that was more a salute than a wave as Adam pulled up the ropes and the *Queen Ahmes* shifted away from the jetty.

The small knots of hungry-looking young men were still there, watching our departure as they'd watched the dahabeeyah's arrival. I could only hope, if my mission proved successful, they might one day return to the cruise boats that once employed them.

I acknowledged Saleh el-Sayed's gesture with a small nod, then turned my attention to the others waving and, in Shukura's case, blowing exuberant kisses. Adam, Ahmed and I stood at the handrail on the upper deck until they were nothing more than small specks on the distant dock. The *Queen Ahmes* picked up speed, the wind snapping in her sails and the engine thrumming with life as Khaled steered her into the centre of the Nile. The current would flow against us all the way to Luxor. Adam dropped a kiss on the tip of my nose, an affectionate little habit of his that I love. 'We're on our way, Merry!'

I heard the excitement in his voice, and matched it with a rising anticipation of my own. This was our true homecoming, sailing the Nile onboard our adored dahabeeyah, watching the Egyptian scenery drift by.

An early morning haze swathed Cairo in a smoggy shroud and obscured our final sighting of the pyramids. It had the opposite effect as we left the suburbs behind, softening the harsh sunlight and turning the riverbank – busy with families gathering onions and potatoes and loading donkeys with hefty sheaths of watercress – into an Impressionist painting.

The river widened out as we left the city far behind, and rippled like an inland sea. I felt a spreading sense of peace and contentment. Cairo had been like a sensory storm before the calm of the Nile. After the noise, clamour, bustle and pollution of the capital, this soft-focus scenery felt like paradise. We drifted past small towns punctuated by lush green farmland dotted with swaying palms.

I doubt it looked very much different when the Belzonis set off on their Egyptian adventure up the Nile: the same lean, brown labourers at work in the fields with their hoes; slim young girls carrying water from the river in jars upon their heads; bat-like women swathed in black robes washing pots in the shallows; patient donkeys; scrawny, flea-bitten, disdainful camels – a living frieze of figures on the riverbank that repeats itself endlessly.

I knew it had taken the Belzonis three weeks to reach Luxor, with plenty of time for sightseeing along the way. I was lucky to be able to take my time too and follow in their footsteps while writing my travelogue. Indeed, since my mission was to entice tourists back, it would be remiss of me to omit a single one of the historical sites from our journey southwards on the mighty river. Especially since this stretch was now back on the tourist map after two whole decades off limits to travellers due to the terrorist threat of the fundamentalist Al-Gamaa al-Islamiya group in the 1990s and, more recently, the chaos following the election and removal of Mohamed Morsi.

The so-called 'long cruise' from Cairo to Luxor re-opened in late 2014, but it was clear booking numbers remained at rock bottom. We saw only one cruise boat throughout the entire duration of our journey south. Even in the larger towns the docks were either empty, or full of ageing cruise vessels leashed together and rusting at the quayside.

So each day we fell into the habit of visiting a major site or two, all so I could whet potential travellers' appetites with my write up of the ancient wonders to be found along this largely unknown stretch of the Nile.

The sites are smaller, quieter and more personalised than those on the once-popular Luxor to Aswan sailing. And would be otherwise almost impossible to reach. They include Tuna el-Gebel (the necropolis of the city of Hermopolis), Beni Hassan (where Howard Carter started his career in Egypt painting the wall reliefs), and the wonderful temples of Abydos and Denderah. Not forgetting my personal favourite of our stops, Amarna. This was once the glorious new capital city Akhet-Aten, built by the heretic pharaoh Akhenaten. Now two stumpy pillars and a few foundation walls are all that remain of the once magnificent new city. Nevertheless, the place exudes a desolate sadness that never fails to send shivers down my spine. It holds a special place in my heart being the setting for part of our previous adventures.

What the Belzonis made of these ancient sites I can only imagine. It's fair to say they didn't actually have any clue what they were looking at. Until the world gained some idea of the vast length of Egyptian history, thanks to Champollion's decipherment of the hieroglyphs, early nineteenth century visitors were understandably at a loss to appreciate the relics of ancient civilisation along the Nile.

With visitors now in short supply, I could well imagine we were seeing the archaeological wonders very much as the Belzonis had experienced them, without the modern hawkers and other tourist detritus.

Even with all our stops, it only took us a week to reach the familiar bend in the Nile that betokened Luxor. This was just as well, I suppose. If Adam and I wanted one day to include it in our cruise itinerary, we'd need to be able to offer nice neat 7-day packages.

Aside from all the sightseeing, our time had passed pleasantly enough. Georgina Savage did indeed make free with our onboard gin supply, but never overdid it to the extent that I could accuse her – even if only inside my own head – of having a drink problem. If anything, the alcohol sharpened her wit. I found I quite enjoyed her company, although I still wasn't sure what her motivation was in wanting to join us. She seemed quite content to cast herself in the role of one of the holidaymakers it was my task to lure back to this antique land. In between our little excursions to see the sites, she spent most of her time sunning herself on one of the loungers on the sundeck, usually with the ubiquitous gin and tonic at her side, and one of our Egyptological books on her lap. She showed no sign of undertaking any kind of journalistic enterprise herself. I decided maybe she was giving herself a little holiday – time out to recover from her most recent divorce. It struck me those with broken hearts could do worse than give themselves over to Egyptian history and archaeology, the romance of the Nile, the sunshine, and the pleasures of a gin and tonic... or three.

If Georgina Savage spent her time at leisure, Mehmet Abdelsalam was the opposite. I don't think I ever saw him without his camera slung around his neck. He'd set up some hi-tech computer equipment in his cabin and when he wasn't actually taking photographs, he was usually to be found uploading his SD card, and editing his images with focused concentration. Even this early on it was clear he would provide a stunning photographic record of our travels. We'd sent off a couple of his shots taken from the top of the Great Pyramid when I submitted my first article. And each day he provided me with beautifully composed photographs to accompany my regular blog posts. He even went so far as to leave the dahabeeyah for a day and hire a scooter as we journeyed southward, so he could take some pictures of the *Queen Ahmes* under full sail; meeting up with us at Asyut, where we docked that evening.

Khaled kept himself busy, variously steering the dahabeeyah, furling and unfurling the giant sails, keeping the engine well oiled, and touching up the paintwork here and there – quite unnecessarily in my view. He also proved himself an unexpected dab hand in the kitchen. Each evening we sat down to an Ottoman-inspired feast. He prepared cumin-scented lamb kebabs, grilled Nile perch, tahini salad, falafel and freshly prepared pitta served with aubergine dip and peppery hummus.

'Och, Rabiah's recipes,' he confided with a grin when I quizzed him on how he'd kept his culinary light under a bushel until now. 'She gave me a crash course before I came away. But you just wait until you taste her version when she comes onboard. Mine aren't a patch!' I decided I was very much looking forward to meeting Khaled's rather wonderful-sounding wife.

Ahmed spent his time nursing his wounded pride and his perhaps-rather-less-than-we'd-feared wounded body. A trip to get him medically checked out proved thankfully unnecessary.

He'd bought himself a security guard uniform, modelled closely on his police uniform, although without the gold epaulets. Nevertheless, the steel-toe-capped black boots, black trousers, black belt, black beret – oh, and big black gun of course – were very much in evidence on each of our trips ashore. He had a large supply of crisp white shirts, which he ironed with military precision to ensure the only creases were the ones he put there. A big man with a stomach perhaps not quite so ample as it had once been (I'd noticed he'd trimmed down after meeting Habiba), he looked every inch the professional bodyguard. It was a role he took with deadly seriousness, and just a touch of his characteristic puffed up pride.

On board he unbent a little, dressing in a grey or light blue galabeya, with sandals on his feet. His gun was nevertheless always within reach. I noticed he wore a smooth stone carved with an image of the Eye of Horus on a leather cord around his neck. I felt there was something vaguely familiar about it, although I'm not sure I'd ever seen him wearing it before. But of course the Eye of Horus was a popular item of jewellery, the ancient Egyptian symbol of protection, royal power and good health.

'My eldest sister Atiyah gave it to me after the incident at Karnak,' Ahmed said when I commented on it. 'It is for my protection. It has been in my family for many generations.'

I managed to refrain from asking whether he'd been wearing it during his unfortunate experience with the camel. Humour was uncalled-for. The gift clearly meant a lot to him, given in response to an attack that could have killed him. 'I would very much like to meet your sisters one day,' I said instead.

'Inshallah,' he nodded, beaming.

He spent long hours standing at the front handrail up on deck scanning the river and both banks for any sign of anything amiss. I'm pleased to report our days passed with a marked lack of the kind of incident he was employed for. Out on the Nile it was almost impossible to believe Egypt had suffered any of its recent tribulations. The scenery was as serene, timeless and unchanging as ever. Indeed, there was very little to give away that we were travelling in the twenty-first century at all. It could have been just about anytime in the last thousand years or so, and beyond.

Habiba spent much of her time up on deck too. Unlike Georgina Savage, she sat in deep shade and sipped water in preference to gin and tonic. Habiba's exotic beauty seemed as natural a part of the setting as the sunlight sparkling on the water or the palms swaying along the riverbank. It took no great leap of imagination to picture her as a young Egyptian queen travelling between her palaces in ancient Memphis and Thebes.

She carried out detailed official inspections of each of the sites we visited, and typed lengthy reports into her laptop for filing back to Director Ismail at the Ministry. I glanced at her screen once, trying for a sense of what she was writing. But of course the text was all in Arabic so I was none the wiser.

When she wasn't typing I noticed her gaze strayed often to Ahmed, standing erect and alert at the prow of the dahabeeyah. He never once turned to look at her, and she never approached him. Yet the air between them positively fizzed.

I sighed. So much for the ringside seat I'd promised Adam and myself for any theatrics that might play out. It seemed the pair of them were determined to stay stuck in this no-mans-land of stiffness and silence indefinitely. Maybe we'd end up knocking their silly heads together after all.

It was getting dark as we approached Luxor on our final day of cruising. Adam and I were up on the sundeck, excited by our first glimpse of the city we loved, and where we'd first met. Ahmed was keeping watch at a discreet distance. Everyone else was below deck. Standing hand-in-hand, we turned to gaze in wonder at each other as the evening call to prayer, marking the end of sunset, swirled over the river. It was almost as if it were welcoming us home. Tonight the muezzins calling the faithful to prayer seemed somehow to be competing, but unusually for musicality rather than sheer volume.

We stood, mesmerised and spellbound, watching the familiar shapes of the city hotels and buildings drift by in the gathering dusk and listening to the familiar chant. As prayers ended, darkness descended, and the moon appeared at the stern – an upturned crescent, just like the moons that top minarets. I could see Venus too, close to the horizon. The Nile was a black mirror. The peace was total. Adam slipped his arm across my shoulder and pulled me close against him. 'Home, at last!' he whispered against my hair. 'I wonder what adventure it has in store for us this time.'

Little did he know how quickly we were due to find out. Although I'm not sure we recognised it as such to begin with.

* * *

To Belzoni, arriving in Luxor in July 1816, "...*it appeared like entering a city of giants, who, after a long conflict, were all destroyed, leaving the ruins of their various temples as the only proofs of their former existence*". Or so he tells us in his published *Narrative*. But Belzoni had time for no more than a cursory glance at the ruins of Karnak and Luxor temples before he crossed over to the west bank of the Nile to seek out the famous bust it was his mission to shift.

In Belzoni's day a simple track led across the cultivation in front of the two seated Colossi of Memnon on the plain. Nowadays the modern town of Gurna sprawls from the riverbank almost to the feet of these once monolithic statues of Amenhotep III. Cracked and eroded or crudely restored, they're all that's left of the pharaoh's once magnificent mortuary temple. Today the main road runs directly alongside them, and the modern excavation site behind them has recently turned up some rather wonderful statuary.

A right-hand fork in the main road at the foot of the Theban hills leads to the Ramesseum, known – confusingly – to Belzoni as the Memnonian. Belzoni reached it by the same dirt track that cut in front of the Colossi on the plain.

I imagine Belzoni, Sarah and James Curtin approached either on foot or by donkey. My small party tumbled out of the two taxis we'd hired at the quayside, once we'd moored the *Queen Ahmes* at her old landing platform – another detail organised by the indispensible Khaled.

Mehmet Abdelsalam reached immediately for his tripod. Habiba pulled her notebook from her bag and set off on her usual inspection. Ahmed lifted his gun strap onto his shoulder, released the safety catch and marched off to patrol the perimeter. Georgina trailed along with Adam and me, as she usually did. Of other tourists there was no sign whatsoever. Just a couple of galabeya-and-turban clad locals observed us with lazy disinterest from the shade of the portico.

The name "Ramesseum" – or at least its French form, Rhamesséion – was coined by Jean-François Champollion, who visited the ruins of the site thirteen years after the Belzonis in 1829 and first identified the hieroglyphs making up Ramses' names and titles on the walls.

Even in Belzoni's day the temple was in picturesque ruins. The inexorable passage of three millennia was not kind to Ramses' "temple of a million years". This was mostly due to its location on the very edge of the Nile floodplain, with the annual inundation gradually undermining the foundations. But, then as now, visitors were still able to enjoy measuring themselves against the earthquake-toppled hands and ruined feet from the enormous seventeen metre high statue of Ramses II which once stood in front of the first pylon to the temple.

'It probably weighed at least a thousand tonnes,' Adam said, as we stood and gaped at its mass of tumbled stone.

Belzoni can't fail to have been impressed, as was I.

'The Ramesseum is pretty standard in design for a mortuary temple, with a pylon, an open court and a hypostyle hall of pillars,' Georgina informed us. 'Its true historical significance comes in its being the site of the first arches in history.'

I decided I shouldn't be surprised by her ability to lecture since she'd claimed some Egyptological knowledge when I'd first met her. Besides, she'd thumbed her way systematically through our small library of Egyptian reference books on the journey south from Cairo. I directed my gaze where she pointed and acknowledged these could still be seen today in the surrounding mud brick walls.

'They were granaries, storerooms of the grain and corn whose value was as great as gold to the ancient Egyptians,' she added. 'As such, the granaries served as lavish representations of the pharaoh's great wealth.'

To me, the beauty of the Ramessuem lay in its position, a tumbledown mass of golden stone with the Theban hills rising at a little distance behind it, tawny gold against the intense blue sky. I found it irresistibly romantic, and could well appreciate why this was a favourite moonlight picnic spot of the Victorians.

I knew Belzoni's first thought as he entered the ruins was to find the bust he was here to transport. He had little time to spare for the fallen colossus in the forecourt and none at all for the sculptured reliefs on the pylons and inner walls of the temple. The battle of Kadesh – these vigorous but repetitive scenes, assiduously re-enacted wherever this vainglorious pharaoh found a suitable expanse of wall – meant nothing since the picture language remained unintelligible.

Adam took my hand as we approached the spot where the head and torso bust we'd seen in the British Museum had once lain. 'Belzoni left his mark here,' he said, leading me up the ramp and into the inner court. 'Look, you can see where he scrawled his name into the stone up there…'

I followed his pointing finger and saw the name 'Belzoni', and underneath it the year '1816' carved into the rock.

Somehow I could quite easily picture him here using some metal object to carve his name for posterity. I had a spine-tingling sense of communion with Belzoni's spirit. 'Don't look now,' Georgina hissed from behind me, interrupting the moment. 'We have company.'

I turned to find Saleh el-Sayed approaching along the wooden planks of the modern boardwalk erected to access the site from the car park. I'll admit to a corresponding sinking in my feelings.

'Ah,' he called out a greeting when he saw we'd noticed him. 'You are early. I was meant to be here to welcome you, and introduce you to this wonderful site – the location of Giovanni Belzoni's first triumph.' As before, his words, which may have sounded polite coming from anyone else, managed to convey a subtle reproachfulness that had the effect of an open rebuke. As before, I felt my hackles rise.

'Saleh! How lovely to see you!' I wondered if my own insincerity was beaconed as clearly as his.

'I hope you had an enjoyable trip from Cairo,' he said, joining us. 'I have been reading your blog with interest.' Again, if it hadn't been for the expressionless visage and toneless voice, I might have taken this at face value, even as a compliment. As it was, I sensed enough subtext to fill the Book of the Dead.

'Yes, thank you,' I managed.

He looked as suave as ever in another crisp linen suit, teamed with a pink shirt this time, designer sunglasses and a less-than-subtle drift of the same expensive aftershave I'd registered last time. But my first impression of a handsome young man was gone. Attractiveness shines through the eyes and comes alive in personality. Since Saleh's eyes, obscured behind his expensive sunglasses, were expressionless at best, and since he had all the personality of an amoeba, it was impossible to appreciate his undoubted good looks beyond the most superficial level.

'I see you are familiarising yourselves with these most romantic of Egypt's ancient ruins,' he went on. 'Sadly, the Ramesseum is not always on the tourist itinerary. It tends to get overlooked among its close competition of the Valleys of the Kings and Queens, Hatshepsut's mortuary temple and the Howard Carter Museum.'

'I think it's rather wonderful,' Georgina Savage piped up.

'Yes,' Saleh el-Sayed acknowledged. 'And of course the Belzonis set up camp here.'

'They walled off a corner of a portico with loosely-piled stones to give them some privacy,' Adam nodded, deciding to meet Saleh's history lesson head-on. 'Their things were brought from the boat and they quickly settled into their makeshift camp.'

Not to be outdone, I added, 'Belzoni says in his *Narrative* – perhaps a little too breezily if you ask me – that "*Mrs Belzoni had by this time accustomed herself to travel, and was equally indifferent with myself about accommodations*".' I felt quite proud that I could quote this from memory, able for once to give Adam a run for his money. It just served to show how much of an impression it had made on me.

'Poor Sarah,' Adam said, meeting my gaze. 'She really didn't have much choice!'

I looked around at the unforgiving rock, stone and unrelenting sand and acknowledged silently I was heartily glad we had the dahabeeyah to return to tonight.

Saleh el-Sayed gave a thin smile. 'Belzoni realised he had to act fast if he wanted to move the head before the annual inundation caused the Nile to burst its banks.'

Adam nodded sagely. 'Under normal circumstances, transporting heavy stone by water was a good thing. The ancient Egyptians cut canals, which took their statuary directly from the quarry, via the Nile, to their temples.'

'But Belzoni didn't have the resources – or the time – to cut a canal linking the Ramesseum to the Nile,' I said. 'So he determined to drag the bust to the river using manual labour.'

Georgina, perhaps bored with our conversation, wandered off.

Saleh el-Sayed, possibly also regretting the historical lecture he'd precipitated, murmured something unintelligible, then added, 'I really must go and congratulate Mehmet on his photographic skill. The portfolio he is putting together is most impressive.'

He, too, wandered off, climbing the shallow stone steps into the hypostyle hall, where I lost sight of him among the columns.

'There's something about that pompous young man that really puts my back up,' Adam remarked, removing his Indiana Jones-style hat, rubbing the back of his hand across his damp brow, then plonking his hat back on his head again. 'He never actually says anything you can openly object to, yet there's this veneer of insolence in every sentence.'

'Ignore him,' I advised shortly. 'I really couldn't care less if he prefers Mehmet's photographic record to my written one. Let's just enjoy being here, shall we? We've got the place to ourselves, so we should make the most of it, don't you think?'

Adam grinned at me; good humour restored, and took my hand. 'Yes, my lovely Merry, I do.'

After our unusually good summer in the UK we'd both arrived in Egypt with a decent base tan. A few days on the Nile was all it had taken to give us both back our healthy Egyptian sun-kissed glow. I pulled my little digital camera from the canvas holdall on my shoulder. 'Go and stand between that broken pair of stone feet,' I prompted, nodding towards the badly damaged statuary of the fallen colossus. Each stone foot reached almost as high as Adam's shoulders. 'Cross your hands across your chest in the same Osirian pose as those statues over there and say "*cheese*".'

Adam was only half way across the scrubby sand ready to pose for my snapshot when we heard it.

There was a sudden loud shout, a sharp crack that might have been a piece of wood splintering. And then a gun went off.

'What the hell…?!" Adam exclaimed in the ensuing silence. Our hesitation was fractional. After a split second frozen in shock, we both turned and started to run.

Chapter 10

We pelted across the open court, through the pillared hall, and out into the sunshine on the more open stones beyond. My eyes darted everywhere at once, trying for a sense of what had happened, while attempting to do a roll call of the others.

Adam and I weren't the only ones running. Mehmet Abdelsalam was racing across the stone concourse within the mud brick enclosure walls. Georgina Savage and Saleh el-Sayed both appeared, although from opposite directions. In Georgina's case it was from the arches she'd mentioned earlier, and Saleh from an expanse of carved stone blocks not far from the perimeter wall. I spied Habiba, on her knees, pulling what looked like palm rushes away from what seemed to be a gaping hole in the ground in front of her. The terrain here was made up of a series of inter-connecting low walls of stone blocks or mud brick, none above waist height. Not so much an excavation site as one of modern reconstruction. It gave a sense of the shape of these outer precincts of the ancient temple. There were no pillars, pylons or columns to obstruct the view. It was apparent at once who was unaccounted for.

'Where's Ahmed?' Adam shouted, a good few paces ahead of me by now.

'Quick!' Habiba called, rising to her feet. 'Over here!'

Mehmet reached her first. Long-limbed, wiry and athletic, he had speed and evident fitness on his side. He peered into the hole and immediately dropped to his knees. Then levered himself forward, swung his legs over the side and sprang, disappearing from view.

The rest of us converged on the spot. Adam wasted no time in following Mehmet's example. He too crouched, steadied himself, and then leapt down to join the photographer.

I clutched at Habiba's outstretched hand and steeled myself to look.

'What is it? What's happened?' Georgina demanded. 'Is the poor man hurt or... or... worse? Was he shot?'

'Did he fall in?' Saleh el-Sayed asked rather more prosaically, his voice overlapping with hers. 'Didn't he see the hole?'

Ahmed was lying sprawled at the bottom of a square stone pit – at a guess some kind of excavation shaft or ancient well. It was about seven feet deep and approximately three or maybe four across. He was utterly still. I caught my breath and stared in horror at his inert frame, seeing the long trickle of blood oozing from his temple.

'He's unconscious but breathing!' Adam called out.

'Oh, thank God!' I exclaimed. 'When I heard that gunshot I...!' But I didn't finish the sentence to add my own worst fears to Georgina's better-left-unspoken conjecture.

Mehmet was scrabbling about in the dust and sand at the bottom of the hole while Adam bent over our friend's motionless body to check his pulse. 'It was Ahmed's gun that went off!' Mehmet said. 'But I can't see what ...' Then he let out a loud exclamation, and grabbed at Adam's arm. 'Look! There's a bullet embedded in the steel toe cap of his boot!'

'He must have somehow shot himself in the foot!' Georgina gasped jumping to the inevitable conclusion. 'But, how on earth...?'

Alongside me, Habiba dropped to her knees again on the hard stone blocks. She reached forward and pulled a thin sheet of plywood from the inside edge of the hole. 'The hole was covered with this.' she stated. 'And with these palm leaves and some sand over the top.' She pointed to the two long dusty rushes she'd pulled away earlier.

'No wonder he didn't see it!' I exclaimed. 'He just stepped right on top of it. Any one of us could have done the same.' Looking around, it was beyond me to understand why the hole had been covered in the first place. The flagstones that made up the flooring of the outer temple were uneven at best. There were any number of ditches and ravines either cut into the stone when the temple was built, or subsequently excavated. Anyone pacing the temple boundary would watch his or her step as a matter of course, and would have spotted the shaft without any risk of falling into it. It made no sense to cover it. It was hardly as if it were hiding or protecting anything beneath. It was just a big empty stone hole.

'So much for health and safety!' Georgina muttered. 'He must have accidentally fired the gun as he fell. Thank God it was pointing at the ground!'

'Health and safety is not something taken particularly seriously by the Egyptians,' I commented with an arch look at Saleh el-Sayed.

'Your bodyguard does seem particularly accident-prone,' he replied thinly with no discernible change of expression.

'Looks like he knocked himself out on the stone when he hit the deck,' Adam said, straightening. 'Thank God the bullet hit the toecap of his boots. He could have shot his foot off! As it is, it's impossible to tell how badly he's injured.'

'Did you see what happened?' I whirled round to ask Habiba. As first on the scene she couldn't have been too far away when Ahmed crashed through the plywood.

'No,' she said, tearing her gaze away from Ahmed's inert frame. 'I'd been concentrating on making notes. I waved at Georgina when I saw her going over there to look at the arches. Then I saw Saleh el-Sayed with Mehmet and thought I'd go and join them. I passed Ahmed. We didn't speak. I only turned back when I heard him yell, and his gun went off. I saw at once what had happened.'

'It was an accident waiting to happen,' Georgina tut-tutted.

'I'll make a full report to the Ministry,' Habiba said, gazing back down at Ahmed.

Her admission that they hadn't spoken as they passed one another pulled at my heartstrings. I could hardly begin to imagine how she must be feeling now. 'There's no point in blaming yourself,' I said, responding to the note of regret in her tone. 'As Georgina says, it was an accident. But, yes, I do think it's a good idea to let the Ministry know. Especially if Ahmed turns out to be badly hurt.' My concern mounted with each passing moment he failed to regain consciousness. 'It's possible there'll be a medical bill to pay.'

'If it had been a tourist, it would indeed be a serious matter,' Saleh el-Sayed remarked, looking at Habiba with a hint of reproach. 'As it is...'

I could have hit him.

But I think it was Habiba's sharp intake of angry breath that stopped him in his tracks. She flashed him an enraged glance; then uttered a volley of rapid-fire and quite obviously furious Arabic. I'd never seen her so incensed.

Saleh dropped his gaze, muttered something unintelligible – impossible to tell if it was in English or his native tongue – and then he too crouched at the edge of the shaft. 'I will help you pull him out,' he offered, looking down at Adam. 'Unless you think he may be too badly injured?'

A groan from Ahmed suggested this might indeed be the case.

'Ahmed, mate, can you hear me?' Adam said, falling once more to his knees on the hard stones beside our prone friend as he appeared to come to.

Ahmed's head lifted and immediately lolled backwards again. His eyes fluttered open and closed.

Habiba, alongside me, sucked in an audible breath and didn't release it. I too held my breath, willing him to come to.

'I falled into a hole,' Ahmed grunted, lifting his head once more as Adam eased an arm under his shoulders and propped him up.

I let out my breath in a long sigh, as Habiba exhaled hers in a rush of air, murmuring something to herself in Arabic. It may well have been a version of the same thankful prayer I myself was silently sending up. That Ahmed's first words on regaining consciousness were in his usual execrable English surely must be a good sign.

'I think he'll live,' Adam said with obvious relief, still supporting Ahmed's broad shoulders. 'Ahmed, my friend, how many fingers am I holding up?'

* * *

It was no simple matter to hoist Ahmed out of the hole and get him back to the *Queen Ahmes*. While his most critical faculties appeared unimpaired – he answered Adam's cognitive questions readily enough – he remained blank-eyed, no doubt with shock and possible concussion, and weak as a kitten.

'I wish Dan were here,' Adam muttered at one point, when the combined efforts of Mehmet, himself and Saleh proved unequal to heaving the almost-dead-weight that was our big friend up a seven foot sheer drop. It seemed falling or jumping into the shaft was one thing. Scaling its sheer walls of smooth stone to climb out again was quite another.

Eventually we had to enlist the help of both taxi drivers to achieve it. It's the habit of cabbies in Egypt to wait for their fares having dropped them off. There's patently nothing else for them to do. They've no doubt realised they may as well be napping on the back seat in the car park, waiting to make the return trip – for which a tariff has been negotiated and agreed up front – than dozing in the front seat at a rank in Luxor with no real hope of any trade at all.

Habiba ran back to the parking lot to demand their urgent assistance, while Georgina and I did what little we could to help the men.

Georgina kept up a commentary the whole time, exclaiming over the 'poor man' and how unfortunate it was that he should have fallen from a bolting camel, and now, just as he was healing up so nicely, fallen into a stupidly concealed stone pit; and all after being injured in last year's terrorist attack at Karnak. 'Too bad I left my medical kit on the boat,' she mourned.

Saleh, on the other hand, said nothing at all – although I couldn't fault his efforts, now he'd decided to lend a hand to extricate Ahmed from his current predicament.

Finally it was achieved with the aid of some rope from the car boot of one of the taxis and the combined efforts of five men and three women, alternately pushing from below and pulling from above.

Once again, as at Giza, Ahmed found himself strung between Adam and Mehmet, with an arm looped across each of their shoulders as, like a pair of human crutches, they supported his slow progress back through the temple.

Inside the taxis, I didn't dare reprise the trip back from the pyramid plateau. To find his nose wedged in the ample bosom of our unexpected houseguest for a second time might surely add insult to undoubted injury. I nodded Georgina into a car with Habiba and Mehmet, while Adam and I rode with our bruised and battered friend.

I wasn't sure how Saleh el-Sayed had made his way to the Ramesseum, or now expected to leave it. There was no sign of a third vehicle, or a scooter, or any other mode of transport, in the parking lot.

I decided it wasn't my problem. Nor did I see it as my responsibility, under the circumstances, to offer him a lift. Getting Ahmed back to the dahabeeyah so we could call a doctor was my only concern. Still, I managed to bring myself to bid Saleh a civil farewell and thank him for his help; even as I wondered if he wasn't perhaps an unlucky charm with the power to disrupt each of our main Belzoni-related stops.

* * *

Once back onboard it was obvious Georgina was positively dying to fuss over Ahmed with her medical kit. I hadn't seen her so animated in days. Habiba on the other hand seemed like a flower plucked from its stem and left in the harsh Egyptian sunlight to wilt. She didn't appear to know what to do with herself but sat listless, staring sightlessly across the Nile from one of the steamer chairs up on the open deck, apparently oblivious to her surroundings.

Firmly, I thanked Georgina for her concern and reassured her we had a well-stocked medical supply of our own on board. Besides, it was quite clear Ahmed needed professional attention, and so a doctor was duly called.

Adam and Mehmet saw Ahmed into his cabin, while Khaled made the call to summon the medic. While all this was going on, a doe-eyed, soft-featured woman swathed in long robes hovered uncertainly in the background. This I deduced was Khaled's wife Rabiah. At a smile and a nod of welcome from me (I wasn't so distracted as to have lost my manners altogether) she snapped into action, busying herself making hot, sweet, peppermint tea. She pressed a cup into each of our hands with an earnest look but no words.

There are few ills in life that a good cup of tea can't improve. Egyptian tea, made with fresh mint leaves and sugarcane is in a league of its own. I felt immediately calmer and able to grapple with this latest misadventure. I smiled my thanks, welcomed her onboard properly, and apologised for our distracted state. She smiled back, squeezed my hand, and said nothing. But I sensed she would come to be a valued, trusted and welcome addition to our little crew. Small, unobtrusive, watchful and attentive, she was exactly what we needed; a quiet, calming influence after the unlooked-for drama. No wonder Khaled treasured her.

The doctor came, checked Ahmed over, diagnosing a mild concussion and a badly bruised toe. 'He'll lose the big toenail,' he prophesied in careful and heavily accented English. 'It will turn black and drop off. But, with luck, it should grow back in time.'

'All things considered, it could have been worse,' Adam said, returning to the upper deck after thanking the doctor for his time, and seeing him safely ashore via the gangplank. 'Thank heaven for Ahmed's boots. I'm not a fan of steel toecaps myself; but they've certainly done their job today. The doctor's given him something to help him sleep. After a couple of days' rest he should be as right as rain.'

Khaled helped Rabiah collect up the teacups and they descended below deck in preparedness for making dinner. I hoped Rabiah would like our state-of-the-art stainless steel kitchen. After all, her husband fitted it. But I doubted she could boast so many mod cons in her own home.

Georgina Savage, after a few moments protesting her thankfulness for the miraculously minor nature of Ahmed's injuries after such a close call, excused herself also. I hope I won't be considered too mean if I say it was always a source of some entertainment to watch her negotiate the spiral staircase. A big girl, she had to descend sideways, almost crablike; and take it rather more slowly than the rest of us for fear of getting stuck.

I tore my gaze away and let it rest instead on Habiba's unhappy face. 'Why don't you go and check on him?' I suggested.

'He'll be sleeping,' she said. 'I don't want to disturb his rest. Sleep is the best thing for him. Besides, I'd hate to cause him any further upset.' Her gaze drifted off across the Nile again.

'Habiba, at some point one of you is going to have to break the ice,' I pointed out gently. 'And since you're the one who refused his offer...'

She looked at me uncertainly, her unusual bronze-flecked eyes troubled. 'But, what if he rejects me?'

I felt my patience give out. 'Then you'll know exactly what it feels like,' I snapped, somewhat more harshly than I'd meant to. After all, Ahmed was my friend first and foremost, a musketeer alongside Adam and me, and she was mad to have turned down his proposal. I wanted to be even-handed and not interfere. But the silly girl was infuriating. Perhaps she thought I'd forgotten the tirade I'd seen her launch at the slimy Saleh el-Sayed this afternoon.

'I think perhaps Ahmed might appreciate a kind word and a warm hand to hold his right now,' Adam said softly. Lovely Adam! Unlike me, he always knows exactly the right thing to say.

Habiba looked between Adam and me; clearly found something in his expression that wasn't in mine, and got up. 'You're right,' she said. 'At the very least we should be friends.'

We watched her descend the spiral staircase, with rather more grace and poise than Georgina before her. Habiba is slim and beautiful after all.

Adam sat back and rubbed his eyes. 'That was not quite the end I was expecting to our little excursion to the Ramesseum,' he said. 'Poor old Ahmed, he really is in the wars, isn't he?'

'Careful,' I smiled. 'You sound like Georgina Savage.'

He chuckled and fixed his lovely blue-eyed gaze on me. 'Now there's a woman I don't feel I've worked out yet. She calls herself a journalist and yet I don't see any evidence of the reporter in her. She asks a good many questions, usually to get whoever she's talking to to agree with something she herself has just said...'

'You've noticed that too, have you?' I murmured.

'...But she doesn't seem to write anything down. I haven't seen any sign of her notebook since we left Giza, and there's no evidence of a laptop, or even a tablet...'

'She has a phone.' I pointed out.

'Yes, but that's hardly a device she can use to write and file news stories,' he frowned. 'Maybe all that stuff at Giza was just an act to get you to believe she's a journalist.'

'Oh, she's a journalist all right,' I said. 'I Googled her. She used to work for Trinity Mirror. She wrote quite regularly for the national newspapers.'

He stared at me. 'So you've had your doubts about her too,' he surmised.

'Yes,' I admitted, 'Not that I've been able to discover much. When we first met, she was at pains to tell me she's an *independent* journalist – freelance I suppose – and had turned her back on working for one of the major news corporations after they fired her for writing a journalistic piece they objected to.'

Adam raised an eyebrow. 'Hardly sounds like a sacking offence,' he remarked. 'Couldn't she sue them for unfair dismissal?'

'That's just it,' I said. 'I haven't been able to find any trace of her article, even though she told me what it was about.'

'Maybe the newspaper pulled it before publication,' he pointed out reasonably enough.

'Perhaps,' I acknowledged. 'But I find the timing a bit suggestive. She said she was let go a year or so ago. Well, last year Trinity Mirror had to fork out damages totalling nearly one-and-a-quarter million quid after a high court ruling. It was as the result of that big phone hacking scandal, if you remember? A number of Mirror Group journalists were involved.'

'You think Georgina Savage was one of the phone hackers?' His eyes widened.

'As I said, I just find it suggestive, that's all,' I shrugged. 'It's possible all her bluster and bravado about her sacking are some sort of smoke screen. I'm certainly not accusing her of anything. But, like you, I think it's a bit odd that she muscled her way on board so forcibly yet has shown no sign so far of wanting to use the trip for anything media-related.'

'Maybe she's decided to give herself a holiday,' Adam suggested; then grinned. 'Unless you think she phone-hacked one of us, and is here with some nefarious intent...?'

I smiled and shook my head; sure he'd accuse me of letting my imagination run wild again. 'I don't think that for a second. We're hardly household names worthy of hacking, are we? And I'm not aware of much in this trip that could possibly provide an ulterior motive for wanting to join us, even if we were. No, you're probably right that she's simply decided to give herself a break for a few days,' I decided. 'She's recently divorced, after all. And we haven't exactly been doing anything especially reportable, sailing down from Cairo. My travelogue is on the web. Maybe she's planning on penning a more properly journalistic piece. She told me she wants Egypt to be taken seriously as a tourism destination again. So we seem to be here for the same purpose.'

'Well, all the time she's paying us good money, I'm happy to humour her,' Adam said.

I was about to concur when Habiba interrupted us. The spiral staircase isn't really made for running up but somehow she managed it. The expression on her face told me at once something was wrong.

'Oh, please don't tell me you've had another falling out...'

'...Or that he refused to see you...' Adam added.

'Nothing like that,' she said sounding panicked. 'But I can't wake him!'

I looked quickly at Adam. 'You said the doctor gave him something to help him sleep. What was it? I thought sleeping tablets weren't allowed in cases of concussion!'

'No, it wasn't pills' Adam frowned, getting up. 'It was a packet of camomile tea, and some Paracetemol to ease the pain of his toe.'

'Camomile tea?' I repeated stupidly.

'I shook him but couldn't rouse him at all,' Habiba said on a rising note of hysteria.

'Oh God, perhaps it's worse than concussion after all!' I cried, jumping up. 'Maybe we should get him to a hospital!'

Adam was already half way down the spiral staircase.

Ahmed's cabin door was standing open. Whilst all the cabins were fitted with locks, we'd never quite got into the habit of using them. Besides, on this trip in particular, it seemed a bit unnecessary.

Adam strode into Ahmed's room with Habiba and me close on his heels. Ahmed was sprawled across the bed, still fully dressed – excepting the big black boots, which Adam and Mehmet had helped remove when we got back from the Ramesseum.

'If he wanted to sleep, why didn't he get undressed and into bed?' I asked the obvious question. My gaze darted about. The packet of camomile tea, together with the Paracetemol, were both lying unopened on Ahmed's bedside cabinet. I noticed the carved Eye of Horus on its leather cord was there too in front of a framed photograph of an older woman with her arms circled around the waists of two younger women; all three dressed in Egyptian hijabs. From their resemblance to Ahmed, I deduced this must be his mother and two sisters. But after the briefest glance my attention snapped back to Ahmed.

'He said he was happy to rest awhile,' Adam reported. 'But that, provided his headache subsided, he had every intention of joining us up on deck "to resume his duties" later.'

'Silly man!' I exclaimed. 'Surely he knows we don't expect him to play bodyguard 24/7, not at home here in Luxor; and certainly not after what happened today!'

'You know Ahmed!' Adam grunted over his shoulder, kneeling at the bedside. He took hold of Ahmed's shoulder and shook him gently, 'Ahmed, mate? Can you hear me?'

'I tried all that,' Habiba said impatiently, moving to the other side of the bed. She looked down at Ahmed's once more inert frame, anxiety creasing her brow.

'I'll call for an ambulance,' I announced, turning abruptly to fit the action to the words and almost colliding with Georgina Savage filling the doorway with her bulk.

'What is it? What's happened?' she demanded, pushing past me into the room.

'He's out for the count,' Adam said grimly.

'Good Lord, unconscious again?' Georgina gasped. 'Perhaps my smelling salts will rouse him!'

'Smelling salts?' I said before I could stop myself. 'Didn't they go out with the Victorians?'

'Ammonia inhalants,' she corrected. 'But they're the same thing really. Awful pong. Great for revival. Though not pleasant of course. I have some in my medical kit. We should try them first, don't you think? Before calling for an ambulance? I'm sure you agree?'

'Get them, by all means,' I said shortly, knowing how desperately keen she'd been all along to reprise her Florence Nightingale routine. 'But I'm still calling for an ambulance. He might have a blood clot on his brain for all we know!'

I caught Habiba's horrified glance before I turned and marched from the room.

Georgina followed, almost breathing down my neck in her eagerness to collect her cherished medical supplies. The speed of her appearance on the scene suggested she'd been hoping for just such an opportunity to play nursemaid, a role she clearly relished if her performance at Giza was anything to judge by.

The nearest telephone was in the reception area just steps from Ahmed's cabin. The gangplank was still lowered, connected to the causeway as I presumed it had been since the doctor's departure.

I was just reaching for the phone when a movement outside on the crumbling stone jetty caught my eye. It was enough to make me pause and look up. Look up and freeze.

'What the hell is *he* doing here?' I muttered to myself.

It was none other than Saleh el-Sayed glancing nervously from side to side, as if frightened he were being watched.

As indeed he was: by me! He caught my narrow-eyed stare and jolted to attention.

'What are you doing here?' I repeated aloud, none too politely, calling it out so he could hear me.

He hesitated, shifted about looking a bit uncomfortable, then stepped forward towards the gangplank. 'I was concerned about your security man,' he called back. 'That was a very nasty accident back at the Ramesseum today. His second nasty accident,' he added. 'I thought I should come to enquire after his health.'

'How did you know where to find us?' I asked suspiciously, unable to help it.

'There are only so many landing platforms in Luxor suitable for a dahabeeyah,' he said, answering me at face value.

'Actually, he's not too well at all,' I confided. It struck me, since he'd taken the trouble and had the decency to come here to ask after Ahmed, I should perhaps treat him a trifle more civilly. 'I'm calling for an ambulance.'

A quick frown crossed his features. 'But the doctor told me it was a minor concussion, nothing to worry about.'

Now it was I who frowned. It was a while since the doctor's departure. If Saleh had bumped into him as he was leaving, and been reassured about Ahmed's clunk on the head, then why was he still here? And what had he been doing in the several minutes since the doctor had bidden us farewell?

'You'd better come on board and see for yourself,' I said, snapping to a decision.

'No, really, I don't want to intrude,' he protested.

I marched down the gangplank and only just about managed to check myself from physically hauling him on board. 'Please, after you,' I said, stepping aside so he had no choice but to step up onto the gangplank ahead of me.

Saleh and I almost collided with Georgina returning with her smelling salts – by which I mean ammonia inhalants.

'Saleh has kindly come to see how Ahmed is faring after his accident today,' I announced. 'As you can see Saleh,' I said, turning to look at him keenly, 'he's somewhat the worse for wear.'

'He was fully conscious when the doctor left,' Adam said. 'A bit bleary, I'll grant you. But awake, at least!'

Uninvited, Saleh approached the bed, leaned forward and lifted one of Ahmed's eyelids. It immediately dropped closed again. 'Very worrying,' he agreed, placing a hand on Ahmed's shoulder, and leaning forward with his ear against our friend's nose. 'But his breathing at least seems normal.' He sounded relieved.

I didn't know what to make of this. Perhaps his concern was genuine after all. Or perhaps if our journey were to be delayed due to Ahmed's injuries there was some risk to ~~him in~~ his role with the Egyptian Tourism Authority.

Georgina bustled forward with her inhalants. 'I'm sorry, Habiba,' she said kindly. 'But there's not room enough here for both of us.'

Poor Habiba was forced to come and stand by me in the doorway. I reached out and gave her hand a sympathetic squeeze. Georgina was a bulldozer in human form but, to be fair, she didn't know about the relationship – such as it was – between Habiba and Ahmed.

Georgina waved the inhalants under Ahmed's nose. He grunted and his body suffered a sudden involuntary spasm, but he didn't wake.

'Right, that's it!' I announced. 'You all stay here. I'm calling that ambulance!'

But back in the reception area, I didn't immediately make the call. Acting on gut instinct, I descended the gangplank onto the causeway. A couple of stray cats mewed and darted away as I approached. I didn't really know what I was looking for as my eyes scanned the crumbling stone jetty and the bank beyond. But I knew it when I saw it floating in the

Nile between the landing platform and the dahabeeyah. A medical syringe.

I kneeled on the gangplank and gingerly reached forward, scooping it out of the water.

Whatever it had contained, I could only hope the dose injected wouldn't prove to be lethal.

Chapter 11

'He's awake!' Adam yelled, and Habiba came running to fetch me.

I darted up the gangplank, slipping the empty syringe into my pocket.

When I got to his cabin Ahmed was indeed conscious and struggling to sit up. I let go of some of my suspicious concern in the simple joy of seeing him alive, if not exactly kicking. 'Ahmed! Thank God! How are you feeling?'

He was given no chance to respond. Georgina Savage pressed him back against the pillows with a firm hand and a matronly air. 'The smelling salts did the trick in the end,' she said over her shoulder to me. Then she turned her attention back to Ahmed. 'But, my dear man, you really must rest. We don't want you passing out on us again.'

'Is the ambulance on its way?' Adam asked.

'Not yet,' I admitted. 'I heard your shout and Habiba came running to get me before I could make the call.'

'I'm sure there's no need to cart him off to hospital,' Saleh el-Sayed said smoothly, stepping away from the bed. 'If the concussion is more serious than first thought then bed rest and sleep must surely be the best thing for him.'

Habiba rounded on him sharply, 'Who made *you* a doctor all of a sudden?'

He shifted uncomfortably under the angry weight of her stare. 'I simply think we shouldn't be too quick to move him,' he protested.

'I agree,' Georgina nodded firmly. 'It's perfectly normal for people to suffer blackouts in cases of concussion, and to be a bit confused for a while.'

'*Is it?*' I demanded with disbelief. 'That's not my understanding. 'Surely his loss of consciousness suggests there may be something more serious going on.' Georgina Savage might be a strong personality, but I was determined to be stronger. For once, she hadn't finished her sentence by asking me to agree with her, so I could only presume she wasn't quite as sure of herself as she sounded.

'He should probably have a brain scan,' Adam agreed, nodding and taking Saleh's place at Ahmed's bedside.

'And a blood test,' I added.

'A blood test?' Habiba frowned. 'Why on earth would he need that?'

Saleh el-Sayed's gaze come to rest on my face. I felt a corresponding heat sweep into my cheeks. Georgina Savage also turned from her fussing to frown at me. Even Adam looked surprised.

I toyed with the idea of brandishing the empty syringe. It would be interesting to see if it sparked a reaction.

200

Something stopped me. The Nile is full of all sorts of rubbish. While suggestive, the syringe proved nothing. It could have floated towards the dahabeeyah from just about anywhere. Looking at the varying expressions on the faces all turned towards me, I decided not to play my hand just yet. 'I just think we should get him thoroughly checked over,' I said weakly.

'What I would really like...' – Released from Georgina's ministrations, Ahmed succeeded in sitting up on the bed – '...is to be left alone with a cup of the camomile tea the doctor left me.' This was delivered in such an imperious tone it had us all jumping to attention. Maybe he was not just alive but also kicking after all.

'Ahmed, do you remember what happened after the doctor left?' I demanded, rallying quickly.

'I must have fallen asleep,' he confessed, his chin lifting defiantly, daring me to chastise him for this all-too-human frailty.

'But I couldn't wake you!" Habiba cried.

'*You*?' He glared, forehead scored with deep creases, dark colour rising in his cheeks.

'None of us could wake you,' I clarified quickly. 'We all tried.'

'I don't think he should be left alone.' Georgina addressed me in authoritative tones. 'I'm happy to sit with him. Just in case he passes out again.'

I saw Ahmed's horrified expression. He reached for his Eye of Horus and secured it around his neck, almost as a talisman to ward off meddling medics.

Adam stepped forward. 'I'll stay with him,' he said firmly, to Ahmed's evident relief.

'What about the hospital?' I persisted.

'I have no wish to go to the hospital.' Ahmed's tone brooked no argument, even from me. I'd have stood up against Georgina Savage indefinitely if need be. But the implacability in Ahmed's expression warned me not to try it with him.

It's possible I imagined the relaxing of Saleh el-Sayed's shoulders. But I certainly didn't misinterpret the triumphant look Georgina Savage shot me. 'I'm well equipped with medical supplies,' she assured, turning to Adam. 'I can take his pulse and his blood pressure. Just call me at any sign of him drifting off again.'

It occurred to me to ask her why she felt the need to be a walking apothecary. But before I could open my mouth, Saleh stepped forward. He addressed himself to Ahmed in Arabic. I raised an enquiring eyebrow at Habiba.

'He said he's relieved to see Ahmed sitting up again and hopes he'll be well enough to resume his full duties soon,' she translated.

Since I was unable to see Saleh's expression, it was impossible to get a sense of whether this was his genuine wish, or delivered with his usual bland insincerity. The good news was it heralded his departure.

I saw him off the dahabeeyah with as much civility as I could muster. Then pulled up the gangplank and bolted the door.

* * *

'He slept like a baby,' Adam said the following morning, re-joining me in our bedroom. He'd spent the night camping on the floor in Ahmed's room using a cushion from one of our recliners as a mattress. 'I set the buzzer on my phone so I could check on him every half-hour.' Adam looked tired, as well he might, but the crease of worry had left his brow.

'That's a relief,' I said with feeling, taking as much reassurance from his expression as his words. 'But I still think we should get him medically checked over.' I knew it was too late to demand a blood test. If Ahmed had been injected with some kind of drug, I doubted its traces would still be in his bloodstream now, so many hours later. The speed with which he'd regained consciousness proved that, if anything had been administered at all, it hadn't been in a sufficient dosage to do him any permanent damage. I decided I'd allowed my suspicious mind and fertile imagination to team up and get the better of me. The sensible thing seemed to be to let the matter drop.

'I'll call the doctor back to look him over,' Adam nodded. 'I'm quite sure he'll repeat that all Ahmed needs is plenty of rest and relaxation over the next few days. Remember, I speak from experience. The best cure for concussion is peace-and-quiet, and plenty of sleep.'

I lost myself for a moment in pleasant reminiscences of the time Adam had been the one suffering concussion. If peace, quiet and plenty of sleep could be converted into energetic activity between the sheets followed by a pleasantly sated torpor, then Adam could indeed claim an understanding of Ahmed's condition. Sadly for Ahmed, the situation between him and Habiba didn't appear in its current state to lend itself to such fast-track recuperation. It was a shame. If the doctor could only write this remedy on his prescription pad, I couldn't help but think it might be just the tonic Ahmed – and poor misguided Habiba – might need right now.

'Ah well,' I said cheerfully, snapping out of my reverie. 'It won't hurt us to hole up here in Luxor for a while. Belzoni took three whole weeks to drag the bust from the Ramesseum to the banks of the Nile. I'm sure I can find something to write about while we're here. After all, Luxor must surely remain the jewel in the Tourism Authority's crown. For holidaymakers wanting more than a swimming pool, a sunlounger and some snorkelling, this must surely take some beating.'

Adam met my gaze and smiled. 'You'll hear no complaints from me about a stopover. Besides, I'm sure we can keep your readers engaged with titbits from Giovanni and Sarah's experiences here. Their young servant James Curtin had to be sent back to Cairo, you know. He found it utterly impossible to cope with the climate. Even the great Belzoni himself succumbed.'

'He suffered heatstroke.' I nodded, recalling my research. 'Small wonder, since he dressed in the stuffy clothes of a Georgian British gentleman.'

Adam poured himself a glass of the purified water from the nightstand. 'Not forgetting Sarah,' Adam said. 'She too was completely inappropriately dressed. But she spent her days with the local women, sheltering in the shade and cool of the tombs cut into the mountainside beyond the Ramesseum. She was the only one not to get ill.'

I opened the shutters and glanced out at the unchanging scenery of the Nile riverbank. A donkey trudged mournfully through the copse of palms above the stone causeway. For a moment I experienced one of those strange time-shift moments, realising Sarah Belzoni must have gazed on just such a scene. The donkey might belong to anybody or nobody, and just about any period of history.

I turned back to Adam, re-grounding myself in the twenty-first century. 'You know what?' I murmured. 'I have never, not even for a second, forgotten Sarah Belzoni. It may be Giovanni's story I'm telling. But it's Sarah's footsteps I'm following in.'

An hour later, I was sitting in deep shade up on the sundeck with Sarah Belzoni's original journal spread across my knees, anticipating a quiet hour alone with this treasure. It was remarkably generous of Rashid Soliman to have loaned it to Adam and me for the duration of our trip. But of course Rashid was no fool and had access to the British Museum's archives. He knew the story of Sarah Belzoni's brave bid to mount an expedition of her own back to Egypt, and the rebuttal she'd received from the Trustees before Henry Salt wickedly stole this very journal from the grieving widow. And he was understandably proud of the fact that his ancestor, the Belzonis' *reis* Abdullah, unceremoniously stole it back.

I ran my fingers softly over the leather cover of the journal on my lap. Sarah Belzoni had touched this same soft leather two hundred years ago. So too had Abdullah. So too had Henry Salt.

In truth, I found it hard to think of that man, the British Consul General, without a shudder of distaste. His enmity with Giovanni Belzoni was one thing. They were both grown men, whose quarrel might have been avoided had they only communicated a little more clearly. But Salt's theft of Sarah's diary – recording her adventures in Egypt alongside her beloved giant of a husband, and so shortly after Belzoni's death – was something I was unable to forgive. It was a despicable act of malice and petty jealousy.

I pulled back the leather cover, and turned a couple of the thick, yellowing pages. Sarah Belzoni's flowing copperplate covered the first few sheets. I'd read these entries a thousand times: her impressions of the alien country her husband had brought her to in search of his fortune, of the overwhelming heat, poor sanitation, disease, and even plague the couple encountered on arrival. She described her disgust at the lack of cleanliness and basic education that allowed mothers to make no attempt to clear the flies clustering around the eyes of their children, and the ignorance that allowed sickness to be treated with stifling darkness, closed shutters, filthy water and prayers. Even in Georgian London medical awareness was not quite so prehistoric.

But, in truth, it was the entries a few pages in that fascinated me most. Here Sarah's prose was accompanied by a set of beguiling sketches. Abdullah Soliman first joined Giovanni Belzoni as his *reis* in Luxor. He was instrumental in the gargantuan effort to shift the bust of Ramses II from the Ramesseum to the Nile.

My impression was of a man who toiled for Giovanni during the day under the ferocious glare of the sun. And sat alongside Sarah in the evening, sketching images from the day's work into her journal.

Abdullah's drawing of the Ramesseum, with the crew of men heaving the bust on its rollers – was not so very different from the temple ruin I'd visited yesterday.

I lost myself for a moment in the reverie of asking Mehmet Abdelsalam to recreate exactly the scene-and-angle I was looking at now, so I could compare the two-hundred-year-old sketch with a modern photograph. This was something I felt sure my travelogue readers might find as compelling as I did.

Lost in thought, I was unprepared for the sudden interruption to my time travels.

'What's that?' Georgina Savage joined me, wedging her bottom into the seat alongside me in the shade of the wide canvas awning.

Jerked in such unwelcome fashion from my happy musings, I hesitated, not really wanting to share this treasure. I realised I'd been stupid to bring it out here. Too late now to retreat with it to my cabin, away from prying eyes. In my defence, I'd thought Georgina had gone with Mehmet on his early morning excursion to photograph Karnak Temple. I'm sure that had been the plan they'd hatched yesterday. I said as much, stalling for time in the hope I might somehow spirit the journal away under a cushion, out of sight, and forestall further questions.

'Oh, no,' she said breezily. 'I had your lovely new housekeeper – Rabiah, is it? – bring me breakfast in my cabin. I decided I really wasn't in the mood for a crack-of-dawn start after all the excitement of yesterday.'

'That's one word for it,' I murmured a trifle acidly, still not willing to accept that my cherished time alone communing with Sarah Belzoni's ghost had been so brutally cut short. And it wasn't lost on me that Georgina had wasted no time pressing Rabiah into her service.

'I popped a note under Mehmet's door to let him know I'd changed my mind,' she went on. 'A little lie-in this morning was just the ticket. After all, I spent a good part of the night only half-asleep, constantly on the alert in case dear Ahmed should need further medical attention.'

'That's kind of you,' I managed, wondering why her determination to play Florence Nightingale riled me so. 'But I'm pleased to say he slept soundly.' I closed the journal, laying it down on the small table beside me, beyond her reach. 'The doctor is with him now. Adam and I are hopeful all he needs is rest to put him back on his feet again.'

'Please God,' she nodded, then went for my jugular, 'It's a journal of some sort, am I right?'

'I'm sorry?' Her lightning strike caught me off-guard.

'The book,' she said, indicating the leather-bound tome beside me. 'It looks like a journal. An old one.'

'Er – yes,' I stumbled.

'How old exactly?' She probed, looking at me with keen interest.

Asked a direct question I find it impossible to dissemble. It's a definite shortcoming, one I've had cause to curse before. 'A couple of hundred years,' I murmured reluctantly, and as vaguely as I could.

'How fascinating! And illustrated too, from the glimpse I caught. Can I see?'

'Er – well – it's not exactly mine to share.' This was a quite frankly pathetic attempt to put her off. I recognised at once that my ineffectual dissimulation would have the exact opposite effect. Of course, quite naturally, it served only to pique her interest more. Let's not forget, Georgina Savage was far from stupid. A journalist, for heaven's sake! Professionally trained to sniff out a story. And no doubt drilled in the interrogation techniques necessary to winkle out every last detail.

'Two hundred years…' she said inevitably, adopting a musing tone. 'So it dates from Giovanni Belzoni's time here in Egypt…?'

She'd have had to have the brainpower of a gnat not to make that particular deduction. Impossible to hitch a lift on this particular trip and not have a clue whose coattails we were riding on. 'Er – yes,' I admitted, wishing with all my heart I'd left the diary in my cabin. It seemed to have become radioactive, positively thrumming alongside me.

She reached out and gripped my forearm. 'You have a journal contemporaneous with Giovanni Belzoni's travels in the Nile Valley?'

'Er – yes,' I said again, realising there was really no way out. I'd have to tell her in the end.

'But that's *wonderful,*' she exclaimed thrillingly. 'Who's is it? By which I mean to say, who wrote it?'

Another direct question; two in fact. I looked unhappily across the Nile at the smudge of tourist hotels strung out in the soft-focus of the morning mist on the opposite bank. Rippling waves lapped gently against the dahabeeyah. Usually the combined effect of the view and the soft rocking at the moorings soothed me. Not today. I'd made barely an attempt at the first hurdle and I was falling fast, aware of her hand clutching my lower arm.

Suddenly I felt my blood fizz. I found myself wanting to impress this infuriating steamroller of a woman. 'It's Sarah Belzoni's journal,' I said flatly, giving in to the inevitable. 'At least, it was.'

I've heard pauses described as *pregnant* before. I hadn't known what it meant until now. All I can say is if the expectancy in Georgina's expression was anything to go by, she was awaiting a great delivery of some sort. I decided to make her work for it.

'*Sarah* Belzoni?' she repeated, when I failed to elucidate. 'Belzoni's *wife*?'

'Uh huh!'

'Oh my good Lord! How on earth did you come by *that*?'

'It belongs to the British Museum; or, more accurately, to the Chief Egyptologist there, Rashid Soliman. He's kindly loaned it to Adam and me for this trip.'

'Wow! I mean, my goodness! I mean, how incredible! You have a little piece of history right there on your lap!' I'd picked it up again while she was speaking, was holding it rather protectively across my knees. 'I'll bet it makes for interesting reading?'

'Er – yes,' I conceded, a deliberately undramatic – if repetitively inarticulate – response to her onslaught. Though I was unable to prevent myself from adding, 'I rather think his wife was the unsung hero – heroine, if you prefer – of Belzoni's adventures in Egypt.'

'The first European woman to travel the length of the Nile Valley!' she gleamed. 'A true trailblazer for the likes of you and me, don't you agree?'

'She was certainly intrepid. And probably ahead of her time,' I allowed.

'So, are you going to sit there gripping it as if it's about to spontaneously combust in your hands, or are you going to let me take a look?'

'I'm really not sure I can,' I demurred. 'You see, it's rather a family heirloom to Rashid Soliman.'

'I thought you said it was Sarah Belzoni's journal.'

'Yes, it is. Er – well, it was.'

212

'Then what possible familial claim can your Rashid Soliman stake?'

'His ancestor illustrated it,' I said shortly. I was quite determined not to tell Georgina how Abdullah Soliman had acquired it in the first place, even while Sarah still lived. Or how it had come to be passed down through generations of the Soliman family.

Georgina Savage surprised me very much with her next utterance. Rather than pursue the dubious provenance of the journal – stolen more times than I care to count – she made an astonishing claim of her own. 'You know, I attended an auction in London a while back. One of the lots was a set of papers once belonging to Sarah Belzoni, including a journal – although definitely not that one. Strange coincidence, don't you agree? Someone called Samuel Bane wrote the one at the auction. I wonder what his connection was to Sarah Belzoni.'

I stared at her, curiously frozen.

'Sadly, I was outbid,' she volunteered.

'Yes,' I said, grappling with this unexpected revelation. 'By Adam!'

'That's the trouble with being a freelance,' she lamented, almost as if I hadn't spoken. 'It was a while since I'd had a commission. I simply couldn't afford to keep bidding; even though I'm sure they went for less than they were worth.

I'd have given my eye teeth for that little slice of history. I've always thought Sarah Belzoni an intriguing woman.'

I had a sudden flash of insight. 'So, that's why you muscled your way onboard?' I challenged. 'Because actually your interest was in Sarah Belzoni all along?'

'I hope I didn't *muscle*,' she raised an eyebrow at my choice of words. 'I'd like to think I'm a tad more delicate than that! But, yes, I'll admit a passing fascination with your Sarah Belzoni.'

'*My* Sarah Belzoni?'

'Meredith, my dear girl…' I'm not quite sure how she thought she could get away addressing me that way when I'd swear the difference in our age was less than five years. '… I read your articles on the British Museum website, and I visited the exhibition your husband put on more than once. Sarah Belzoni was quite clearly the thread that tied it all together.'

'She was a lioness alongside her husband.' I knew I had to qualify my interest somehow.

'And yet so little is known of her life after his tragic and untimely death…'

'A desperately sad tale of oblivion and penury,' I said.

'Yet Adam bid so hard for those papers.' Her gaze was fixed on mine.

'Only because he wanted to out-fox his ex-wife,' I forced a laugh. 'Can you believe Adam's ex is now married to a direct descendent of the Belzonis' servant James Curtin?'

'I think I can stretch credulity that far,' she smiled. 'After all, we all have to be descended from someone. So why shouldn't Adam's ex-wife's new husband be from James Curtin? And why shouldn't Adam's boss be from the *reis* who illustrated Sarah Belzoni's journal? Life moves in mysterious ways, don't you think?'

I narrowed my eyes on her face. I was quite sure I hadn't described Abdullah Soliman as the Belzonis' *reis* – a kind of excavation foreman. I'd swear I'd simply referred to him as Rashid's ancestor. I had a horrible feeling Georgina and I were engaged in a game of verbal ping pong.

I latched onto the one thing that was becoming screamingly obvious. 'So it was no coincidence you happening to be at the Giza plateau that day. It wasn't an accidental meeting. You were there quite deliberately.'

'I made no pretence of my interest in your assignment,' she parried, since there was clearly no point in denying it.

'That's not the same thing as admitting you deliberately sought us out.'

'Perhaps not,' she conceded. 'Ok, look, I'll come clean.' She sat forward in her chair and met my gaze levelly. 'I've always had an interest in Egypt and its history. I've made no secret of that.'

'You said your family had links here generations ago.'

'Well remembered,' she acknowledged. 'Yes; and it's always been my holiday destination of choice. I think the opportunity to get a suntan while also enriching one's cultural life beats sitting by a pool with a trashy novel, wouldn't you say? I'm particularly fascinated with the early explorers. I learned about Giovanni Belzoni when I was a small child.'

I raised an eyebrow at this. 'Most people have never heard of him, even now.'

'Adam's exhibition last year has gone a long way towards righting that particular wrong,' she observed. 'But in my case, my parents had a book originally published in the late fifties. A sweeping biography of Belzoni: the circus strongman who discovered Egypt's treasures.'

'Yes,' I murmured. 'I've read it.' I still had no idea where she was going with all of this.

'I found it impossibly romantic,' she confided. 'I spent hours and hours poring over that book, imagining the thrill of discovery; of literally digging Egypt's lost civilisation out of the sand. I always thought it a terrible tragedy that Belzoni died on his reckless and ill-fated mission to find the lost city of Timbuktu just a couple of years before Jean-François Champollion cracked the hieroglyphs. Poor Belzoni never knew the story of ancient Egypt that he unearthed almost single-handedly. Horribly sad, don't you think?'

'An awful waste,' I murmured.

'When I saw there was to be an exhibition at the British Museum celebrating Belzoni's contribution to the early days of Egyptology, I was first to snap up tickets. I must say; it was a triumph. Whoever had the idea to recreate some of the chambers from Seti I's tomb, complete with sarcophagus, and get actors along to stage the moment of discovery was really quite brilliant.'

'That was Adam,' I said, trying not to sound smug.

'And, as I say, I read your articles and the pamphlet you produced to accompany the exhibition.'

'So you knew he and I shared your interest in Giovanni Belzoni,' I concluded. 'But that still doesn't explain how you found out about our assignment here in Egypt. Or why you've left it until now to tell me all this.'

She continued to meet my gaze squarely enough. 'I really only started to get interested when I was outbid at the auction for Sarah Belzoni's papers. I enquired about whom it was I'd lost out to and was told it was an Egyptologist from the British Museum.'

'Adam bid for those papers personally,' I said. 'He paid for them out of his own wallet. It was nothing to do with his job. The Museum doesn't own those papers, we do. He gave them to me as a wedding present.'

'You really are a lucky girl,' she said. 'As I think I may have had cause to mention before.'

'Yes, thank you,' I said. 'But we're still not getting to the point.'

'After the auction, I put two and two together and realised Adam Tennyson must be the mastermind behind the

Belzoni exhibition. I decided there and then I had to interview him. Of course, I had no idea that you, his wife, were responsible for the website articles or the pamphlet. The British Museum doesn't credit its authors, as you know. I only discovered that when I contacted the Museum's press and public relations department...'

'...And no doubt spoke to Carrie,' I said.

'She shrugged. 'I have no idea who I spoke to. Only that she told me it wasn't possible to interview you since you were no longer there. It took minimal prompting from me to get her to tell me you and Adam had accepted an assignment on behalf of the Egyptian Tourism Authority, and partly-sponsored by the British Museum, to retrace Giovanni Belzoni's footsteps here in Egypt. Well, as I'm sure you can imagine, I was on the next flight out ...'

* * *

'The trouble is,' I said to Adam – having excused myself to check on Ahmed-and-the-doctor back in the privacy of our cabin – 'eighteen whole months elapsed between the auction and our departure from London. So why did she wait so long?'

'You didn't ask her?'

'I was rather hoping if I gave her enough rope she might just hang herself,' I confessed.

'You don't think she's told you the whole story,' Adam surmised.

'I'm damned sure of it. Given the timing, I rather think she must still have been employed when the auction took place, not freelance at all. She has an ulterior motive; of that much I'm sure.'

'But you managed to get away without showing her Sarah's diary?'

'When I heard you say goodbye to the doctor on the gangplank I seized my chance to make my excuses. But I don't doubt she'll badger me now until I give in and let her see it.'

'For someone so keen to interview me, or you...' he mused, '...she's shown a marked lack of urgency. What is it now, ten days we've known her?'

'Maybe she decided to wait it out,' I speculated. 'Once on board she could bide her time and get a measure of things, and us.'

'You don't trust her.'

'She knows more about Sarah Belzoni and her return trip here than she's letting on,' I said.

'Oh?'

'For a start, she knows Abdullah Soliman was Belzoni's *reis*. But it was the comment she made about the auction papers she bid for and lost to you that really made me wonder...'

'Go on...?' he invited.

'She said it would be interesting to know who Samuel Bane was, and what his connection may have been to Sarah Belzoni.'

Adam's eyes widened. 'She's no fool, is she?'

'The trouble is, in an auction the bidders are allowed to study the lots before bidding. Why would a journal purporting to be written by a *Samuel Bane* turn up among papers bequeathed by Sarah Belzoni to her one-time servant James Curtin? I can see why it got her journalistic juices flowing.'

'*Investigative* juices?' Adam qualified unhappily.

'Maybe so,' I nodded. 'Let's face it; it takes only seconds of Internet searching to discover that Bane was Sarah's maiden name. Georgina senses a story, and she's here to sniff it out.'

But we were given no time to pursue this particular line of enquiry. Adam's mobile rang even as we were looking at each other trying to decide whether it might be a good idea or not to show Georgina the diary and simply get it over with.

Adam's expression froze and he immediately hit the speakerphone button on his iPhone so I could hear. 'Walid,' he said. 'I think you need to repeat that so both Merry and I can take it in,' he said to our friend in Cairo.

I heard Walid suck in a breath in preparation for re-delivering whatever bombshell it was that had Adam's eyes turning from deep blue to violet.

'I can't speak for long,' he said. 'You need to go and see Ibrahim Mohassib at the Luxor Museum.' He spoke in his careful English, his voice filling our small cabin with its curious mixture of authority and apology. 'Those stone tablets you've had me searching high and low for ... the ones you think could shed light on Nefertari and her origins...I have a feeling he may be able to help...'

Chapter 12

You might suppose I'd forgotten about the elusive origins of Queen Nefertari. Not a chance. Just because this little mystery had not been uppermost in my mind with everything else going on, it certainly didn't mean I'd neglected to give it any thought at all.

I'd wondered all along if the simple matter of placing myself back in the Nile Valley might act as a catalyst of some sort. As I've had cause to note in the past, Egypt has a way of whispering its secrets to me. I hope I don't sound too ridiculously kooky when I admit I'd been wishing all along for some revelation or other. So I received Walid's suggestion with a small thrill of inevitability. But a small thrill nonetheless.

Nefertari's origins may never have been far from my thoughts but truth to tell I'd forgotten all about Ibrahim Mohassib. I had to shut my eyes and concentrate hard for a moment or two to call him fully back to mind. Of course Walid had provided the reminder with the reference to the Luxor Museum. This rather wonderful small museum is situated on the Corniche on Luxor's east bank. It's modern in design, beautifully air-conditioned, and packed with magnificent ancient Egyptian treasures. Ibrahim Mohassib, lucky man, holds the distinction of being the museum's curator.

My brain struggled to dredge an image of him from my memory banks. He'd played a tiny bit part in our previous adventures, lending us – or Walid, to be accurate – one of his museum's state-of-the-art lab rooms as somewhere to study the papyri we'd "discovered" in an old briefcase once belonging to Howard Carter.

Eventually I pieced together the image of an unremarkable, mild-mannered man in his middle years. I had a feeling he knew rather more of our story than was entirely comfortable, having been there when we coaxed Habiba through the clues towards what we'd intended to be the "staged" discovery of our tomb. But Director Ismail, on exiting Adam, Ted and me from Egypt, had made it clear he was also intent on tying up all loose ends that could possibly pertain to our secret tomb. And in that I'd placed my faith. I hadn't given Ibrahim Mohassib so much as a passing thought in years.

So it was with some considerable excitement and lots of nervous energy that Adam and I approached our visit to the Luxor Museum towards closing time that same day.

I took the precaution of advising Habiba to keep an eye on Ahmed. The doctor had checked him over, and he seemed very much better but I was unwilling to leave him. Seeing her gaze lock with mine, and the determined set of her jaw, my qualms left me.

We'd sold our scooters on leaving Egypt three years ago, so had to hire a taxi to pick us up at our jetty on the west bank. Luckily, during our time here before we'd struck up some easy acquaintanceships with a good many of the local taxi drivers. This was to our great advantage as it saved us the whole bartering rigmarole.

Hani, who came to collect us, knew we knew the fare. Knew also we'd give him a generous tip. So it was smiles all round. We greeted each other like long lost friends, then Hani jumped in behind the wheel and Adam and I slid onto the back seat. I let Adam do the talking, answering Hani's excited questions about our return to Egypt and our time in England. For myself, I preferred to watch the oh-so familiar landscape as we crossed the bridge over the Nile and drove along the east bank through the suburbs into Luxor.

This route was as familiar to me as if I'd lived here all my life. Nothing had changed. The same multi-colour bougainvillea dripped from bushes along the central reservations, pink and orange, and white, sometimes all flowering in profusion on the same bush. There were perhaps fewer chunks of random masonry to negotiate than before, and not a single flock of sheep or goats to hamper our progress. But the raggedy children were out in force, and stray cats and mangy dogs roamed the streets as they always had. Sand proliferated, banked up at the kerbside in wind-blown drifts. This was Luxor. This was home. I sighed contentedly, and let it settle back into my soul.

The Luxor Museum is a long, low-slung building with a wide grass bank behind tall metal railings on the Corniche. This grassy bank is dotted with stone statues of pharaohs gazing impassively towards the ever-shifting Nile and the Theban hills of the west bank beyond.

I took Adam's hand after he'd paid Hani the fare and we strolled towards the security booth. Adam showed his credentials at the kiosk. He mentioned Ibrahim Mohassib by name. 'We have an appointment,' he said. 'Mr Mohassib is expecting us.'

The security guard was given no chance to check the British Museum identity card Adam held out politely for inspection. Ibrahim Mohassib himself almost knocked the young man off his feet in his rush to come forward and greet us. 'Mr Tennyson! Miss Pink!' he shouted eagerly, pushing unceremoniously past the guard. 'I wanted to be here to welcome you personally. I hope you have not been kept waiting long!'

'We've literally just arrived,' I assured him, 'It's Mrs Tennyson now. We've married since we were last here.' I decided to dispense with the Tennyson-Pink appellation on this occasion. The whole double-barrelled business was quite honestly proving more of a mouthful than it was worth.

'My congratulations,' he said warmly, peering closely at each of us in turn through his glasses. 'You know, I had forgotten what you looked like. I was unable to call to mind a clear image of either one of you. I just had a vague impression in my memory of a young English couple, friends of Dr Massri. But, now you are here, I know I would have recognised you both anywhere! Welcome! Welcome! I have been most anxious to see you both again!'

It was impossible not to warm to this effusive bonhomie. Especially so since he'd owned up so openly to exactly my own inability to conjure him up with any clarity in my memory. But now he was in front of me I shared in the experience of instantaneous recall and recognition.

He was a plain-featured and unremarkable chap of fifty-something at a guess, with a crop of closely cut frizzy grey hair; wearing dark trousers and a short-sleeved white shirt. His blue-and-yellow tie was patterned with small Egyptian ankh symbols.

'It's good to see you again, Mr Mohassib,' Adam smiled, gently extricating his hand when it seemed the museum curator might stand delightedly pumping it for the rest of the evening.

'Now you must please excuse my poor attempts at your language,' Ibrahim Mohassib appealed, turning immediately to take my own hand, which he raised in a gallant gesture to his lips.

I acknowledged this gentlemanly conduct with a smile and a small squeeze of his hand before he released mine and let it drop back to his side.

There was absolutely nothing wrong with his English. That much I most certainly did remember from last time, despite his apologetic protestations about his inadequacy on that score. Now I was witness to it again, I was also forcibly reminded of the excitability of his nature. Whether this was a natural facet of his character or simply the product of his short previous acquaintance with us was impossible to say. He'd had good cause on that occasion to be excited. Let's face it; we'd presented him with three genuine ancient Egyptian papyrus scrolls dating back to the 18th Dynasty. These seemed to point towards buried treasure at the very least, the possibility of an undiscovered royal tomb at the other end of the spectrum. Surely reason enough for a bit of jumping up and down.

I had no idea what Director Ismail had told him to throw him off the scent when he ejected us from Egypt. I cherished some small hope I was about to find out. At the same time, despite the warmth of the curator's welcome, I was very conscious of not letting my guard drop. In reality I was far more interested in learning what light Ibrahim Mohassib might be able to shed on Sarah Belzoni's discovery than I was in raking over the coals of ours. But it was naïve to think we could avoid the subject altogether since it was the reason we'd made the museum curator's acquaintance in the first place.

Adam and I had made a pact to watch our own step and each other's. We exchanged a quick glance as if reaffirming this promise as Ibrahim Mohassib took us each by the arm and ushered us out of the security kiosk. 'Come, come! We have much to talk about!'

He led us across the grassy bank past the stone pharaohs. A moment later we stepped inside the blissfully cool interior of the building.

Ibrahim Mohassib kept up a steady stream of animated conversation as he led us through the ground floor gallery. We could do little more than glance at the magnificent statuary of the pharaohs and their gods lining the walls as he steered us towards the door that led from the public display space to the behind-the-scenes and no less state-of-the-art off-limits part of the museum. These rooms were set behind the public gallery and descended into a hi-tech basement we'd visited before. He nodded to the security guard posted there, who stood back respectfully and held the door open. I spied a gun propped against the side of his chair, regretting the need for such precautions in these terrorism-rife times but grateful for the reassurance it provided all the same.

We entered a sterile corridor. We'd been here before, and I was reasonably familiar with the layout. The third door on the right was the one into the laboratory – if that was the correct word for the ultra-modern space housing the hi-tech preservation equipment used to examine our ancient papyri. But Ibrahim Mohassib led us past its closed door, instead throwing one open a little further along. His office was furnished with a big desk and a soft-cushioned seating area in one corner around a low rectangular coffee table. He waved us into the seats with a flourish, clapping his hands together in a gesture that brought a slim young woman in Western dress running through another door on the far side of the room to offer us refreshments.

Settled a few minutes later with tall glasses of iced tea in front of us, Ibrahim Mohassib beamed and adjusted his glasses, apparently to see us more clearly. 'You are most welcome here,' he said, adding an expansive hand gesture to reinforce his words. 'Now, you must tell me all about your assignment. Dr Massri mentioned the Egyptian Tourism Authority has engaged your services? Sadly, I have not seen Walid since you were all last here, but we keep distantly in touch through our profession.'

Adam sat back, crossing one leg across the other, an ankle resting on the other knee in a studiedly relaxed pose. 'We're following in the footsteps of Giovanni Belzoni,' he said conversationally, answering the question rather than the comment. 'We were both involved in staging one of the British Museum's most successful exhibitions last year.'

'Ah yes,' the curator nodded. 'Alas, I was unable to visit personally, but I did look at the website. I was particularly impressed with the life-size replica chambers you built minutely recreating the interior of the tomb of Seti I. An inspired idea.'

His English wasn't just good, it was flawless, his accent soft and unobtrusive.

Adam gave a modest shrug. 'I really can't take the credit. I simply copied what Belzoni himself did when he set up his own Egyptian exhibition in London nearly two hundred years ago.'

Ibrahim Mohassib tilted his head to one side. 'It may interest you to know,' he said, his alert gaze darting from Adam's face to mine and back, 'that Director Feisal Ismail from the Ministry for Antiquities has decided to re-open two of our most famous tombs to the public. That of Seti I is one of them. There's an 'official' opening this weekend for local dignitaries, ahead of the public opening next month.'

I sucked in a breath, hearing this.

Adam sent me a quick look. 'That was your idea as I recall it, Merry.'

'Don't tell me,' I ventured. 'The other is Nefertari's tomb in the Valley of the Queens. They've both been closed to the public for years. How I'd love to see Nefertari's final resting place.'

'Your idea?' Ibrahim Mohassib pounced on this, eyes snapping. 'You are acquainted with our Director Ismail from the Ministry?'

Luckily, I saw the trap and had the good sense not to fall into it. I wasn't so blinded by my fascination with Nefertari, nor flattered by the unexpected news that Director Ismail had taken my advice, to lower my defences. 'Yes of course,' I said smoothly. 'Director Ismail accompanied the junior Tourism Minister Zahed Mansour to London back in the spring to offer me this job.'

I heard Adam let out a slow breath alongside me. Ibrahim Mohassib looked a bit crestfallen. 'Ah. I had thought maybe you and he were already acquainted.'

Since he hadn't asked this as a direct question, I was able to give a small regretful shrug and say nothing. Instead I volunteered, 'During their visit to London Director Ismail and Mr Mansour were bemoaning the fact that the replica tomb of Tutankhamun hadn't attracted large numbers of visitors as hoped. I merely suggested they might consider opening a couple of genuine tombs that may prove a stronger draw.'

Some of the speculative light came back into the museum curator's brown eyes. 'And of course all the talk about secret chambers behind Tutankhamun's tomb came to nothing.' His tone was conversational.

Adam and I maintained a watchful silence.

'I followed those investigations with extreme fascination, as you might imagine,' Ibrahim Mohassib added. 'I couldn't help but be reminded of the suggestive text of the papyri Dr Massri discovered. You'll recall, I'm sure; it seemed to point to an undiscovered Amarnan royal burial. Of course, most scholars accept that the skeleton in KV55 was Akhenaten. But Nefertiti has never been found. I was quite breathless with Nicholas Reeves' conjecture that the hidden chambers might contain her burial.'

'We followed the story avidly too,' Adam acknowledged, perhaps feeling it was riskier to stonewall the curator than make some attempt to join in the conversation normally. 'I'm honestly not sure whether I was disappointed or relieved when those infrared scans failed to identify any cavities behind the walls.'

'So, you think Nefertiti might be out there somewhere in a hidden tomb awaiting discovery?' He was watching us closely. Whatever it was Director Ismail had told him, it clearly hadn't satisfied his curiosity. Of course, I didn't dare ask what it was for fear of giving the game away.

'It would be nice to believe there's an undiscovered royal tomb out there to rival Tutankhamun's,' Adam said, neatly side-stepping the question. 'But whether this is the right time and Egypt can cope with such a momentous find is another matter.'

'And that's where Adam and I come in,' I said brightly, deciding it was time to take control of the conversation; steer it away from treacherous waters and back in the direction I really wanted to go. 'We're here in an attempt to put Egypt back on the international holiday map. The success of the Belzoni exhibition in London has encouraged the Tourism Authority to think it might be possible to market Egypt as a vacation destination once more to those with more than a passing interest in ancient history, as well as in sunshine, sand and sea. Oh! And it gives Adam and me the chance to investigate the small mystery we've stumbled across as well, of course.'

I'd thrown this in quite deliberately, and was gratified to see it have the desired affect, landing squarely where I'd aimed it. Ibrahim Mohassib's bright gaze swung in my direction. 'Mystery? Ah yes, now I perceive we may be getting to the nub of the reason Walid Massri asked me to turn my storerooms inside out.'

I offered him my most dazzling smile, deciding to fill in some background. 'You've heard of Professor Edward Kincaid?'

'Naturally. He delivered a seminal lecture series many decades ago, now used as study notes by Egyptologists the world over.'

'Well, a couple of years ago he was coaxed from retirement to catalogue a bequest made to the Ashmolean Museum in Oxford.'

'I have heard of it,' he nodded.

'It contained papers bequeathed by descendants of Joseph Bonomi. He was an epigrapher from the Robert Hay expedition to Abu Simbel in 1825, nine years after Giovanni Belzoni dug it from the sand. There was a pen-and-ink drawing by Bonomi of the inside of the smaller temple in Nubia...'

'…Nefertari's Temple…' Ibrahim Mohassib said.

I inclined my head in acknowledgement. '…As well as a papyrus scroll we believe was taken from the same place…'

'These are both highly suggestive about the origins of Queen Nefertari, great royal wife of Ramses the Great,' Adam interjected. 'And perhaps even shed new light on the character of Ramses II himself.'

'Suggestive but not explicit,' I added.

Ibrahim Mohassib was nodding slowly in comprehension. But he wasn't yet ready to play his hand and divulge what he may or may not know that might help us in our quest.

There was no way I was willing to reveal our knowledge of Sarah Belzoni's brave excursion back to Egypt to join the Robert Hay expedition alongside Joseph Bonomi, disguised as the young male draughtsman Samuel Bane. That remained her secret and I was determined to keep it. But the auction lot Adam had successfully bid for was another matter. It was on the public record. Even Georgina Savage knew about it, for heaven's sake!

'But now we've come by some auction papers that strongly suggest the Belzonis may have come across further textual evidence in Nefertari's Abu Simbel temple,' Adam intervened. 'We think this may have taken the form of stone tablets, stele if you prefer. It's our belief they'd been removed by the time of the Robert Hay expedition. But we don't know by whom.'

'We've scoured the storerooms of the museums of the western world with notable Egyptian collections,' I explained. 'But we've so far drawn a blank. Of course, it's possible they were destroyed, but we're hopeful that didn't happen.'

'We felt they might be languishing among the uncatalogued artefacts in the Egyptian Antiquities Museum in Cairo,' Adam added. 'But Walid – by whom of course I mean, Dr Massri – conducted a thorough search and has so far turned up nothing.'

Ibrahim Mohassib met my gaze. We were all – or, in my case, had been – employees of some of the finest Egyptological museums in the world (Walid in Cairo, Ibrahim Mohassib here in Luxor, and Adam and myself in London). We were colleagues in a sense. I hoped that meant we could be comrades of a sort too.

'Stone tablets, you say…?' Why did I have the sense Ibrahim Mohassib was drawing this moment out, milking it for all it was worth?

'Well, we don't know for sure,' Adam qualified. 'But that's what the evidence we've studied seems to suggest. We were just thinking what an incredible epitaph it would be if, without knowing it, the Belzonis discovered the genealogy of one of Egypt's most famous queens.'

'It would certainly add a certain piquancy to your Belzoni opus,' Ibrahim Mohassib mused, once again proving his command of our language was anything but inadequate.

Neither one of us attempted to deny this; just stared at him expectantly. It was me who broke first. 'So, Dr Massri suggested you may be able to help? Do you have any evidence that these stele existed, and may perhaps have survived the last two hundred years?'

The airwaves seemed to grow heavy as he contemplated us across the coffee table and slowly sipped his iced tea. I wondered if perhaps the air-conditioning had developed a sudden malfunction. I felt I could almost hear the cogs of his brain whirring, as if he were weighing up how many brownie points he might earn by sharing whatever he knew or had found. Whether if, in revealing his knowledge to us, we might be more inclined to return the favour. I was damned sure he'd clocked that we knew more than we were telling about the story those three papyrus scrolls had offered up three years ago.

I decided to nudge him along a little. 'Think what a coup it would be for the Luxor Museum if you were able to shine a light into one of the most fascinating periods of ancient Egyptian history,' I coaxed. 'Visitors would be falling over themselves to come here. Surely that's what we all want? And to unveil another chapter of history, of course.'

I wondered if I might have overdone it a bit when he sent me a quizzical glance. I watched indecision flicker across his rather plain and unremarkable features. Then he seemed to make up his mind. 'I'm sorry to say I don't have a set of hitherto unknown stone tablets from the early 19th Dynasty in my storerooms,' he said.

I felt my shoulders slump and only then realised how much pent up anticipation I'd been suppressing.

'No,' Adam cut in smoothly. 'As a relatively new museum, we knew that was too much to hope for.'

I looked at him askance, wondering why he hadn't chosen to share this little insight with me. Then I realised the foolishness of my own conjectures. Of course it was impossible for the stele – if indeed they still existed – to be here. Luxor Museum was inaugurated in the seventies, recent enough for modern techniques to have been used in cataloguing and itemising each artefact, whether on display or not. I let go of that little shred of hope with a small puff of disappointment. Then looked at Ibrahim Mohassib every bit as enquiringly as he'd earlier looked at me.

He met my gaze steadily, and I saw a softening in his expression. 'Let me ask you a question,' he said.

'Yes?' I leaned forward.

'Have you heard of a certain Abdullah Soliman?'

I caught my breath, and heard Adam gasp alongside me.

'He was Giovanni Belzoni's *reis*,' Adam spluttered, recovering his composure more quickly than I was able to. Images from Sarah Belzoni's original journal were swimming before my eyes. But Adam had studied Giovanni Belzoni's life and times academically in order to stage the exhibition. He had legitimate reason to have heard of him.

'An unusually highly educated man for his time,' Ibrahim Mohassib commented. 'Very few Egyptians could write Arabic in those days. But Abdullah Soliman was an exception. Able to write as well as being a skilled artist.'

'He would have been a key member of Giovanni Belzoni's team when he was in Abu Simbel in both 1816 and 1817,' Adam said excitedly. 'He may well have been there on the spot when the Belzonis first entered Nefertari's temple, for all that they were unable to decipher the hieroglyphs.'

'Better than that, my friend,' Ibrahim Mohassib said tantalisingly. 'Abdullah Soliman returned to Abu Simbel in the years after the Belzonis left Egypt for England, and before Robert Hay and others beat a path to Nubia.'

'Of course!' I cried. 'Abdullah rescued the tablets!'

Who knows where the conversation might have gone from there? Sadly – frustratingly – I wasn't destined to find out.

Because that was the point at which the inner door from the secretary's office crashed open and a man disguised by a balaclava and wielding a long, ugly looking knife stormed into the room. He had the young female secretary who'd so kindly brought us our iced tea pinned against his chest. She looked terrified; as well she might with the blade of that vicious looking knife against her throat.

'I have waited a long time for this day,' our assailant barked out in thickly accented English. 'Now you will tell me everything I want to know.'

Chapter 13

I felt I ought to be shocked by this sudden intrusion. Only somehow I wasn't. Adam and I had after all encountered enough knife-wielding maniacs during our adventures in Egypt to be fairly well inured to the scenario.

'Saleh el-Sayed!' I breathed. Then I looked twice – no, not Saleh, after all. I frowned in confusion. The balaclava was a definite attempt to conceal his identity. But, looking closely, there was nothing so familiar about the individual with his knife at the poor secretary's throat that I could positively identify him as the unloved and unpleasant Marketing Manager. He was too tall for a start. I was really at a loss as to why his name had escaped my lips so readily.

We all leapt up of course. Adam was trying very hard to manoeuvre me behind him. Naturally I was having none of that. Whatever this was, we'd face it together.

'What is the meaning of this?' Ibrahim Mohassib demanded furiously. 'Who are you? And how dare you barge into my office like this? Let that poor young woman go at once! Jamira, are you alright?'

The secretary just stared back at him with frightened eyes round like saucers. I thought it was a bit much to expect her to speak, but was impressed by the curator's bravery, squaring up to our uninvited guest.

'You will tell me what I want to know,' our assailant repeated.

Adam inched forward, raising one hand and holding it out towards the man. 'I'm sure you don't want anyone to get hurt,' he appealed. 'Why don't you give me the knife and let Jamira go? Maybe then we can have a civilised conversation and find out how we can help you.' He stepped forward.

The movement was too sudden for our attacker. He'd been watching Adam warily. But at the movement, he shoved poor Jamira away from him and slashed out with the knife. Jamira screamed, and I shouted a warning. Adam neatly sidestepped the flashing blade. Ibrahim Mohassib wasn't quite so lucky. He'd moved when Adam did. The knife caught the side of his neck, just under his left ear. Blood spurted from the wound. Ibrahim Mohassib clutched at his neck and slumped to his knees.

Adam didn't waste another second. He flung himself bodily against the man, knocking him off balance. The knife clattered to the tiled floor as he fell against the desk. I darted forward and kicked it away. Jamira moved in the same moment, punching the side of her hand against the glass alarm on the wall behind Ibrahim Mohassib's desk. The glass shattered. A deafening wall of sound rent the air as the alarm started wailing.

Our assailant kicked out at Adam, attempting to get a grip on him. Adam dodged the kick, but stumbled against the coffee table, losing his balance. It was all the opportunity our assailant needed. I wasn't quite quick enough to trip him up as he jolted past me, shoving Jamira and sending her slamming against the wall as he made for the door he'd come through.

Even so, he only just made it. The other door leading from the corridor flew open, smashing against the wall. The guard who'd so politely held open the entrance door for us earlier stood there with his gun unslung and aiming into the room. In one horrified glance he took in the sight of Ibrahim Mohassib slumped on the floor clutching his bloody neck, Adam sprawled across the coffee table, Jamira regaining her balance where she'd been shoved against the wall; and me gesturing urgently at the door our attacker had just escaped through. 'Don't let him get away!' I yelled.

He was off after him in a heartbeat. I steeled myself for a volley of gunfire. Instead I heard a thumping sound, a grunt and a crash. It was evident from Jamira's frightened face what had happened. She was nearest the doorway and able to see through into the next room. Balaclava man had clearly assaulted the guard with something heavy.

I dreaded to see our deadly attacker returning through the door again. Hunting around urgently, I spied the knife sticking out from under the edge of the desk, and darted forward to retrieve it. Unarmed, there was little he could do, and I might just be able to launch a counter attack should it prove necessary.

But, of course, the alarm was still wailing, and there were other guards. I could hear them shouting and running towards us along the corridor. Moments later they burst into the room; two of them. They also took in the scene at a glance. But this time reached a slightly different conclusion.

One of them darted forward towards Ibrahim Mohassib, who had blood trickling wetly through his fingers where he was clutching his slashed neck. The other guard trained his deadly looking gun on me. I can only presume this was because I was the one now holding the knife. I don't mind admitting to heart failure looking down the long barrel of that lethal weapon. Knives are one thing. In a fair fight, you stand a chance against a knife-wielding opponent – as indeed we had just proved. But a gun; well, a gun doesn't leave much room for manoeuvre, especially in the hands of someone trained in how to use it.

Jamira jabbered something in rapid Arabic.

The great expulsion of air I released as the gun swung away from me was probably the biggest sigh of relief of my life. The guard could have fired first and asked questions later. Now, properly directed by Jamira, the guards ran across the room to give chase to our escaping assailant.

Back on his feet again, Adam followed. But valuable seconds had been lost. He called back to us a moment later… 'Too late! He's made a run for it!' I heard doors slamming, shouting but no gunfire.

Even before Adam re-joined us, Jamira and I were bending over Ibrahim Mohassib, frantically trying to see how badly he was injured.

'You need to let me see the wound,' I entreated, trying to prise his slippery wet, bright red fingers away from his blood-soaked neck.

Jamira was unwinding her headscarf ready to use as bandages.

Ibrahim Mohassib had suffered a long gash from just under his ear to the top of his collarbone. It was enough to have slashed through the collar of his shirt, tie and all. Thankfully it didn't appear to be deep but it was bleeding copiously. 'Thank God it didn't catch you a couple of inches lower,' I breathed. 'It's missed your jugular. 'You're going to be ok.'

'I am not dying?' he sent me a look of desperate hopefulness.

'I think you'll live,' I said grimly. 'Let me clean you up a bit so I can see if you need stitches.'

Adam and the guards came back. 'It was pointless trying to pursue him,' Adam panted. 'He was on the other side of the road by the time we got outside, and running as if he had the hounds of Hell in pursuit.' He came and dropped down on his haunches alongside the museum curator. 'That was remarkably brave Mr Mohassib,' he remarked. 'You launched yourself straight at the blade!'

'Your wife tells me I will live,' the curator murmured. 'Even so, I admit to feeling quite dizzy.' His eyes rolled up in his head and he passed out.

The guards came forward. The two who'd arrived last on the scene were propping their colleague up between them. I raised an enquiring eyebrow at Adam.

'Our attacker threw a metal waste paper bin at his head,' he explained. I could see the deep gash above his right eye, oozing sticky blood.

Jamira jumped up, ran from the room and returned a moment later with a first aid kit.

We patched both men up as best we could. But, in both cases it was clear a trip to the hospital was advisable. Jamira instructed the guards to return to their posts and then called for an ambulance.

The curator regained consciousness while we were waiting for it to arrive.

'Do you have any idea who that man was?' Adam asked him the obvious question as soon as he was compos mentis again. Jamira was on the other side of the room tending to the wounded guard; too far away to hear our conversation. Besides, I'd ascertained her English wasn't good.

'He was wearing a… a…' It was clear Ibrahim Mohassib was groping for an unfamiliar word in our foreign language.

'A balaclava,' Adam supplied. 'Yes, I've been wondering about that. Of course, it could just have been a precaution against CCTV cameras and the like. But, in view of what he said about waiting a long time for this day, it did rather make me wonder if he might be someone you'd recognise?'

Ibrahim Mohassib looked blank.

I glanced up at Adam. 'Did he put you in mind of anyone?' I couldn't help but recall that sudden inexplicable reference to Saleh el-Sayed that had escaped unbidden from my lips.

'Not a soul,' Adam said. 'You?'

I toyed with confessing it, but shook my head. Our assailant had not been Saleh el-Sayed, of that much I was certain.

'So we have to conclude it was you he wanted to threaten.' Adam returned his attention to Ibrahim Mohassib.

'And yet, the whole conversation took place in English,' I interrupted with a frown as this simple fact dawned on me.

Adam met my troubled gaze. 'So, whoever it was, he knew we were here.'

'We never did discover what it was he wanted "to know",' I said, making speech marks around this direct quote with my fingers. 'How frustrating! Maybe we shouldn't have been in such a hurry to disarm him.'

'Forgive me, Merry.' Adam murmured in a tone laced with heavy irony. 'I was rather more concerned for your safety, and that of poor Jamira over there, than I was with interviewing him.'

'Yes, I know,' I conceded. 'But it does rather leave me wondering how much he might already know, and about what.'

The sound of an ambulance siren cut off further conjecture.

A few minutes later both men were carted out of the museum on stretchers.

* * *

'The only thing we can say for sure about that visit is that we came away with more questions than answers,' I said in frustration. 'That man barged in just as Ibrahim Mohassib was about to tell us what he knew about the *reis* Abdullah Soliman. As it is, we know virtually no more about the mystery of Nefertari – or what happened to Sarah Belzoni's missing tablets – now than we did when we set off.'

We were back on board the dahabeeyah in the privacy of our own cabin with the door firmly closed. I stripped off my blood-stained t-shirt, replacing it with a clean one. It had been impossible to clean up Ibrahim Mohassib without coming away looking as if I'd been the one to inflict his injury.

'We need to call Walid,' Adam said. 'He may know more than he was able to tell us earlier.'

It had been impossible to have this conversation in the taxi on the way back to the *Queen Ahmes*. We'd called Hani to come back and collect us. He'd been appalled to see the blood stains on my top. I'd had no choice but to tell him I'd had a nosebleed, hence our earlier than expected departure from the museum. He'd exclaimed loudly and profusely over this, and then driven like a bat out of hell to get me back to the dahabeeyah, presumably before I suffered another and bled inconveniently all over his nicely upholstered back seat.

'I'm not sure we should mention the knife attack,' I said as Adam picked up his phone.

'But surely he'll find out?' he frowned. 'Both he and Ibrahim Mohassib are employed by the Ministry for Antiquities.'

'We could say he was taken suddenly unwell?' I suggested. 'You know what a worrier Walid is. And the last thing I want is for Director Ismail to get wind of anything amiss and decide to take it into his head to abort our mission.'

'You don't think Ibrahim Mohassib himself will report the incident to the Ministry? Or the police?'

'Yes, of course, he might,' I acknowledged. 'Then again, perhaps not.'

He sent me a quizzical glance.

'I'm starting to get a sense that maybe everything on this trip is not exactly as it seems. I'm seriously starting to wonder who we can trust.'

Adam gazed at me unhappily. 'You think we were deliberately targeted today?'

I shrugged. 'Honestly, I have no idea. But it's starting to feel as if we've been dogged with unwelcome drama on every step of this trip. Ok, so I know Ahmed's the one who's copped it until now, but...'

He cut me off, his brows drawing together sharply. 'Hang on a minute. Are you suggesting Ahmed's mishaps were somehow deliberate attempts to harm him? Even the *camel*?'

'I don't think the camel itself set out to hurt him,' I said with a grim smile. 'But someone could have arranged for those kids to let off firecrackers once they saw any one of our party up on one of the animals. Ahmed wasn't necessarily the intended victim. He just happened to be the first of us to mount. The camel's reaction to what sounded like a gunshot was entirely predictable.'

'And the accident at the Ramesseum?'

I returned his gaze steadily, and then shrugged. 'Any one of us could have stepped on those flimsy coverings concealing the hole, fallen in and been badly hurt.'

'You suspect it was set up as a trap?' The groove between his brows was deeper than ever.

I answered question with question. 'Why would anybody attempt to cover a hole like that? It doesn't make sense.'

'Agreed. But it was hardly a sure fire way of sabotaging our visit. I mean, it was equally possible none of us would go anywhere near the damned hole. It was in the outer precinct of the temple, not exactly part of the usual tourist stomping ground.'

'We're not casual tourists,' I reminded him. 'Anyone familiar with our movements would have known Ahmed was in the habit of touring the perimeter of each of the sites we visited with his gun unslung and at the ready.'

'They couldn't possibly know he'd shoot his own foot,' he argued.

'No,' I agreed darkly 'Perhaps they were hoping for worse.'

'Merry, are you sure you're not letting your imagination run away with you?' he asked gently. But I could see I'd worried him.

'If it hadn't been for the syringe, and what happened today, then yes, probably,' I admitted.

'Syringe?' he asked blankly.

I told him about finding it floating in the Nile underneath the gangplank on the evening of Saleh el-Sayed's unexpected visit to check on Ahmed's condition. 'Don't you think it's suspicious?' I finished.

'I wish you'd told me at the time,' he said.

'I thought I probably *was* letting my imagination run riot,' I confessed. 'After all, if someone had wanted to do Ahmed permanent damage and injected him with something lethal, he'd hardly have responded so quickly to Georgina's smelling salts, or whatever the hell she called them. Let's face it, he's pretty much back to his old self again now, barely twenty-four hours later.'

He gazed at me, and I could see him looking at our entire trip from a different angle. 'Everything you've described could have been accidents, pure and simple...' he started.

'...Until what happened today...' I cut across him. 'Today's little attack was certainly not pure and possibly very far from simple.'

Adam tilted his head to one side. 'You know, whoever that balaclava-wearing, knife-wielding individual was, I don't think he ever seriously had any intention of hurting the secretary. Jamira, was it? He shoved her away at the first sign of us fighting back.'

'Yes, Ibrahim Mohassib simply moved at the wrong moment,' I agreed. 'Unlucky for him, it was into the path of the blade.'

'It's possible he just wanted to use the threat of the knife to frighten us, with no intention of actually using it,' Adam speculated.

'Which brings us full circle back to wondering what it was he imagined we might be terrified into telling him.'

Adam slumped on the edge of the bed. 'I can think of two possibilities.'

I sat alongside him and voiced what I was sure he was thinking. 'Either someone knows we're seeking to unearth evidence of stone tablets that may shed light on Nefertari's elusive origins...'

'...And they want to steal a march on us,' he nodded, unperturbed by my interruption. He was well used to it by now. Since we think and speak as one, we barely notice when we finish each other's sentences.

'...Or somebody knows about – or, at least, suspects about – our tomb,' I concluded. 'Marvellous though it was, in some ways that dratted tomb has been a damn sight more trouble than it's worth!'

'Amen to that!' he said, taking my hand. 'I suggest on this trip, Merry, we give the place the widest possible berth. At least, that way, we can have some confidence we'll not end up incarcerated inside and facing the prospect of a lingering, suffocating death.'

I lost myself for a moment in happy recollections of the times we'd spent trapped in those hidden chambers contemplating just that. In truth, I can think of worse ways to depart this mortal coil. Then I snapped back into the present. 'So we're agreed? We don't mention our run of mishaps to Walid?'

'Agreed.'

He pressed the speakerphone button on his iPhone so we could both participate in the call. After a few minutes exchanging pleasantries we came to the point. 'So, you see Walid, it would be helpful to know exactly what you said to Ibrahim Mohassib,' Adam prompted. 'The curator was taken ill just at the point he was about to tell us what he may have sitting in his storerooms in the Luxor Museum...'

Walid made the appropriate noises to register his concern at Ibrahim Mohassib's sudden and unfortunate malaise but thankfully didn't probe for details. I suspect, like us, he was far more interested in any historical insights Mr Mohassib might be able to impart than he was in the person of the curator himself.

'I asked him to search for anything in the museum's catalogue that he could confidently date to the period between Giovanni Belzoni's excavation of Abu Simbel in 1816 and the Robert Hay expedition in 1825,' he said.

'And did he tell you what he'd found?' I pressed eagerly. 'You were very mysterious on the 'phone earlier.'

'No,' he said regretfully. 'I was merely pushed for time. I called you on my way to a meeting. Ibrahim told me only that he'd turned up some evidence to suggest it wasn't only European travellers interested in beating a path to Abu Simbel in the requisite period.'

'Abdullah Soliman,' I breathed, looking at Adam. All the evidence pointed to the Belzonis *reis* being the one to remove the stele from Nefertari's temple. It made me desperate for another look at the illustrations in Sarah Belzoni's journal.

But before ringing off I decided I might as well use the opportunity of speaking to Walid to find out something else I wanted to know. 'So, Walid, is it true the Ministry of Antiquities is opening the tombs of Seti I and Nefertari?'

'Yes, quite correct,' he said. 'They will be open to the public next month. The private opening ceremony – or, more accurately, *re*-opening ceremony is scheduled for this weekend. Sadly, I am unable to be there due to a family commitment. But Director Ismail will be in attendance, plus a delegation from the Tourism Authority.'

'Do you think you could somehow wangle us a place on the guest list?' I asked. 'After all, Giovanni Belzoni was the one to discover the tomb of Seti I. So even if not strictly in the chronological order of this trip following in his footsteps, I feel I should include it in my travelogue.'

'Leave it with me,' he said. 'I'll see what I can do.'

* * *

We joined the others up on deck for a nightcap before turning in.

Nobody objected to our proposition that we remain in Luxor for a few days before journeying further south on the Nile to pursue the next leg of the Belzonis' travels through Egypt and Nubia.

'I want to take some time out to write a couple of proper articles,' I explained, '…while also giving Ahmed as much time as possible to heal before he needs to attempt to wear his boots again. As it is, I don't see much prospect of his toe being comfortable in anything besides flip flops for a little while yet.'

It's possible I imagined the speculative light in Georgina's eyes as she regarded me. But since she raised no demur, I let it go, and dismissed it from my thoughts for the time being.

My real purpose in remaining, of course, was to reassure myself of Ibrahim Mohassib's recovery. Naturally I was concerned to know he had suffered no long-term ill effects from his brush with the blade, so to speak. But I'm honest enough to admit – to myself at least – that I very much wanted to get to the crux of what he'd been about to reveal when we were so brutally interrupted. I felt rather as if I'd had a much-anticipated gift snatched away just at the moment of untying the ribbon.

If our hanging around a while also meant Adam and I were available should Walid prove successful in his attempt to wangle us an invitation onto the guest list of the re-opening of the two tombs, so much the better.

Later that night, I sat up in bed while Adam towel-dried his hair from the shower and brushed his teeth. 'There's a clue in this journal somewhere, I'm sure of it.' I said.

He climbed into bed alongside me, smelling clean and wholesome, of shampoo and toothpaste. 'A clue?'

'Yes, a clue to what Abdullah Soliman did with the stone tablets he took from Nefetari's temple after he stole Sarah's diary from Henry Salt.'

'Salt must have told him that he intended to travel back to Abu Simbel and claim the tablets for himself,' Adam speculated.

'Thankfully ill health prevented him making the journey,' I said. 'Not so Abdullah; he must have decided there and then to be the one to retrieve them, out of loyalty to the Belzonis if nothing else.'

Adam lifted the journal so it was resting across both our sets of legs on top of the cotton sheet.

We were both intimately acquainted with its contents. Yet somehow knowing now of Abdullah's daring, I felt sure there must be something we both had missed.

As I had done a number of times before, I frowned in frustration over the binding at the back of the journal. It was clear the very last page had been torn out. It was impossible not to wonder why, and what it might have contained. But since it wasn't there now, there was no point in pursuing this conjecture. I shrugged and dismissed it from my thoughts. The clue I was searching for was more likely to be found in what was there than what wasn't.

We turned the pages together in an almost reverential silence. The first three-quarters of the book belonged to Sarah. Her flowing script covered each sheet, interspersed after the first few pages with Abdullah's sketches of the scenes and events she was describing.

Abdullah joined Giovanni's work team in Luxor, so there were no pictures to accompany the first part, which described Alexandria, Cairo, and the journey southwards on the Nile. But once Belzoni was engaged on his mission to transport the head and torso bust of Ramses II from the Ramesseum the prose and the sketches competed for our attention.

Those I loved best were the entries completed by Sarah and Abdullah jointly at Abu Simbel; Abdullah's sketches showing it still mostly submerged in drifting sand. These sheets recorded the initial discovery of the stele in Nefertari's 'smaller temple'. If only Sarah had transcribed the complete hieroglyphics and Abdullah had drawn the entire set of tablets, rather than each of them contenting themselves with fragments, this mission Adam and I were on would be unnecessary. But then, of course, at that time Sarah and

Abdullah had no inkling the ancient Egyptian picture writing was so close to decipherment. They believed they were recording mere snapshots for Sarah's personal reminiscences once back in England. They couldn't possibly have known they may have stumbled across a narrative recording the origins of one of ancient Egypt's most alluring queens.

The Abu Simbel scenes came about half way through Sarah's narrative, dated to late August of 1816. There were pages and pages after that recording her husband's discoveries in the Valley of the Kings the following year.

'We're wasting time,' I said after a while. 'There's no point re-living all the bits of Sarah and Giovanni and Abdullah together. We've looked at them a thousand times. We need to focus on the pages that are Abdullah's alone, now we know he returned to Nubia for the tablets.'

We flipped forward and re-familiarised ourselves with the final quarter of the journal. The first page once it was in Abdullah's sole custody described in florid Arabic how he had boldly stolen it back recognising it among Salt's possession and suspecting foul play.

'Such a shame that Sarah and Abdullah couldn't stay in touch,' I murmured. 'It might have saved her an awful lot of heartache.'

'And an abortive mission back to Egypt,' Adam agreed.

There were far more pictures than writing in the last quarter of the journal. This was just as well since I don't read

Arabic. Adam has made a study of the language and was able to decipher a fair bit. But we already knew Abdullah, far from recording his own experiences in writing after taking custody of the journal, actually used the space to record his own remembrances of his cherished times with the Belzonis. He clearly knew he'd touched greatness in Giovanni; and that he worshipped Sarah was evident in every word. Even so, not every sketch in the last few pages was a repeat of those he'd penned earlier in the company of the Belzonis. Some, quite clearly, dated from the time after he'd claimed the journal as his own. The last couple of sheets were sketches of people he'd obviously known, young men in turbans and Moorish tunics and pretty ladies swathed in dark robes. The same pretty lady, I should say, lovingly drawn to capture her fine dark eyes and a Mona Lisa smile. I felt sure this was Abdullah's sweetheart. These images were intrinsically interesting for their own sake. We'd gazed at them time and time again, wondering at the personalities of these people Abdullah had known so long ago. But as they could shed no light on our current mystery we didn't turn forward to study them again now. Instead, we concentrated on the Abu Simbel pages. I'd always assumed these to be drawn from memory, a re-living of his trip with the Belzonis. Now I looked at them with fresh eyes, knowing they depicted the route of Abdullah's personal pilgrimage to retrieve the tablets.

'The trouble with these smaller temples in the most southern part of the Nile in ancient Nubia,' Adam said dampeningly, '...is that they were all flooded to create Lake Nasser in the 1960s. Some of this stuff that Abdullah sketched simply isn't there any more.'

I knew this to be sadly true. If Abdullah had rescued the tablets from Nefertari's temple and then hidden them somewhere among the monuments of ancient Nubia, they were indeed lost forever, sunk beneath the floodwaters of Lake Nasser.

But it made no sense for Abdullah to collect them only to hide them again so far from home. Abdullah was a man of Luxor, and I felt sure he'd have brought the tablets home, and then kept them somewhere safe.

There was really only one obvious location.

I flipped forward a couple of pages. Now I was looking at sketches of a far more familiar territory. The Valley of the Kings was clearly recognisable. And one tomb in particular was featured. 'Look!' I cried excitedly, struck by something in one of the images. 'I've never noticed *that* before!'

Chapter 14

When Giovanni and Sarah Belzoni departed Egypt, they left Abdullah behind employed as a *ghaffir* – a kind of guard/guide protecting Belzoni's greatest discovery: the tomb of Seti I in the Valley of the Kings. Even now it's known colloquially in certain circles as Belzoni's tomb. This was where Henry Salt found him when he returned to Egypt with Sarah's stolen diary. And this was the employment Abdullah returned to after his break with Salt as the Consul General's health declined and he returned to Alexandria – with Abdullah now safely in possession of Sarah's journal. To Abdullah, Seti's tomb represented a safe hiding place. He could keep watch on anything he may have hidden inside.

The sketch I was staring at was one I'd studied many times before. It was a meticulous drawing of the inner chambers of Seti's tomb. Adam and Rashid Soliman had even used it to help them reproduce faithful replicas for the British Museum exhibition.

The thing I'd never noticed before – or, more accurately, had *noticed*, but, knowing what it was, had never particularly *remarked* on before now – was the tunnel that burrowed into the rock from the place beneath where the king's sarcophagus once stood in the burial chamber.

In Abdullah's drawing it was quite clear, a deep hole tunnelling into the bedrock. That it was central to the sketch seemed somehow significant, now I knew Abdullah had rescued the tablets.

'I think you can forget that, Merry,' Adam said flatly. 'The first attempts to excavate that tunnel were made in the 1960s. Even Belzoni didn't risk it. The 1960s team gave up, fearing further digging would bring the tomb crashing down. Zahi Hawass, while he was still Minister for Antiquities, tried again in 2007. His hypothesis was a secret burial chamber carved into the bedrock. In 2010 he was forced to admit defeat, despite finding a number of small antiquities as his workmen excavated the tunnel. There was no secret burial or hidden chamber. Instead it looks as if the ancient artisans simply abandoned whatever the original project was, possibly because the king died.'

I continued to stare at Abdullah's sketch of the opening into the tunnel as it had been almost two hundred years ago. My senses were fizzing. 'But...' I started to object.

'Merry, my love,' he said gently, lifting the journal off our laps and pushing it under the bed, 'if Zahi Hawass failed to find anything of significance in that tunnel despite a three-year search, do you really think we stand any better chance?'

'P'raps not,' I conceded reluctantly. 'But I'm thinking maybe the chance of another look around inside Seti's tomb might be a good idea after all. We know Seti was a pharaoh who harboured secrets. Maybe he kept one for Abdullah without even realising it.'

* * *

'First thing's first,' I said the following morning, disentangling myself from Adam's arms after a thoroughly satisfactory start to the day. 'We need to pay Ibrahim Mohassib a visit in hospital. I want to know what light he can shed on Abdullah's retrieval of the tablets from Nefertari's temple.'

After securing Sarah's diary safely inside our lockable chest, we hired a taxi – the driver another local we knew, although less well than Hani – and set off after breakfast.

Luxor has two hospitals: an international one catering for foreign travellers located on Television Street in the town centre, and a general hospital for locals on the Corniche near Karnak temple. It was to this latter medical centre Ibrahim Mohassib had been carted off by ambulance yesterday.

We spent a frustrating few minutes trying to explain to the reception staff that we were in the correct place when they tried to re-direct us to the international hospital. Eventually we made ourselves understood, only to discover Ibrahim Mohassib had discharged himself last night against medical advice. Despite his refusal to stay in overnight for observation, the staff nurse assured us the patient was as well as might be expected after his treatment, and should make a full recovery, albeit with a scar. The wound had not been deep enough to need stitches. Instead it had been cleaned, dressed and secured with surgical tape.

'Well, it's a relief to know he's ok at least,' I said as we left the air-conditioned interior and stepped outside into the hammering heat. 'But I can't help but wonder if he discharged himself so quickly because he was worried about what happened yesterday. Perhaps he feared our attacker would make another attempt.'

Adam frowned and took my hand. 'Let's go to the museum and see if he's there.'

The Luxor Museum was walkable from the hospital, a stroll along the Corniche on the upper east bank of the Nile. We went slowly, forced by the suffocating temperature and blinding sunshine not to rush. I'd forgotten how difficult it was to go at my normal pace in upwards of forty-degree heat.

The museum was quiet, sadly bereft of all but a very few tourists studying the exhibits and reading the printed cards on each display case. It was blessedly cool inside.

We approached the guard on duty at the door separating the public and staff spaces. I recognised him as the one who'd aimed his gun at me yesterday. He recognised me in the same instant.

His startled expression could have meant anything or nothing. Perhaps it was simply a jolt of awareness at how close he'd come to riddling me with bullets. 'You return,' he said in less than friendly tones, and somewhat unnecessarily in my view since our standing here in front of him was ample evidence of exactly that.

'Yes,' Adam said with a smile of greeting. 'We're hoping to see Ibrahim Mohassib. We want to check he's ok after that nasty incident yesterday.'

I wasn't quite sure what to make of his reaction. He moved and blocked the doorway, barring us entry.

'Is he here?' I asked, frowning. 'We know he was discharged from hospital last night.'

'No. Not here,' the guard said flatly.

'He's probably recuperating at home,' Adam surmised. 'Reasonable enough in the circumstances.'

Despite the guard's unwelcoming demeanour I was determined not to leave until I'd satisfied myself there was nothing else to learn here. 'Jamira?' I asked. 'Could we see her?'

'Alas. Jamira also not here,' he said with a regretful shake of his head.

'Shock,' I said, nodding, and telling myself the guard was probably just being extra vigilant given what had happened on his watch. 'She had an unpleasant time of it yesterday.'

There seemed little more to be gained by staying any longer. A little put out by the coolness of our reception and disappointed to find Ibrahim wasn't here, we turned to go. Then Adam abruptly turned back, pulling me around with him. 'Tell me,' he said. 'Did you or anyone else call the police yesterday?'

The guard was unable to mask the quick, hunted look that flashed across his features. 'Police?' he jabbered, as if he had no idea to whom Adam might be referring.

'Yes, Adam said pleasantly. 'You know, the people you tend to call when someone breaks in, wounding your boss and threatening two foreign visitors with a knife.'

The guard recovered himself quickly and managed to look affronted. 'We are armed security,' he said. 'We have no need of police.'

'Ah, just as I thought,' Adam said in the same cordial tone. 'But it's a shame the attacker got away, don't you think?'

'You are here to make complaint?' the guard asked suspiciously.

'Not at all, Adam assured him smoothly. 'We are merely concerned for Mr Mohassib and wish to assure ourselves of his recovery.' Then he turned to me, speaking almost as if as an afterthought. 'You know what, Merry? I'm wondering if we shouldn't report the incident to the Luxor Chief of Police, just so he knows there's a knife-wielding maniac on the loose in his city. Remind me of the officers name…?'

'Commander Abdul el-Saiyyid,' I supplied, dredging up the name of Ahmed's former Chief Superintendent from my memory banks.

It was quite remarkable to behold the affect this bit of judicious name-dropping had on our companion. He dropped all pretence of stonewalling us.

'Please, you will allow...?' He looked from Adam to me and back with a cringing expression. 'The times they are desperate. This job, it is all that keeps the food in the mouths of my children.'

I stared slack-jawed at his fearful countenance. I'm no Sherlock Holmes, but it struck me there was something decidedly odd going on, something Adam had sensed and decided to check out.

'My wife and I were threatened here yesterday,' Adam said. 'Give me one good reason why I shouldn't report that to the police, seeing as nobody here appears to have had the simple good sense to do so.'

'Please, sir...' the guard entreated. 'You must allow... I have not been truthful. Mr Mohassib, he is here. He ordered me to admit no visitors.'

Adam and I exchanged a glance. Something was clearly not as it should be.

'Let us through,' Adam said abruptly, shoving past the guard with no further ceremony, and pulling me after him.

I stumbled through the door and down the few steps that led to the basement conservation areas, archives and offices. I don't honestly know if I could have said if it was a surprise or not when the siren started wailing overhead. The guard had clearly whacked his fist against the security alarm the moment we were past him. I daresay it was preferable to him training his gun on us.

Adam started to run. The trouble was, Ibrahim Mohassib's office was at the furthest end of the corridor. It was certainly no surprise that by the time we flung ourselves bodily through his office door it was to find the room empty. The interconnecting door with Jamira's little cubbyhole office was standing ajar. We were just in time to see the curator fleeing through the outer door, still wearing yesterday's blood-stained clothing.

Adam called out to him in a loud voice. 'Mr Mohassib! Stop! What's the matter?'

The curator glanced over his shoulder but didn't turn back. 'Please!' he shouted back to us instead. 'I cannot stop! I have a problem but I am dealing with it! Do not follow me. And please tell no one! I am in trouble enough!' And he started running again. There was no point chasing him. He had too much of a head start.

Adam hesitated undecided then turned from the doorway and slumped onto one of the comfortable seats around Ibrahim Mohassib's coffee table. I sat opposite him.

For a long moment we stared at each other in open stupefaction.

'What are we to make of that?' I questioned blankly.

'Your guess is as good as mine, Merry,' he admitted.

'Do you still think we should call the police despite what he said?'

He met my gaze and I could see him thinking it through. 'Perhaps,' he said. 'But it's risky. They'll ask how we know him and what we were doing here. It begs too many questions. Maybe we should tell Director Ismail.' But I could see he wasn't keen.

'I have no desire to be flung out of Egypt having only just arrived back,' I said emphatically. 'Goddammit Adam! I was looking forward to an uneventful trip fulfilling the Tourism Authority's mission, whilst also doing a little bit of quiet independent sleuthing to see if we could find out what happened to the tablets Sarah discovered. Why do we keep getting caught up in these ridiculous scenarios? It was all going so well until that madman with the knife pushed his way in here yesterday. Now I have no idea what's going on. I'm starting to wish Walid had never suggested we should come here.'

'You and me both,' he said with feeling.

We abandoned the idea of a search of the curator's office and the museum's strong rooms for anything that might shed light on Abdullah Soliman or Queen Nefertari. The guard who'd seemed so cowed earlier had proved himself anything but. Even though I was sure his intention had been only to warn Ibrahim Mohassib he had visitors and buy a little time, it was clear whose side he was on. I sympathised with his need to keep hold of his employment in these straitened times – he was one of the few still lucky enough to have a job to go to. Still, hanging around here was risky. We simply couldn't take the chance of getting locked in, as had been our unfortunate habit in the past. Perhaps we were learning not to take unnecessary gambles.

'I suggest we beat a hasty retreat,' Adam said. 'Ibrahim Mohassib knows we've come looking for him. Hopefully he'll be in touch once he's sorted out the spot of bother he's in.'

We received the hoped-for communication much sooner than expected. But when the note came it wasn't at all what we'd imagined. Delivered to the *Queen Ahmes* that afternoon by a lad on a scooter (who immediately zipped off again), it said in typed script:

"I have Ibrahim Mohassib in my custody. If you wish to see the curator again you will await my further instructions. DO NOT call the police. DO NOT inform Director Ismail."

We stared at each other in open shock, glad to have had the sense to come to the privacy of our cabin to open the note.

'Do not inform Director Ismail,' I repeated, re-scanning the contents. 'That's a bit specific, isn't it? Can we assume this individual knows Director Ismail and our relationship to him?'

'It can only be our attacker from yesterday,' Adam said, hunching his shoulders and rubbing his chin with the back of his hand. 'When Ibrahim Mohassib said he was in trouble, I didn't anticipate kidnap! He must have run out of the museum this morning and straight into the man's clutches. I wonder who the man is.'

'I don't know what to make of all this,' I confessed. 'Do you think it can possibly have anything to do with our tomb?'

Adam looked at me unhappily. 'It's starting to look like an unavoidable conclusion. You know, I'm wondering if we should tell Director Ismail regardless. After all, he's the one who told us he'd tie up all the loose ends when he chucked us out of the country three years ago.'

'Well, he'll be here tomorrow,' I said. 'The ceremonial re-opening of the two tombs is scheduled for the afternoon. I'd like to think he might spot for himself if Ibrahim Mohassib isn't in attendance, and make a few enquiries of his own. We might have received these "further instructions" before then. If not...'

We were interrupted at this point. Someone was banging on our cabin door. Adam unlocked and opened it. Ahmed loomed in our doorway.

271

'Everything, it is alright?' he asked, peering at us closely.

Adam and I exchanged a quick guilty glance. Ahmed was our bodyguard and best friend, and yet we'd told him nothing.

Ahmed saw the glance. He's not trained as a police officer for nothing. 'What is it you have failed to confide in me?' he demanded with a direct stare and a frown.

'Ahmed, mate; you'd better come in,' Adam invited.

Ahmed limped forward into our cabin, squeezed his bulk into the armchair in the corner and propped his foot on the little footstall in front of my antique dressing table. The room immediately felt half its former size.

Adam and I sat alongside each other on the edge of our bed. Between us we told the story of our visit to Luxor Museum to see Ibrahim Mohassib, the light we'd hoped he might be able to shed on the little mystery of Nefertari's missing tablets, and everything that had happened since.

Ahmed's facial expressions went through a number of contortions while we told the tale. Ahmed is a man who loves a story. His frowns, grunts and popping eyes were really quite gratifying. If I weren't quite so confused by everything that had happened, I might have quite enjoyed the re-telling of our recent drama. As it was, setting out the whole sequence of events aloud left me more baffled than ever. I could see it had the same affect on Adam. We finished by handing Ahmed the typed note we'd just had delivered.

He frowned over it for a moment, then looked up and met my gaze. His first words couldn't have surprised me more had he admitted to penning the note himself. I'd thought he might have something to say on the matter of Ibrahim Mohassib and his apparent kidnap, but no.

'This Abdullah Soliman,' he said. 'I have heard of him.'

I stared at him in shock. His next words took my breath away completely.

'He was murdered.'

'Murdered?' I gasped. A word I knew and understood, I suddenly felt rather as if I didn't know what it meant, grasping for a translation of something said in a foreign language.

Ahmed looked a bit discomfited for a moment. 'Yes, by one of my ancestors,' he admitted. 'He slit his throat, a bit like your Mr Mohassib.'

Adam recovered his wits more quickly than I did. 'I knew you were descended from a bunch of tomb-robbing rogues and villains,' he remarked. 'But I didn't know you counted cutthroats and murderers among your family tree.'

'It was in the act of robbing a tomb that the killing took place,' Ahmed said, his chin jutting out as if this were some sort of defence. 'My ancestor broke into a tomb where Abdullah Soliman was on guard.'

'Let me guess,' I found my voice at last. 'Seti's tomb.'

'Indeed, yes,' Ahmed affirmed, although it hardly needed confirmation.

Adam and I traded glances, disbelief and incredulity vying for supremacy in our expressions. That Ahmed, of all people, should be in a position to shed light on what happened to the Belzonis' *reis* nearly two hundred years after his death seemed beyond all reckoning. But perhaps we shouldn't be so surprised. Ahmed was raised on rip-roaring tales of the exploits of the family of miscreants he was descended from. He was as proud as punch to have such infamy in his ancestry. The real miracle was that Ahmed himself – when he wasn't playing fast and loose with the strict letter of the law – was such a fine, upstanding pillar of his profession. Even so, the Abd-el Rassul history was in his blood, part of his genealogical DNA. He thrived on stories of their treachery. Really, we should have known he'd have the inside track.

Ahmed leaned forward, warming to his theme. 'There was a trial,' he went on. 'My ancestor, Hakim Abd el-Rassul claimed Abdullah got drunk one night and bragged about something he'd hidden in the tomb, something of great value.'

'Nefertari's tablets,' I breathed.

'But Abdullah's family said Abdullah was a devout Muslim who never touched so much as a drop of alcohol. They claimed Hakim had been sent to kill Abdullah by someone who knew what he had hidden there.'

This time it was Adam who commented. 'Henry Salt,' he murmured.

I stared at him. 'Henry *Salt*? The British Consul General? Really Adam? I mean; I know he was a thief... But to commission a contract killing...! That's a whole different ball game!'

Adam shrugged. 'Who else knew about the tablets?' he asked rhetorically. He clearly didn't expect a response and went on, 'It might just fit with one last unsuccessful attempt to get his hands on them, if he realised Abdullah had re-stolen Sarah's diary and retrieved the stele from Nefertari's temple. His health was failing of course. It's possible he died soon after realising he'd failed in his attempt to claim them back.'

'Hakim was sentenced to five years in jail for the crime,' Ahmed offered.

'That doesn't sound very long for murder,' I exclaimed.

'Hakim protested his innocence saying he killed Abdullah in a fair fight. He said he approached the tomb with no intention of hurting anyone. He didn't know Abdullah would be there.'

'And the penalty for breaking into the tomb?' Adam queried.

Ahmed shrugged. 'Nothing was taken. Abdullah prevented Hakim from entering the tomb. When he realised he'd killed the *ghaffir*, Hakim ran away. He was identified as the murderer because in his panic he left his knife at the scene. It was carved with his name.'

'Pretty compelling in the days before forensics,' Adam commented.

'So, what happened to the tablets?' I brought us back to what seemed to me the crux of the matter. 'Surely by now, with the trial and whatnot, it was clear to anyone with half a brain that Abdullah had hidden something of value in Seti's tomb. I'd have thought all the enterprising thieves in the area would have made a beeline for the place!'

'The authorities made a search of the tomb, and nothing was found.' Ahmed declared. 'My ancestor Hakim died in jail. The conditions, they were very bad in those days. No sanitation. Dirty water to drink, and unbearable heat in the summer.'

I stared at him in frustration. 'So if he knew anything about the tablets, the secret died with him. It feels as if every time we get a step closer to finding out what happened to them, they move further away. I'd cherished some small hope that, even after all this time, they might still be hidden there, but even I have to concede the chances of that are virtually nil.'

Adam turned his head to look at me with sympathy in his expression. Or perhaps it was pity for my unwillingness to let go of the dream of finding those stele in Seti's tomb, when he'd told me quite plainly about all the excavation and preservation work that had gone on there during the last two hundred years.

Ahmed leaned back in the chair. It creaked under his weight. 'Is it possible whatever Ibrahim Mohassib has found in his storerooms may reveal more of the story?'

'I doubt it,' I said forlornly. 'Anything he's found written by Abdullah would date, by necessity; to before Abdullah's murder, presumably while the tablets were still in his custody. Heaven alone knows what happened to them after his death.'

Adam turned to look at me again. 'Still, I'd love to know what it was. But now Ibrahim Mohassib has been kidnapped, our chances of finding out are slim. Damn that crazed knifeman. I guess all we can do is wait for his next move.'

'I can do some investigations about this Mr Mohassib,' Ahmed said, brightening. 'I can find out where he lives. I can go under cover and keep watch on the museum to see if his attacker shows his face.'

'But your toe…!' I protested.

'I need to get off this overgrown felucca,' he said. 'I will go mad if I have no work to do. Now I know you are in danger, I must use my police training to return to my duty as your bodyguard. My toe, it is of no consequence. If I go under cover I do not need to wear my boots. I can mix with the locals in a galabeya, turban and sandals.' His eyes were snapping with excitement at the prospect of turning detective.

'I will find out what is going on here. You can leave things to me.'

Much as I hated to curb his energy and evident enthusiasm, I couldn't help but ask, 'And Adam and me? What are we supposed to do while you take over the investigation?'

'Ah yes,' he said. 'You have reminded me of my purpose in knocking on your door. Walid, he called while you were out this morning. Your invitations to attend the re-opening tomorrow of the tombs of Nefertari and Seti await you in your email letterbox. Walid said when he asked Director Ismail, the Director told him he had already sent them.'

'You'll get your chance to see inside Seti's tomb again after all,' Adam smiled. 'Until we receive these "further instructions" there's nothing more we can do to help Ibrahim Mohassib beyond letting Ahmed see what he can turn up.' Then he smiled at me. 'Let's face it, Merry; unlikely though it is; if those tablets are still there two hundred years after Abdullah hid them there, you'll be the one to find them!'

Chapter 15

I tried to settle to writing my article. But the typeface on my laptop screen kept dancing, the letters jumbling in front of my eyes. My fingers on the keyboard felt like a bunch of bananas. It was hard to write sensibly about the drama of Giovanni Belzoni's life when my own was so full and confusing. At any moment, I expected another communication from the balaclava-clad knifeman issuing his instructions. I could only hope these wouldn't get in the way of our attendance at the 'official' re-opening of the tombs tomorrow. My eagerness to see inside those tombs knew no bounds. It was nigh on impossible to concentrate on anything else. But no doubt Director Ismail and Zahed Mansour would expect a progress report of my professional activities. So it was important to crack on and have something to show them.

Even so, it was almost a relief when I heard a knock on the door to the cabin I'd commandeered as an office. I looked up to see Georgina Savage standing there wearing another of her ubiquitous tent dresses. This one was pale yellow, a colour that suited her, setting off her tan to perfection.

She launched into speech without preamble. 'I offered to treat Ahmed's big toe with some arnica for the bruising.' she informed me. 'But now I find the annoying man has given me the slip. Habiba seems to think he's gone ashore. Were you aware he'd left the dahabeeyah?'

'He has family in Luxor,' I murmured vaguely.

'Is it wise for him to be moving about so soon after his accident?' she frowned. 'I thought some time resting with his feet up was what the doctor ordered. I really thought the arnica was a good idea. And I have some non-steroidal anti-inflammatories I thought might aid his recovery. Surely rest and recuperation would be the thing, don't you agree? Rather than traipsing off to see the rellies.'

I raised an eyebrow at her ongoing determination to play nursemaid. Ahmed seemed to me to have made it perfectly clear he wished to avoid at all costs the ministrations of our hefty houseguest. Yet the message didn't seem to be getting through. 'Ahmed is a grown man and a free agent,' I said mildly. 'He doesn't have to ask permission to take some time out.'

She made a small tut-tutting noise, but seemed to realise further argument was pointless. I would not be drawn on Ahmed's whereabouts or comment on her thwarted attempts to minister to him.

I thought she might turn to go. Instead her gaze alighted on my computer screen. 'Have you come up with an angle for your article?' she asked.

I shrugged. 'I'm working on a Luxor past and present theme. But it's not really coming together if I'm honest. I'm struggling for inspiration.'

She stared at me, then plopped herself, uninvited, onto the upholstered armchair alongside my desk. 'I know I'm a journalist rather than any other sort of a writer,' she started. 'But it seems to me folk prefer reading about people rather than places.'

I stared back at her, trying to decide if I was aggravated or appreciative of her unlooked for advice. 'Oh?'

'Oh yes,' she nodded. 'And it strikes me you've got all the inspiration you need locked away in your cabin.'

'Sarah Belzoni's journal,' I said flatly. It hadn't taken her long to launch her assault. Still, I could hardly claim surprise since I knew full well her determination to see it. I'd long since resigned myself to having to share it with her. I just hadn't got round to doing so given everything else going on.

'If you want to bring Luxor past and present to life,' she urged, 'I think you could do worse than describe it through the eyes of those who knew it.'

'You think I should quote directly from Sarah's diary?' I said doubtfully.

'I can see no harm in comparing her experiences and yours,' Georgina shrugged. 'Two intrepid women, two hundred years apart; both travelling in the Nile Valley while others deemed Egypt unsafe. Ok, so hers was a journal and yours is a blog, but aren't they both travelogues of a sort? If Sarah recorded her impressions of the temples her husband was literally digging out of millennia-worth of sand, you can compare them to yours of those same places after two-centuries-worth of Egyptology. The difference is, she didn't know what she was looking at, and you do. So you can tell the ancient story at the same time. Hey, maybe you should make it a tale of three women!'

'Three women?' I parroted, not following.

I was unable to interpret the expression on her face as she met my gaze. With a dramatic wave of one arm meant I'm sure to illustrate that she was casting about at random for a suitable candidate, she plumped for a name that had my eyes narrowing sharply. 'What about Nefertari?'

'Nefertari?' Why the sudden feeling that this wasn't an off-the-cuff conversation after all; rather a carefully choreographed verbal dance leading me exactly where she wanted to go?

'Sure!' she nodded eagerly, the movement causing some of her hair to escape the clip she had it caught up in, and fall around her face. She re-secured it absently, still nodding. 'I think we can safely assume Sarah Belzoni spent time in Nefertari's 'smaller' temple in Abu Simbel while her husband was digging away at the mountain of sand that obscured the Great Temple of Ramses.' Her eyes gleamed as she stared into mine. 'It's possible Sarah got to know

Nefertari quite well – even if only her image staring down from the walls. Of course, it's a shame so little is known about Nefertari's origins, don't you think? Don't you wonder what Sarah Belzoni might have found inside that temple, if only she could read the hieroglyphs?'

This was a bit much. I took refuge in silence, knowing if I failed to speak she'd have no choice but to carry on. Her gaze was fixed on my face. I didn't dare look away for fear she'd pounce and accuse me of hiding something. It felt almost as if she were performing some sort of brain scan, so intense was her scrutiny. I tried my hardest to look pleasantly blank-featured. Now, even without her seeing Sarah's journal, I was certain she knew more than she was letting on. I failed to see how she could possibly know of Neferari's tablets. Even so, they seemed to be dancing silently on the airwaves between us.

At my determined lack of response, Georgina had no choice but to make another attempt. 'Apparently Nefertari herself was a writer, you know. So you and she have something in common.'

I continued to stare at her, unwilling to break.

'Ah yes,' she went on blithely. 'There's a whole section dedicated to her in one of your Egyptological reference books in the lounge bar. I'm sure you've read it. Apparently Nefertari was highly educated and able to both read and write hieroglyphs, a very rare skill at the time. She used these skills in her diplomatic work, corresponding with other prominent royals of the time.'

'Er, yes,' I mumbled. 'I was aware that she was a gifted correspondent.' It was as far as I was willing to go. I was quite sure in her journalistic way Georgina was trying to trip me up, provoke me into making some thoughtless comment to ensnare me in her trap.

Georgina waited to see if I might elucidate further. When I remained obstinately tight-lipped she gave a small shrug. 'Still, I'm sure that, between you, you and Sarah Belzoni can find a way of telling Nefertari's story so that your readers can hear her voice echoing down the centuries, almost as if she were telling a narrative of her own.'

I didn't respond to this. Instead I lifted my fingers over the keyboard as if eager to get back to work. She took the hint. 'If you're looking for a literary hook,' she said, admitting defeat, 'it might interest you to know that next month Nefertari's tomb in the Valley of the Queens is being opened to the public for the first time in decades. There'll be an entry fee, of course; but nothing like the swingeing price those willing to stump up the cash have been required to pay for the last few years.'

'Yes,' I murmured. 'I'd heard the Ministry of Antiquities and the Tourism Authority had teamed up to re-open a couple of the A-list tombs. The other is Seti's, I hear.'

'Let's hope they prove enough of a draw to entice back stalwarts who've been to Egypt before,' she said. 'I'm sure if you could write about them in your travelogue, Merry; you'd have people clamouring for tickets. It's not as if there isn't a Belzoni link. Giovanni discovered Seti's tomb of course. And considering his other Pharaonic achievements brought Ramses II back from obscurity – courtesy of his work at the Ramesseum and Abu Simbel – I can only repeat that Nefertari, as Ramses' Great Royal Wife, seems to me to deserve a mention.'

This seemed so reasonable a suggestion it made me wonder suddenly whether I'd imagined all that subtext a few moments ago. Perhaps in reality she didn't know more than she was letting on, and it had been an innocent suggestion after all. I started to ask myself if perhaps I was becoming paranoid.

Georgina had only paused for breath, and went on, 'I'm only surprised the bigwigs at the Ministry and the Tourism Authority haven't invited you for a sneak preview.'

I'm sorry to say, even despite the modification of my suspicions I was unable to resist the chance this offered me to score a point. There was something about being on the receiving end of her lecture that brought out some demon in me. 'Oh, but they have,' I said airily. 'Adam and I are due to attend the 'official' opening ceremonies, with some dignitaries from here and Cairo, tomorrow afternoon.'

Hah! I thought. Put that in your pipe and smoke it!

* * *

By the time we were ready to leave to attend said ceremonies the following day there had still been no further communication from the individual apparently holding Ibrahim Mohassib hostage. I found this strange, but was way too excited by the prospect of the afternoon ahead to allow myself to dwell on it for long. If anything, it was a relief. It meant we could get on with our plans unhindered. We could worry about Ibrahim Mohassib and what to do about him if there was still no update when we got back. In the meantime, Ahmed had gone ashore again first thing this morning, assuring us he was making progress with his investigations. That he was hell bent on avoiding Georgina Savage and her medical kit might also have had something to do with his early departure.

I'd taken pity on our would-be Florence Nightingale after my bout of childish one-upmanship yesterday. I'd given her Sarah Belzoni's journal. As far as I could tell, she'd been poring over it with slavish absorption ever since.

Today we had no need of a taxi. Director Ismail's email containing our invitations also informed us a car would be sent from the Tourism Authority to collect us at the causeway above our mooring platform.

Sadly Saleh el-Sayed was sitting inside when it arrived.

He leapt out and held the door open for me as I reached the top of the crumbling stone steps. 'It is my honour to accompany you personally,' he said. As this was uttered in his usual expressionless tone, I couldn't help but think he actually meant the exact opposite. It had been a relief to have no reason to see him over the last couple of days. Back in his company, I immediately felt my hackles rise. 'Your bodyguard is not joining you?' he asked in some surprise as only Adam stepped up after me.

'He's visiting family in Luxor,' I lied glibly.

I'm sure I didn't imagine his frown, quickly masked. 'But he is quite well, I hope? And making a speedy recovery from his accident at the Ramesseum and his unfortunate concussion?'

Forcibly reminded of Ahmed's blackout and Saleh's unexpected appearance on the jetty ostensibly to check up on him, his words also brought sharply to mind the syringe I'd found floating in the Nile alongside the dahabeeyah. I still hadn't made up my mind whether these were somehow connected. 'His big toe will take some time to heal,' I managed. 'But in himself, yes; I'm pleased to report he seems back to normal.'

'That is good news,' he said. Pity it didn't sound as if he meant it.

Getting into the car, I wondered yet again why Saleh's name had sprung so readily to my lips when confronted with the balaclava-wearing, knife-wielding maniac who presumably now had Ibrahim Mohassib in his clutches. It was unanswerable. Saleh el-Sayed, here in the flesh and greeting Adam with a veneer of polite civility, was a world away from that opportunistic ruffian. Equally loathsome, I'll grant you; but hardly out of the same mould.

Adam joined me on the back seat, and Saleh moved to sit in the front passenger seat alongside the driver. Thankfully this relieved us of the need for much in the way of further conversation. Saleh informed us events would start with a small opening ceremony in Nefertari's tomb in the Valley of the Queens and then we'd drive on to the Valley of the Kings for the official re-opening of Seti's tomb. This information imparted, he subsided into silence.

I'd worn a nice dress for the occasion. Even so, I'd had the sense to team it with my low-heeled sandals and, of course, my broad-brimmed straw hat. It was a little bit of a walk from the car parks in each of the Valleys to the tomb entrances. Whilst there was blissful air-conditioning in the car, Mother Nature hadn't seen fit to provide the same outside. The sun beat down – bludgeoned us, I should say – from a hard, hot sky so intense a blue it was almost purple.

I was unsurprised to see a small crowd already gathered when we pulled to a standstill in the dusty parking lot leading to the Valley of the Queens. The buff-coloured foothills of the Theban hills rose around us. I spotted Zahed

Mansour and Director Ismail deep in conversation in the shade of an awning. Saleh el-Sayed spotted them too. After holding open the door for me with as much solicitude as he could muster he wasted no time in stalking off to join them.

I was about to follow when a hand touching my forearm in a jabbing gesture forestalled me. I turned to see who was seeking to detain me so urgently and nearly fell over in shock.

He was wearing a loose cotton scarf tied loosely around his neck, with a turban wound around his head and a ceremonial galabeya resplendent with gold braiding rather than Western dress. But there was no mistaking him.

'Ibrahim Mohassib!' I breathed.

'Please!' He raised one finger to his lips in an unmistakeable gesture meant to silence me. Not that I was feeling particularly capable of further speech. He might be the one with a knife-wound the length of his neck, but right now it was I myself feeling as if my windpipe had been abruptly severed at the unexpected sight of him. All my startled brain seemed capable of processing was the ridiculous thought that his traditional costume was doubtless necessary. A livid gash from ear to collarbone held together with surgical tape surely would be impossible to hide in a shirt and tie.

Adam's strangled exclamation, clapping eyes on him provoked a repeat of the same frantic gesture.

'Please!' the curator whispered urgently. 'We have no time to talk now. I managed to get away. I knew I had to be here today. My absence would be remarked upon and checked. But let me tell you this…! I know the identity of the man who attacked me! He is dangerous! Please! You must help me!'

Adam recovered himself more quickly than me. 'I have a few questions,' he said. 'First, why did you discharge yourself against medical advice from the hospital? And second, why did you flee when we turned up at the museum, presumably straight into the ambushing arms of your attacker?'

I was really quite impressed with his elucidation given the shock of this surprise encounter. I never would have been able to call the essential questions back to mind with such precision.

Ibrahim Mohassib stared wild-eyed and forestalled him. 'I can explain! But not now! There is no time! Please! I beg you! Can we meet after the ceremonies today? Not at the museum. It is too exposed. I can come to your dahabeeyah; yes?'

So, he was quite happy to bring the danger to us, I noted. I thought of Ahmed, engaged on his fruitless investigations. Suddenly I wished we'd had the simple good sense to bring him with us today.

We were given no opportunity to respond. I could hear footsteps crunching on the loose scree covering the parking lot. I watched Ibrahim Mohassib's expression freeze, just as a familiar voice called out in greeting.

'Ah, Meredith, and Adam; I am so glad you were able to accept my invitation.' Director Ismail approached, trailing Zahed Mansour and Saleh el-Sayed in his wake. Ibrahim Mohassib melted away, almost as if he'd never been there. 'I'm delighted to have this opportunity to catch up with you both,' the Ministry director went on warmly. 'And Meredith, let me congratulate you on the early success of your blog. You already have a following, I see. The number of 'Likes' gets higher with every new post, and people are starting to leave comments. Most impressive, my dear.' His golden molar glinted in the sunshine as he smiled. I couldn't see his eyes, hidden behind dark sunglasses.

'I think it's Mehmet's photographs that have sparked most of the positive comments,' I said demurely – and truthfully. 'He's very talented.'

Zahed Mansour stepped forward. 'We wanted only the best people on this project,' he preened. For the first time in my short acquaintance with him the creases on his forehead matched the expression on his face. 'I'm pleased to say early signs are good. The number of hits on our website has gone up significantly since we started publishing your travelogue. Remind me of the latest metrics Saleh?'

I caught the sour expression on the Marketing Manager's face before he managed to mask it, and felt an unexpected stab of sympathy. It couldn't be easy to have his nose rubbed in it every day. He clearly wasn't deemed 'the best', and was now relegated to the humble role of number cruncher. No wonder his tolerance of me was paper thin.

'We have recorded a ten percent increase in traffic in just the last week,' he said thinly.

'Now we must hope to see a corresponding rise in holiday bookings,' Zahed Mansour remarked.

'Fingers crossed,' I murmured, glad that even through the events of the last few days – although without yet managing to draft a fully-fledged article I was satisfied with – I'd still managed to publish a new blog post every day.

While saying this I was looking over their shoulders as unobtrusively as I could trying to spot Ibrahim Mohassib. He'd disappeared into the small crowd of local dignitaries and invited guests. I don't mind admitting I was thoroughly unsettled by his sudden appearance, and by everything he'd said. It was impossible not to wonder what had happened to his assailant. I could only fervently hope the curator had somehow incapacitated him, even if only temporarily.

It was no mean feat to carry on a semblance of a normal conversation while feeling so off balance. I wasn't at all sure I wanted the museum man turning up at the *Queen*

Ahmes later. But unless Adam and I could somehow get to him first, I really didn't see how we could stop him

'I am optimistic,' Zahed Mansour smiled, pulling my attention back from the crowd. The contrast in his demeanour when I thought back to my first meeting with him at the British Museum couldn't be starker. He looked like a man coming back to life after a period of cryonic preservation; literally thawing out after a deep freeze. This was quite a thought given the hammering heat. 'You are still in the early part of your retracing of Belzoni's travels. You have yet to write about the ruins on the island of Philae and, of course, the magnificent temples of Abu Simbel.'

I told myself to forget about Ibrahim Mohassib for now. 'I'm looking forward to all of that very much,' I said earnestly. 'And, thank you, both of you. It's a real honour to be here today.' I meant this quite sincerely, so hope I didn't deserve the arch look Saleh el-Sayed sent me. I ignored him, feeling my sympathy explode like a burst balloon. I went on, 'I hope our readers won't mind too much if I take things a little out of sequence and write about Belzoni's discovery of Seti's tomb in my next post as the tomb is going to be back on the tourist trail after such a long time off limits.'

'That, my dear, is why we invited you,' Director Ismail said with a smile. 'We owe you the credit, after all, for making the suggestion in the first place. I'm sure the chronology of Belzoni's adventures is not well known. So I can see no harm in getting maximum value from your time here in Luxor by writing about Seti's tomb before you embark on your voyages further up the Nile and across Lake Nasser.'

Saleh el-Sayed shifted his feet. 'Er, gentlemen, and Meredith, I think it is time we made our way to the tomb for the grand opening.'

Director Ismail and Zahed Mansour stood back so Adam and I could proceed along the dusty path in front of them. Saleh brought up the rear. We passed the ubiquitous row of souvenir outlets as we walked towards the Queens' Valley. Their owners stood outside their cubbyhole shops, silent and staring. They knew this was an official delegation. There was no point in wasting energy on the hassle that was their stock in trade. Yet I had no doubt they were as hopeful as Zahed Mansour that the re-opening of Nefertari's tomb would prove an inducement to lure repeat-visitors back to the Valley of the Queens and give them some much needed victims.

The Valley of the Queens is a dustier, less impressive Valley than that of the Kings. For a start, it lacks the pyramidal shape of the mountain of Meretseger – *she who loves silence* – looming over it. It doesn't have the impressive stone entrances of some of the sepulchres in the Kings Valley. Some of the tombs here are gaping holes in the rock, accessed through metal-grilled gates. Nefertari's is the exception. It has a shaded rest area outside and is reached through a domed concrete entranceway.

Adam and I proceeded ahead of our hosts, but behind some of the other local dignitaries. I recognised the Mayor and the Governor of Luxor respectively.

'What a shame Walid couldn't be here,' I murmured to Adam. It was all the conversation we were able to have. With our hosts within earshot we didn't dare broach the subject of Ibrahim Mohassib and his unexpected reappearance, even though I was quite sure we were both itching to discuss it.

The Governor of Luxor called us to a halt in the shade of the rest area. He stepped forward as a kind of master of ceremonies. 'It is my great pleasure to welcome here Director Feisal Ismail from the Ministry of Antiquities to re-open this most beautiful of tombs to the public after so many years. Please, Director Ismail…' He led the polite applause.

As the director came forward, I scanned the small assemblage for Ibrahim Mohassib. I spotted him standing towards the back of the rest house, furthest from the tomb entrance. He looked edgy – or perhaps furtive – glancing this way and that. I rather wished he hadn't put in an appearance today so I could simply enjoy this moment. As it was, there was no denying it. I was on edge too.

Adam reached for my hand as Director Ismail cleared his throat in readiness to begin his speech. 'This is a lifelong dream of yours, Merry,' he whispered. 'Don't let anything spoil it. I'll keep an eye on our friend the curator.'

Lovely Adam, my soulmate; he always puts me first. I squeezed his hand, knowing the same was true for him. 'Thank you.'

'Friends and esteemed colleagues,' Director Ismail started, raising his voice so as to be heard by all. 'I shall give my small speech out here, if you will forgive the heat. To give speeches inside Queen Nefertari's final resting place seems somehow disrespectful.' He paused, and repeated this same introduction in Arabic.

'We are about to enter the most exquisite of all our ancient Egyptian royal tombs – and we are lucky enough to have a few. But Nefertari's trumps them all, a token of the enduring love a Pharaoh bore his Great Royal Wife, even beyond death.'

Unexpectedly, I felt my throat tighten and my eyes prick. I pulled myself together while Director Ismail gave the Arabic translation. But the pressure of Adams hand on mine told me he felt it too.

'As many of you will know,' Director Ismail continued, 'Ernestino Schiaparrelli, the director of the Egyptian Museum in Turin, discovered Nefetari's tomb in 1904. It has been called the Sistine Chapel of ancient Egypt.'

After the Arabic repeat he went on, 'Nefertari, which means "*beautiful companion*", was Ramses II's favourite wife.

Ramses went out of his way to declare this to the world, referring to her as "*the one for whom the sun shines*" in his writings, as well as building temples in her honour, most notably at Abu Simbel in ancient Nubia.

'Ramses' affection for his wife, as written on the tomb walls we are about to see, shows clearly that Egyptian queens were not all simply marriages of convenience to accumulate greater power and alliances. In some cases at least, they were based on genuine emotional attachment. Poetry written by Ramses about his dead wife is featured on some of the walls of her burial chamber.' He glanced down at his notes and quoted, "*My love is unique — no one can rival her, for she is the most beautiful woman alive. Just by passing, she has stolen away my heart*".'

This time my chin wobbled and I had to press my lips together and dig my fingernails into the palm of my hand so as not to make my emotional response obvious.

'Nefertari's origins are unknown except that it is thought she was most probably a member of the nobility,' Director Ismail went on rather more prosaically.

Adam squeezed my hand again and I knew we were sharing a single thought. If only we could just find the elusive stele we might be able to lift a veil on her background.

'Regrettably, by the time Schiaparelli rediscovered Nefertari's tomb it had already been found by tomb raiders, who stole all the treasure buried with the Queen, including her sarcophagus and mummy. Parts of Nefertari's knees were found in the burial chamber, which Schiaparelli took home to the Egyptian Museum in Turin, where they are still kept today.'

I tried not to mutter at the indignity of this. After all, who robbed a mummy but left its knees in situ? Ancient tomb robbers, apparently. I guess no amulets were wrapped around the body at mummification to protect the knees.

'The tomb has been closed to the public since World War II because of the deterioration and sometimes disintegration of the wall reliefs,' Director Ismail finished. 'Since then, a very few visitors have had the privilege of seeing inside. As you know, the humidity created by thousands of visitors caused salt crystals to form on the walls, eroding the murals. The Getty Conservation Institute completed a major conservation project between 1986 and 1992. It is now my belief – providing we restrict visitor numbers and control the humidity – we can, and should, re-open this marvel of ancient Egyptian artistry – the symbol of the love a great Pharaoh bore his Great Royal Wife.' He paused and ran his gaze over the small gathering. 'So welcome... Welcome to this, the official re-opening of Nefertari's tomb. Come with me and feast your eyes on the very best ancient Egyptian art has to offer...'

Chapter 16

There's no point trying to pretend I was unmoved by Nefertari's tomb. If my eyes were pricking, throat tightening and chin wobbling just listening to Director Ismail's speech, there was really no hope for me once inside. I walked around with a lump the size of a golf ball in my throat. It left me quite incapable of speech. My eyes pricked with hot tears.

I'm not sure I'd ever had myself taped as highly-strung or especially sentimental. But there was something about Nefertari's tomb that really got to me.

Georgina Savage was quite right. It wasn't the place. It was the *person*. So exquisite were the wall reliefs, it felt almost that Nefertari herself were here. Her image was everywhere, featured in every scene. She was so beautiful, so regal, so serene; so eternally youthful. In short, so *alive*. And so *present* somehow. It seemed impossible I was gazing at images of a woman dead for over three thousand years.

Sure, the brilliance of the images was courtesy largely of the Getty Institute's six-year multi-million-dollar restoration and preservation project. It didn't matter. The sense of seeing the tomb in pristine condition, just as it must have been when Ramses brought his Great Royal Wife here for burial was overwhelming. If it's possible for love to endure through art then this tomb was truly testament to a marriage that transcended time, was stronger even than death.

Each chamber burst with colour, reliefs, hieroglyphs and images painted on a white plaster background in vigorous shades of russet, ochre and olive. The ceiling was deep indigo patterned with bright yellow stars, masses of them.

The ancient artists had given the queen's face a lot of attention. This emphasised her beauty, especially the almond shape of her eyes, enhanced with black kohl, the blush of her cheeks, and the curve of her eyebrows.

Somehow the tomb managed to be at once a celebration of Nefertari's life and her death, and of the love a husband bore his wife. Adam pointed out the poetry Director Ismail had referred to, the texts written by Ramses himself and transcribed faithfully onto the walls of his wife's tomb. He brushed tears from my cheeks with the pads of his thumbs and carried the salty wetness to his lips. 'I feel the same way about you, you know,' he murmured – which actually did nothing whatsoever to stem the flow of my tears.

'Oh, Merry,' he said, pulling me close. 'You great big softie! I thought *I* was supposed to be the romantic one!'

Turning to go, I knew I wanted to learn more about this woman who had been queen during a golden age in Egypt. Now I really knew how Sarah Belzoni must have felt. As Georgina Savage rightly said, Sarah spent untold time in Nefertari's temple in Nubia. The wall reliefs there are no less exquisite, although perhaps less beautifully preserved. I felt sure Sarah too had known this feeling of Nefertari brought back to life through the skill of the ancient artisans' artwork. She, like me, must have wondered at the personality of this woman who had clearly inspired the man who loved her to immortalise her in stone. One didn't need to be able to read the hieroglyphic text for this simple fact to be inescapable.

It brought me closer to Sarah. And it brought me closer to Nefertari. I wondered if, just perhaps, my destiny and theirs might somehow touch. There might be some small part I could play in bringing them back from obscurity. And, as such, fanciful as it may sound, I could claim to have known them.

You see! That's what being inside Nefertari's tomb did to me!

Director Ismail greeted us as we stepped out into the blazing sunshine. 'Oh, my dear,' he said, observing me swiping at my wet cheeks. 'I see I do not need to ask you whether you will feel able to write about something of the atmosphere of the place rather than just the number of chambers and the amount of dollars spent in preservation.'

Adam smiled and spoke for me. 'I'm not sure she took a proper breath the whole time we were in there.'

Zahed Mansour stepped forward. 'Just wait until you see Seti's tomb. While perhaps it may not pack the same emotional punch, the sheer size, and the quality of the wall reliefs is unsurpassed.'

I didn't have the heart to tell him I'd already seen it; had in fact held my wedding ceremony in an exact replica of its most impressive chamber. Yes, it was spectacular. But no, outside of my marriage vows, it had not reduced me to tears.

Once the official viewing was over and all the invited guests had filed outside again, we made our way back to the car park. I glanced over my shoulder to see Ibrahim Mohassib trailing the small procession by a few paces. He hadn't fallen far enough behind to separate him from the group. But neither was he exactly part of the pack. Perhaps he'd simply decided he didn't want to speak to anyone. I guessed he was perhaps going through the motions of attendance without really engaging in the event itself. It was possible I'd feel the same way if I'd been knifed and then captured. He looked quite agitated, still glancing this way and that as if expecting to be ambushed at any moment. I found myself also nervously scanning the rocky terrain for any sign of danger. But the number of armed security guards patrolling with us surely made any attempt on him unlikely.

I gave up fretting about it after a moment or two. There was nothing I could do in the here and now to make sense of the last few days or Ibrahim Mohassib's strange behaviour. I determined to not let it worry me. I was quite sure Adam and I, between us, could get to the bottom of things later if the curator did indeed decide to show his face onboard the *Queen Ahmes*. For now, I simply wanted to enjoy being part of this historic day.

It was a fifteen-minute drive between the Valleys of the Queens and Kings once back on the main road running along the edge of the cultivated land. I gave myself up to the blissful air-conditioning and the view of the Theban hills rising up at some distance, tawny gold in the sunshine, looking for all the world like the hide of a lion stretched out across the desert landscape. Saleh el-Sayed enquired whether we had enjoyed our visit to Nefertari's tomb. But as I was quite sure he had no interest whatsoever in our response, I limited myself to a vague murmur of appreciation.

The Valley of the Kings was open for business. The few knots of tourists looked at our small party curiously as Director Ismail and Zahed Mansour led us towards Seti's tomb, located in the southeast branch of the wadi. Our dressed-up-ness made it clear we were an official delegation of some sort. I took Adam's hand, re-acquainting myself with the Valley and taking a moment to remember the part it had played in so many of our previous adventures. Bleached rock rose all around us, blinding now the sun was high in the sky. This surely must be one of the hottest and most barren places on earth. That the pharaohs conceived of carving their sepulchres out of the bedrock here was frankly astonishing. I didn't envy the ancient workmen their labours. But it was impossible not to admire their enterprise.

In view of the temperature and the tourists, Director Ismail led us inside for the ceremony to re-open Seti's tomb. Saleh el-Sayed stood back so Adam and I could enter ahead of him to descend the steep staircase of the entrance corridor. Before we went in I turned and noticed Ibrahim Mohassib still bringing up the rear, glad to see he'd made it here without being kidnapped or attacked or whatever else it was he feared.

Portable fans had been set up in the first chamber when we reached the bottom of the staircase. Whilst not cool, it was a definite improvement on the suffocating heat outside. I took a moment to admire the familiar pillared hall and wall reliefs of Seti being embraced by the gods, nostalgic for my wedding day.

Once Director Ismail saw we were all assembled, leaving the armed guard stationed outside at the top of the staircase, he cleared his throat and took a small notebook from his breast pocket.

'My friends and esteemed colleagues,' he began in much the same way he had outside Nefertari's tomb. 'I see you are already gazing in wonder and awe at the remarkable wall paintings. What this tomb has in common with that of Nefertari – who was Seti's daughter-in-law, of course – is that it counts among the greatest works of art in the world. This tomb is the largest and the finest Pharaonic rock-cut tomb in all of Egyptian history. It became the model others copied down the centuries, although none ever achieved the sublime quality you will see here.'

As before, he repeated his introduction in Arabic, and then flipped open his notebook. 'I think I can do no better on this, the official re-opening of the tomb to visitors from all corners of the globe, than to quote from the *Narrative* of the man who first discovered it, the one-time circus strongman and great nineteenth century adventurer and explorer, Giovanni Belzoni.' And he proceeded to read:

'"*On the 16th October 1817 I recommenced my excavations in the valley of Beban el Malook (the Valley of the Kings), and pointed out the fortunate spot, which has paid me for all the trouble I took in my researches. I may call this a fortunate day, one of the best perhaps of my life. Fortune has given me that satisfaction, that extreme pleasure, which wealth cannot purchase - the pleasure of discovering what has been long sought in vain, and of presenting the world with a new and perfect monument of Egyptian antiquity. A tomb which can be recorded as superior to any other in point of grandeur, style, and preservation, appearing as if just finished on the day we entered it.*"'

Director Ismail broke off and gazed around at our rapt faces. I was familiar with this passage, having read Belzoni's *Narrative* from cover to cover. But I'd never expected to hear it read aloud in a deep male voice made exotic by its subtle Arabic accent, and inside the very tomb Belzoni was describing. A shiver snaked down my spine, goose bumps rising on my flesh.

'So now,' the director finished. 'Let me say that it also gives me the greatest of pleasure to present back to the world this perfect monument of Egyptian antiquity. Ladies and gentlemen, I give you the tomb of Seti the First!'

The polite applause had barely died away when I heard someone yell.

A cry of alarm went up among the assembled guests. My blood froze and I craned my neck to see what the noise was about. It was Ibrahim Mohassib shouting the warning. Somehow I felt I had known this even before I turned. Standing at the back of the small crowd just at the foot of the steep staircase we'd all just descended, he was gesturing wildly and at something further inside the tomb, fear writ large across his features.

Perhaps you'll forgive me when I say my over-riding sense was irritation. I wanted nothing more than to get on with our private VIP tour of this tomb, eager to re-familiarise myself with its vast and superbly decorated interior now Director Ismail had whetted my appetite so effectively. I especially wanted to see for myself the tunnel; inaccessible to visitors though I knew it to be, dug into the bedrock beneath the place Seti's sarcophagus once lay in the burial chamber.

Perceiving at once what was going on, I let out a puff of irritation. I had little patience with the notion that the curator's opportunist attacker may have followed us here, somehow managing to gain admission to the tomb ahead of us. It was an ill-timed and aggravating interruption, just as his first at the museum had been. And I was quite sure, if called upon to do so, we could bring it to an equally rapid, yet hopefully rather more satisfactory conclusion.

Ibrahim Mohassib's pointing gesticulations were aimed at the space just beyond where Adam and I were standing. Among the first to enter the tomb, we were furthest from the entrance, standing with our backs to the darkness of a further chamber set behind this pillared hall inside the ancient sepulchre. But, looking at the curator, I quickly discerned he was in the grip of a very different sort of fear. Barely had the thought registered, and before I'd had half a chance to spin around to see what he was pointing at with so much agitation, I felt myself roughly grabbed from behind and hauled backwards.

I cried out in fright. Adam reacted in a heartbeat, trying to wrest me back again. But I watched stark horror dawn on his features as he took in whatever it was I couldn't see.

'Don't move, Merry,' he commanded.

His tone, used so rarely, issued an extra instruction to obey.

'My God!' a woman standing next to Adam exclaimed in a terrified whisper. 'He's wearing a suicide vest!'

The man holding me captive uttered an incomprehensible string of guttural Arabic. I recognised one word only. 'Allah.'

All my worst fears crowded in on me at once. I'd come back to Egypt, only to get caught up in a terrorist attack on my first public engagement. I should have known the ceremonial re-opening of these two spectacular tombs – the finest Egypt has to offer – was far too tempting an opportunity for Islamic State to pass up. An attack here would capture headlines around the world, and make last year's attack at Karnak seem little more than an aperitif before the showstopper main course at a banquet.

To my way of looking at it, there's something especially chilling about suicide attacks. It's terrifying to contemplate how someone of whatever religion or creed can be willing – eager even – to catapult himself into whatever version of the afterlife he's been brainwashed into believing is so supremely preferable to the life he's living, in many cases leaving behind a spouse, parents, friends; small children even.

It's a warped ideology, impossible to counter. How does one fight an enemy that places no value on human life?

In a moment of dazzling clarity I saw each of the faces of the people here with me, staring transfixed in this moment of paralysed shock and horror. These were the people who would die with me; people I did not know, in the most part had never spoken to. Our faces would appear alongside each other in police reports. We'd make up a photographic montage on the BBC, and on every other major News channel around the world. Our families would come together in grief, and all right-minded people across the globe would stand together in denouncing this cowardly act.

That was what terrorism did. It united every bit as much as it divided – possibly more so. That's what the terrorists would never understand.

I don't know how many seconds passed while these riotous thoughts tumbled through my brain. Perhaps no more than two or three. I've noticed that about the brain. It can go into overdrive while the body and everything else around it seems to slow to a snail pace.

It was the thought of Seti's tomb being the setting for this atrocity – more than the loss of my own life; more even than the loss of Adam's – that upset me the most. It sent my brain into super-overdrive for another second or two.

I'd read of course of so-called Islamic State's motivation in destroying Middle Eastern cultural heritage sites. ISIS – or ISIL as it had been re-named in the media of late – justified the destruction of these sites with its extreme following of *Salafism*. This, according to its followers, placed great importance on establishing *tawhid* (monotheism), and eliminating *shirk* (polytheism). So I knew that while it was often assumed ISIL's actions were mindless acts of vandalism, there was in actual fact an ideology – no matter how twisted to our Western way of thinking – underpinning the destruction. ISIL viewed its actions in sites like Palmyra in Syria and Nimrud in Iraq as being in accordance with Sunni Islamic tradition.

Beyond the ideological aspects of the destruction, I was fully aware also of the other, more practical, reasons behind ISIL's targeting of historic sites. Grabbing the world's attention was easy through the razing of such cultural heritage, given the extensive international media coverage that followed.

Also, as I well knew thanks to my time at the British Museum, despite the images showing extreme destruction, ISIL had also been making use of looted antiquities to finance its activities. Disregarding the United Nation's 2011 ban on the trade of items looted from Syria, the group had been smuggling artefacts out of the Middle East and on to the underground antique markets of Europe and North America for years.

All at once I was super determined Seti's tomb would not succumb to either vandalism or destruction. I had not come here today just to see terrorists claim it. The very thought of explosives blasting through this tomb in this Valley, obliterating sepulchres that had lasted through thirty or more centuries from the highest point of ancient Egyptian civilisation and artistry, brought my blood boiling to the surface. While there was breath in my body, I would fight to save it. I just needed to figure out a way to incapacitate this self-styled soldier of Islam who'd grabbed me so precipitously before he blasted us all to kingdom come.

At this thought my thundering brain stopped short as if I'd run headlong into a roadblock. I realised the illogic in a man with a suicide vest needing a hostage. Surely all he required was a detonator. I wondered what he was waiting for. Ok, so it was maybe only five or six seconds since he'd hauled me from the assemblage. Even so, I failed to see why we were all still standing here, a frozen tableau of paralysis. From what I knew of suicide bombers they struck without warning, blowing themselves and their victims sky high at the first opportunity. This one seemed to be thinking about it, which struck me as decidedly odd.

Adam was still staring at me with the same agonised expression. Alongside him, it was Saleh el-Sayed, astonishingly, who moved. What he said, uttered in an urgent whisper, shocked me even more.

'Eshan! Not this way! Don't be a fool, man! Let her go!'

I felt the heavy breath of the man holding me captive hot on the nape of my neck. He uttered a short burst of furious-sounding Arabic in response to Saleh's English appeal, also in an undertone. That Saleh's choice of language was for my benefit I did not doubt. Considering he disliked me so much, I could only wonder at this. That my assailant had understood every word was equally apparent.

'This isn't the way,' Saleh whispered again.

I narrowed my gaze on Saleh's smooth-skinned face. I didn't want to believe he operated on the fringes of terrorism, but one could never tell.

I felt the hesitation, or maybe it was indecision, raging in the man holding me from behind. My shoulder was starting to hurt, his fingers pressing into the flesh exposed by my sleeveless dress. A moment later he shoved me away. I stumbled forward and fell into Adam's outstretched arms.

Righting myself, I immediately spun around to see his face. 'You!' I exclaimed. Not a terrorist of Islam after all, for all that, this time, he sported a suicide vest instead of a balaclava.

His resemblance to the Marketing Manager was not pronounced. Nevertheless there was something in the indefinable way of family likenesses that was unavoidable. Now I knew why I'd breathed his name so instinctively back at the museum. Related, obviously. I was starting to deduce that my first instinct on hearing Ibrahim Mohassib's shout had been correct. This wasn't an ISIL terrorist incident after all. But there was no doubting the suicide vest. It posed a far more devastating threat than the knife had done.

Adam found his voice. 'What the hell is this all about?' He looked from Saleh to our attacker while a frisson of alarm quivered through our little gathering, thankfully no one standing close enough to hear what was being said. 'Who is this man?'

'This,' Saleh said in quiet tones of the most abject discomfort, 'is my cousin.' It was the most natural I'd ever experienced him, quite a nice change from his usual polite incivility.

Director Ismail had seen enough. He shoved his way forward to join us, anger radiating from his tall frame. The dignitaries shrank back behind the richly decorated pillars. I didn't blame them. Such anger in close proximity to a suicide vest felt...felt...well... In truth it felt suicidal. 'I know you!' he looked as if he'd very much like to grab hold of our assailant and shake him until his teeth rattled. But he kept his voice down. 'You work at the Antiquities Museum in Cairo!'

'Worked,' Saleh corrected. 'Past tense, sir. Eshan lost his job three years ago in the cutbacks after the Morsi administration wiped Egypt off the tourist map.'

Our would-be suicide bomber glared at the director. I daresay he considered the sheer quantity of explosives he was wearing gave him the upper hand. 'It was you!' he spat. 'You took away my job and left me in the gutter. Not because of cutbacks. It was because of what I knew. But now I don't suppose you even remember my name! Do you?' While his Arabic accent was pronounced, his grasp of English was impressive.

313

'For the sake of Allah, keep your voice down,' Saleh hissed as his cousin 's temper flared. 'You're signing your own death warrant!'

My darting glance flicked from our attacker to Saleh el-Sayed as I tried to keep up. Finally my gaze settled on Director Ismail to gauge his reaction. I saw the light of comprehension dawn in his eyes. 'Eshan,' he murmured, groping for a surname to match. I guessed it wasn't el-Sayed.

'Eshan Abadi,' our attacker provided. 'Do you remember me now, Director?' There was a definite sneer in his voice, although he dropped it to a whisper once more. 'I worked at the Egyptian Museum as a...'

'As a philologist!' I gasped as the pieces fell into place. 'You're the man who was sent from Cairo to translate the papyrus scrolls!'

'Enough!' Director Ismail held up one hand. 'Stop talking!' Collecting himself, he went on more calmly, speaking in hushed tones to once more keep the assembled guests from overhearing, although they must surely be wondering what was going on, even with their view obscured by the pillars plastered with images of the ancient king. 'Eshan Abadi. Yes, I remember you.' His eyes narrowed on the other man's face, his gaze moving to take in the threat implicit in the suicide vest. 'Ok, Mr Abadi, I am willing to go ahead with whatever conversation you have come here to have. But I refuse absolutely to say another word with all of these innocent people present. I demand that you release them. And then, perhaps, we can talk.'

'Great job he did of tying up the loose ends, I don't think,' Adam muttered sarcastically beneath his breath so only I could hear him. 'Talk about hand a man a grievance and enough ammunition to make trouble!'

'Literally,' I mouthed in response.

'We will talk now,' Eshan Abadi asserted, touching his suicide vest as if to remind us all of how real a threat he posed. 'I think you care less for their lives than you do about revealing what you have been hiding for the last three years. I translated those papyri. I read all about the "precious jewels"! So, where are they?'

My blood congealed in my veins and pounded in my ears all at once. I knew it would take only a few more words and a raised voice to alert the assemblage to the existence of a tomb that would make those of Nefertari and Seti seem scarcely worthy of mention.

That suicide vest, I realised, was less about blasting people to smithereens – although I was sure that remained a very real risk. It was more about blowing the cover on the no less explosive secret we'd vowed to keep. There were people here with the clout to demand it be brought out into the open.

Not for the first time, I rued the day Adam and I had sleuthed our way through Howard Carter's clues to find the hidden entrance to that tomb. The tomb itself would have been far better off – and, right now, we would be too – if we'd left well alone!

Saleh el-Sayed appeared to be reading my mind – not the last bit about the tomb, but the bit before about the level of threat posed by his cousin.

'I very much doubt the suicide vest is real,' he said flatly. Perhaps he realised that despite his best efforts to gag his cousin, his only chance of saving his own skin was to make clear they were not in cahoots, and side with his employers.

I couldn't help but wonder if he'd called it right when Eshan Abadi's right fist flew out, striking the Marketing Manager squarely on the jaw. He grunted and reeled backwards, losing balance and dropping to the hard floor.

It was the cue the onlookers needed to panic. Until then shock, inertia and possibly interest in trying to hear the low-toned discussion taking pace in one corner of the chamber had held everyone tense, watchful and rooted to the spot. Now, released by this more normal brand of violence, there was a sudden swell of movement towards the staircase. Fake or not, the threat of the suicide vest was enough to spark pandemonium now the freeze-frame spell was broken.

As Adam spun instinctively to help Saleh up from the floor, I jerked my head sideways. The momentum towards the way-out of Seti's tomb was the scene of a new commotion.

I searched for Ibrahim Mohassib among the melee. He was nowhere in sight. To my surprise I spied a familiar form thrusting forward through those gathered at the foot of the steep staircase. His gun was unslung, ready to enter the fray.

'Ahmed!'

Dressed informally in galabeya, turban and flip-flops, he lacked the authority of his uniform. Nevertheless his sheer bulk and the determined set of his shoulders showed he meant business. The gun was a further inducement to fall back rather than get in his way. No wonder the panickers were having second thoughts. Dressed like that, they had no idea who Ahmed was of course. I could well see it was a toss up between taking one's chances with a would-be terrorist wearing a – possibly – fake suicide vest, and an aggressive-looking unknown assailant with a cocked-and-at-the-ready firearm in his hands.

Well, it was and it wasn't – in his hands, I mean.

No sooner had Ahmed thrust himself forward than suddenly Ibrahim Mohassib sprang up from where he'd been presumably crouching on the floor, keeping – literally – a low profile. Don't ask me how he knew to stamp on Ahmed's foot. Perhaps from his position cowering on the floor he'd had a birds-eye view of Ahmed's injured toe and spotted his chance. Our police pal let out a howl of pain and crashed to the floor. As he toppled forward, Ibrahim Mohassib wrestled his gun from him. What happened next unfolded in slow motion.

Ibrahim Mohassib lifted the gun and took aim. At first I thought it was at me as I was full-square in his line of sight. For the second time this week, I found myself staring down the barrel of a gun and let out an involuntary yelp of terror. Then I discerned I was not his target. The shot rang out before this thought fully registered. I wasn't quick enough to follow its trajectory, although I'd swear I felt it whistle through the air and past my left ear. But I couldn't fail to be aware of its impact. Eshan Abadi's body convulsed and crumpled to the floor. He uttered not a sound. The bullet had hit him in the neck. The significance of this was not lost on me. Neither was the thought that a suicide vest – fake or not – was no use whatsoever as a life jacket if the aim was high enough.

Saleh el-Sayed let out a cry and jolted forward. Adam grabbed him, gripping his upper arms, and held him back. It was too late. Eshan Abadi was very clearly dead.

Chapter 17

A cry went up from the assembled guests. I recognised at once it wasn't of the same horror I was feeling staring at the dead body at my feet. It was actually more of a cheer. And I figured, from their point of view, I could see why. To their way of looking at it, this brave man had taken swift and decisive action. He'd wrested a gun away from an unknown possible assailant and used it to shoot the terrorist. Ibrahim Mohassib had every chance of being lauded a hero.

Even so, I couldn't help but be sickened by his cold-blooded killing of the former philologist. But then I realised the curator had no reason to think the suicide vest a fake. That being the case, he'd spotted his chance and taken it. To be fair, looked at like that, his shooting of Eshan Abadi was commendable. The only trouble was – Ibrahim Mohassib was still brandishing the gun.

He wasn't the only one. The unmistakable sound of a gunshot brought sounds of the armed guards starting to descend the steep staircase, shouting as they came.

'Don't shoot!' Ibrahim Mohassib cried as they came into view at the bottom of the entrance passageway and the sights of newly assembled firearms were trained on him. 'I ask only for the opportunity to speak to Director Ismail alone!'

Oh God, I thought. *Here we go again.* The miracle was he hadn't included Adam and me in his request.

'Who is that man?' the director whispered alongside me, clearly not recognising the curator in his traditional garb.

'Ibrahim Mohassib of the Luxor Museum,' I replied. 'He and the dead man at our feet are the two loose threads you promised to tie up three years ago.'

Comprehension dawned and he paused to collect himself. 'It seems I failed to secure the knot tightly enough,' he breathed.

'You can say that again,' I muttered.

On the other side of the pillared chamber, Ahmed groaned and tried to push himself up from the floor at the curator's feet. Ibrahim Mohassib spied another chance once more and grabbed it. 'This man was in cahoots with the terrorist!' he shouted out, making me gasp in outrage. 'Please… nobody shoot him, or me! I will take him into police custody so he can give a full account of himself! Director Ismail, perhaps you will do me the honour of meeting me at the police station.' Then very deliberately, he lowered the weapon aiming it at point blank range at Ahmed's head.

I sucked in a painful breath and felt my knees go weak, wondering what he was playing at. But, of course, Ibrahim Mohassib knew just enough to use this opportunity to flush out the truth. My panicked gaze fixed on the Eye of Horus secured around Ahmed's neck on its leather cord. If ever our police pal needed protection from the ancient god that time was surely now. Ibrahim Mohassib had quite clearly taken leave of his senses. The silly man could have milked his apparent heroism for all it was worth. Instead, he seemed hell bent on turning himself into the villain of the piece.

'For God's sake Feisal, *do* something,' I appealed to the director in an undertone, using his first name quite unconsciously in my distress.

'Guards!' Director Ismail rapped out, making me jump with his sudden shout. 'Withdraw with your weapons. Let this man do as he says. He has done our country a great service today.'

I wasn't at all sure this was quite what I'd had in mind. I looked at him askance. Saleh el-Sayed muttered something under his breath in Arabic but had the sense not to say it aloud. I had to give the Director full marks for playing along with Ibrahim's little drama. But then, what choice did he have? We had an undiscovered royal tomb to protect. And, to my way of looking at it, Director Ismail was more than a little complicit in today's unwelcome turn of events. He was possibly just trying to buy himself some time.

Ibrahim Mohassib nudged Ahmed with his foot. Grunting with pain as he put weight on his newly re-injured toe, Ahmed heaved himself up from the floor. Ibrahim Mohassib kept the gun trained at his head. This became his heart when the curator realised what a big man he'd felled.

Ahmed towered over him. But sheer size was no match for a bullet through the chest. Even though I felt sure the curator was using Ahmed to bring the director to heel, it was impossible not to baulk at the sight of our big friend with his own gun pointed at his heart.

We had no choice but to watch as Ibrahim Mohassib started shunting Ahmed towards the foot of the staircase. At a command from Director Ismail, the guards dropped their weapons and fell back, letting them pass. Even the millennia-old wall reliefs seemed to shrink.

I could see rivulets of sweat running down Ahmed's temples. I had no doubt he'd come here today fearing an incident of some sort. His police instincts are pretty well honed. I could well imagine his investigations on the east bank into Ibrahim Mohassib's apparent kidnap and whatever evidence he'd perhaps uncovered had brought him hot-footing it (as far as his mangled toe would allow) to the Valley. Ahmed was our bodyguard and his first thought would be to protect us. That he arrived on the scene a bit late for all that, and was now the one who'd ended up with a gun at his back seemed to me particularly unfair.

Adam moved to stand alongside me. We watched together, gripped with anxiety, as Ahmed limped onto the staircase to climb out of the tomb with his own gun pressed against his ribcage. Seeming to realise that allowing Ahmed to ascend ahead of him would expose him, Ibrahim Mohassib barked a command in Arabic and muscled his way in front of Ahmed, turning so that his gun was still trained on our police buddy while Ibrahim himself climbed up the steep staircase backwards.

'Please God, don't let Ahmed try anything brave, reckless...' Adam started.

'...Or stupid,' I finished. 'Let's hope Ibrahim Mohassib is bluffing.'

An almost unnatural silence descended in the moments after the two men reached the top of the staircase and left the tomb. It was as if the very airwaves were holding a collective breath. Everybody seemed to be looking at everybody else. And yet nobody was making eye contact.

I was aware of Saleh el-Sayed dropping to his knees alongside his cousin's dead body. I think I even tried to care. I'm sorry to say I failed. My entire being was attuned to Ahmed, senses quivering in fear for his safety in case Ibrahim Mohassib wasn't bluffing after all. I wasn't sure how many heartbeats I was supposed to count before we were allowed to move. I could feel each one thumping painfully against my ribcage. Never before had I been quite so acutely aware of the blood pumping through my veins, or the seconds so slowly ticking by.

I have no idea quite what I expected to happen next. What I didn't predict was the bone-chilling scream echoing back into the tomb from above – undoubtedly a female voice – that immediately preceded the sound of a gunshot.

'*Ahmed*?' Adam and I both cried out in a single voice, jolting from our paralysis and moving as one.

'Stop!' Director Ismail commanded.

We both ignored him, making for the staircase.

A cry went up from the assemblage. They too were breaking out of their torpor but, unlike Adam and me, it wasn't their best friend up there. I was aware of the hesitation in the general shift towards the exit. Director Ismail took full advantage of this to wrest back some control and assert his authority.

'My friends; stop!' Director Ismail ordered again. This time I knew he didn't mean us since I didn't consider myself his friend, so felt completely at liberty to disobey. 'For your own safety, remain here!'

I was aware of the uncertain shuffling as Adam and I pushed and shoved through the hesitating guests.

'Guards!' Director Ismail re-directed his orders. 'Protect these people with your lives! I will assess the danger outside. For now, let no one re-enter this tomb, unless it is me.'

Adam and I bolted up the staircase as fast as the steep gradient would allow and burst from the tomb entrance into the harsh sunlight outside. Director Ismail was a scant few paces behind us. I'm not sure in a million years I could have imagined the scene that greeted us as my eyes adjusted.

The sight of Ahmed sprawled on the dusty bedrock of the Valley floor only a stone's throw from the entrance was the only part to align with my fearful expectation. That he'd sustained a gunshot to his right shoulder was obvious from the spreading pool of blood seeping across the bedrock.

Habiba – yes! *ohmygod Habiba* – was draped across his inert frame, tears coursing down her beautiful face, Ahmed's blood ruining her rather-lovely tunic as she ripped off her headscarf to press against his bullet wound to stem the bleeding.

Georgina Savage – yes! *Georgina Savage* – was slumped on the ground, clearly winded, gasping, and trying to recover her breath. 'I tried to trip him up!' she wheezed. 'The man with the gun, that is. But he shoved me aside and I just collapsed!'

My gaze flew along the branch of buff coloured rock leading from Seti's tomb towards the central stem of the Valley and I spied Ibrahim Mohassib running as if all the demons of Hell were in hot pursuit.

Director Ismail gave chase. For Adam and me it was different. In that moment, I knew we couldn't care less about Ibrahim Mohassib and whether he was the hero or villain of the day. Our only thought was for Ahmed.

My gaze jolted back to Ahmed and Habiba. I'd never seen Habiba without her headscarf. I'd expected her hair to be long. The short pixie-cut took me completely by surprise.

This incredibly modern and oh-so-beautiful look almost diverted my attention from Ahmed and his bullet wound. Almost, but not quite.

'OhmyGod, Ahmed!' I cried, dropping to the dust alongside him. 'Are you ok? Can you hear me?'

'I am not dead,' he grunted in a muffled voice.

Habiba's cry of relief was like nothing I have ever heard. It held joy and heartbreak and a good many other emotions I wouldn't know how to name. Suffice it to say it spoke volumes.

'Come away Merry,' Adam coaxed gently, reaching forward to pull me to my feet, and tugging me away.

Habiba lapsed into Arabic, crying over Ahmed with deep hiccupping sobs. I discovered I didn't need to speak the language to understand every fervent and gulping word. Love has a language all of its' own after all.

Had I been in any doubt as to her meaning, the slow spreading smile across Ahmed's features before he passed out would have told me everything I needed to know.

'Make no mistake, they're engaged to be married,' Adam murmured.

'She saved his life!' Georgina piped up, recovering her breath but not yet getting up. 'We arrived here just in time to see Ahmed leaving the tomb at gunpoint. Habiba was awesome! She assessed the situation in a heartbeat while I was still drawing breath. She let out the most deafening scream and hurled herself bodily between Ahmed and the gun. I think her scream made the attacker jump. He pulled the trigger as she moved. It was enough to divert the bullet. Rather than hitting either Habiba or Ahmed directly, the bullet struck poor Ahmed in the shoulder. Hearing movement from the tomb, the man decided to leg it! You arrived on the scene just as he made off.'

I couldn't help but think their timing unfortunate. I was pretty sure Ibrahim Mohassib had no real intention of hurting Ahmed. But it was possible I was wrong. 'Director Ismail will catch him,' I said confidently.

Except, he didn't.

The Ministry Director returned, puffing and shaking his head. 'He had too big a head start and was too fast for me,' he panted. 'It is of no matter. We know who he is and where to find him. I can only dare to believe it wasn't a deliberate shooting on his part, and that he still wants to meet me.'

'But he still has Ahmed's gun,' Adam pointed out 'And he clearly suspects about the tomb. We'll need additional security for the *Queen Ahmes* while Ahmed is being patched up.

Director Ismail considered this for a moment, clearly realising there was more to all this than he had perhaps supposed. 'Had Mr Mohassib somehow threatened you?'

'No,' Adam admitted. 'It was Ibrahim himself who was threatened – by the chap he just killed in Seti's tomb. Eshan Abadi turned up brandishing a knife while Merry and I were visiting the curator at the museum the other day.' He managed to tell the whole story in a few short sentences – omitting any mention of the stone tablets – and ending up with Ibrahim Mohassib's unexpected appearance at the Valley of the Queens just before the re-opening of Nefertari's tomb today. 'How Eshan Abadi got into Seti's tomb ahead of us I can only imagine,' he finished. 'Perhaps he still had his ID card from his old job at the Cairo Museum.'

I listened to all of this with half an ear, watching Habiba still crooning over Ahmed's prone form. It was clear we needed to get an ambulance out here. And there was the small matter of a dead body needing removal from Seti's tomb. Not to mention the invited guests still under guards' protection inside. I imagined the Governor of Luxor taking control in Director Ismail's absence. But he couldn't hold them inside the tomb indefinitely.

Georgina Savage hefted herself off the floor to help Habiba stem the flow of blood from Ahmed's bullet wound, no doubt delighted to have yet another opportunity to play nursemaid. Her propensity for being on the scene for each of his mishaps was really quite remarkable. They were both far enough out of earshot that I knew I could speak to the Director candidly.

'It's clear to me that either singly or jointly Eshan Abadi and Ibrahim Mohassib figured out those papyrus scrolls led to a discovery of some sort that you hushed up,' I said uncompromisingly. 'I'd like to think the tomb itself is not in danger since they didn't have all the pieces of the puzzle. But it strikes me, as well as providing additional security for Adam and me while Ibrahim Mohassib is in possession of Ahmed's gun, it wouldn't hurt to double up the guard at Hatshepsut's temple.'

'You're telling me I must take responsibility of clearing up the mess I have made,' Director Ismail remarked.

'In a word, yes,' I admitted. 'Ahmed needs an ambulance, and Eshan Abadi's body should be taken to the morgue. You also have some damage limitation to do with those people inside the tomb. They seem to accept the dead man was a terrorist. But it's possible some realised he was in actual fact a disgruntled ex-employee with just enough knowledge to be dangerous. You'd better have a good story to tell, just in case.'

Director Ismail looked at me levelly while I told him how to do his job. 'Strange how these occurrences have coincided with your return to the Nile Valley, my dear,' he said mildly. I wasn't deceived for a moment by his gentle tone. I remembered he'd spoken in just such a way when we'd first encountered him and he'd relieved us of the tomb. I bit my lip, wondering if perhaps I'd overstepped the mark. I felt sure he wouldn't leave it there. No doubt I had just invited a more thorough interview about exactly why Adam and I had gone to the Luxor Museum the other day.

But right now, Director Ismail had no choice but to acknowledge he had more pressing matters to sort out. Little knots of tourists were starting to gather, pointing and whispering to each other. I could see security guards stationed here at the Valley running down the track towards us. Director Ismail was a man with a lot on his hands. 'I will ask Zahed Mansour to arrange a hotel for you all tonight,' he said. 'I agree it is not advisable for you to return to your dahabeeyah. I suggest you bolt her securely and tell your captain to return to his own home tonight. We will meet again before I leave Luxor, by which time let's hope Ibrahim Mohassib has made himself known to me.'

Unsure if this was a threat or a promise, I watched him turn and stride towards the tomb entrance, pulling his mobile phone from his pocket as he went.

* * *

The prospect of a night or two away from the *Queen Ahmes* was not something I relished. But, as things turned out, I couldn't have been more delighted with the hotel Zahed Mansour chose. He arranged rooms for Adam and me, plus

Georgina Savage at the Jolie Ville hotel situated on Kings Island a little way out of downtown Luxor on the east bank.

Habiba was resolute in accompanying Ahmed to the hospital. She said she would contact his mother and sisters to let them know of his injury. She felt sure they would give her a bed if needed. Since I had no doubt she would soon be part of the Abd el-Rassul family, I was sure she was right. Mehmet Abdelsalam had friends in Luxor, happy to be granted a couple of days paid leave to stay with them.

Khaled and Rabiah proved immovable in their decision to remain onboard the dahabeeyah, promising to guard and protect her should it prove necessary. That Khaled loved the *Queen Ahmes* could be in no doubt. He'd restored her from the rusting hulk of disrepair she'd become in the latter half of the twentieth century.

I have to say it settled my mind to know they'd be on board ensuring she came to no harm while we were away. So, with everything arranged, we packed an overnight bag each and relocated to the Jolie Ville.

I daresay the fact of the hotel's location on its own private island was the reason Zahed Mansour chose it. Access was across a single-lane bridge complete with guard post. If someone wanted badly enough to sail up to the island on the Nile, scale the perimeter boundaries and creep across the gardens to interview Adam and me at gunpoint that may well be possible. But security was tight.

My delight in his choice had nothing to do with the security arrangements however. I had a deep and enduring affection for this hotel. It was here I'd been staying during my first adventures in Egypt; where I'd met and fallen in love with Adam; where the first secrets from Egypt's ancient history had revealed themselves to me. In short I felt right at home.

The sun was setting by the time we arrived. There'd been no opportunity yet for the interrogation of Georgina Savage I planned on having. It was a situation I was determined to rectify now she was here with us on her own. But no sooner was I about to suggest a quiet drink on the outside terrace, just the three of us (we were standing in the huge lobby finishing our check-in arrangements) than I looked up and spied none other than Saleh el-Sayed coming towards us from the entrance.

He was the very last person I expected to see. And, to judge by the look on his face it was plain he'd rather be just about anywhere else right now.

I turned to Georgina Savage, who'd not yet spotted him. 'Why don't you go and freshen up and order yourself some dinner? I suggest we meet for a nightcap outside on the cocktail terrace a bit later.'

She seemed willing enough to agree to this proposal, picking up her overnight bag. A porter immediately stepped forward and took it from her in readiness for escorting her through the gardens to her room.

Adam and I spun around the moment she was out of sight.

'Saleh!' Adam greeted him.

'What are you doing here?' I demanded, not bothering with a greeting of my own.

'Zahed Mansour sent me to check you have arrived safely,' he said.

'I'm surprised he and Director Ismail are prepared to let you out of their sight!' I exclaimed.

He dropped his gaze from mine and stared at the floor. 'I'm aware they could see me as somehow culpable in what happened today,' he murmured. 'For now they seem inclined to be lenient.'

I wondered if perhaps I discerned Director Ismail's hand at play in this, possibly hoping if he gave the Marketing Manager enough rope he'd hang himself.

'Right,' Adam said. 'We've got some talking to do. Let's order up some drinks.'

The huge lobby doubled as a lounge, furnished with deep sofas grouped around a central fountain, with a bar set against the wall opposite the reception desk. We virtually frog-marched Saleh el-Sayed across the room to a grouping of padded chairs and a sofa set around a marble coffee table. Adam caught the waiter's eye and ordered bottled beer for each of us.

'I assume after a day like today you're willing?' he asked Saleh.

The Marketing Manager inclined his head. In truth I'm not sure the younger generation of Muslim Egyptians is quite so abstemious with alcohol as those that went before.

We waited for the beers to arrive, sitting in an uncomfortable silence. I was quite sure each of us was mentally re-living the events of the afternoon.

'It was a fake suicide vest,' Saleh volunteered as soon as the waiter had poured our beers into tall glasses and departed. 'He'd made it with aerosol cans and chicken wire.'

'I'm sorry for your cousin's death,' I said automatically, wondering if I meant it. 'Were you close?'

'Not really.' He looked up and met my gaze. Without the designer sunglasses and having dropped the air of insolent civility, he seemed a different character – a lot less prickly for a start. Even so, I remained wary.

'Are you going to try to tell us you knew nothing about what he was planning today?' I challenged.

He looked away as I continued to stare at him. 'I thought he might try something,' he admitted at last, letting out a sigh. 'But I had no idea he was planning to dress himself as a terrorist.' He let this trail off, and then looked back at me. 'I think that's why he grabbed you. When the man from the museum shouted that warning, Eshan must have thought it would bring the armed guards running. Perhaps they didn't hear as they were stationed outside. Anyway, I think he grabbed you as an insurance against being shot. When the guards failed to materialise he realised he didn't need you.'

'And you told him to let me go,' I reminded him.

Adam took a sip of his beer. 'Why don't you start at the beginning and tell us the whole story?' he invited. 'I imagine you can shed light on the various misfortunes our security guard has suffered throughout this trip?'

I looked askance at this. But of course, it was all starting to make a horrible sort of sense.

Saleh fiddled with his beer bottle for a bit. The waiter had left the bottles on the table so we could top up our own glasses. I noticed Saleh was picking at the label with his fingernails, perhaps wondering where to start.

'Eshan lost his job three years ago,' he said eventually. 'We, the family, knew of the cutbacks at the Museum and the Ministry of State for Antiquities in the wake of the ousted Morsi administration. But Eshan's was a specialist role. He studied for years to become a philologist. We decided he must have done something wrong and been dismissed, although it was clear he'd had a pay-off of some sort.

'When he failed to get another job he started drinking. When drunk, he would ramble on senselessly about a papyrus scroll he'd translated, and about "precious jewels". None of us could figure out what he was going on about. When he was sober and we asked him about it, he'd clam up.'

'So what changed?' Adam prompted when he trailed off.

'What changed,' Saleh said, 'was that I mentioned your imminent arrival and the new project the Tourism Authority was sponsoring, with me as your baby-sitter.'

I baulked at this. Not so much the insult, but the insinuation. 'Hang on!' I argued. 'Your cousin Eshan Abadi had no idea who we were! He never met us!'

No,' Saleh acknowledged. 'But Ibrahim Mohassib did.'

'Of course!' I exclaimed, reminded of Ibrahim Mohassib's motivation in taking Ahmed temporarily hostage. 'Eshan Abadi and Ibrahim Mohassib worked together on translating the papyrus scrolls. It's possible they stayed in touch, trying to figure out why they'd both been bought off by Feisal Ismail. But in Eshan's case, he'd lost his job, so the sense of grievance ran deep.'

'When I happened to mention my new assignment he went nuts,' Saleh confessed. 'It brought everything to the surface. Eshan tried to enlist me in a plan to force you to reveal what you knew so he could blackmail the Director.'

'And?' Adam prompted.

'And I told him I wasn't willing to lose my job, too,' Saleh said. 'Employment is scarce in Egypt right now. Those of us that have a job will do anything to keep it.'

'So, you're telling us it wasn't you who arranged for those kids to let off firecrackers at Giza?' Adam pressed, narrowing his gaze on Saleh's face.

Saleh fiddled with his beer bottle some more and let out a sigh. 'Ok, yes, it was me,' he admitted. 'I didn't – don't – like you, I'll admit that. I resent my boss giving paid work to rich foreigners like you when there are skilled Egyptians on the bread line. It seems to me you're the reason my cousin lost his job and wound up dead today.'

I took a moment to absorb this. It was the most genuine he'd been in our company. And, put like that, it was impossible not to see where he was coming from. I felt an uncomfortable stab of mortification as his manner towards us suddenly made sense.

Saleh took a slow sip of his beer, swallowed, and went on, 'But I didn't want to get involved in his plans. The camel incident was meant as a warning. I thought if someone was injured you might decide to abandon the project before you got started and go home. That way I could perhaps take your place and maybe Eshan would come to his senses.'

'So, what did you do to Ahmed when he was sitting in the back of the car?' Adam asked. 'Weren't the sprained wrists and twisted ankle enough for you?'

Saleh looked blank. 'I'm sorry?'

'Did you asphyxiate him with something? He fell out of the car in a dead faint.'

There was no doubting Saleh's bewilderment was genuine. 'I did not go near your security man from the moment the car came to collect him.'

Somehow I believed him.

Adam also seemed willing to let it go. After all it was possible Ahmed had simply passed out. 'So, what about the concealed hole Ahmed fell into at the Ramesseum, nearly shooting his foot off?' he challenged.

Saleh picked at the label on his beer bottle again. It was quite shredded by now. 'That was not me,' he said. 'But I have a feeling it may have been Eshan.'

'Go on...?' Adam invited.

'When it became clear you were intent on making the trip, Eshan decided to follow you. When I saw what happened to your security man that day, I admit I wondered if Eshan had laid the trap hoping one of you would fall into it. Why do you think I was so worried at the prospect of your companion from the Ministry – Miss Garai, is it? – making a report to her superiors? I did not wish to alert them to trouble or spark an investigation.'

'Which is why you suddenly decided to be helpful in hauling Ahmed out.' I deduced. 'You realised that his gun going off could have changed everything. He was lucky not to be dead!'

'Why do you think I came to your dahabeeyah that night?' he hit back, suddenly animated. 'I realised he could have been killed, and knew I could perhaps have prevented it. My relief at the assurance it was a minor injury was genuine, I assure you.'

'And the syringe?' I asked guilelessly.

'Syringe?' he looked confused.

'I found it floating in the Nile close to where you'd been standing on the causeway.'

He frowned and shrugged. 'I don't know anything about a syringe.'

And somehow, yet again, I believed him. Although I saw in his face, as perhaps he saw in mine, a suspicion that maybe his cousin had paid a visit to the riverbank intent on finishing what he'd started.

'So, what do you know of your cousin's relationship with Ibrahim Mohassib of the Luxor Museum?' Adam asked. 'And about his movements over the last couple of days?'

'Nothing!' Saleh professed.

'You knew nothing about Eshan's knife attack while we were at the museum the other day?'

'He attacked you?' Saleh gaped.

'Not very successfully,' Adam murmured. 'I imagine he thought the knife would frighten us into submission. He reckoned without our instinct to fight back. It took him by surprise and he panicked.'

'Ibrahim Mohassib was the one who got hurt,' I added. 'You're sure you didn't know about it?'

'I swear it.'

And somehow, yet again, I believed him.

Saleh could obviously sense our scepticism. 'Where the blame rests with me,' he volunteered, 'is for telling him Director Ismail was coming to Luxor for the private re-opening ceremonies of Nefertari's and Seti's tombs. I suggested it might be better to direct his vigilante tactics at the Director himself.'

'That advice almost got Ahmed killed today,' I said coldly.

'It got Eshan killed,' he returned without emotion, trumping me very effectively. And then he turned the tables. 'So, was my cousin's death really necessary?' he demanded. 'Was that the price he had to pay for translating the papyrus scroll you found? I heard all that talk about "precious jewels". Does Ibrahim Mohassib, even now, know something that could have saved his life?'

I felt these questions settle in my conscience and had no idea how to answer them.

'I think the bigger question,' Adam interrupted, 'is whether Ibrahim Mohassib shot your cousin to save his own skin and pursue the "precious jewels" himself.'

Chapter 18

'A man died today,' I said to Adam a little later, shaking my head at his suggestion of dinner. 'I really don't think I have any appetite for food. I feel quite sick if I'm honest. I can't help thinking it's all my fault.'

The truth is it had taken a while for today's events to really sink in. But there was no escaping it. A man was dead. An apparently innocent man, only caught up in all this because we'd wanted to 'stage' the discovery of the tomb three years ago, and he'd been called from Cairo in his professional capacity to translate the larger scroll.

'There's been too much of this sort of thing,' I added. 'I've started to lose count of the number of people who've wound up dead because they've found out about the tomb.' And I started to reel off their names. 'There was Mustafa Mushhawrar, Abdul Shehata, Gamal Abdel-Maqsoud, and now Eshan Abadi; and that's without even mentioning the unholy triad of Said brothers. And, let's face it; wherever he happens to be right now, it's possible Ibrahim Mohassib is headed the same way. I don't like it, Adam. It makes me quite ill to think about it.'

He looked at me unhappily in the gathering darkness. We were sitting on the little terrace outside our room in the gardens. The inky Nile flowed beyond the palm trees across the lawn. Normally the riverbank scene and the caress of warm evening air soothed me, but not tonight. Tonight I felt cursed. 'Eshan Abadi's death was sickening,' he agreed. 'But I'm not sure I feel the same degree of sympathy you do. To my way of looking at it, a man who chooses to dress up as a terrorist in this day and age is asking for everything he gets. Those people in Seti's tomb today didn't ask to be frightened out of their wits. I rather think Eshan Abadi got what was coming to him.'

'If he hadn't lost his job three years ago...' I started to argue.

'I think we can lay the blame for that squarely at Director Ismail's door, not yours Merry,' Adam asserted firmly. 'He was the cause of the man's unemployment.'

'But, if I hadn't found Howard Carter's damned hieroglyphics...!'

He reached across and took my hand. 'Then we wouldn't have met,' he murmured. 'And, speaking for myself, that doesn't bear thinking about.'

I turned my head to look at him, uncaring of the single tear that escaped my brimming eyes to trickle down my cheek and drip off my chin.

'Merry, I've been thinking about what Ted said. Do you remember? When you shared your anxiety about encouraging holidaymakers to come back here?'

I stared at him with a wobbling chin.

'He said you couldn't take responsibility for their actions. That people acted on their own free will, made their own choices. All we've ever done since finding that tomb is try to protect it. You are not responsible for the Arab Spring, or for President Morsi being deposed, or for Egypt's sinking economy, or the rise of Islamic State on this country's doorstep. These, more than any action of yours or mine, are the factors that have pushed possibly good men over the edge to a place where the temptation posed by the tomb – however much or little they actually knew about it – proved irresistible.'

I knew he was right. But still the sick sense of guilt was gnawing away at me. 'I don't want Saleh el-Sayed to go the same way.' I said. 'It may be too late for Ibrahim Mohassib. Even allowing for the apparent suicide vest, he killed a man today. And I am not impressed by the way he used Ahmed. Whatever he may have feared for himself was no excuse. He could have been hailed a hero. Instead he made matters worse. I have no idea what got into him. But Saleh is a different matter. I understand now why he resents us so much. He's right when he says we've taken food from the mouths of professional Egyptians. His cousin was a prime example. Saleh had to stand by and watch his cousin go steadily loopy before witnessing his violent death. No wonder he hates us. I'm not sure it sits comfortably with me anymore to take paid employment here when there are so many Egyptians out of work.'

Adam was quiet for a long time, staring through the darkness towards the Nile. 'But remember our purpose in being here,' he said at last. 'Our goal is to put Egypt back on the tourist map. If we succeed then we'll create employment, not take it away. People will get their jobs back. And that will be because of you, Merry. It's a very worthy cause you're pursuing.'

I wrestled with my conscience for a few moments more, and then sighed, recognising the sense in what he was saying. 'Do you think Saleh meant it?' I asked after a while. 'When he said that personally he couldn't care less about any "precious jewels" that may or may not be out there waiting to be found?' It had been his parting shot as he left us earlier.

'I believed him,' Adam said. 'I don't think Saleh el-Sayed is interested in his country's ancient history beyond its ability to appeal to foreign visitors. He never would have been the right man for your job, Merry.'

'But I have to make sure both Zahed Mansour and Director Ismail let him keep his.' I decided. 'I am not willing to be responsible for another associate of ours going over to the dark side.'

The telephone rang in our room. Adam got up to answer it. 'It's Director Ismail,' he said, returning after a moment.

'I thought I had better give you a progress report, my dear,' the Director said without preamble as I took the receiver from Adam and put it to my ear. 'I felt quite sure you would expect an update on the action I have taken so far against the list of tasks you gave me.'

I wasn't at all sure how to respond to this, since I didn't know if he was being sarcastic. I mumbled something unintelligible deciding my best bet was to keep quiet and let him go on. I pressed the speaker button on the phone so Adam could listen in too.

'Ibrahim Mohassib has not returned home and has not been seen at the museum. I've decided if he does not show his face within the next twenty-four hours I will have no choice but to put the matter in the hands of the local police superintendent. The Governor of Luxor is understandably concerned about what he witnessed today, especially now he knows the suicide vest was a fake. He is starting to ask some difficult questions. I have to be seen to take appropriate action since Ibrahim Mohassib is on the loose with a gun.'

'But...' I started to interrupt as Adam and I exchanged a worried glance.

'Don't worry, Meredith. I'm sure I can keep you and your husband out of any investigation. As you rightly pointed out, I created this situation, and must be the one to put it right. But we cannot escape the fact that Ibrahim Mohassib killed a man today, heroic though that action may have appeared at the time. I will also ensure Eshan Abadi's family are fully compensated for their loss.'

'It's a shame you felt the need to dismiss him in the first place,' I muttered, finding my voice.

'That's just it,' Director Ismail said. 'I didn't dismiss him. I treated him in exactly the same way I did Ibrahim Mohassib. That is to say, I acknowledged that his translation of the scroll was suggestive of an undiscovered royal tomb. I explained that, in my judgement, Egypt was too politically unstable to search for it. Remember, neither Eshan Abadi nor Ibrahim Mohassib knew you had already found it. I paid him some money by way of a small bonus for his hard work and to buy his silence.'

'So how exactly did he lose his job?' I asked in confusion.

I heard him sigh. 'The trouble was, because I had personally paid him off, he thought he was invulnerable. He was found guilty of misconduct. One of the young ladies in his team reported him for paying her unwelcome attentions. I admit I don't recall all the details now. But it was rather unpleasant.'

'It's called sexual harassment where I come from,' I murmured, feeling a tad less sympathy for the dead philologist.

'There's no doubt he was in the wrong,' Director Ismail went on. 'He expected me to intervene on his behalf. But of course I couldn't, not without raising eyebrows, and begging questions. Given the genuine cutbacks to our services following all the political upheaval, my only option was to stand back and allow events to run their natural course.'

'But he blamed you,' I concluded.

'So it would seem,' the Director acknowledged. 'And perhaps I could have done more. But Eshan Abadi was the architect of his own dismissal. Sadly plenty of good, blameless men and women have lost their employment over recent years, and through no fault of their own. The majority have not taken to petty terrorism as a result.'

'And now Ibrahim Mohassib is out there with a gun, and just enough knowledge to be dangerous,' I remarked.

'If it should prove necessary to tell him more about the "precious jewels", I am planning to throw up a smokescreen,' the Director said. 'I'll say I hope there may yet prove to be secret chambers behind Tutankhamun's tomb containing the secret and until-now undiscovered burial described in the scroll.'

Adam raised an eyebrow. 'Clever!' he mouthed.

'But it does all rather make me wonder why you went to see Ibrahim Mohassib at the Luxor Museum the other day,' the Director said. I didn't miss the hardening of his tone despite the mildness of the enquiry.

Luckily, I'd had time to give this some thought since Adam had brought the Director up to speed with the events of recent days. I decided to stick as closely to the truth as possible, without telling the whole story. 'Adam and I have been on a bit of a quest for the last year or so to discover more about the origins of Nefertari,' I admitted, explaining how the Joseph Bonomi papers from Abu Simbel were suggestive of royal titles. 'We believed you when you told us you'd tied up all the loose threads,' I finished. 'We had no reason to think Ibrahim Mohassib posed any sort of risk. We just wanted to ask him to search his storage vaults.'

'I see,' he said again. 'And was the curator able to help in your quest?'

'I don't know,' I admitted. 'Eshan Abadi jumped us with a knife before we had a chance to ask him.'

It was as much as I was prepared to say right now.

'Royal titles you say…?'

'Suggestive of…' I repeated. 'We don't know anything for sure.'

'Ah well,' the Director said, apparently dismissing the subject. 'I agree it would be lovely to find out something new about Nefertari to coincide with the re-opening of her tomb.

But I can't help but think the tomb itself would be the place any royal titles would have been transcribed. Suggestive or not, I think you're heading down a blind alley.'

I didn't want to admit he might well be right. Besides, his mention of the re-opening of the tomb brought another thought spinning to the front of my mind. 'Will you still be able to go ahead with the public re-opening of the tombs next month?' I asked. 'I'm sure the media will have a field day with what happened in the Valley of the Kings today, coming only a year or so after the Karnak suicide attack.'

'I think I have been successful in ensuring it will stay out of the Press,' Director Ismail said sternly. 'Zahed Mansour and I spoke with the Governor of Luxor and agreed it is not in Egypt's best interests to let the story get out. The main perpetrator is dead, and, despite appearances, was not a terrorist after all. Ibrahim Mohassib is known to us and cannot have gone far. I am quite sure we can apprehend him.'

'But there were tourists there today,' I pointed out. 'They heard the gunshot and saw the ambulance take Ahmed away.'

'But they didn't see the removal of Eshan Abadi's body. I ensured the Valley was emptied of people and closed before I allowed it to be moved. I reassured those visitors I was able to speak to that there had been an unfortunate accident, nothing to cause alarm.'

I'll say that for him, he was proving adept at covering his tracks. It was just a shame he hadn't shown such skill three years ago.

'So, there are two things we've got to do,' I said to Adam as Director Ismail rang off. 'We need to find Ibrahim Mohassib before the police do. I still want to know what he came across in his storage vault. And we should ask Georgina to explain why she and Habiba came to the Valley of the Kings today.'

We found Georgina Savage sitting, as arranged, on a padded sofa on the outside cocktail terrace sipping a gin and tonic.

'Nice place this,' she commented as we joined her. 'Not up to the lavish standards of your dahabeeyah, of course. But it's rather wonderful to have a choice of swimming pools, and the chance to walk about a bit among some greenery. All in all, it's no hardship to hole up here for a day or two.'

Adam ordered a beer and I opted for a cocktail. While we waited for the waiter to deliver them, we each stared out over the shifting waters of the Nile, listening to the whispering palms and letting the warm darkness envelop us. A few bats flapped lazily among the trees and frogs kept up a chorus along the riverbank. There's something almost physical about the Egyptian night, a bit like being wrapped in a warm cloak. I took a moment to savour it while I mentally rehearsed the conversation I planned to have with Georgina.

As it happened, she was the one to break the silence. 'So, any news about how Ahmed's getting on at the hospital?' she asked once we were settled with our drinks.

'Habiba called a few minutes ago,' Adam said. 'Thankfully the bullet skimmed rather than penetrated his shoulder. They're keeping him in for observation tonight, but hope to release him tomorrow.'

'I hadn't realised they were an item,' she remarked, eyeing me over the rim of her glass.

'Until now, I'm not really sure they were,' I admitted.

'They'll make a fine pair,' she prophesied. 'They certainly look good together. I imagine they'll have beautiful babies.'

As this was a moot point, I decided to change the subject. 'So, tell us, what brought you and Habiba to the Valley of the Kings today? You weren't on the guest list.'

She sipped her gin and tonic slowly, and then gazed out over the black waters of the Nile, which shimmered with the reflection of the hotel lanterns strung between the palm trees lining the terrace.

'I was following Ahmed,' she said at last, without looking back.

This was unexpected. I'd presumed she'd come looking for me, although heaven knows why. 'I beg your pardon?'

She did not return her gaze from the Nile, but talked staring into the darkness. I got a sense that this was a conversation she wasn't entirely sure she wanted to have, but now she'd started on it she'd determined to see it through. 'I wanted to see if I could get him on his own. The wretched man has been giving me the slip for days. Until today, it didn't really matter. But today I started to make sense of things and decided it couldn't wait any longer. Since he refused to come to me, I decided I should pursue him. When he came back to the dahabeeyah from wherever he'd been this morning, seeming in such a hurry, and left immediately having stopped only to pick up his gun, I decided to follow him.' Finally her unfocused gaze came back to settle on my face, seemingly daring me to challenge her.

I decided the challenge could wait a moment or two. First I needed to put all the pieces together to get a full picture of this afternoon's events. 'And Habiba? I questioned. 'How come she was with you?'

Georgina's eyes were dark pools in the lantern light. After a moment she smiled. 'I presume she was following me in much the same way I was following Ahmed. Luckily there were plenty of taxis for hire on the riverbank at Gurna near the dahabeeyah's landing platform. I've always wanted to say,

"Follow that cab". Today I got my chance. I imagine Habiba did too. It's clear she had no intention of letting me out of her sight. She doesn't trust me much, that one, I think. I daresay she suspects me of having designs on her man! Anyway, the first I realised she was on my tail was when the guards at the entrance to the Valley refused to let me in. I didn't have a ticket of course. Ahmed had some sort of security badge and was allowed through without a murmur. I was just thinking I'd have to get quite high-handed with the security personnel when Habiba stepped forward waving her Ministry of Antiquities ID card and rescued me. Naturally I told her I'd come to meet the pair of you. I don't suppose she bought it for a second. But that's how we came to be together approaching Seti's tomb when Ahmed emerged at gunpoint. I will never forget the way she shrieked or threw herself forward in front of that gun. I did my best to trip the man up as he ran past me. But he shoved me and I fell. Of course, I had no idea then who he was.'

I was determined not to get side-tracked talking about Ibrahim Mohassib and his dubious motives and behaviour. We'd given Georgina a potted version of events on the way back to the *Queen Ahmes* from the Valley earlier, just enough to satisfy her curiosity without giving away the whole story.

She shrugged now she'd finished recounting the movements that had brought her to the Valley. 'The rest you know.'

'Not quite,' Adam said, leaning forward to issue the challenge I'd delayed. 'It is not at all clear to me why you were following Ahmed. You said today you started to make sense of things. What things? And why did you want to get Ahmed alone since I presume you don't actually have designs on him?'

She gave a small chuckle. 'As if he'd so much as look twice at me,' she said with a gentle touch of self-deprecating humour. 'Especially with a stunner like Habiba under his nose.'

'You haven't answered my question,' Adam prompted when Georgina returned her attention to her gin and tonic.

'No, I don't have designs on Ahmed,' she sighed. 'I think it's fair to say I'm off men for a while. I've a singularly unsuccessful track record in that department.' She took another sip of her drink while her gaze shifted from Adam's face to mine. 'But I'm not bad at piecing together a puzzle and sniffing out a story.'

All of a sudden my patience gave out. I was not in the mood to have carrots dangled in front of me. If she had all the pieces of whatever puzzle she was engaged in resolving I was damned if I was prepared to sit here and work for them, one by one. Frankly she was on borrowed time, and it had just run out. 'Why don't you just cut to the chase?' I snapped. 'Tell us who you are and exactly what you're playing at!' No sooner were the words out of my mouth than my brain started to whir madly and the blood zipped and fizzed through my veins. 'No! Forget that!' I amended. 'I know exactly who you are, and I think I can probably hazard a pretty safe bet about why you're here and what you're playing at!'

I was aware of Adam's head swinging in my direction, surprise and confusion in the movement. But my eyes were fixed on Georgina's face. Not by a flicker did she betray alarm or consternation. Annoyingly, she just kept on looking right back at me, still with that same slightly deprecatory smile on her face. 'Go on then,' she invited mildly. 'If you're right, I promise to lay all before you. I have a feeling it will need both of us in any event.'

Ignoring this rather cryptic remark, I sucked in a breath and blurted, 'You're here on the trail of the stele Sarah Belzoni found in Nefertari's temple at Abu Simbel!'

I heard Adam's sharp intake of breath alongside me. Georgina's expression didn't change but her eyes glinted darkly in the lantern light.

'But Merry...' Adam started to protest.

I held up my hand in a peremptory gesture, almost knocking over my cocktail glass. I righted it automatically.

'She knows about them,' – answering the question I'd cut off before he had a chance to utter it, and addressing myself now to Adam, while still looking Georgina squarely in the eye – 'because the story has been passed down through her family tree. She talked about having links here in Egypt generations ago. Unless I'm very much mistaken, she is descended from the British Consul General and Giovanni Belzoni's bitter enemy Henry Salt! Aren't you?' I challenged, narrowing my gaze.

She let out a shout of laughter. 'Meredith, my dear girl, you've holed it in one! As I once said, we all have to be descended from someone. After his death, Henry Salt's papers passed to his sister. She was my several generations removed great-grandmother.'

'And you phone-hacked us!' I went on, really on a roll now. 'After you attended that auction and saw Adam bid for the Belzoni lot, you listened in on our calls and learnt about this trip. That's when you decided to muscle your way on board. You've been stringing us along the whole time!'

She still managed not to look even in the slightest bit contrite. Infuriating woman. She kept right on smiling at me as I fired these accusations at her, not once attempting to excuse herself or contradict me. 'I sincerely hope it won't put us on opposite sides,' she said. 'I might be distantly related to Henry Salt but I've always had a bit of a crush on Giovanni Belzoni. I hope you won't hold my ancestry against me. I'd very much like to become firm friends, not bitter enemies!'

'Tell me where Ahmed fits in and I'll consider it,' I parried.

Chapter 19

But I was already piecing it together quite nicely for myself. 'His name...Abd el-Rassul,' I said as Adam motioned to the waiter for another round of drinks. I watched Georgina's face as I spoke. 'You clocked it when we were at Giza, and thought he might be a missing piece of the puzzle. I imagine your family papers inherited from Henry Salt mention Ahmed's ancestor, a certain Hakim Abd el-Rassul, employed by Henry Salt to ambush Abdullah Soliman at Seti's tomb and steal Nefertari's tablets from him.'

This was all guesswork of course, but Georgina didn't baulk.

In the absence of contradiction, I decided to go on with the story. 'The trouble was, a fight broke out and Hakim killed Abdullah, whether accidentally or deliberately, who knows? Hakim, having stupidly left his knife presumably sticking out of Abdullah's dead body, fled, was duly arrested and inconveniently died in jail. Of course, your ancestor Henry Salt also succumbed to ill-health about the same time and died in Alexandria. So the key question must be: what became of the tablets?'

Georgina thanked the waiter as he replaced her gin and tonic. Adam and I also acknowledged delivery of our refreshed drinks. Adam made no attempt to interrupt the conversation. He hadn't seen it coming – but then neither had I – and was content to let it unfold.

'I had thought maybe Hakim didn't immediately flee the scene,' Georgina mused. 'A dead Abdullah could hardly stop him making a search for the tablets. Henry Salt offered him a large reward so it seems strange that he apparently came away empty handed.'

Adam leaned forward with a frown, finally minded to re-join the conversation. 'And you seriously thought Ahmed might be able to shed some light on this two hundred years later?' His raised eyebrows were eloquent. 'You're forgetting the Victorian Abd el-Rassul brothers who came a generation or so after the Georgian ones known to your ancestor. They were an enterprising bunch of tomb robbers and gave the Antiquities Service the run-around for years. I'll bet if they had even so much as a whiff of stolen stele hidden and somehow handed down through the family, they'd have sold them onto the burgeoning antiquities market faster than you could blink!'

'I always knew it was a long shot,' Georgina admitted. 'But it seemed worth a try.'

So, all your attempts to play nursemaid...' I was still piecing it together. '...They were all in an attempt to get Ahmed on his own, in a weak spot, so to speak, so you could quiz him?'

Georgina met my gaze steadily. 'When he had the accident on the camel, I realised he was my best chance of hitching a lift. You'll remember I gave him a couple of anti-inflammatories to take while he was sitting in the back of the car after I bandaged him up at the Giza plateau?'

'I'm guessing one of them wasn't an anti-inflammatory at all,' I deduced, frowning.

'A sleeping tablet,' she confessed. 'But it had the desired affect. Actually, he passed out quicker than I expected. I'd thought I might have to keep you talking about Muon technology, or whatever else I could think of, for ages.'

A sudden suspicion dawned. 'And the syringe I found floating alongside the *Queen Ahmes* after Ahmed's accident at the Ramesseum?'

'It was only Ketamine,' she declared. It's a mild anaesthetic, but can leave people woozy. I'd thought I might be able to ask him one or two friendly questions. I reckoned without Habiba turning up to bid him goodnight. Luckily I heard her coming. When she raised the alarm and you all started to panic, I injected him with Atropine to bring him round again.'

'So much for the smelling salts!' I exclaimed. 'They were just a ruse to get you close enough to inject him, right under our eyes!'

Georgina had the grace to look abashed for the first time. 'My mother was a nurse,' she said, as if this explained everything. 'I'm always well kitted out with medical supplies, and I know how to administer them. I never would have done him any serious harm.'

'It strikes me between you and Saleh el-Sayed, not to mention the events of today, Ahmed is extremely lucky to be alive!' I didn't much care how accusatory I sounded. If Georgina wanted to be friends she had a funny way of going about it!

'As I say,' Georgina shrugged, 'I wouldn't have hurt him and I always knew it was a long shot. But today I saw something that made me wonder if actually I've had it right all along. But perhaps I've been looking at it the wrong way up. I'll swear the Abd el-Rassul family, certainly past and possibly present, hold the key to the mystery of Nefertari's tablets; whether they know it or not.'

'You *saw* something?' Adam repeated quizzically.

'Yes.' Georgina sipped her drink and lifted her gaze to mine. 'The portraits Abdullah drew in Sarah Belzoni's diary…'

I remembered Abdullah's sketches of the same doe-eyed Egyptian woman, her beautiful face framed by her traditional hijab.

'It wasn't so much the woman herself who captured my attention,' Georgina went on. 'More something she was wearing.' She lifted a carrier bag onto her lap. I hadn't noticed it resting against her chair.

'You brought Sarah's diary here with you?' I accused.

'There was no time to return it to you earlier on the dahabeeyah,' she shrugged. 'I wanted to keep it safe. Anyway, look, here, see?' I have to say, she was the most maddeningly unapologetic woman I'd ever come across. She flipped the tome open turning to the last few pages, then passed it across to me.

I lifted it onto my lap, feeling its familiar weight across my knees. Adam shifted closer alongside me.

'Look at what she's wearing around her neck,' Georgina prompted. 'And tell me where you've seen it recently.'

I sharpened my gaze. Alongside me, Adam's breathing quickened.

'It's Ahmed's Eye of Horus!' Adam exclaimed.

'The lucky talisman his sister gave him after he was hurt at Karnak!' I added. 'My God! I *felt* I'd seen it somewhere before when I saw it around his neck!'

'And you thought there was a clue in Sarah's journal,' Adam reminded me.

'I just didn't put two and two together.'

'So, who is this woman Abdullah sketched?' I demanded. 'And how did Ahmed's sister end up with the Eye of Horus before giving it to Ahmed?

Georgina finished her gin and tonic and leaned back in her chair. 'Those are the questions I've wanted to put to Ahmed. But I daresay we can make a couple of wild guesses, don't you think? Have you seen the family photograph on

Ahmed's bedside table in his cabin? I made a study of it this morning, comparing his sisters to the portrait in the diary. There's quite a resemblance, even after two hundred years.'

'Do you make a habit of snooping through our cabins when we're not there?' Adam challenged mildly.

'The doors aren't locked, and the photograph was there in plain sight on the cabinet,' Georgina defended herself. 'I noticed it when we were all in his room that night.'

'The night you injected him,' Adam said uncompromisingly.

She met his gaze without flinching. 'So I contend that Abdullah's sweetheart was also an Abd el-Rassul; one of Ahmed's female ancestors.'

'I think he said something about the Eye of Horus being passed down through his family,' I recalled.

Georgina's gaze darted between Adam's face and my own, her eyes gleaming in the reflected lantern light. 'So I repeat, whether he knows it or not, your Ahmed Abd el-Rassul holds the key that might yet unlock the mystery of what happened to Nefertari's Narrative.'

***

Adam and I were still several paces away from the entrance to the hospital next morning, planning to see Ahmed, when we were accosted.

I use this term loosely. It implies we were set upon aggressively, whereas in actual fact the manner of our being waylaid was really quite timid, if determined. It took me a moment to place the young woman who stepped out of deep shade into our path with a mumbled apology and an entreaty for us to stop.

'Jamira!' I exclaimed, recognising Ibrahim Mohassib's young secretary, though today she was engulfed in a voluminous black robe rather than the Western dress she'd favoured at the museum.

'Please!' she appealed, her dark-eyed gaze shifting from my face to Adam's and back. 'You help me, yes?'

Adam automatically stepped forward. 'Are you hurt?'

'Me, no hurt,' she shook her head, reminding me of her less than perfect English. 'My boss ...!'

'Ibrahim Mohassib!' I cried. 'You know where he is?'

She cringed, darting a glance around her, and raised one finger to her lips in an unmistakeable plea for me to keep my voice down. The Corniche was busy enough but nobody seemed to be paying us undue attention.

'Please!' she said again. 'He need help.'

'Jamira,' I said as gently as I could. 'Do you have any idea what happened yesterday?'

'Yes!' she nodded her head emphatically. 'Even before he tell to me, I know.'

'Luxor is a small community, for all it's a big city,' Adam murmured. 'Something like that will have spread like wildfire. The guards were all local men. Feisal Ismail might be successful in keeping it out of the Press, but he can hardly gag the locals.'

'The man killed ... bad man.' Jamira said earnestly, fixing us with her big dark eyes. 'Very bad man.'

I didn't know quite what was going on here. But with those words she convinced me she did indeed know the essentials of what had transpired yesterday.

'Jamira,' Adam matched his gentle tone to mine, addressing her as I had done. 'Ibrahim Mohassib could be in a lot of trouble. If he hasn't come forward by tonight, the Director from the Ministry for Antiquities is going to hand the matter to the police. It wasn't a good idea running off like that with a gun.'

'Yes. He telled this to me,' she nodded. 'You are here to see your friend, yes? Mr Mohassib, he send me to check Mr Abd el-Rassul alive. Mr Mohassib no want hurt him. He no mean gun go off. He very worried.'

I wasn't at all sure what to make of this, wondering if I dared take it at face value.

'Mr Mohassib, he telled to me to watch for you,' Jamira offered. 'He say tell you he have something for you ... you come help him, yes?'

Adam caught my arm as I moved to follow her. 'Merry, it could be a trap,' he warned. 'We know Ibrahim Mohassib is unpredictable.'

I thought of the effusive, excitable and hospitable man who'd welcomed us to the Luxor Museum. He'd greeted us like long-lost friends. True, his behaviour since had been bizarre. Yet somehow my instincts were urging me to give him the benefit of the doubt.

I reached out and caught Jamira's arm in much the same way Adam had taken mine. She allowed herself to be turned fully to face me. 'Jamira, has Ibrahim Mohassib threatened you in any way?' I asked searchingly. 'We can help you if you're in trouble.'

Initially clouded with confusion, her face cleared into a guileless smile. 'No trouble. No threat,' she assured me. 'My boss come to me for help. I help.' She shrugged. 'All good. All happy. Mr Abd el-Rassul no badly hurt. You here. You help Mr Mohassib, yes? He have something for you.'

Adam and I exchanged a glance. 'He has a gun, Merry,' he said. But I could see in his eyes he was torn, as hopeful as I that, this time, we might finally learn what Ibrahim Mohassib had unearthed in his storerooms at the Luxor Museum. And, let's face it: if Director Ismail got to him first it was almost certain we'd never get to find out what it was. It was a pretty powerful incentive to do as we were bid. He shrugged, 'I guess we can come back and see Ahmed later.'

'Hopefully they'll have discharged him by then,' I nodded. 'Habiba can be relied upon to see him safely into the bosom of his family while the *Queen Ahmes* is out of bounds.'

He took my hand as Jamira gestured for us to follow her 'At the first sign of trouble, we run. Pact?'

'Pact.'

We were quickly threading our way through the back streets of Luxor. These were dusty and malodorous, littered with rotting vegetable and fruit husks, animal waste and a strange assortment of old junk – we'd call it fly-tipping at home. In these less than hygienic surroundings children dressed in brightly coloured raggedy clothes played noisily, oblivious to the obvious health hazards. I watched my step as we followed Jamira into the back alleys, which I doubted had changed much since Belzoni's time.

Jamira didn't speak at all as she led us into this Luxor backwater. She glanced back once or twice to ensure we were following, but mostly just kept on moving with a quick light step.

I expected her to take us to a house, or what passes for one. Instead, Jamira ushered us through a broken wooden gate from an alleyway into a dusty yard containing a sort of stable. At least, that's what it looked like, with its cradle of hay, bridle tack hanging on the wall and piles of manure swept into the corner. There was no horse in evidence right now.

'My father has caleche,' Jamira said by way of explanation. I took this to mean he was currently out plying his trade.

There was a pile of none-too-clean straw in the corner behind a partition wall. From this rose a bleary-eyed and dishevelled Ibrahim Mohassib, still wearing the embellished traditional costume he'd worn to the tomb opening ceremonies. It's fair to say it was in nothing like the pristine condition of yesterday, sweat-stained, creased and caked in dust. That he'd slept in it, probably here in the stable, was self-evident. He'd unwound his headscarf. It trailed over his shoulders, revealing the livid scar on his neck.

He blinked at us a couple of times, then came rushing forward, almost tripping over the rope I assume was used to tether the absent horse in his haste to greet us.

'My friends, my friends, I knew you would not fail me. I placed great faith in Jamira's ability to find you and bring you here. I am delighted to see this was not misplaced! I didn't dare approach your dahabeeyah. I am a wanted man, I imagine.'

Adam gripped my wrist, holding me back when I would have stepped forward. He addressed the curator in uncompromising tones. 'You have some serious explaining to do,' he warned.

'Officer Abd el-Rassul, he is alive?'

Jamira jabbered something in Arabic.

'Allah be praised,' Ibrahim Mohassib said fervently. 'I would not wish his death on my conscience. I fired by accident. It was a reflex reaction when the woman outside the tomb screamed.'

'What on earth were you playing at?' Adam quizzed him. 'One moment everyone was cheering you, the next you were taking Ahmed hostage at gunpoint!'

'I was not thinking straight! After I killed that man, I panicked. I am a murderer!' he wailed.

'I don't think a single other person saw it that way,' Adam pointed out. 'I'm not sure shooting dead a terrorist really counts as cold blooded murder.'

'I knew he was not a terrorist,' Ibrahim Mohassib admitted. 'But I saw my chance to silence him and I took it. He paused to pick bits of straw from his clothes. Then he turned away and groped about behind the partition for a moment. When he straightened he was once more brandishing Ahmed's gun.

I sucked in a painful breath, aware of Adam going utterly still alongside me. I tensed, ready to put our pact into action and run for my life.

'Here,' Ibrahim Mohassib said, holding it out handle-side forward towards Adam. 'You take this. I have no further use of it, and it sickens me to look at it.'

My brain performed another mental cartwheel. Perhaps he wasn't planning to interview us at gunpoint after all.

Adam gingerly accepted the gun, checking the safety catch, and then gestured for me to pass him my cavernous canvas holdall. He zipped the gun inside without a word, slipping my bag over his own shoulder rather than handing it back to me.

Jamira watched this with satisfaction. 'Now you help, yes?'

Seemingly reminded of his young secretary's presence, Ibrahim Mohassib turned to her and murmured a few sentences in Arabic. She immediately smiled, bowed slightly in a respectful gesture, nodded at Adam and me and left us.

I turned to Adam for a translation. 'He thanked her for her loyalty, and asked to be allowed to talk to us privately,' Adam provided.

'I imagine I am a wanted man,' Ibrahim Mohassib said, sinking down onto the dusty floor and crossing his legs as if in readiness for a long cosy powwow.

I looked around for somewhere to sit, loathe to join him on the ground. I spied a plastic drinks crate, pulled it forward and perched on it gingerly. Adam crouched alongside me.

'I think it's fair to say you lost your chance of being lauded a hero,' Adam shrugged. 'Even so, Director Ismail is clearly reluctant to involve the police. I think he'd rather play it down given half a chance.'

Ibrahim Mohassib picked some more straw from his outfit, addressing Adam as he did so. 'Eshan Abadi was not a good man. I regret to say I feel no remorse for killing him. But I am not a man accustomed to having blood on my hands. When those guards came running into the tomb with their guns at the ready I saw your friend Officer Abd el- Rassul as my chance of getting away before they shot me. Please don't judge me too harshly.'

'Why don't you start at the beginning and tell us the whole story?' Adam invited.

Ibrahim Mohassib let out a heavy sigh. 'There were reports from the female staff of unwelcome attentions even during the time he was sent from Cairo to help translate the papyrus.'

'Yes, I understand he got into trouble for something similar at the Cairo Museum and it led to his dismissal,' I nodded.

Adam reached for my hand, his way of silencing my propensity to interrupt. 'Go on…?' he prompted.

'I'm ashamed to say I didn't pay it too much heed at first. I was caught up in the excitement of the story the papyri were telling. Of course, Eshan Abadi was sent back to Cairo as soon as he'd finished the translation. But I was there if you recall when you, your associate Ms Garai and Walid Massri started putting the pieces together to determine what the "precious jewels" might actually mean. It was clear you were all talking about the possibility of an undiscovered royal tomb.'

Looking back, I was appalled we'd allowed Ibrahim Mohassib to witness our step-by-step piecing together of the puzzle. It had been done for Habiba's benefit of course. Back then, we'd been intent on "staging" the discovery of the tomb. We'd planned to lay the whole matter before Director Ismail. We couldn't possibly have known he was already several steps ahead of us and had planted Habiba to discover the extent to which we were complicit in the tomb's cover-up.

If Director Ismail had let us stick to our original plan, the tomb would be known to the world and neither Ibrahim Mohassib nor Eshan Abadi would have had any reason to pursue their speculations further.

I understood, indeed agreed with, all the reasons for keeping the tomb under wraps. Even so, it was hard not to regret the consequences of our continued oath of secrecy.

'When Eshan Abadi was fired from his job in Cairo, he beat a path to Luxor asking me to hire him,' Ibrahim Mohassib went on. 'Despite having no need of a philologist, I felt sorry for him and offered him a temporary role. He'd only been in the post for a fortnight when Jamira reported him for indecent assault. Naturally I terminated Abadi's contract on the spot. He bore a grudge against me from that day forward. Periodically he would turn up at the museum, usually drunk, and threaten me with all sorts if I didn't tell him what he wanted to know. He said we should team up to search for the "precious jewels". I admit I didn't really take him seriously. I always ordered the guards to remove him.'

'Why did you claim not to recognise him when he stormed us with a knife that day at the museum?' I quizzed. 'Surely the balaclava wasn't that much of a disguise.'

Ibrahim Mohassib sighed heavily. 'I wanted to contain the situation. I thought him more demented than genuinely dangerous. I didn't translate his fondness for fondling young women into a real risk of violence or criminality. I saw I'd exposed you both to danger and hoped to deal with it myself.'

'Did you know he was in Luxor?'

'I had no idea. I was as shocked as you when he burst into my office brandishing that knife against poor Jamira's throat. At first, I thought he was simply back to repeat his threats. But then I realised he was speaking in English. I guessed at once he must know who you are. It put a whole new slant on things. I hoped by sustaining some small injury I could bring the incident to a rapid conclusion while I tried to figure out what to do.'

'You could have been killed!' I said aghast. 'An inch lower and he'd have severed an artery!'

'I misjudged that,' Ibrahim admitted. 'I assure you I had no intention of martyring myself to his cause. I value – valued – my job too much.' He gave a small fatalistic shrug as if to say he realised, as things had turned out, his job was a goner in any event.

'Why did you run when we showed up at the museum the next day? Adam pressed.

'Eshan Abadi had already tracked me down at home after I left the hospital. He insisted there must be more to the gagging order Director Ismail placed on us than we first imagined. Of course, I'd always wondered ... but your arrival in Luxor, coinciding with Eshan Abadi's re-appearance got me imagining all sorts. I wasn't at all sure what was going on. I persuaded him to allow me to return to the museum that morning to collect the item I promised you. I suggested I may be able to use it in a trade of some sort to get you to tell us what you knew. I was trying to play for time.'

I raised my eyebrows at this.

'We thought he'd somehow managed to kidnap you as you ran from the museum.' Adam pushed on, not wanting to be distracted from the point.

'Not quite,' Ibrahim Mohassib corrected. 'My poor wife was the one he used to bring me to heel. The man really was a monster where the fairer sex was concerned. I knew I had to get back with all possible haste.'

I tried not to imagine what torment his wife had been subjected to.

'I convinced him I needed to be at the ceremonial opening of the tombs, so as not to raise suspicions,' Ibrahim

Mohassib went on. 'I tried to enlist your help, you may remember, but the bigwigs from Cairo interrupted us. I had no idea Abadi would try anything so stupid as to turn up in a suicide vest – fake or otherwise!'

Adam and I exchanged a glance. Ibrahim Mohassib had been caught up in events as they'd spiralled out of control. I pitied him, realising he'd been thrashing about, clearly out of his depth, for the last couple of days.

Ibrahim Mohassib tilted his head to look at us now his story was told. 'So tell me my friends, did you find anything else to suggest an undiscovered royal tomb after Eshan Abadi and I translated those papyrus scrolls?'

He looked straight at me as he posed the question. But even though I felt sorry for him I wasn't stupid enough to drop my guard. Thankfully the way he asked the question provided the let-out. Since we had discovered the tomb a long time *before* he and the philologist translated the scrolls I was able to cross my fingers behind my back and answer with perfect truth. 'Sadly not.' I thought of Feisal Ismail's planned smokescreen, knowing I had to offer him something to satisfy his curiosity. 'I understand there remains some hope of finding hidden chambers behind Tutankhamun's tomb.'

Ibrahim Mohassib looked disappointed, as well he might.

I decided it was time to take control. 'You said you'd returned to the museum for whatever it was you found in the stores. Jamira said you had something for us. We have nothing to offer you a trade, but we'll certainly be willing to fight your corner with Director Ismail should it prove necessary.'

He met my gaze and reached inside the breast of his braided tunic. Drawing out a package he held it towards me.

No sooner had my fingers closed over it than there was a commotion at the gate leading into the stable yard from the alleyway.

I twisted to look over my shoulder in shock. Two familiar-looking men thrust the gate aside and strode into the yard. One was Director Feisal Ismail. The other was Ahmed Abd el-Rassul.

Chapter 20

My joy at seeing Ahmed upright and alert was marred by the sheer quantity of bandages wrapped around his left shoulder. He was dressed in a galabeya; or, more accurately, most of a galabeya. The left sleeve of this garment had been cut away to accommodate the bandages and sling he was wearing presumably to keep his shoulder as still as possible. Inevitably, he was limping.

The sight of the small woman pushing past the two men distracted me from a greeting. No sooner had the gate banged shut behind her than she launched herself at Ibrahim Mohassib. I wasn't able to understand her volley of high-pitched Arabic. That she was berating him with all the energy of a small human tornado was only too evident.

'Enough!' Director Ismail stepped between them. 'There will be time for marital recriminations later!'

So it was his wife, just as I suspected. I have no idea whether she understood the English. Perhaps Director Ismail's peremptory gesture was enough to silence her. Thankfully she shut up and let her arms fall back to her sides.

Jamira came out, no doubt drawn by the commotion. It was badly timed. At the sight of her, Ibrahim Mohassib's wife let out a shriek. It was only Adam's quick thinking in pulling Jamira forcibly behind him that prevented an attack.

I tried to look everywhere at once. My gaze fixed on Ibrahim Mohassib, shrinking backwards. Whether he was more frightened of his wife or Director Ismail was impossible to say. His stricken gaze darted from one to the other.

I had the presence of mind to slip the package he'd given me into my pocket while everyone's attention was diverted elsewhere.

'Silence!' Director Ismail barked. He looked around with distaste at the dirty stable yard as it fell quiet. 'Where is the gun?'

Adam pulled it from my bag and handed it over. 'Ibrahim Mohassib has not in any way threatened us,' he said.

Director Ismail took it and handed it across to Ahmed. Then he jabbed a pointing finger towards the cowering museum curator. 'You! Come with me! I am not prepared to talk to you in this pigsty! We will return to the museum. You can account for yourself there!'

He stepped forward and hauled the curator towards him. 'Ahmed, I suggest you accompany Meredith and Adam back to their dahabeeyah. I have no idea what they are doing here, but I will handle the matter personally from now onwards.'

'What about Jamira and Mrs Mohassib?' I ventured. Adam continued manfully to stand between them. They looked very much like a pair of circling ravens.

Typical Egyptian man that he was, Director Ismail looked as if he couldn't care less about the two women. I wouldn't swear it but I think he shrugged, as if this domestic matter were beneath him.

Ahmed stepped forward and with his good arm lifted Mrs Mohassib up off her feet. She screeched but made no attempt to fight him. Thank God! One more injury might just finish him off. He deposited her by the gate with a fierce look and a few words muttered in Arabic. She looked mutinous but stayed put, contenting herself with poisonous glances at the young secretary.

'Jamira, go inside and stay there,' Adam advised, giving her a gentle shove towards the door.

Director Ismail was already manhandling Ibrahim Mohassib towards the gate. As they passed, Mrs Mohassib hawked and spat in her husband's face. I gaped. Ibrahim Mohassib made no attempt to wipe the spittle from his cheek, allowing the director to push him out into the alleyway.

I couldn't help but think right now that as far as Ibrahim Mohassib was concerned maybe an interview with Director Ismail was the lesser of two evils. I wondered if he's been entirely honest with his wife about the events of the last few days. That she'd had a rough time and blamed him seemed clear.

Ahmed, Adam and I exchanged glances as the two men moved along the alley. 'Director Ismail is responsible for creating this unholy mess,' Adam said. 'I'm sure he's glad of the chance to sort it out himself. It was always clear he wanted to avoid getting the police involved.'

'Too many awkward questions about his own actions that he wanted to avoid,' I agreed sagely. 'It will be interesting to see if and how he can extricate himself – and maybe even Ibrahim Mohassib – from this one.'

At the sound of her husband's name – clearly recognisable even in English – his wife launched into another torrent of Arabic, this time directed at Ahmed.

He caught her flailing arms in his one big free hand and propelled her towards the gate. Adam and I followed them into the alley. Ahmed directed a steady stream of Arabic at the tormented woman, pointing her in the opposite direction from the way the Director and her husband had departed.

'I will ensure she gets home,' he said, turning back to Adam and me briefly. 'Her marriage, it is on the stones, but now it is not the time for all this. She did well to bring us here today. I am glad to see you are safe. But now she must go. I will see you back at the *Queen Ahmes*.'

'Wait,' I said, reaching out a hand to detain him as he started to move away. 'How did you know we were here?'

He flashed his megawatt smile. 'I am a good detective, no? My investigations yesterday led me to Ibrahim Mohassib's house. His wife was angry even then. Some man had turned up and attempted to rough her up – this is the

English expression, yes? She assumed this to be a jilted lover. He was threatening to kill her husband and said he would strike at the tomb opening ceremonies. I realised this may be the same individual who jumped you with a knife at the museum. I knew you were at the ceremonies and realised you may be in danger. The next bit you know. Then Jamira came to the hospital this morning. I recognised her from the last time I was at the museum with you. She thought I did not see her as she spoke to the nurses. Habiba had told me Ibrahim Mohassib was on the run after shooting me. I suspected he may not go home. I put together the pieces. When Director Ismail turned up at the hospital with Ibrahim Mohassib's wife – shrieking about her husband not coming home because he was either dead or with another woman – I guessed Jamira might hold the key.'

'But how did you know we were here?' I asked, still confused.

His smile flashed again. 'As I left the hospital with Director Ismail and this lady, Habiba was arriving. She said she had seen you both walking away in the company of a young woman in a hijab. She called after you but you did not hear her. I put two and two together – this is correct, yes? I asked this lady if she knew where her husband's secretary lived. It was as if a firework exploded inside her head! Believe me, she marched the Director and me here as if she were on a righteous crusade!' He beamed again, apparently very pleased with this turn of phrase.

'Poor Jamira,' I murmured to Adam. 'I'll bet she's just an innocent caught up in all this.'

'Just as we are,' he said tersely, then glanced back at Ahmed. 'Ok mate, you've proved yourself a fine detective. We'll see you later at the dahabeeyah. Oh, and by the way, it's rocks not stones. Her marriage is on the rocks.'

Ahmed frowned, then grinned. He never minded having his English corrected. 'Habiba, she is probably there already,' he said. 'I telled to her to wait there in case you came back before I found you.'

Habiba was indeed there when we arrived back at the *Queen Ahmes*. But she wasn't alone.

I recognised the three women sitting with her in the lounge bar, despite never having met them. If the photograph on Ahmed's dressing table wasn't clue enough, the family resemblance was certainly sufficient for me to identify his mother and two sisters at a glance. The older woman was dressed in the ubiquitous black burka. Habiba and Ahmed's sisters favoured Western dress; in Habiba's case a khaki patterned knee-length tunic over nipped-in-at-the-ankle trousers, while the sisters wore modest dresses in dark fabric. All three had headscarves covering their hair. I found it impossible not to mentally remove Habiba's and picture the pixie-cut underneath, glimpsed so tantalisingly yesterday. But there was no time for the image to settle. Habiba was quite clearly hopping mad.

'Where's Ahmed?' she jumped up from the sofa as Adam and I entered the room, her gaze darting behind us.

Adam moved towards her. 'He'll be along shortly. He's just seeing Mrs Mohassib safely home.'

'And you let him go?' she challenged, beautiful bronze-flecked eyes flashing fire.

'I could hardly stop him,' Adam pointed out mildly, taking a quick step backwards.

'Men!' Habiba spat, raising her eyes heavenwards. 'Only yesterday he was shot, and could have been killed, all because he was frightened for your safety. Today, when we came to collect him from hospital to take him home,' – she indicated Ahmed's relatives with a sweeping gesture – 'he marched off with Director Ismail because he once again supposed you to be in danger!'

'Ahmed *is* our bodyguard,' I pointed out gently.

'Yes! A bodyguard who seems to have had one mishap after another on this trip!' She stared at Adam and me with a hard accusatory gaze.

While I knew it was love and fear talking, I was taken aback, uncertain how to respond.

Thankfully Ahmed's mother chose that moment to intervene. She got to her feet, a large woman with an ample bosom and a gentle face. Moving forward, she drew Habiba's hands into hers, uttering a few softly spoken words in Arabic. Habiba hesitated then subsided, contenting herself with one last mutinous glance at us from under her lashes. She allowed herself to be led to the sofa she had just vacated and sank down onto the cushion.

Then Ahmed's mother turned and approached Adam and me with hands outstretched. 'Hello,' she said with a timid smile. 'My English no good. Ahmed try teach me.' She shrugged to convey it was a battle she had not yet won. 'You friends my son.'

I smiled and took one of her hands while Adam took the other. 'We love him every bit as much as Habiba does,' I said earnestly, and for the benefit of both women.

'But not in quite the same way,' Adam added with a smile of his own, also communicating with them both, his blue-eyed gaze landing on each in turn. Adam, when he chooses, can charm the birds from the trees. I recognised the assault and watched it work its magic.

Habiba jumped up again. 'I know you do,' she cried, taking my spare hand and squeezing it. 'I'm sorry! But I've been so worried! And I was so horrible to him before!'

I daresay we made quite a nice tableau, the four of us standing there, clasping hands. I'm sure Ahmed must have thought so, choosing that moment to burst through the door. (I should perhaps explain that Adam and I got a little lost trying to find our way through the back streets of Luxor to the more familiar parts of the city. Ahmed, of course, knew all the short cuts, so it was no surprise to find him a scant minute or so behind us.)

'Ah, I see you have met my family!' he boomed, the old Ahmed in everything but the bandages.

Rabiah followed him into the room, no doubt having seen our arrival. She brought homemade lemonade and cookies to welcome us back onboard, while Khaled offered to bring our bags from the hotel.

We settled ourselves around the lounge bar with our drinks. Habiba fussed over Ahmed to ensure his foot was propped on a stool, his shoulder amply protected with cushions. He submitted to her attentions with a blissful smile, dark eyes snapping with enjoyment.

'She'd better watch out,' I murmured in an undertone to Adam. 'She's at risk of turning herself into exactly the submissive little woman she's so frightened he wants!'

There was a rather strange moment once we were all seated with drinks in hand and the biscuits within reach on the coffee table. I was aware Ahmed's mother and sisters were staring at Adam and me, perhaps fitting the images and personalities of their imaginations with the reality of meeting us in the flesh.

For myself, I was no less inquisitive. I'd grown used to Ahmed's descendency from the most notorious and enterprising family of tomb robbers Luxor has ever known. But now with his mother and sisters in the room it was a bit like looking at a little slice of history. I was a tad awestruck if I'm honest, and certainly as interested in Ahmed's relatives as they appeared to be in me. Especially so, I must say, since – if Georgina Savage was correct – it seemed this family may hold the key to our current mystery of the missing tablets from Nefertari's tomb. The likeness of one of Ahmed's sisters in particular to Abdullah's sketches in Sarah Belzoni's diary was even more striking now I was looking at her in person.

All at once I'd swear the package in my pocket started to emit an electromagnetic energy as if it might hold a clue. But I didn't dare get ahead of myself. This was the female branch of the family. And in Arabic nations there are still social rituals to be observed when meeting ladies for the first time. It would be a mistake to launch straight in.

'So Ahmed,' I invited. 'Will you perform the introductions? We literally beat you back here by less than five minutes and haven't had a chance to become properly acquainted.'

Nobody loves the opportunity to hold court more than Ahmed. He sat forward eagerly, managing to puff out his chest in the same movement. This was quite a sight given the bandages.

'My mother,' he said grandly, accompanying the words with an imperious gesture and a respectful nod towards the lady herself. 'Her name is Kafele Abd el-Rassul.'

'Mrs Abd el-Rassul,' I also nodded towards her and smiled. 'I'm glad to meet you at last.' In truth, I knew little about his mother beyond the fact that Ahmed lived at home and had taken on the role as man of the house after his father died. Even so, my pleasure was genuine. It was great to be filling in some of the blanks in Ahmed's life at last.

She smiled back at me. 'Meredithd,' she said, pronouncing my name in the way Ahmed used to (before his new teeth and years of correction); that is with a definite 'd' on the end. 'And Adam.' She had no such difficulty with Adam's name, allowing for the unavoidable accent. She didn't need say more. Her beaming expression was enough to communicate how she felt at meeting us. I wondered if she'd be half so delighted if she knew of the scrapes we'd landed her son in.

'And these are my sisters,' Ahmed waved his hand again. 'Atiyah, my elder by two years...' He gestured towards the woman seated on the divan watching us with alert dark eyes. She looked so like Abdullah's drawing I caught my breath. '...And Tahirah, the baby of the family, who is five years my junior. Their English it is not good, but they will understand some of what you say. Forgive them please if they do not speak.'

Adam and I expressed all the necessary – and expected – niceties of first acquaintance, accompanied by lots of smiles, nods and gestures. Naturally these consisted of complimenting Ahmed excessively and lavishly. The Abd el-Rassul ladies nodded and smiled at us in response, conveying their pleasure without words. It was all very sociable and friendly. But in truth I was itching to get to the nub of the matter, wondering how to lead up to what I really wanted to say.

'Your family is famous in all of Egyptian history,' I ventured, looking at Mrs Abd el-Rassul shyly. I knew this was a risk. She must know of her family's notoriety. But I wasn't sure it was exactly polite to remark upon it. Still, I've never been known for reticence. Adam has called me a bull in a china shop on more than one occasion. I watched Kafele Abd el-Rassul's expression flicker.

Of course, the story of how her ancestors found the fabled mummy cache – containing several of the A-list pharaohs from the New Kingdom – is as old as Egyptology. It's one of those pieces of Egyptian folklore, made all the more fascinating for being true.

'Fame, it does not bring riches,' Ahmed's mother said. 'Perhaps only ...' she trailed off and turned to Ahmed, completing her sentence in Arabic.

He looked at Adam, at a loss for the translation. 'Joking?' he attempted. 'Funny? Bad laugh?'

'Ridicule?' Adam supplied.

'Yes!' Ahmed pounced. 'No riches but ridicule.'

'That's a shame,' I remarked. 'In my view it's one of the most romantic chapters in the rediscovery of Egypt's ancient past. Even the great Giovanni Belzoni, for all his fabulous finds, couldn't lay claim to actually unearthing the human remains of Seti I and Ramses II! And all because a goat fell into a pit shaft! It's quite a story!'

'Yes! My family should be hailed as heroes,' Ahmed boasted with a broad grin. 'The Abd el-Rassul brothers were true Egyptologists!'

Adam laughed, blue eyes twinkling teasingly. 'Perhaps you're right. Who's to say where the line should be drawn between collecting for the museums of the world and plundering for profit? Tomb robbery is tomb robbery, right?'

Thankfully Ahmed has a sense of humour and relishes his descendency from Luxor's most enterprising gang of antiquities thieves. 'Alas, my ancestors' motivation was not so pure as some.'

Mrs Abd el-Rassul and her daughters watched this exchange with indulgent smiles. I'm not sure how much they followed given the language barrier but they seemed to enjoy the banter batting back and forth. Having pursued their villainous antecedence this far apparently without causing offence, I decided the time had come to broach the subject I was really interested in. I reached into my pocket.

'It's quite fitting you're all here,' I said, pulling out the package. 'You were telling me about another ancestor of yours Ahmed – the one who murdered Abdullah Soliman.'

'Ah yes! Hakim Abd el-Rassul.' Ahmed nodded; eyes alight with lively interest at the sight of the package. 'You have information?'

'Ibrahim Mohassib gave me this just before you and Director Ismail arrived on the scene.' I set the package on the coffee table alongside the plate of biscuits.

Ahmed uttered a few sentences in Arabic, no doubt bringing his family up to speed on our knowledge of this other less than glorious chapter in their genealogy.

My gaze flicked between the faces of his mother and sisters to check if I'd over-stepped the mark. Thankfully they appeared perfectly sanguine with our discussion of the tomb robbers and cut-throats in their family tree. All three ladies looked at the package with avid curiosity.

'I'd forgotten all about that!' Adam exclaimed, staring at the little parcel.

'What is it?' Habiba leaned forward excitedly.

I shrugged. 'Walid asked Ibrahim Mohassib to search his museum storerooms for anything he could confidently date to the early 1820s.'

'We believe Sarah Belzoni spotted some tablets in Nefertari's smaller temple at Abu Simbel,' Adam provided, aiming to condense the whole story into a few short sentences. 'We think Henry Salt intended to lay claim to them but ill health prevented him making the trip into Nubia. It's our belief Abdullah Soliman, who was the Belzonis' *reis,* made it his secret mission to recover them behind Salt's back. We think he brought them back to Luxor and hid them in Seti's tomb. It seems Henry Salt may have got wind of this and possibly employed a certain Hakim Abd el-Rassul – ancestor to Ahmed and these ladies – to steal them back. From what Ahmed told us, a fight broke out and Abdullah was killed. Hakim was tried for murder and died in prison. We have no idea what became of Nefertari's tablets.'

Ahmed provided a quick translation for his sisters. All eyes were on the package resting on our coffee table. I couldn't help but notice the sudden stillness that settled over Atiyah, the eldest sister.

'So, are we going to sit around staring at it, or are we going to open it?' Habiba asked impatiently.

I dragged my gaze away from Atiyah's face and slipped forward onto my knees alongside the coffee table. The parcel wasn't very big; about the size of a smallish envelope; wrapped in brown paper and tied in string. I assumed this was Ibrahim Mohassib's doing.

We held a collective breath while I reached forward and pulled on the ends of the string to loosen the bow. Then I folded back the brown paper to reveal what was inside.

'What is it?' Habiba asked again, sounding no less breathlessly impatient than before.

It was a folded piece of white parchment paper. In fact, I recognised that paper at a single glance. 'Oh my God Adam! It's the missing sheet torn from Sarah Belzoni's journal!'

It was folded around a small notebook filled with closely packed Arabic script. This, I deduced was Abdullah's written record of his mission to Nubia to retrieve the stele. But that wasn't all. As I picked it up and carefully unfolded the sheet an object slipped onto the coffee table from between the parchment folds. It was a small wooden carving.

Adam reached for it while I opened up the sheet of paper. I heard the sharp intake of breath from one of Ahmed's sisters.

It came as no real surprise when I glanced up to see that Atiyah had visibly blanched. Even allowing for her Arabic complexion, she was as white as a sheet, staring at the small wooden carving as if she'd seen a ghost.

'What's the matter?' I looked in some panic at Ahmed. Her reaction was impossible to ignore.

He too was staring at the carving. 'It is her name,' he said. 'The carving spells out "Atiyah" in Arabic.'

I looked from the carving to Atiyah's ashen face and then down at the sheet of parchment torn from Sarah Belzoni's journal, which I'd now unfolded and smoothed out on the coffee table.

There was no mistaking the date – 1824 was recorded plainly at the top of the sheet in a black charcoal script. The year before Sarah made her abortive trip back to Egypt disguised as a young male epigrapher commissioned to join the Robert Hay expedition to Abu Simbel.

Underneath were two sketches. The first was a fine rendering of the Great Temple at Abu Simbel, showing two of the four colossal seated statues of Ramses II still semi-obscured by a mountain of drifting sand. On the other side of this huge sand dune the smaller temple of Nefertari was depicted entirely free of the choking desert.

The second drawing alongside the first was of the burial chamber in Seti's tomb, an exquisite rendering showing the alabaster sarcophagus still in situ.

Adam picked up the notebook, saw it was impossible to decipher right now and frowned instead over the drawings. 'I don't understand,' he frowned. 'Ok, so I know Abu Simbel and Seti's tomb were Belzoni's greatest triumphs. And I know Abdullah worshipped the Belzonis and was there for both discoveries. But why did he sketch them both on a page torn from the diary? And why are they each shown as they'd have looked when Belzoni was there rather than in 1824, which is the date shown at the top? We know Belzoni shipped the sarcophagus to England almost as soon as he discovered it, so it definitely wasn't still there in 1824.'

I shrugged, equally at a loss, staring blankly at the beautiful drawings. Then my eye alighted on the line of text at the bottom of the page. 'Look! There's a transcription!' I pointed. 'Oh!' – in disappointment – 'It's also in Arabic. Of course it is. What does it say?'

Habiba crouched alongside me to squint over the line of writing. She frowned, hesitated, then read aloud, 'It says *"A curse on anyone who destroys this page. It is a gift. A gift for my gift. She knows."* And then his name, *"Abdullah Soliman"*, and his titles, *"Reis to Giovanni Belzoni and Ghaffir to Henry Salt."*'

'Well, even if that doesn't explain how these items found their way into the Luxor Museum storerooms,' I said. 'It's clear why they kept them. That's two pretty hefty names from Egyptology!' Then I wrinkled my brow. 'But, "*A gift for my gift*"?' I parroted the text. 'That doesn't make sense.'

Ahmed sat up straighter. 'In Arabic, the meaning of the name Atiyah is "gift",' he said. 'Literally translated it is, "Gift from Allah".'

I lifted my gaze to stare back at his elder sister. Even though I knew she wasn't the Atiyah Abdullah was writing about two hundred years ago, it was an uncanny experience to look at her and see a face from the latter pages of Sarah Belzoni's journal staring back at me. She was still pale and transfixed. And there was something else in her expression.

393

She looked as if she were stepping through a minefield and expected one to blow up in her face at any moment.

While I registered this, Adam was putting the pieces together. 'So, it looks as if Abdullah is saying it's a gift for Atiyah – what though? The carving? The sheet with the sketches? Or both? And Atiyah knows... Knows what...?'

Nobody was given an opportunity to respond. The lounge bar door was flung open and Georgina Savage barged into the room. In a white tent-dress and with her chin thrust forward she looked like a galleon in full sail. 'Hello everybody,' she launched into speech as she came purposefully forward. 'Please don't let me stop you. I too would very much like to discover what Atiyah knows. You are that lady, yes?' she approached Ahmed's elder sister with the deadly accuracy of a heat-seeking missile. 'I spotted Khaled when he came to the Jolie Ville to collect your bags, Merry and Adam,' she explained as she plopped heavily into the armchair alongside the divan where Atiyah and Tahirah were sitting wide-eyed. 'He told me about your unexpected guests. Now Atiyah,' – turning to skewer Ahmed's big sister with a look – 'perhaps you can start by telling us where you came by the Eye of Horus talisman you gave to your brother? I know for a fact it came originally from Nefertari's temple in Nubia.'

I saw Ahmed's hand go automatically to his throat. He pulled the carving on its leather string from among the folds of his bandages and held it protectively in his big fist. 'Now, hang on a minute,' he started imperiously. 'This object has been handed down in my family for generations.' I wasn't sure he realised it, but in his agitation his English was faultless and almost without accent.

Georgina lifted her chin. 'Yes, no doubt since Abdullah Soliman gave it to the Atiyah Abd el-Rassul of his own generation, his sweetheart; having stolen it from Henry Salt, his employer.'

'And your forebear,' I muttered. 'Let's not pretend you're unbiased.' With Georgina here my chances of carefully stepping up to the conversation I hoped to have about the likeness between Ahmed's sister and the lady Abdullah sketched in the journal had been snatched away. If I was a bull in a china shop, Georgina had all the finesse of a T-Rex on the prowl.

Georgina's chin jutted even further. 'It is listed among Salt's excavation notes from his one and only trip to Abu Simbel not long after Belzoni was there. Alongside the original entry he's added a single word... "missing" ...So I can only presume Abdullah was as light fingered with the carving as he was with Sarah Belzoni's diary.'

'Salt stole it first!' I defended hotly.

'Two wrongs do not make a right,' she shot back.

Atiyah sat forward staring fearfully at Georgina. 'No understand,' she said tremulously.

'Oh good grief!' Georgina exclaimed. 'Don't tell me she doesn't speak English!' She didn't wait for a response but launched a volley of Arabic at Ahmed's poor sister. This was unexpected. I'd had no idea she spoke the language so fluently.

Ahmed had heard enough. A big man, he can be quite commanding when he chooses. He heaved himself out of his chair and loomed over Georgina. 'Stop! Do NOT bully my sister. I will not have it!' Then he turned to me. 'Can you explain to me please what is going on here, and what my sister has done to deserve this onslaught from this... this... this tractor of a woman?'

I knew the word he was really groping for was steamroller or possibly bulldozer, but I didn't have the heart to correct him. I sent a frowning glance at Georgina, and noticed she'd brought her bag with her when she came storming into the room. I spied a familiar leather-bound tome poking from its unzipped opening. Getting up from my position still kneeling on the floor by the coffee table, I lifted it from the bag. I approached Atiyah, sitting alongside her younger sister on the divan. Both Ahmed and their mother moved forward to join her. So it was in fact the entire Abd el-Rassul I approached with Sarah Belzoni's journal.

Trepidation was writ large in Atiyah's expression as she watched me. I smiled reassuringly, sinking into a crouch in front of her and opening the diary across my knees. I flipped the pages, found the one I was looking for towards the back, and turned the book around so she could see the portrait sketch Abdullah had drawn.

'Atiyah,' I said gently and slowly, enunciating carefully to give her the best chance of understanding me. 'We've all been struck by the incredible likeness between you and the picture of this young woman...' I gestured to the sketch, looking up at Ahmed so he could translate for me as necessary. 'As you can see, in this drawing she's wearing the Eye of Horus that Ahmed has around his neck. We're all wondering what, if anything, you might be able to tell us about it?'

My gaze went back to Atiyah's face as she stared at the sketch. I watched her eyes swing to the carving of her name resting on the coffee table. She muttered a single strangled sentence in Arabic. Then her eyes rolled upwards and she fell backwards on the divan in a dead faint.

'What did she say?' I demanded urgently of Ahmed, jumping up in distress at having caused this reaction.

Atiyah's mother and sister reached for her with strong womanly arms.

Ahmed also jolted forward at the sight of his sister passing out. But there was more than just concern on his face. There was surprise and confusion too. 'She said, "*At last, the curse it is broken*".'

Chapter 21

Thankfully, Atiyah regained consciousness quickly. We fussed around while she gathered her composure. Even Georgina – that maddeningly unapologetic human wrecking ball – managed to look discomfited at creating such a stir.

I was pleased to see colour return to Atiyah's face. Recovering from her shock, she seemed eager to talk. She turned towards Ahmed and launched into a rush of Arabic. I watched the changing expressions on Ahmed's face, always eloquent. It was fascinating to see his eyebrows inch higher and his eyes bulge. Whatever he was being told was clearly news to him.

It's hard to say how much Adam understood. He speaks a little Arabic and can usually translate the essentials. But he'd grown rusty during our years back in England. That Georgina understood every word was plain from the unmasked excitement in her eyes. Which left just me as the only person in the room at a loss. I decided there and then I really must make more effort to learn the language.

As Atiyah finished I turned to Ahmed for a translation. But Georgina Savage pitched in before Ahmed could draw breath.

'What a strange, superstitious lot these Egyptians are!' she started, quite rudely I thought. 'You'd never believe we're in the twenty-first century! All this talk of curses and deadly spells! Honestly!'

'Please Georgina,' Habiba interjected sternly, leaping to her prospective sister-in-law's defence. 'You insult Ahmed's family.'

'I apologise,' Georgina addressed herself stiffly to Ahmed's mother who, I have to say, seemed far less surprised than the rest by whatever Atiyah had divulged. She simply inclined her head as Georgina went on, no less rudely in my opinion, 'But it astonishes me that a hex can have the power through hundreds of years to part intelligent individuals from all rational thought.'

Habiba gave up on that lost cause of social graces, Georgina Savage, and instead took pity on me, providing the explanation I craved. 'Atiyah is the current holder of a secret handed down through the female line of the family for many generations in the belief that to break silence will mean the death of the eldest son of the family.'

It sounded almost biblical. But it wasn't the curse I immediately latched onto. 'A secret?' I'm afraid I couldn't help myself. I do try to curb my tendency to jump in but sometimes it gets the better of me. I was also unable to stop the quick glance I sent at Ahmed to check he was alive and well.

Habiba saw this. 'Atiyah has been worrying herself sick that instead of the Eye of Horus protecting Ahmed as she intended since his brush with death at Karnak, it has in fact been the cause of his various mishaps, casting some sort of malevolent spell over him.'

I was aware of Georgina Savage rolling her eyes heavenwards at this but thankfully she refrained from comment.

Ahmed finally managed to get a word in edgeways. 'My sister says she has followed the message given to her by our Aunt Atiyah who had only boys. But she stepped outside her instructions when she gave the carving to me.'

'Instructions?' I asked inevitably, willing to work for it. 'Message?'

Habiba perched on the arm of Ahmed's chair, perhaps wanting to align herself with him in the re-telling of Atiyah's story. Whatever, it was touching to see after so much misunderstanding between them. 'The message passed down through the female line of the Abd-el-Rassul family was,' – and she made speech marks with her fingers to indicate this was through word-of-mouth – "*Until you receive my gift, keep what I have given you safely hidden in our secret place. It is cursed. Your brother will surely die if you break this promise. You must not visit that place. My gift is the only thing that can release the evil spirit and prevent his death. The Horus Eye is for your protection. It will keep you safe. Wear it always.*"'

Georgina sat up straighter with satisfaction. I heard her poor chair creak in protest as she shifted her bulk. 'I told you so!' She looked at me in triumph. 'I don't think we need take too wild a guess at what Abdullah and the original Atiyah hid away. All his hokum-pokum was probably just to scare her into keeping it secret until he decided on his next move. He probably didn't want her going back there in case she was followed. I don't suppose he expected to be murdered.'

I was too caught up in the revelations to mind her self-congratulatory tone. 'And then, of course, the curse came true and Hakim died in jail,' I breathed on a note of discovery.

'None of which explains how the sheet torn from Sarah Belzoni's journal with Abdullah's notebook and the carving of Atiyah's name inside it wound up in the storerooms of the Luxor Museum,' Adam said. 'Or what Abdullah intended to do with them had he lived.'

'Perhaps Abdullah *did* know his life was at risk,' I conjectured. 'From what we know, Hakim Abd el-Rassul wasn't only in Henry Salt's employ, he was also Atiyah's brother. There could be all sorts of reasons for bad blood between them. It's possible these things' – I indicated the sheet of parchment and the carving of Atiyah's name – 'were discovered among Abdullah's things after he was murdered and simply filed away somewhere. Anyhow, one thing's clear. The original Atiyah never received them, and therefore believed strongly enough in the curse to pass it on through the generations. I daresay the deaths of both her sweetheart and her brother in quick succession were enough to convince her of its potency.' I turned to Ahmed as another thought struck me. 'It's strange both your sister and your aunt are called Atiyah.'

He shrugged, and winced as the movement shifted his bandaged shoulder. 'In our family the first-born daughter is always named Atiyah, and the first-born son Ahmed,' he said. 'This is not strange. This is family tradition.'

'Can we cut to the chase?' Georgina Savage cut in testily. 'I know for a fact that Eye of Horus came originally from Nefertari's temple at Abu Simbel,' she pointed at the talisman around Ahmed's neck. 'I'll bet whatever Abdullah and the original Atiyah hid in their secret hidey hole came from there too. The point you folks all seem to be missing is there's someone with us in the room who would seem to know where it is!' Her hard-eyed gaze landed on poor besieged Atiyah once again.

At this point my lovely husband proved his worth. 'I think you've said enough, Georgina.' His eyes were steely blue as he fixed her with a stare.

It's rare for Adam to use that uncompromising tone but when he does I've found it commands compliance. Georgina sat back heavily in her chair, folded her hands in her lap and clamped her jaws together. Adam approached Atiyah with a gentle expression and an outstretched hand. 'Atiyah,' he said softly. 'I think you may hold the key to a two-hundred-year-old mystery. If you can help us, maybe your family can become famous for more than just the discovery of the fabled mummy cache.'

Atiyah looked to her brother for a translation. He provided it, and her gaze went back to Adam's face as he let his blue eyes do the talking. 'The curse has been broken. You're the one who has received Abdullah's gift, and you are now able to do what your ancestor and namesake was unable to do, and reveal the hidden location of the secret your family has passed down through the female line through the centuries. You can release future Atiyahs from the heavy burden you have borne...'

I watched Atiyah's eyes brimming and realised just what that curse had meant to the Abd el-Rassul women through the last two hundred years. A heavy burden indeed – although I couldn't believe it was what Abdullah had intended. As Atiyah's gaze once more sought her brother I felt guilty all over again for the various misadventures we'd caught him up in. In all the years I'd known him, it had never occurred to me Ahmed had someone at home worrying for him and taking responsibility for anything that might threaten his life. He might not have a wife – yet – but the love of a sister was clearly no less intense. Superstition was one thing, familial love another. It was a curiously sobering thought.

All of which explained how Ahmed, Adam, Habiba, Georgina Savage and I came to be clambering through the foothills of the Theban Mountains that evening.

Ahmed and Habiba had flicked through Abdullah's notebook. It did indeed record his pilgrimage to Nefertari's temple to claim the tablets, his last entry noting his storage for safekeeping of them in Seti's tomb. But without time to translate the whole thing, I'd woven a story in my head – some of it from what Atiyah had been able to elucidate, and some, admittedly, a product of my own imagination. Putting the pieces together, I reckoned Abdullah Soliman and Hakim Abd el-Rassul were once buddies. Atiyah was able only to talk about the story that had been handed down about their employment by an Italian and an Englishman respectively. It took no great leap to arrive at Giovanni Belzoni and Henry Salt. It seemed this was when the rot set in. While Abdullah's star was in the ascendency, Hakim struggled on as a labourer. And when Abdullah Soliman became friendly with the Italian's wife, visiting her camp at night – I could only imagine this was when Abdullah spent time with Sarah to illustrate her journal – Hakim forbade his sister to continue the relationship with his erstwhile friend. I'm quite sure Atiyah-the-original knew Abdullah's relationship with Sarah was both innocent and professional, and continued seeing him in secret. But men are men, and allowances have to be made. It was perfectly possible Hakim discovered the clandestine relationship and determined to put a stop to it. Add this to Henry Salt's commissioning of the Abd el-Rassul brother to recover Nefertari's tablets after Abdullah Soliman hid them in Seti's tomb, and it's perfectly possible to see how emotions got out of hand. Whether or not murder was an inevitable outcome is anyone's guess. The fact is all the major protagonists – Abdullah Soliman, Hakim Abd el-Rassul, Henry Salt and the original Atiyah – died some two hundred years ago so we would never know for sure. It was a strange lesson in mortality. Even so, I felt I could sense their spirits drifting on the airwaves. Never one to believe in ghosts, I'd swear I could sense the echo of ancient voices and personalities. Of course I didn't dare mention this to Georgina Savage!

I was unsurprised when the pathway Ahmed was leading us along started to ascend. We found ourselves climbing steeply towards the escarpment that separates Deir el Bahri from the Valley of the Kings. As we reached the top, panting and, in Georgina's case, pressing the stitch in her side and dabbing her perspiring face with a tissue, we stopped to take in the view and catch our breath.

I've always loved this particular spot. It was possible to see Hatshepsut's mortuary temple nestled against the cliff in the desert basin far below us. Down there carved into the rock behind the temple was our secret tomb. I spared a fleeting thought for Ibrahim Mohassib, wondering how he'd fared in his interview with Director Ismail, whether the Director had been able to throw him off the scent, and how close we'd come to having the lid blown off our secret.

Adam reached for my hand as we gazed at the temple, and I knew he was thinking about what lay hidden down there too. But it was another secret we were here to explore today so I didn't allow our proximity to the tomb to distract me for long.

The sun was sinking behind us as we stood with our backs to the stretching cliffs and gazed across the strip of desert separating the mountains from the cultivated land with the mighty Nile flowing through it. In the far distance, smudged charcoal in the dusky golden light Luxor sprawled along the riverbank, twinkling with early evening lights.

'Right!' Georgina said after a short pause. 'Lead on Ahmed...' She'd recovered her breath remarkably quickly for such a stout girl. It said much, I thought, about her eagerness to reach our destination.

We turned from the view and stared instead across the tawny rock turning graphite grey in the stretching shadows. We'd brought flashlights, knowing how quickly night falls in Egypt. There really is no discernible twilight. Once the sun disappears on its nightly journey through the underworld darkness sweeps in on swift wings. It's an old joke that night falls in Egypt with a thud.

I'd made a half-hearted attempt to persuade Georgina to wait until morning to make this trip. But she was having none of it. She'd been on this quest for years. Now, with the end in sight she was like a hunting dog, nose aquiver with the scent of its quarry. As this search had become something of a personal crusade for me too I hadn't tried very hard to dissuade her. I glanced around and realised what a strange bunch we were, yet with so much in common. In Georgina's case, Henry Salt's papers handed down through her family. In Ahmed's, the story he'd heard today passed down through generations of Atiyahs. And in ours, Sarah Belzoni's diary on loan from Rashid Soliman who'd inherited it like his forefathers.

Only Habiba had no direct mission of her own. Even so, while I was sure she'd insisted on coming primarily to ensure no further injury befell Ahmed and to insist he kept his sling on when he would have discarded it, I couldn't help but think she'd realised that in marrying into the Abd el-Rassul family she may one day have a small Ahmed and Atiyah of her own – despite her protestations to the contrary. All things considered, it was a pretty compelling reason for joining us.

But there were risks to an evening trek into the mountains. Poisonous snakes and scorpions abound in Egypt and I had no doubt this was their favourite time of day, freshly alert after basking in the heat of the sun as it set.

As a precaution we were all wearing stout walking boots. All, that is, except Ahmed whose big toe, having been stamped on by Ibrahim Mohassib, was still swollen and too painful to squeeze into shoes. But, in common with most Egyptians, his feet are like leather. Even allowing for his limp he was making short work of the arduous terrain in his sandals. He carried a long stick, but barely used it. Ahmed, of course, is as fit as a flea and agile as a mountain goat, so I shouldn't have been surprised. He knows the inhospitable gullies, ravines and plateaus of the Theban hills like the back of his hand. This was his childhood playground after all.

But he'd never known he was so close to the hiding place his female relatives kept secret for generations but apparently never visited. I wondered how he felt about what he'd learned today. Ahmed is not a man to share his feelings lightly, for all his gusto and bravado. He could be forgiven for being a little shaken up by the revelations.

I felt vaguely uncomfortable that Atiyah herself was not accompanying us on this trek. After all she – or at least her namesake – was the original intended recipient of the "gift". But her look of horrified refusal was enough to persuade us from bullying her into joining us. Ahmed assured us she was relieved to be released from the curse and had no particular interest in trudging through mountainous terrain as night fell to uncover whatever her ancestor and Abdullah Soliman had hidden among the cliffs. She trusted Ahmed to find whatever it was and keep Georgina at arms length.

I decided I admired her. Even with all the talk of ancient curses, I'm not sure I could have grown up with a secret like that in my family and not gone rushing off into the hills at the first opportunity to see for myself exactly what all the fuss was about. But then, as Adam has often told me, I'm all too quick to rush in where angels would fear to tread. I'm also Western born and bred. Atiyah was my polar opposite, seemingly content with her traditional role and happy to live life in the background. In fairness, I was really starting to see what Habiba had been getting at with all that talk of putting her career in a marital cul-de-sac. Death by domesticity wouldn't be high on my bucket list either in her shoes.

If Atiyah's response was underwhelming, even if only in deference to her brother or as a result of deep-seated superstition, Ahmed's more than made up for it. I'd seen the gleam in his eyes. Of course, we all knew what we hoped to find. If the notorious Abd el-Rassul family was instrumental in unearthing something Nefertari-related, it could make headlines around the world.

I hoped he wouldn't be disappointed. There was every chance we'd follow Atiyah's directions only to find that whatever she and all the Atiyahs before her guarded so fearfully was gone, or possibly of no value. It didn't bear contemplating so I cut the thought off before it had a chance to settle.

I wasn't surprised to find the secret hiding place was here in the Theban hills. It seemed a thoroughly sensible location for anyone looking to keep something safe. Let's face it; this place was once a landscape full of buried treasure.

What *did* surprise me was when Ahmed started leading us down a scree-covered slope. Even in the darkness beyond the range of our flashlights I recognised the Valley of the Kings spread out like a giant oak leaf below us.

Atiyah had provided Ahmed with directions in Arabic, out of earshot from the rest of us. So I had no idea where we were headed. Actually I think it was Georgina she wanted to avoid overhearing our destination. Unsurprisingly, Atiyah seemed more than a little intimidated by our buxom houseguest. Or maybe she just wanted to ensure Ahmed got there first, so it was indeed an Abd el-Rassul who made the discovery.

Whatever, this was a familiar decent. Adam and I had slip-slided down this treacherous slope on more than one occasion on clandestine visits, arriving on the Valley floor alongside the tomb of Seti I. The significance of this was not lost on me. But after a scramble downwards, Ahmed veered off before we reached the bottom.

It was truly dark now. The slope was steep enough in places to demand a descent on our bottoms, hands out for balance. Adam waved his flashlight in wide arcs when he wasn't gripping my elbow to steady me. We kicked at the stones, hoping the combination of light, noise and ground vibrations would scare off any curious cobras. Luckily we were still a long way from the Valley entrance, obscured by a jagged overhang of rock, so I had no fear the night patrol would spot us.

Even so, we knew not to talk. Our descent was punctuated only with soft grunts and the occasional swear word as one of us missed our footing. I tried to keep my bearings. I guessed we were descending in a wide arc in a fissure in the cliff face behind Seti's tomb.

'Here!' Ahmed puffed at last. 'Dis should be de place!' In his excitement he forgot all about the pronunciation of his t-h's. He pointed at a petrified tree, gnarled and blackened charcoal in the beam of his torch. 'Dis is de landmark. Now, ten paces further on ...'

I admit my heart was in my throat as he counted the steps northwards from the grizzled old tree. I wondered at the centuries it had stood there. The cliffs around the Valley of the Kings must surely be one of the most arid places on the planet. To imagine the tree growing here where not a single blade of grass enlivened the rock was beyond me. But its skeletal branches stood testament to a different terrain. Its survival as signpost to Abdullah's stash seemed downright spectral.

All at once I shivered. In this ancient graveyard under the pinprick stars glittering coldly to life in the heavens, and with not a breath of wind to stir the dense air, it was all too easy to believe in curses.

I hesitated, suddenly wanting to call Ahmed back.

But a voice other than mine split the night. 'Stop right there!'

Our flashlights jolted wildly as each of us jumped out of our skins then froze, rooted to the spot with fright, before slowly turning.

My first thought was that the Valley guards had spotted us. Then I realised I recognised that voice, especially as it went on coolly, 'Would you mind telling me exactly what you're doing?'

I peered into the darkness on the slope behind the petrified tree. Slightly beyond the range of our torchlight stood a familiar figure.

'Saleh el-Sayed.' I breathed.

He stepped forward into the beam of our joint flashlights. The effect was rather like seeing him shrouded in a glowing halo. I felt another chill go through me.

'Director Ismail has returned to Cairo,' he informed us, rather shattering the other-worldly illusion with this prosaic utterance. 'He has taken the museum curator with him.'

My eyes bulged hearing this. Had Ibrahim Mohassib been given any choice, I wondered, and had the curator perhaps decided accompanying the Director to Cairo was somehow preferable to returning home to face his wife? Either way, it was a surprise, representing swift and decisive action on the part of the Director to remove the curator from the scene of yesterday's misadventures. Perhaps, still intent on damage limitation, he'd seen it as his only option to let the dust settle.

'Zahed Mansour has gone too,' Saleh continued. 'He sent me to let you know he will be in touch. I approached your dahabeeyah in time to see you depart, and decided to follow. With Director Ismail and Zahed Mansour gone, you once more report to me. So, I will ask again – what are you doing?'

We all stared at him, and the silence drew out.

'Let me guess,' he said when nobody volunteered an explanation. 'You are pursuing the "precious jewels", yes? My cousin Eshan was right all along. His words have forced you to make a move.'

My blood started fizzing. I suddenly realised what a gift of an opportunity he'd handed us. If we could convince him we were here on a quest to discover whatever Eshan Abadi had translated from the scrolls – let's face it, Saleh el-Sayed wasn't exactly hot on his ancient Egyptian history – there was a chance we could throw him off the scent and protect our tomb just that little bit longer, or at least until Director Ismail decided what to do with it. My brain started firing like a rocket launcher as I worked out that Ibrahim Mohassib already knew about our search for Nefertari's tablets. We'd even hinted as much to Director Ismail. In reality half the museums in the world – all those with notable Egyptian collections at any rate – knew Adam and I were searching out something alluding to

Nefertari's origins. It could do no harm to bring Saleh el-Sayed into the fold, and might also ease my conscience about the various accusations Saleh had fired at Adam and me last night.

'Saleh! I am so glad you're here!' I exclaimed. 'I'm only sorry we didn't think to invite you along!'

Adam and Ahmed knew me well enough to follow my lead. Even Habiba, after a quick startled glance at me, pressed her lips together and waited to see what would transpire. Only Georgina lacked the instinct, subtlety, or perhaps enough of the inside track to realise what I was trying to do.

'I can assure you quite categorically, young man, that I do not report to you, or indeed anyone else!'

'No, of course not, Georgina,' I leapt in smoothly and intently. 'But we do; and you are our guest.'

'Even so,' she was clearly unwilling to concede, and carried on in similar vein. 'I fail to see what business it is of this tourism chappie to demand an explanation for your movements when you're not on duty!'

I reacted quickly. 'You weren't in Seti's tomb yesterday' I said. 'We told you what happened. Saleh was related to the man who died. It is of course only right that Saleh should be here to see whether his cousin was correct in believing there might be "precious jewels" buried somewhere out here in the Theban cliffs.'

'"Precious jewels"?' she demanded suspiciously, eyes narrowing sharply on my face.

Oh God, I thought. *In throwing Saleh off the scent, I've succeeded only in putting her onto it!* I'm not sure I'd mentioned to her the part about Eshan's translation of the scrolls, saying only he was a disgruntled ex-employee of the Ministry of Antiquities intent on disrupting yesterday's ceremonies.

Saleh stepped forward before I could open my mouth to respond. 'My cousin long believed there was something buried secretly here in the hills; something to do with Nefertiti.'

'*Nefertari*,' Georgina corrected him waspishly. 'For heaven's sake, if you're going to muscle in on it, you could at least get your facts straight!'

The rest of us held a collective breath and, I felt quite sure, shared a single thought. Saleh was in fact one hundred percent correct in naming the Amarnan queen. When, after a pause, Georgina failed to make the mental leap that he was referring unknowingly to another secret burial altogether, I dared to believe we might just get away with the smokescreen I was throwing up.

It was Adam who held out a welcoming hand towards Saleh, helping him down the steep slope beside the petrified tree to join us. 'I've never understood the term "precious jewels",' he said, making me wonder if he had his fingers metaphorically crossed behind his back. 'We've always

415

believed we were searching for some stele originally from Queen Nefertari's temple in Nubia.'

When nobody argued I allowed myself to breathe again. I looked at Saleh. 'I know you don't approve of our employment by your Tourism Authority, and I understand the reasons why,' I said warmly. This much was certainly true. 'But we're very much hoping – if we do discover something here tonight – it may be enough to entice tourists to once more consider Egypt a holiday destination of choice.' This was stretching things a bit. But I was already resigned to the fact that, with so many people already in the know – one a journalist for heaven's sake – there was no way we could hope to keep this find to ourselves.

'The hiding place,' Ahmed announced grandly from a few paces away. 'This must be it!'

Chapter 22

Ahmed's words succeeded in cutting off further debate, even if anyone wanted it. We turned and trained our collective flashlight beams on the spot he was indicating. It was quite clearly the mouth of a small cave set into the rock.

We almost fell over ourselves in our haste to join him. Unsurprisingly, Georgina managed to barge Adam, Habiba and me out of her way so she was the first to crouch and shine her torch into the dark cavity. The cave looked to be about five metres deep after a drop from the entrance of a metre or so. At the far end I could see a wooden board wedged into a hole at waist height.

'That's been put there by human hand,' I breathed on a rising note of excitement. 'It looks a bit rotten, I'll grant you. But promising nevertheless!'

'I should be the one to check it out,' Georgina asserted, pushing me aside. 'After all, my relative Henry Salt would have brought Nefertari's tablets to light two hundred years ago if only that scoundrel Abdullah Soliman hadn't stolen a march on him!'

'Interesting choice of words,' I remarked tartly, recovering my balance and glaring at her, '...considering Henry Salt only knew about Nefertari's tablets because he stole Sarah Belzoni's journal. She's the one who discovered them first! And I'm the one following in her footsteps!"

'You could argue that Rashid Soliman ought to be here to make the discovery,' Adam said with quiet authority. 'Sarah's journal has been passed down through generations of his family after all, thanks to Abdullah's sketches. As Rashid is sponsoring me to make this trip, perhaps I should be the one…'

Ahmed cut him off with a muffled roar. 'But my family have kept this place secret through two centuries. Without us, it might never be found.'

Habiba spoke up, proving that, much as she may love Ahmed, she was her own woman and a career one first and foremost. 'Really, the Ministry of Antiquities…' she began.

'No!' Ahmed cried in alarm. 'I will not have you crawling into this hole!' To prove the point, he dropped down on his knees, cursing his sling as it stopped him going further.

At Ahmed's sudden motion, I caught a movement at the mouth of the cave from the corner of my eye. But before I could pull him backwards, Saleh el-Sayed darted forward. 'Your employment in Egypt is thanks to the Tourism Authority. As its most senior ranking official here, I will be the one to investigate.' And with no further ado he slid forward into the cave.

As he did, a long black shape uncoiled, reared up and spread its hood.

418

We froze.

The swaying cobra was caught in the harsh beams from five separate flashlights. Adam, Ahmed, Habiba, Georgina and I stared in horror.

'Don't move, Saleh!' Adam commanded urgently.

But the deadly snake already had him in its sights, the glare from our combined flashlights not enough to blind it. As it reared back I acted without thinking, hurling my big torch with all my strength.

It hit the rearing cobra between the eyes, snapping its swaying head backwards. The impact lifted the snake fully off the ground, spinning it backwards. It landed heavily with a furious hiss, coiling around itself as it regained balance and prepared once more to strike. My flashlight clattered against the rock, smashed to the floor in a cascade of shattered glass and went out.

Adam reacted in a heartbeat, reaching forward to grab Saleh and haul him backwards. With his good arm, Ahmed reached too so, between them, they heaved him upwards. When the strike came, seemingly in slow motion in the glare from Georgina and Habiba's joint flashlights, it connected with Saleh's foot. I watched with my heart lodged in my throat as the snake's fangs locked around the toe of Saleh's right shoe. Unlike the rest of us, he had not come out tonight expecting a trek through the cliffs. He was wearing smart loafers in brown leather.

While I'll admit there was a time I might have rejoiced in the Marketing Manager's misfortune, right now I could only pray the leather was thick enough to prevent the venom penetrating.

It was a curiously frozen moment as we all watched the deadly snake hanging by its jaws from Saleh's foot while Adam and Ahmed pulled him fully from the cave. Of course, as Saleh came, the cobra came too, fangs still clamped around his shoe.

I'm not sure what any of us would have done if it hadn't been for Georgina's quick thinking. Free of the cave now, we were all within striking range. But as Habiba kept her flashlight trained on the snake, as Adam and Ahmed pulled Saleh back onto the slope and as I watched paralysed with fear, all bravery and strength extinguished along with my broken torch, Georgina was easing her rucksack off her shoulders and unbuttoning her shirt.

As the snake let go of Saleh's foot, falling to the floor near the mouth of the cave and coiling in preparation for another strike, Georgina shrugged out of her shirt and threw it over the cobra.

There are advantages to being a big, buxom girl. The shirt was large, completely covering the snake, which did not lack for size itself. I watched in a kind of primordial fascination as the creature writhed beneath the cotton, causing the fabric to ripple and roll.

'They think it's a place of safety,' she murmured. 'Habiba, don't train your flashlight on it directly. Let it think it's back in the dark.'

I saw what it cost poor Habiba to pull the beam from her torch away.

Georgina was now emptying out the contents of her rucksack. I observed her medical kit and a large bottle of water drop onto the dust. Quick as a flash, as the snake's motion beneath her shirt stilled, she slid the opening of her bag firmly along the ground, scooping up the snake, shirt and all, into the rucksack, quickly pulling it closed and securing the buckle. Then she stood back in satisfaction, holding her rucksack aloft with the snake inside.

I was so impressed I managed not to be in the least perturbed by the sight of her standing there with her ample bosom spilling from a too-small pink-and-lace bra unequal to the task of containing it, and the great white mound of her stomach protruding above the elasticated waistband of her jeans.

'Bloody hell, Georgina; that took some doing!' Adam congratulated her, the first to recover his voice. 'Here,' you'd better wear this...' And he shrugged out of his own shirt.

The gesture was chivalrous, as I've come to expect from my husband, but fell somewhat flat when it became clear there was no way the buttons were going to do up across Georgina's bust. The sight of her pink bra and white flesh straining at the buttonholes was almost worse than seeing her semi-naked.

'Allow me... please...' Ahmed eased out of his sling, averting his eyes from our buxom heroine. It was clear his galabeya, although cut away at the shoulder to allow for his bandages, was the only garment big enough to give Georgina her modesty back.

I watched Ahmed, with Habiba's help, prise it over his head, my gaze almost as riveted as it had been a few moments ago fixed on the snake. I'd long wondered what, if anything, Egyptian men wore beneath their galabeyas. In Ahmed's case it turned out to be a pair of knee-length, drawstring cotton pants. I don't mind admitting the sight of him standing there with the musculature of his tanned torso on display, bandaged though it was, was a damned sight easier on my female eye than Georgina's wobbly bits had been. A big man, Ahmed had toned up in the years since knowing Habiba. What had once been an ample stomach of his own was now taut beneath his broad chest. I refused to allow my gaze to stray lower after that first glance at his underwear. While not transparent, the fall of the fabric hinted at certain male shapes beneath. Habiba was a very lucky woman, I decided, before snapping my attention back to the rucksack.

'What are we going to do with the snake?' I asked.

Clad now in Ahmed's galabeya, Georgina regained her directness along with her decency. 'We came in search of

Nefertari's tablets,' she said. 'I, for one, have not come this close to finding them only to retreat! We can decide what to do about the snake later. Now, Saleh, are you quite recovered?'

I'd almost forgotten about poor Saleh, lying shaking on the ground. In the reflected beam of the flashlights dropped at our feet I could see the long trail of venom dripping from his shoe.

'You'd better take that off and check the fangs didn't penetrate,' I advised. He sat up jerkily and Adam helped him prise the shoe off his foot, holding it carefully by the heel. We inspected his toes closely. 'No harm done,' I nodded, satisfied. 'Thank God it wasn't Ahmed in his sandals!'

Saleh gazed up at me. He was dusty and sweating, a long way from the sneering, sartorial young man who'd accompanied us to the top of the Great Pyramid. 'You saved my life!' he murmured.

'Nonsense, I said briskly. 'Georgina did that. She probably saved us all.'

'If you hadn't thrown your torch at the snake when you did…'

'I was just the first one to move,' I shrugged. 'Adam and Ahmed were the ones who hauled you out of the cave.'

'Thank you,' he said quietly. 'Thank you all. I know I have not welcomed you back to my country. But I hope now we may wipe the slate clean and perhaps be friends.' He was sitting up as he said this, putting his bare foot on the ground in readiness to get up.

I was about to respond warmly when he yelped. Pain swept across his handsome face. My heart lurched, instantly fearing another deadly cobra.

Adam swung his torch. Thank God, not a snake; but a small black scorpion scuttled out of the beam of yellow light. In fact, now I looked closely there were a number of them scurrying about the mouth of the cave, no doubt disturbed by all the unaccustomed commotion in their quiet, dark sanctuary.

'Scorpions!' I cried out in alarm. 'One's stung Saleh!'

Saleh was clutching his foot, sweating and grunting with pain. 'It's burning,' he muttered.

Adam dropped on one knee. 'Scorpions give a nasty sting but it's not usually life-threatening.'

I watched the red welt coming up on the side of Saleh's foot and remembered Atiyah's fixation with curses. Snakes and scorpions might occur in Egypt in nature but they were still pretty strong maledictions, the ancient snake god Apophis and scorpion goddess Serqet respectively.

Ahmed was using the fabric of his sling to sweep away the horrid black creatures as they emerged from the cave, their tails curled up and quivering.

I could see Saleh's eyes starting to bulge, his breathing dry, rasping and irregular. 'Unless you happen to be allergic to them,' I said worriedly, meeting Adam's gaze in the torchlight. 'Then a sting can cause anaphylaxis.' I knew this because my brother was allergic to bee stings. Looking at Saleh I recognised the signs. 'Georgina!' I called her over. 'If ever there was a need for you to play Florence Nightingale, it's now!'

'Habiba, keep an eye on that rucksack,' Georgina said tersely. She scooped her medical kit out of the dust and came forward. 'I don't have a cold compress,' she muttered.

'It's not so much a cold pack as a shot of Adrenaline he needs,' I advised, knowing that's what worked for my brother. 'And some Antihistamine.'

Georgina rooted around in her supplies. 'Yes! I think I have both!'

The woman really was a walking pharmacy. Right now I could only be grateful for it. I was really quite relieved to hand Saleh over into her care.

Georgina prepared her syringe. Habiba kept her flashlight trained on her. Ahmed, wearing only his drawstring pants, bandages and his sandals kept up his work clearing away the scuttling scorpions with his sling. Adam and I lifted our heads and locked gazes.

'So, are we going to check out what's behind that chunk of wood?' he asked quietly, cocking his head towards the back of the cave.

'I think we'd better so we can get out of here,' I said in the tones of one making a sacrifice for the greater good. In truth, the snake and scorpions notwithstanding, I was raring to go. Perhaps it was the sight of Ahmed in his underpants and Georgina firing up her syringe making the energy zip through my bloodstream. I felt I had adrenaline enough for both Saleh and me, and probably more besides.

This, in part, was what I had come back to Egypt for. This was me, Meredith Pink – ok, Tennyson-Pink – doing what I loved best: throwing caution to the winds alongside the man I loved, allowing Egypt to reveal her hidden secrets to me. There was no way on earth I was leaving without exploring that hole.

Even so, now it was just the two of us contemplating entering the cave, common sense reasserted itself. We did what any sensible person would have done in the first place, rather than standing around quibbling over whose privilege it should be to go in first.

Adam reached into his rucksack and pulled out a flare. Lighting the end with a match he threw it forward into the cave. It popped, flashed fire and filled the cave with acrid smoke.

'That should clear it of anything else that might be inclined to bite or sting us,' Adam said, standing back to allow the smoke to clear.

We took the precaution of several long, slow sweeps into the cave with the flashlights even so. I'd commandeered Georgina's torch to replace my smashed one.

'My friends, I beg of you to be careful,' Ahmed entreated as we crouched in readiness to swing ourselves down inside the cave. 'The scorpions, they can drop into your hair from above. You need fire.' With no further ado, he unwrapped a section of bandages from around his shoulder, winding them around the big walking stick he'd brought with him but barely used.

'What are you doing?' Habiba demanded furiously. 'Ahmed, you have a bullet hole in your shoulder!'

'I am body guard, yet even I realise I cannot accompany them with my injuries in case swift exit is needed,' Ahmed said imperiously. 'So I must do what I can to protect them from afar.' He took a match from the box Adam had used earlier and set light to the bandages, making a flaming torch. 'I have no oil I can dip it in,' he said seriously, 'So it will not burn for long, but it should see you to the other side of the cave. Wave it at the roof to deter the scorpions.'

'Wait!' Georgina said from her position crouched over Saleh on the ground. 'I have some hemp seed oil in my medical kit. That should increase the flammability.' She rummaged some more and offered Ahmed a plastic bottle, then turned back to her patient. 'Right, Saleh, let's get this Adrenaline into you. I hope you don't mind needles.'

I didn't watch her inject the raggedy-breathed Marketing Manager. Instead I focused on Ahmed as he uncapped the bottle and poured oil onto the flaming bandages.

'Goddamit, Ahmed; it's like something from Bonfire Night!' Adam exclaimed as the already flaming torch exploded into a blazing inferno atop the stick. 'If the scorpions aren't lethal, that thing damn well is!'

'Hurummph!' Ahmed intoned eloquently. 'Just take it. It will protect you.'

Adam accepted the stick.

Ahmed met my gaze. 'But just in case...' The next thing I knew, he'd pulled the Eye of Horus on its leather string over his own head and lowered it over mine. 'This will keep you safe.'

I didn't like to remind him that it had failed quite spectacularly in this regard for him. His superstitious belief was well meant and touching. In truth, it brought tears to my eyes.

As it settled heavily against my chest, I felt the weight of history not just the ancient stone come over me. Glancing at our small party, I had a strange out-of-body experience. Adam, holding the flaming torch aloft and seeming bigger in its glare could have been Giovanni Belzoni about to explore an ancient tomb. Ahmed, in his long cotton briefs might well have been his Egyptian *reis*. Georgina, in the torn galabeya, with her hair coming out of its clips to cascade around her face, and tending to the man sprawled on the ground looked like one of Abdullah's sketches brought to life. It was a curious time slip moment.

'Ok Merry; let's go,' Adam said. Rather thrillingly he leaned forward and kissed me full on the mouth, reminding me of all the other times we'd risked life and limb to uncover Egypt's ancient secrets. Then he allowed Ahmed to grip his upper arm, helping him drop forward into the cave; where he turned, holding the flaming torch behind him so he could lift me down to join him.

Caught up in the magic of the moment, I forgot all about cobras and scorpions. Forgot even about the little glimpse of history I'd just had. I recognised the light in Adam's eyes. This was just him and me and the thrill of discovery. This was just as it was meant to be. Events had transpired to keep Saleh and Georgina away from the critical moment of discovery – whatever it may prove to be – with Ahmed and Habiba looking on, as Adam and I allowed fate to steer us.

'Are you feeling the same overwhelming sense of destiny I am?' Adam whispered. 'Don't you just know we're going to find something?'

'Egypt called us back for a reason,' I murmured, reaching out to touch his free hand.

Adam held the flaming torch aloft and I kept my flashlight trained on the ground as we took one step, then two forward into the cave. One and two swiftly became three and four, then five and six. No cobras reared up from the shadows. No scorpions fell into our hair. I felt an inexplicable sense of predestination. Sarah Belzoni was watching. Of that much I was certain.

The wooden board we'd spied from the entrance was firmly wedged into the cavity at the back of the cave. Did Abdullah Soliman put that there? I wondered, feeling his ghost brush against me.

I could see it was disintegrating even as Adam punched at it with his fist, still holding the flaming torch above our heads.

But I was unprepared for the squirming motion his action set off. 'Snakes!' I shrieked.

But they were babies, each of them no more than a pencil-length long and just as thin.

'Bloody hell!' Adam cursed, kicking his feet as they cascaded to the floor all around us.

It was a strangely Indiana Jones, *Raiders of the Lost Ark* moment. And not in a good way.

'We've disturbed the nursery,' I murmured, waving my flashlight in all directions and stamping my feet. 'I'll bet the cobra in Georgina's rucksack is their momma.'

The baby snakes slithered away, probably more frightened by us than we were of them. I thanked my maker for fire and the bright white light of a modern flashlight. I certainly wouldn't have fancied being in here without them.

My stout leather walking boots, lacing up to above my ankles with my jeans tucked into them, were another definite plus.

Adam punched at the wooden board with increasing desperation and ever-louder grunts until finally it gave way. I'm not quite sure what we expected to find on the other side, but it certainly wasn't a hole backed by a solid stone wall, plastered and stamped with a hieroglyphic cartouche.

'What the hell...?!' Adam exclaimed. 'Bloody hell, Merry; it's the cartouche of Seti I...!'

Don't ask me why this didn't surprise me. 'I'll bet you any money you like if you smash through that wall you'll find yourself in the tunnel that burrows into the rock beneath Seti's burial chamber,' I said triumphantly. 'We're simply approaching it from the outside!'

'I'm sure you're right, Merry,' Adam acknowledged. 'I was clocking the topography as we veered off the main path to the Valley earlier. But, right now, I'm much more interested in that!' He pointed to a fissure in the rock just above head height. It was actually more a ledge or shelf cut into the cliff.

He reached forward into the cavity he'd created holding the flaming torch, still just about alight. A couple more small snakes dropped out. 'Here, hold this.' He passed me the makeshift torch and took my flashlight. 'There's no way I'm reaching in there with my bare hands.'

I held the flare aloft, still stamping my feet while Adam used the flashlight to clear the splintered wood from the gap and scrape around inside, ensuring the last of the snakes were cleared out. The jerky light in the dense blackness seemed to take on a life of its own, almost as if some ancient *djinn* were jumping around in anger at having its peace disturbed. I watched with a kind of morbid fascination, knowing it was just torchlight but finding it impossible not to think of evil spirits and sinister spells.

'Please be careful,' I entreated.

'I should have thought to bring gloves,' he muttered, wedging the flashlight into the corner of the space he'd cleared so it shone upwards into the hole. 'Ok, here goes...' Squaring his shoulders and flexing his knees, ready to spring back in a flash, he reached forward, stretching upwards towards the shelf.

I held my breath, heartbeat thundering against my breastbone. Instinctively, I brought my free hand up to hold the Eye of Horus resting against my chest.

'There's definitely something up here!' Adam's voice was a thrilling whisper. 'God! But it's heavy!'

The makeshift torch chose that moment to give a final flare and go out. In the shadowed darkness I felt sudden fear clog my windpipe. Reality pressed me down. I was in a deep black pit running alive with baby cobras and home to multitudes of scorpions. Even at this critical moment of discovery, I asked myself if we'd gone out of our minds coming here. Maybe the place was cursed after all. Adam had his hands on whatever Abdullah had hidden here two centuries ago. He might even now be calling down the wrath of ancient gods for daring to touch it.

'Get a grip, Merry!' I schooled myself silently. I knew it was just the darkness spooking me. Taking a deep, steadying breath, I reached forward with curiously numb fingers and fumbled for a moment, finally unhooking Adam's spare flashlight from his belt. The light as I snapped it on was a benediction. My hammering heartbeat slowed to something more like its normal pace. I breathed again.

Adam was grunting and sweating with the exertion of dislodging whatever was wedged into the cavity behind the ledge. 'It's some kind of box, I think,' he puffed.

All at once it came free. Adam fell backwards with a cry, landing heavily on his back, a huge casket covered in cobwebs pinning him down. Dust, chunks of rubble and splinters of wood rained down on him. Baby snakes slithered in all directions.

'Pah!' he spat dust from his mouth and heaved the casket off him, scrambling to his feet. I reached forward and yanked him upright, kicking at the snakes and waving my flashlight wildly.

Adam stamped his boots and brushed the worst of the dust and rock chippings from his clothes and hair. We both stared at the casket. It was rectangular with a domed lid, covered in ornamental inlay oriental in design. It looked like something straight out of the Ottoman Empire. Impossible in the torchlight to tell what it was made of.

Ahmed was kneeling at the entrance to the cave shining the beam of his flashlight towards us. 'You finded something?' he shouted out excitedly.

'Yep,' Adam called back. 'We sure did. Right, Merry; let's get the hell out of here.'

We lifted the casket between us. It was impossible to hold our flashlights and the ornamental chest, so we secured our torches, still on full beam, to our belts. I watched my step as we heaved the box towards the entrance, shuddering at every wriggly movement as the small snakes slithered away from the light.

'You climb out first,' Adam advised. Ahmed won't be able to help lift this out with a bullet hole in his shoulder. I'll need you above so I can hoist it up to you.'

I've never been more pleased to get out of somewhere. Considering some of the places I've found myself that's saying something. Putting down the casket, Adam gave me a leg up. Ahmed and Habiba hauled me upwards, Ahmed reaching forward with his good arm.

A quick glance was enough to tell me Saleh el-Sayed had not succumbed to his allergy to scorpion stings. It was great to see him alive. But I guessed from the acrid smell he'd been sick. He and Georgina both came forward as I scrambled from the cave.

434

I immediately turned back. Adam, bathed in torchlight, reached down and, knees bent, hoisted the casket into his arms. Then, bracing himself, he heaved it upwards. We all reached out and between us managed to pull it from the cave, setting it heavily on the dusty slope.

Adam was already hauling himself out, using his hands on the cave edge to push upwards like a swimmer emerging from a pool. Ahmed and I reached forward to pull him the rest of the way. 'Well, now I can say I've been in a snake pit!' he grunted, collapsing heavily onto the ground. 'I may have hero-worshipped Indiana Jones since I was a lad, but I could quite happily have lived my life without sharing that particular experience!'

Chapter 23

It took over two hours to get back to the *Queen Ahmes*; impossible to make swift progress considering the weight of the casket, not to mention two limping men. Adam, Habiba, Georgina and I took turns with the heavy lifting while Ahmed led the way with a single flashlight and Saleh brought up the rear, looking constantly over his shoulder to ensure the Valley guards didn't spot us.

Our last action before climbing past the petrified tree was to release the cobra. As this was potentially more dangerous than catching it, Georgina simply undid the buckle on her rucksack and tossed it, snake, shirt and all into the cave. We figured the cobra could be relied upon to find its way out to be reunited with its babies.

Once back on the main path, we avoided the track leading down from the escarpment above Hatshepsut's temple in fear of more guards. None of us fancied explaining what we were doing in the dead of night out in the Theban hills carrying a weighty antique casket between us. Instead Ahmed led the way down another steep pathway a little further south.

If it had been a treacherous hike at sunset, given the steepness of the cliff path and quantity of rock chippings and loose scree covering the ground, it was nigh on suicidal in full darkness, and carrying a dead weight. I lost count of the number of times we nearly dropped the casket. Suffice it to say I had my heart in my mouth the whole time, which wasn't much good for my breathing. My lungs felt as if they were about to explode by the time we reached the main road.

Khaled knew to expect our call. He'd borrowed his brother-in-law's car to bring us back from our excursion. Luckily it was one of those big estate-type vehicles. With the back seats down we were able to squeeze inside with the casket wedged against the driver's seat and Ahmed – in deference to his size and injuries – travelling in the passenger seat. Adam, Habiba, Georgina, Saleh and I squashed against each other, gritted our teeth and submitted to the discomfort. It was either that or travel back in shifts. It was clear none of us was prepared to let the others go ahead with the casket leaving the rest to make the second trip. We all wanted to be there together for the moment of its opening.

And now it was upon us. We assembled in the lounge bar, sweat-stained, dirty and dishevelled, but fired up with thrilling anticipation. Rabiah fussed around with hot flannels and peppermint tea but we didn't pause to avail ourselves of these niceties. All eyes were fixed on the ornamental box, which Adam and Khaled hoisted onto our large dining table. Cobwebs and dust notwithstanding, it was beautiful, made of dark wood inlaid with mother of pearl, with intricate brass clips.

It took Adam several minutes to prise these open after their centuries of disuse. Finally it was done. 'Ready?' Adam looked up and into my eyes.

I nodded, speechless with excitement.

Adam lifted the lid. It creaked in protest. In view of the evening we'd had I half expected it to emit an eerie glow and release ancient spirits into the room; or poisonous scarab beetles at the very least. When nothing supernatural happened, I shrugged off these fanciful thoughts and leaned forward as eagerly as the others for a first glimpse of whatever was inside.

Tablets? Yes, there were tablets! I clamped my mouth shut on a shout of elation, thinking perhaps it wasn't seemly.

Georgina felt no such qualms, letting out a loud exhilarated whoop. 'Saleh, I know you were hoping for precious jewels,' she said. 'But I hope even you'll agree these have way more value! Get them out! Let's see...!' she begged.

Adam needed no further invitation. 'No wonder the casket's heavy!' he grunted. 'These tablets are made from solid granite!' He lifted them one by one from the ornamental box, setting them reverently onto the tabletop. Each was approximately the size of a laptop, made of solid black stone with exquisite hieroglyphics carved into the surface. There were four in total. We stared, awed.

'What do they say, I wonder?' Georgina muttered.

I had another of those weird time slip moments. This, of course, was what Sarah Belzoni had wanted to know. It was the question that got her started on the whole quest to return to Abu Simbel and recover the tablets she'd first spotted there in 1816 – exactly two hundred years ago – on that first fateful trip with her husband. Sarah Belzoni's ghost was here in the room with us now, I'd swear, eager to learn the significance of her discovery. I wondered if perhaps Henry Salt, Abdullah Soliman, Hakim Abd el-Rassul and the original Atiyah might be here in spirit too. Who knows, maybe even Nefertari herself in ethereal form was hovering on the airwaves. Certainly the atmosphere seemed thick with history, the room crowded with both the living and the dead as time became amorphous.

My gaze lifted from its contemplation of the three-thousand-year-old tablets and I looked into Adam's darkly lashed eyes. It's not possible to gain a degree in Egyptology and spend two years working as an Egyptologist in the world-renowned British Museum without learning a thing or two about hieroglyphics. Adam met my gaze. This was his moment. Before, we'd always needed Ted for our translations. But the protégé had earned his stripes.

Ahmed, anticipating the moment, scrabbled about in a drawer and found a magnifying glass. Then he pulled one of our lamps towards the table so its light spilled across the tablets.

Adam pulled out a chair, sat down, lifted the magnifying glass, and started to read…

***

Nefertari's Narrative

The great queen of the land of Egypt speaks thus:

I am Nefertari Meritmut, Great of Praises, Sweet of Love, Lady of Grace, Great King's Wife, Lady of The Two Lands, Lady of all Lands, Wife of the Strong Bull, god's Wife, Mistress of Upper and Lower Egypt.

I leave this written testament in the temple of Hathor in Nubia, that which my royal husband King of South and North Egypt, Usermaatre Setepenre has dedicated to me like Re forever and ever. I write this so that my story may live as I prepare to walk the halls of Amenti.

I was not permitted in my lifetime to use my royal titles. Nor may they adorn my tomb. Yet I was hereditary princess and granddaughter of the royal house before my marriage. This narrative shall serve as my sole testimony to a royal pedigree I have been unable to reveal to any living soul save my husband, the great bull of all the lands of Egypt. He, too, has a lineage he has sworn never to disclose, he, my royal husband and cousin.

We may each count the mighty bull Amenhotep the Magnificent as great-grandfather, though the heretic stood grandfather to us both. We are equally contaminated with the blood of the Habiru through our great-grandparents Queen Tiye and Vizier Ay, he who later became king.

I was begotten of Neferneferure, a younger daughter to the Great Criminal and his royal wife, my grandmother, Nefertiti; may she find ever-lasting happiness in the Field of Reeds.

My Lord was begotten of Setepenre, youngest daughter of that same royal house of Akhet-Aten. His father was raised a prince of the royal house and served as High Priest of the Aten. Queen Tiye begat him of a Habiru; though none knew of it until after the Great Criminal's death, when the priest was banished from all the lands of Egypt. The youngest royal princess went with him as wife.

Many years of chaos followed the heretic's passing. Maat withdrew her balance and order from the two lands. The mighty empire of Egypt crumbled.

Only when the usurper king Horemheb journeyed to the Field of Reeds did my Habiru uncle seek to claim the throne for his infant son. My father-in-law, the great warrior King Menmaatre Seti, declared war and pursued my fleeing uncle into the wilderness. Seti acknowledged the boy's right to rule, yet, having no male heir, determined it would be as his own son. He claimed the child, bringing him back to Egypt as

Crown Prince Ramses. None dared question his legitimacy as Seti's son, not even the great royal wife Yuya. What the king commands all obey.

King Menmaatre Seti bound Ramses and me in marriage before my strong bull inherited the throne. Perhaps my heredity was too dangerous to risk any union save for this. For the sake of peace and stability in the lands of Egypt, Seti made us swear before all the gods to expunge the heresy that was in our blood. Never must we speak of it. I was named Meritmut, for the goddess Mut, Mother in our language. My Lord was named Usermaatre; chosen one of all-powerful Re, to bring balance, security and harmony to the Two Lands.

Seti exercised wisdom in commanding us thus. My husband and I swore a solemn pledge to create royalty through the manner in which we ruled the Two Lands, not through acknowledgement of our contaminated lineage, nor yet the more glorious ancestry that preceded it. To do so would be to invalidate the rights of the current ruling house, risking civil war. Yet, even while we raise monuments to the glory of Amun, Re and all the gods, our shared lineage has united my Lord the King and me, the Lady of the Two Lands through all the years of our marriage. None can encroach upon the unique bond of the secret union we share. He is my universe, my earth, and my sky. He calls me the "one for whom the sun shines". Our sacred bond will transcend mortality and endure for millions of years.

Our marriage has borne fruit, yet Seti's command that my Lord Ramses must beget children of lesser royal wives has been dutifully fulfilled. I see no taint in the sons and daughters of our union, yet I am content that other blood must be used to strengthen the royal line.

My time is short. My mighty bull has paid me great honour, dedicating a temple in my name where I stand shoulder to shoulder with my prince. It will endure through all time so that people may speak of Nefertari Meritmut through all the ages.

This testimony I leave, protected by the Priestesses of Hathor, that none might gaze upon it while yet my royal husband lives. Perhaps a day may come, when my Lord and I walk through the Amduat together, past all caring for earthly matters, when our story may be safely known.

I have spoken in truth and justice while yet mistress of this royal house. Now may I rest knowing it is done.

* * *

We stared at each other as the ancient queen's voice reaching across the millennia faded. The spooky sense of ghosts crowding around us also dissipated.

'Bloody hell!' Adam said, returning to his everyday tones now he was no longer speaking for the great queen. 'That's enough to spin history on its head and get Egyptologists turning somersaults! I'd thought the Amarna period too far back for Nefertari's descendency to be possible. But I suppose it could just about fit.'

'Did I hear that right?' Georgina gaped. 'Nefertari and Ramses were *both* descended from the Amarnan royal house? Grandchildren of Akhenaten and Nefertiti?' Her eyes looked as if they might pop right out of her head.

I nodded, similarly awed although nowhere near so surprised, given what I already knew about Ramses' descendency. 'Yep, through the youngest Amarnan princesses, born late in their marriage.'

'My God! I hoped for a scoop, something to re-boot my journalistic career, but this is beyond all imagining!'

Saleh el-Sayed let out a strangled cry. 'Zahed Mansour is going to go wild when he hears about this!' He pulled his mobile phone from his pocket as if to call him this very minute.

I snapped from my starry-eyed contemplation of the tablets, reminded starkly of more urgent matters. 'Saleh, it's the middle of the night,' I pointed out.

Habiba also got up, a determined look on her beautiful face. 'I think Director Ismail will want to be woken,' she said firmly. 'Those tablets must be passed directly to the Ministry of Antiquities. It will be for the director to decide what to do with them.' She gave Saleh a hard look.

I gazed from one to the other realising that even in this moment of joyous discovery there were those in the room for whom these treasures offered a more prosaic opportunity than simply to re-write history.

'But the potential impact on tourism!' Saleh entreated, all trace of his former insolence gone. 'This trip has been commissioned by the Egyptian Tourism Authority. A find like this, happening within the context of the Belzonis' travels through Egypt and Nubia, and coming so close to the re-opening to the public of Nefertari's tomb, is a godsend! Meredith's blog will explode across the Internet. People will flock to Egypt! It will create a sensation all around the world!'

Even allowing for my disappointment at the inevitability of passing the tablets over to the authorities, I have to say I was warming to Saleh more and more. Enthusiasm is such a lovely contagious characteristic. And his mention of my blog was a point in his favour. Perhaps he really had forgiven me for stealing the job from under his nose at last.

'The Ministry of Antiquities will control exactly how this discovery is handled in the Media,' Habiba said tightly. 'Georgina, I must insist no word of this leaks out until Director Ismail has decided how to manage it.'

I saw Georgina about to react. Saleh too opened his mouth to protest.

Adam stepped bravely into the breach. 'It will certainly be a prize exhibit in the grand Egyptian Museum when it finally opens its doors,' he observed, cutting them both off. 'Last I heard, the official opening has been scheduled for some time in 2018. That gives people plenty of time to book their holiday tickets.'

'Yes, and it gives Director Ismail an opportunity to publicise the contents of those clay jars we found in Amarna,' I murmured to Adam in an undertone while our companions started bickering. 'That's what's needed to explain how Ramses II, son of Seti, and descended from a commoner army general, could also count the great Thutmoside pharaohs of the 18th Dynasty in his heritage.'

'Enough!' This was Ahmed, stepping into the fray as his bride-to-be and the Marketing Manager squabbled while Georgina glared at them both. 'As an Abd el-Rassul, and the one who made this great and historic discovery tonight, I will say what happens!'

I gaped at him. There's no doubting it, Ahmed can be a force to be reckoned with when he chooses. Rabiah had provided him with one of Khaled's robes seeing him return to the dahabeeyah in his drawstring pants. This was all to the good, despite it being slightly too small for him. I'm not sure he could have looked half so imperiously commanding issuing this dictate in his underwear. I didn't even mind his flagrant braggadocio, so impressed was I by his air of authority.

He glared at our warring colleagues. 'Of course, I should be allowed to keep them. Or at the very least be given a great reward for my family's part in bringing them to light.' He let out a heavy sigh. 'But as a fine, upstanding column of the community, I recognise I must do my duty. You Habiba will telephone to Director Ismail. You Saleh will telephone to Zahed Mansour. You will make both of these telephones now, serenditiously!'

'You mean simultaneously,' Adam corrected him. 'I don't think serenditiously is a word! Oh, and it's pillar, by the way – pillar of the community.'

I smiled, watching Habiba and Saleh almost trip each other up in their haste to leave the lounge bar and be first to make their respective calls. 'Who'd have thought it? Ahmed, the great diplomat!' I murmured.

But Ahmed wasn't done. The moment they were out of the room he turned to Adam. 'I'm sure the tablets are very wonderful, but I have to declare my sense of anti-climax. I was hoping for precious jewels at the very least.' He made this pronouncement in tones of the most abject disappointment.

'Ahmed, you knew all along there were no jewels,' I chided gently as he turned his big mournful dark eyes on me. 'As Georgina told Saleh, the historical knowledge contained in these tablets is of much higher value. The wonder to me is this narrative surviving apparently unread and untouched throughout the centuries inside the temple where Nefertari's loyal priestesses hid it.'

Ahmed didn't look in the least bit convinced. 'I know the history of my country is fascinating to many people,' he said pompously. 'So I can hope this is enough to free my family from the...' he looked at Adam for help. '...What was the word you telled to my mother?'

'Ridicule,' Adam supplied.

Ahmed inclined his head, 'Thank you, Adam.' Then he let out another hearty puff of disappointment. 'But, as I was saying, I can only hope this oh-so-wonderful historical knowledge' – perhaps he didn't mean to sound quite so sarcastic – 'is enough to free my family from the ridicule of the many people who see us as nothing more than villainous plunderers of graves.'

'What did you honestly expect us to find?' Adam quizzed him.

Ahmed met his gaze. 'I know you have been talking all along about mysterious tablets. But, speaking for myself, and thinking of the heavy burden of secrecy borne by my poor sister and all the generations before her, I was hoping for something more exciting!'

'More exciting?' I gaped. 'Ahmed, honestly, to anyone with an interest in history or Egyptology, this is a treasure beyond all imagining!'

'But it is not proper treasure,' he said heavily. 'Despite being hidden inside a treasure chest.'

To emphasize his disappointment he reached for the Ottoman box and peered inside as if it might contain some diamond-encrusted riches Adam had somehow missed. His dejection finding it empty was almost unbearable to watch.

Ahmed is not wholly insensitive to the glorious ancient history of Egypt. But I could see how stone tablets perhaps faded alongside the fabled mummy cache discovered by his ancestors.

Ahmed picked up the chest and shook it, perhaps to vent his frustration. We all heard the dull thud of something moving inside.

'What was that?" Georgina gasped.

Ahmed couldn't have looked more surprised if a hand had reached up from inside the chest and slapped his face. His eyes popped and his mouth formed a perfect 'o'.

Georgina, Adam and I leapt forward and crowded around Ahmed and the casket, Nefertari's tablets momentarily forgotten.

Ahmed tipped the chest sideways. The same heavy thud sounded from inside.

'There must be a secret compartment!' I cried.

Ahmed returned the box to the table with its lid up and reached inside. I watched him feeling around the base and sides with the tips of his fingers, a look of rapt concentration on his face.

'What about the lid?' Adam suggested when, with a mystified expression, Ahmed came up empty handed.

Ahmed shook the chest again, trying to identify where the movement was coming from. 'Yes, I think you are right!' he said with shining eyes.

A satin-like fabric, ruched, folded and tacked lined the lid. Very gently, Ahmed prised this away and felt beneath it. 'There is something here!' he shouted excitedly. 'Yes! There is a false lid inside the real one!' He pulled away the fabric altogether, revealing a hidden compartment fixed inside the domed length of the lid. 'I need something to lever it open,' he said when his fingernails proved unequal to the task.

Adam found him a screwdriver with a flat base while Georgina and I struggled to contain our impatience. Ahmed got to work again and finally let out a holler as the fixings gave way under the sustained screwdriver pressure.

He looked around at us, eyes snapping fire. I imagined in that moment he looked exactly like one of his ancestors with that avaricious gleam in his eyes. I prayed he wasn't about to be disappointed.

What he grasped in his big hand and pulled out was an object rolled in a sheet of parchment paper. In fact that paper looked suspiciously familiar. I gaped. 'That's another page torn from Sarah Belzoni's diary!' I choked, feeling my eyes bulge and my breathing stall. 'Quick! Quick! Unwrap it! What's inside?'

Ahmed needed no encouragement. Indeed he was already unrolling the sheet. As he did, another of Abdullah's sketches was revealed. But his drawing didn't distract me for long.

There's something about the glint of gold that magnetises the gaze. I'd swear my heart stopped beating, only to jolt back to life, thundering against my breastbone.

As Adam, Georgina and I gave a collective gasp, Ahmed let out a triumphant shout, holding aloft a statuette. 'From its weight, it is solid gold!' he yelled.

'Is it Nefertari?' I managed, forcing the words through a strangely blocked throat as I stared, wishing Ahmed would stop waving it about so delightedly so I could get a proper look at it.

Ahmed was persuaded to put the golden statuette down on the table. We all gazed in wonder. But it was a wonder mixed with confusion.

'That's not crafted in the ancient Egyptian style at all,' Adam frowned, narrowing his eyes on the statuette. 'It almost looks more ancient Greek than ancient Egyptian.'

I could see what he meant. The figurine was of a woman in flowing Grecian robes, with tresses of hair falling about her shoulders; a diadem of flowers and vine leaves around her head. She was slightly bigger in size than a modern Oscar. 'Are there any markings or inscriptions?' I asked breathlessly.

Adam picked her up and turned her in his hands so he could check the base. This was where any text would be carved. He looked up and met my eyes, a puzzled frown wrinkling his brow. 'I don't read ancient Greek,' he said, and held it towards me so I could read for myself the strange characters carved into the base. It spelled "E_λ_έ_v_η_" We looked at each other blankly.

'Give that here!' Georgina commanded. 'I've studied the classic civilisations of ancient Greece and Rome.' She virtually snatched the statuette from Adam's hands. I saw her register shock at its weight.

She studied it a moment, and then looked up, her gaze darting between us. 'That spells Helénē!' she said thrillingly.

I stared at her in confusion. 'Helénē?'

'The only Helénē – or Helen – I can think of from ancient Greece is Helen of Troy,' Adam said, frowning in perplexity.

'Helen of *Troy*?' I gaped. 'Did she even exist? I thought she was more myth and legend than flesh and blood!'

Georgina turned the statuette in her hands and looked at me. 'Myth and legend often grow up around historical fact,' she said, 'even if they distort it. Look, there's a second word here..." She squinted at the base and pointed it out. My gaze landed on more Greek letters.

'But what does is mean?'

Georgina put the statuette down on the tabletop and stared at it. 'If I'm not mistaken, that spells Lakedaímōn,' she supplied. 'In antiquity that was the city state within Sparta!'

'My God! That proves it,' Adam breathed. 'Helen of Sparta became Helen of Troy!'

This was almost too much to take in. 'But surely Helen, be it of Sparta or Troy, can't be contemporaneous with the time of Ramses II and Nefertari ... can she?' I frowned, picking up the sheet torn from Sarah Belzoni's journal, lying forgotten and overlooked on the tabletop where Ahmed had let it fall. I turned it so I could study Abdullah's drawing. It clearly showed the four colossal seated statues of the Great Temple of Ramses II at Abu Simbel, still partially submerged in drifting sand. He'd sketched the statuette emerging from the entrance to the temple. There was only possible way of interpreting this. The statuette had come from inside.

'Abdullah found it *there*?' Adam gasped, looking over my shoulder and reaching the same conclusion. 'My God! How did all the other explorers miss it?'

'More to the point, what does it mean, and what are we going to do with it?' I questioned.

Ahmed lifted the statuette and held it tightly in his big hands. 'Habiba and Saleh, they do knot know about this extra discovery,' he declared passionately. 'Tomorrow I have no doubt both Feisal Ismail and Zahed Mansour will catch the first flight out of Cairo to claim the tablets of Nefertari. I see no reason why we should let them have them this treasure too! I finded it!'

'Ahmed, you can't possibly keep it,' I said, shocked. 'It's a priceless antiquity!'

'You said it is not Egyptian,' he argued, as if this were a logical excuse for withholding it from his country's authorities.

'That's hardly the point...' I started.

'Once an Abd el-Rassul always an Abd el-Rassul,' Adam murmured. 'Seriously though, mate; if you want your moment of fame and Nefertari's tablets aren't treasure enough for you, then you should hand that over and see what the powers that be make of it.'

'I do not know this Helen of Troy you talked about,' Ahmed said, cradling the beautiful statuette in his hands. 'But if she is famous, then I would not want her competing with the great queen Nefertari for the spotlight in news headlines around the world.'

'He has a point, you know.' This was Georgina Savage, unexpectedly siding with our dodgy police pal. 'I would think these granite tablets are quite enough for the Ministry to be getting on with and to help the Tourism Authority kick start interest in Egypt as a holiday destination. There's such a thing as an embarrassment of riches, I'm sure you'll agree? I see no harm in letting Ahmed here "borrow" the statuette for a while. I'm sure he recognises he'll have to hand it over eventually. But why not let him enjoy it in the meantime, especially as we're headed for Abu Simbel on the next leg of this Belzoni jaunt. What do you say, hmm?'

'But Ahmed and Habiba are engaged to be married!' I exclaimed. 'He can't possibly keep a secret like that from her!'

'You leave Habiba to me,' Ahmed said with the benign air of one who has found an ally and now fully expects to win the day.

'What are you saying?' Adam probed, starting to catch Georgina's drift. 'That we hang onto the statuette as far as Abu Simbel, and then think about how we might go about disclosing its discovery?'

She shrugged. 'Is it such a bad idea? Wouldn't you like to know if there's anything else at Abu Simbel that might shed light on how it came to be there? Helen of Troy is an exotic name from antiquity by anyone's reckoning; I'm sure you agree? If we have to hand over Nefetari, would it really be too unreasonable just to hang on to Helen for a teensy bit longer?'

I could see Adam wavering. Like me, he sensed another mystery. I could tell by the changing colour of his eyes he was hooked.

Ahmed, still clutching the statuette, looked at me hopefully. He knew I would be the one to make the decision. Staring back into his soulful dark eyes, I thought back to all the mishaps he'd endured on this trip. Images of Ahmed atop a bolting camel, sprawled unconscious at the bottom of a stone pit, and bleeding from a gunshot to his shoulder flashed across my inner eye.

'You'd better find somewhere to hide that before Habiba and Saleh come back,' I said briskly, hoping I wasn't going soft in the head as well as the heart. 'We can figure out exactly what to do with it when we get to Abu Simbel.'

Ahmed grinned at me and puffed out his chest, 'Thank you, Meredith.'

Then I turned my gaze on that maddening creature Georgina Savage. 'I didn't expect you to want to come with us on the next leg of our journey,' I frowned. 'I thought you were just tagging along as a way of muscling in on the stele!'

'Oh, I always fully intended coming to Abu Simbel,' she announced breezily. 'Even without this statuette, there are more discoveries to be made following in the Belzonis' footsteps than just the stone tablets, I'll have you know.'

I looked at our ballsy houseguest in shock, not following.

'Oh yes! Of course finding this statuette gives me even more incentive for coming along. But, you see, finding Nefertari's Narrative wasn't my only reason for wanting to join you on this trip. The fact is; I have it on rather good authority there's a stash of treasure hidden away in the walls of the Great Temple of Ramses II. Nothing to do with Helen of Troy I'm afraid; but worth a king's ransom in its own right. What do you say, hmm? Could we have a bash at finding it? I'm sure it would make for quite a story, don't you agree?'

I'll let you imagine for yourself the look on Ahmed's face.

The End

Author's Note

The suggestion of Ramses II being in any way descended, legitimately or otherwise, from the pharaohs of the 18th Dynasty is of course a fiction of my own making. But the possible links between Nefertari and the Amarnan royal house are not necessarily so far-fetched. Ernest Schiaparelli, when he discovered Nefertari's tomb, found a knob bearing the royal cartouche of Ay inside. Ay is widely believed to have been Nefertiti's father, so father-in-law to Akhenaten, as well as being a vizier at the Amarnan court and ultimately the pharaoh who succeeded the boy king Tutankhamun.

Nefertari's tomb had been thoroughly ransacked in antiquity so it's impossible to know how the knob came to be there. Yet it provides great fodder for me and the other fiction writers who've woven stories around Nefertari's possible descendency from the Amarnan court. In truth, her real origins remain unknown, and she certainly never claimed royal titles before her marriage to Ramses in anything found to date.

'Habiru' is a term used by various Egyptian, Akkadian, Hittite and Mitanni sources (dated, roughly, between 1800 BC and 1100 BC) to describe a group of people living as nomadic invaders in areas of the Fertile Crescent from Northeastern Mesopotamia and Iran to the borders of Egypt in Canaan.

Encyclopaedia Britannica states: "Many scholars feel that among the Habiru were the original Hebrews, of whom the later Israelites were [only] one branch or confederation." Others say the link to the Biblical Hebrews is tenuous. As a writer of fiction I have no qualms in using it for the purposes of my story.

The Egyptian Ministry for Antiquities re-opened the tombs of both Seti I and Nefertari to the public after long closure in November 2016. There is a modest charge for admission and visitor numbers are controlled each day to protect the reliefs from humidity.

Nefertari's tomb, like that of her father-in-law, is considered a stunning work of art, beautifully preserved by the Getty Institute. Whether this will be enough to encourage tourists back to Luxor in anything like their pre-Revolution numbers remains to be seen. Terrorist attacks across the globe make people understandably wary.

While this story is set last year in 2016, I've written it throughout 2017, a year that has witnessed three appalling acts of terrorism in London: on Westminster Bridge, in Manchester and on London Bridge. It does rather make me think Egypt is no more or less safe than anywhere else in the world.

The Scan Pyramid project continues at the Giza Plateau, and everything looks to be on target for the Grand

Egyptian Museum in Cairo to open its doors in 2018 – all very exciting.

So, Merry and Adam are back in Egypt and, now they've found the statuette of Helen of Troy, I'm sure more adventures await them.

I hope you have enjoyed this book. Please do leave me a comment on my website www.fionadeal.com. I also read and appreciate all reviews on Amazon.

Fiona Deal
November 2017.

About the Author

Fiona Deal fell in love with Egypt as a teenager, and has travelled extensively up and down the Nile, spending time in both Cairo and Luxor in particular. She lives in Kent, England with her two Burmese cats. Her professional life has been spent in human resources and organisational development for various companies. Writing his her passion and an absorbing hobby. Other books in the series following Meredith Pink's adventures in Egypt are available, with more planned. You can find out more about Fiona, the books and her love of Egypt by checking out her website and following her blog at www.fionadeal.com

.

Other books by this author

Please visit Amazon to discover other books by Fiona Deal. The author reads and appreciates all reviews.

Meredith Pink's Adventures in Egypt

Carter's Conundrums – Book 1
Tutankhamun's Triumph – Book 2
Hatshepsut's Hideaway – Book 3
Farouk's Fancies – Book 4
Akhenaten's Alibi – Book 5
Seti's Secret – Book 6
Belzoni's Bequest – Book 7
Nefertari's Narrative – Book 8
Ramses' Riches – Book 9

More in the series planned in 2019.

Also available: Shades of Gray, a romantic family saga, written under the name Fiona Wilson.

Connect with me

Thank you for reading my book. Here are my social media coordinates:

Subscribe to my blog: http://www.fionadeal.com
Visit my website: http://www.fionadeal.com
Friend me on Facebook: http://facebook.com/fjdeal
Follow me on Twitter: http://twitter.com/dealfiona

Printed in Great Britain
by Amazon